CONCRETE
Angel

CONCRETE
Angel

PATRICIA ABBOTT

The following is a work of fiction. Names, characters, places, events and incidents are either the product of the author's imagination or used in an entirely fictitious manner. Any resemblance to actual persons, living or dead, is entirely coincidental.

Copyright © 2015 by Patricia Abbott
Cover and jacket design by Georgia Morrissey
Interior designed and formatted by E.M. Tippetts Book Designs

ISBN 978-1-940610-38-2
eISBN 978-1-940610-44-3

First trade paperback edition June 2015 by Polis Books, LLC
1201 Hudson St.
Hoboken, NJ 07030
www.PolisBooks.com

POLIS BOOKS

For Philip
...the love of my life.

CHAPTER
One

When I was twelve, my mother shot a soda-pop salesman she'd known less than eight hours. She used the gun Daddy had bought a few weeks earlier, telling her it was to keep us safe now that their divorce was final and he'd be living too far away to protect us. He taught Mother how to fire, load, and clean it, taking her to practice shooting at a nearby gun range.

Daddy was right. There *was* a dangerous, if imperceptible, current coursing down that suburban street because it was only a few weeks later that the incident occurred. Jerry Santini walked out of our bathroom, saw my mother removing bills from his wallet, and headed for the phone—mumbling something about a "thieving bitch" and "not getting away with it."

Mother, adept at identifying potential danger and acting quickly on it, moved toward the drawer where she'd placed the gun, planning only—or so she insisted later—to stop him from making the call.

Stymied by our blood red telephone, a Swedish import with

the dial on the bottom, whimsically called an Ericafone, Jerry's attempt to reach the police was thwarted. Mother caught him in the chest, the ribs, the thigh; she emptied the entire chamber, in fact. He'd been shooting his mouth off when she started pulling the trigger.

"He had this idea I was running a scam, luring men up to our apartment with the intention of robbing them," Mother said. "Can you imagine?"

Jerry couldn't have known my mother had run up against the police and their tactics before, that his reference to her being thrown in jail was anathema to her. Or that his words would send her into a fugue state where her actions were unpredictable, centered entirely on self-preservation. And his particular threat of incarceration was more potent than raising his fist or shoving her around. Physical retribution she would've accepted as fair payback or tolerable, at least. If he'd only kept still after his first threat, he might've survived. But he made the inevitable move toward the phone, persisting in saying what he'd do and seemingly acting on it.

So however it happened, whatever state Mother was in, and whatever Jerry Santini said, or did, or didn't do, she shot and killed him, emptying the gun and letting it clatter on the hardwood floor. Or perhaps I only imagine such a clatter. I couldn't vouch for it having been asleep at the time.

There wasn't much Jerry *did* know after only an hour or two's acquaintance. Our apartment gave the impression of belonging to a woman who wouldn't need to rob a man of, at most, forty dollars. Having her child asleep in the next room would also seem to preclude her undertaking a robbery much less a fatal shooting. These were certainly rational thoughts— they just didn't explain a woman like my mother.

The things Jerry Santini knew were purely physical ones: the feel of her skin, the taste of her lips, her scent, which still wafted on the air he no longer breathed. Some pricey perfume, purchased with the contents of some other guy's wallet he might have reasoned if he managed to smell it while looking futilely for that strangely placed dial.

Mother met Jerry Santini at a shoe-repair shop earlier that day. She was always a sucker for a man who took care of his clothing, and Jerry wore an expensive pair of well-polished, buttery-black wingtips. There were no holes in his socks, an item she examined carefully over the top of the wooden stall. She was disproportionately impressed by appearance, often judging people solely on such things.

"We were sitting side by side in those little cubicles," Mother told me later, an untoward strand of merriment in her voice given the day's outcome. "I wonder why cobblers think nicely stockinged feet need to be hidden. Jimmy—"

"Jerry," I corrected her. "His name is—was—Jerry."

"Right. Well, Jerry made a joke about that very thing."

They kidded around about similar stuff, striking an immediate, although ultimately, deadly rapport.

"I put these socks on clean this morning—so my feet can't smell," he'd said, sticking a foot out as proof. Witty repartee wasn't in his arsenal.

Oh, they were jolly at first, or so she made it seem in the story I heard.

She invited him up to her apartment where she served him stuffed figs, cocktail nuts, dates, and several dry martinis before taking him to bed. She'd given up cooking for men after a nasty episode a few years earlier, but kept prepared foods such as these on hand for potential guests—items looking attractive in a cut-glass bowl. We often made a Sunday dinner of the leftovers if they didn't disappear on Saturday night.

"Good thing you like sardines and chicken liver, kiddo. Dinner will improve when we can split a bottle of wine."

I nodded my agreement, pathetically anxious to take on the role of Mother's confidante rather than her child. Perhaps a glass of wine would seal it.

"It was the briefest of encounters—Jerry's and mine," she told me *much* later, in a half-humorous, half-disdainful voice.

I smiled, pretending to understand what her words meant, not knowing yet what shared information or intimacy would come to mean.

After shooting her date with a degree of marksmanship no one would've predicted given her single lesson in firearms, Mother shook me awake, but failed to convince me, even after several attempts, that he'd tried to strangle her.

"Look at the marks, Christine," she hissed, as if Jerry Santini might be listening. "Right here."

Head cocked, her nails expertly polished a pearly pink, she massaged her throat like Gloria Swanson in *Sunset Boulevard*. I tried to see some marks. I badly wanted to see at least an early blossoming of bruises though its importance was not yet clear to me. But her neck was white and blemishless.

She dropped onto my bed and began to sob, claiming no one ever took her side. It was then she confessed she may have peeked inside this man's wallet, an action she'd been forced to take given our current position.

"I thought the odd ten perhaps."

When I didn't immediately fall in with this idea, didn't know, in fact, what she was talking about, she added, "Your father's so stingy. How he can expect us to live on..."

In order to cut-off a comprehensive recitation of how she'd been wronged over the years, I threw myself on top of her, listening to her hammering heart through the thin fabric of her negligee, crying the next minute myself. I *did* feel responsible for her current unhappiness. If it weren't for my presence, Mother and Jerry might've gone to a nightclub or theater where she wouldn't have been tempted. Or, she might have been able to steal the odd twenty dollars less conspicuously—blaming its loss on a waitress or busboy. I had a vague memory of an incident like this before. Was it a scam after all?

Or maybe they would've gone to *his* apartment, where no gun conveniently waited in a drawer. My role in this debacle was growing large. I listened to her heartbeat, the one I'd first heard in the womb. Its ferocity made it impossible to ignore. I was already setting myself up for the upcoming finale. Preparing myself for the role I'd soon play—the one I'd always perform for my mother. The role I *wanted to* play.

I hadn't heard any of the activity in the living room because my mother had turned on *Saturday Night Live* before Jerry and she made love, and it was still playing. As Mother showed me her throat, sobbing over her ill-treatment by men and me, the Swedish rock group ABBA was singing the eerily appropriate *SOS*. I'd slept right through the early *SNL* skits about bumblebees and cheeseburgers, the lovemaking going on in the next room and, more blessedly, the gunfire. Only Mother, screaming in my ear, was loud enough to wake me.

After our expiating sob fest, we linked hands and tiptoed into the living room—as if we might be disturbing someone—to examine the consequences of Mother's greatest faux pas, me still clinging to the pale hope her imagination had gotten the best of her. Or, at the very least, that the wound was not a fatal one. She continued to jabber away, pretending we were looking at some ordinary mishap—like a broken vase or a ruined piece of furniture— so the oddness and horror of finding a dead body in my living room didn't immediately sink in.

The room had the dreamlike atmosphere of an old crime movie, the ones we liked to watch on late-night TV. But how could the dead body on the floor be genuine when the rest of the room was still the familiar place where I'd watched *Mary*

Tyler Moore and The Bob Newhart Show a few hours earlier? The tableaux seemed to exist on two planes—the everyday and the surreal—as was often the case with my mother.

"Lying there looking so innocent after what he tried to do," Mother said. "He seemed like such a nice guy this morning. You never can tell, I guess," she said, sounding surprised by his sudden change—as if he'd pulled something over on her.

At that moment, I'd no idea how or where she'd met him, vaguely imagining he'd appeared at the door posing a threat of some kind, perhaps deserving his fate.

"How many times did you fire the gun?" I asked, looking at the blood. It'd puddled extensively and it was shockingly red. I'd never considered that blood might come in different shades. Our embarrassingly out-of-date black and white TV had shielded me from the true redness of blood. The black blood on TV was somehow less startling—less of a life force, similar to sludge.

Everything in the room seemed heightened in hue. The color palette had transformed itself into something brilliant: a pale green carpet, two aqua chairs, a chartreuse sofa. And the red, red blood.

"Well, how many bullets were in the thing?" Mother asked, avoiding the menacing word *gun*. "Look, I fired until the gun was empty at the shooting range—the one your father took me to," she explained. "I guess I did the same thing here tonight. I don't remember much."

This seemed reasonable to my twelve-year-old ears. She was probably in shock. I'd often heard such reasoning given on *The Rockford Files* or *McMillan and Wife*, my two favorite TV shows.

"I don't think he mentioned a last name," she said, as if he might not have one. She was on her knees between rivulets of blood, rifling his wallet, examining his license.

Why didn't I find it strange she didn't know the full name of the nearly naked man on our floor? Or that she could talk about it so dispassionately only a few minutes after it happened?

"Santini," she said triumphantly. "Look, he's got a Master Charge." Reluctantly, she slid it back into its slot—wisely forgoing any pleasure stealing it might bring.

Mother continued to forget Jerry Santini's name each time she was asked it in the weeks ahead—I never once heard her get it right. More often than not, she called him Joey Spatini, confusing his name with a packaged spaghetti sauce popular then.

Sprawled on my mother's fluffy carpeting, an item she'd made my father buy as part of their divorce settlement, Jerry Santini was certainly dead, putting to rest any notion Mother had exaggerated or misunderstood the final outcome of their tête-à-tête. It was almost impossible to stop her from immediately spraying the area with rug shampoo.

"My God, what sort of blood did he have?" she said, aiming the can she'd retrieved from the kitchen. A line of rust circled the can's bottom, suggesting its potency was questionable.

"He seemed normal enough this afternoon," she repeated.

Later, when I studied *Macbeth* in high school, the vision of Mother, poised with her can of stain remover, would run through my head in slow motion, her finger moving inexorably toward the button.

"Hey, you're not supposed to touch anything," I said, quickly clapping my hand over the nozzle. My voice and knees were shaking as I began to fully appreciate our situation. "They can find things out from blood samples. Important things."

This was before the science of blood splatter or the discovery of DNA testing, but there was still information to be culled. Blood type, at least. My years of watching TV detective shows hadn't been wasted. It hadn't occurred to me yet that the things they would find in the police lab might not be ones Mother wanted discovered.

She remained motionless with the can pointed at the rug, her still-rouged lips pursed in thought. I wondered if she'd held the gun so steadily fifteen minutes earlier.

"Blood is blood. What could they possibly learn from his blood?" She turned toward me, the can still hovering over the murder scene. "It was an accident, Christine." Her voice was whiney, annoyed. "Why must you insist on seeing this... mishap... as a crime? You make it sound like something it's not. Make sure you use the word *accident* when they come tonight."

"Come?"

"The police or whoever we eventually call. First impressions last longest, you know."

This was the sort of adage my grandmother usually came up with but, in this instance, it was probably on the mark.

"And look," Mother continued, "we have to protect ourselves here. They'll be trying to pin it on me—on us."

Mother's voice trailed off as she stepped back from the body. She'd already linked me with the events although I didn't notice it then. Or perhaps I saw us as immutably linked long before. It was our apartment, our life. I should have been more vigilant and kept her safe.

"I'm gonna call Cy. He'll know what to do."

"Not Daddy?" I whispered, as if this verbal betrayal was being recorded. If she'd kept the door locked, as Daddy suggested after his handiwork a few weeks earlier, we wouldn't be in this mess. And when had my father been stymied by any situation? He may have been away most of the time, may have been at a loss for words with me when he was home, but you could count on him in a crisis. Military training and running a business had prepared him to react with precision in tight circumstances.

I flashed back to *Rear Window*, to Raymond Burr removing his wife in a suitcase. Would this be how we rid ourselves of this body? Did we have the necessary tools, a large enough suitcase?

Mother made a sound of disgust. "How could we possibly call your father, kiddo? Look what's lying on our rug. Think Hank would want to see that—want to figure a way out of this one?"

He was naked except for a pair of extremely tight briefs. The bottoms of his feet were pink and plump, like he hadn't spent much time on them. Good attendance to his feet was fitting given they'd met in a shoe repair shop. I couldn't see his face, pushed into the rug as it was, but I had the impression he was handsome, misled by the idea Mother was rarely drawn to homely men. He had a nice head of steely black hair and wore it long in the back, which was still the style.

Cy Granholm, the man Mother went to call, had loomed large in our life of late. In the last three months, he'd handled Mother's divorce and child custody hearing, gone to court with her on a speeding ticket, and twice filed papers demanding an increase in child support. Mother had begun calling him at home with household predicaments too, questions about financial matters, or advice on how to fix the gurgling toilet. She'd never been much good on her own, and I wasn't old enough to step in. My grandmother often voiced the opinion Mother's body slanted leftward—as if it were made to lean heavily on someone else, preferably a man.

"Cy!" I heard Mother say a few seconds later, using the phone in her bedroom. There was a trace of gaiety in her tone—probably a quality she'd cultivated long ago and couldn't discard now—though it was unseemly. The treacherous Ericafone, with its oddly placed dial, still lay overturned on the living room floor. If the incident had happened in the bedroom, the easier-to-use baby blue princess phone might have saved Jerry's life.

"If it's not too late, I could use your help, Cy." Her words were overly precise—like she was reading a script. "No, no, you'll have to come over here, I'm afraid. Yes, yes, as soon as possible." She laughed a little, pretending it wasn't too awful, that nothing was greatly amiss. "I know it's late but I'd rather not explain over the phone."

Who could blame her? Although I would've liked to have had some warning of what story she'd tell Cy.

It was past midnight and if Cy refused to come, whom could we call next? We'd run out of saviors. One thing was certain from the look on her face when I suggested it, there'd be no calling Daddy. Nor my grandmother. She'd be too full of "I told you so's," for Mother to tolerate. She'd be horrified, maybe having a heart attack, adding to our body count. Our list of possibilities was short, so Cy would have to come.

In the recent past, my father would have handled the situation, found a way to wipe things clean, made the problem evaporate even if Mother disappeared with it. But now there was only the two of us to clear things up. And Cy. Only a month or two into our newly divorced state and we were already in a fix as Daddy had predicted.

CHAPTER
Two

"You have no idea what the world's like," Daddy flung at Mother in the judge's quarters some weeks before Jerry Santini reached for the Ericafone. "I've taken care of you far too well all these years, ushering you straight from your father's bed to mine. You're a child still, Eve. An infant." Daddy knew this was one charge my mother despised.

"I was about to tell him off right there, but Cy grabbed my hand, nearly crushing it," Mother said, dabbing her eyes on the night following their divorce. "And this is the worst part." She blew her nose noisily. "Are you ready for this?" I nodded. "Your father shouted how he could see how things were—suggesting my bed was already waiting for the next guy." She reached for my hand. "Embarrassing me in front of both the judge and Cy," she continued shakily. "Have you ever heard of anything so mean? Deserting us without a thought and then blaming me for hiring a decent lawyer to see us through it. Mocking me for accepting help from my own attorney. He'd prefer to see us on the streets begging pennies from strangers."

I nodded sympathetically.

Mother drew herself up. "Cy's a married man after all." She smoothed the wrinkle in her skirt, adding somewhat sadly, "And he's not my type—not by a long shot."

Cy was a heavy-set man, the kind of guy who was always hiking up his pants, tucking in his shirt, sweating even in winter. He was also balding and wore thick dark glasses completely obscuring his face. No, he wasn't Mother's type. She'd require certain things from Cy, but not others.

I was silent, trying hard to get the childishly mistaken picture of Mother in bed with my grandfather out of my head. The words *from your father's bed to mine* were difficult to excise from my twelve-year old brain.

It'd already occurred to me that Cy's addition to our household, if he married my mother, might take some of the pressure off me. I'd had a good taste of what life alone with her was like over the course of my parents' many separations, and it was wearying. There was always a problem to solve, a slight to be dealt with, Mother's schemes to be derailed, a place to be found for her newest junk. Junk. We haven't gotten into her junk yet.

But now I'd found out Cy was married and unlikely to move in and care for us. And he was *not* Mother's type. His shoes weren't shined. He was fat. He'd fade from our lives quickly once she no longer needed him.

"I kind of like Cy," I said faintly. "Maybe he'll get divorced." A grandfatherly sort of man might suit us both.

"Fat chance," she said with a shrug.

Mother went on to let me in on the entire divorce proceedings. The drama of the hearing came across much like one of the boxing matches Daddy liked to watch on Saturday nights.

Pow! "I'm not picking up your wardrobe expenses. You

have enough clothing to get you into the nineteen eighties. Scratch that—your eighties."

Wham! "You can't see Christine on school nights, and I'm keeping the Thunderbird."

Zing! "That T-Bird was a birthday gift from my parents. You can take the Dart Swinger."

"Swell, you want me carting your kid around in that heap. I can dent it with my elbow."

If there were to be no more boxing matches, perhaps we could watch *Carol Burnett* in peace. But calm, with or without Daddy, didn't last long.

Back to the crime scene: two hours after the soda salesman's death, I told two police officers I'd found Jerry Santini strangling my mother in the living room and pulled the gun Daddy bought for us from the drawer.

"I only meant to scare him," I said, caught in the excitement of the scene and more than half-believing it, "but confusion ensued and the gun went off."

Mature words for a child of twelve, but nobody flinched. I was the sort of child who might say such a thing. "I was barely aware of pulling the trigger," I finished, borrowing Mother's idea, which had left an impression. The notion of the murder being dreamlike felt like a good way to go. "I think I was in a fug state."

"Fugue," Cy corrected me, nodding in the background. I told them what he'd instructed me to say, telling the police officers as little as possible. I was a bit shrill in my delivery, but shrillness established my immaturity—I couldn't seem too well-prepared, too precocious. Reticence was Cy's advice for any situation allowing it. And ladylike tears, if needed.

I didn't mind lying for Mother—I was already dedicated

to an existence of small fibs and truth-shading with neighbors, teachers, grandmothers, Daddy. And it turned out I was pretty good at lying and would grow more skilled over time. When Mother lied, she prattled on. I was the essence of brevity, my tears restrained.

I looked to her for approval, but she kept her eyes pinned on the wall behind me where a chartreuse and aqua ceramic señorita and señor she'd bought at Gimbel's danced the tango. Surreal hues enveloped us, but I was on my own in her neon setting. Neither its brilliance nor hers would fade for years.

Our apartment had a hushed air despite the crowd of men examining the carpet, looking for the bullets' casings, powdering the place for fingerprints, talking to Mother and me, snapping cameras and, finally, carrying Jerry Santini away. A child murderess merits solemnity. Nobody pushed me beyond my practiced confession that day or on any other day over the following weeks. Ordinary men, like cops in 1976, didn't anticipate a mother asking her child to lie — even after the Johnny Stompanato case.

To be honest, I can't remember either Mother or Cy Granholm openly asking it of me — either the lying or taking the rap. It somehow evolved in the hour after Cy arrived and before he called the police. His attempts to cobble a convincing story from Mother's words went awry every time.

"You are amazingly cavalier about what's taken place here tonight, Eve," he said, wiping his forehead. "You did kill the guy. Right? Unloaded the entire gun into his gut? I'm not misunderstanding?" He paced the floor like the bulldog he was.

I could sympathize with Cy. It was hard to remember the fatal events had occurred only an hour earlier given Mother's body language. And as Mother swayed back and forth between anger, helplessness, and a sort of superhuman strength, I tried hard to match it. Were we to play the victims, were we to be hysterical? Sorrowful? Temporarily insane? It was so hard to keep the strategy straight.

"Truthfully, Cy," her eyes fluttered, "I don't remember a damned thing. Not until Christine was standing here beside me." She looked at him, her lashes damp, her lips slightly parted. "And what else could I do?" she added, forgetting herself for a second and changing her tone yet again. "For a lousy twenty bucks, that jerk was willing to see me hang. What's twenty bucks?"

"You sound like a prostitute, Eve," Cy said, frowning. "A cheap one too."

"Now that you mention it, he didn't even buy me dinner. I fed him, in fact."

Cy and I sighed simultaneously, fearing she *would* indeed hang if she made such comments, so I stepped in with my special skill-set. Saving Mother was something I was born to do. It had come into play with great regularity in my twelve years.

Everyone believed me—seemed eager to, in fact. My *statement,* as they called it, was met with subtle sighs of relief, of feet shuffling noisily in tight shoes, the funny crinkling noise nylon stockings used to make, the slight inhale of breath as what I was saying went from nebulous to cogent, the squeak of chairs as people sat down and started to write—relief that the entire sordid episode could be wrapped up quickly.

A sort of giddy freedom set in. No one would have to haul Mother off to jail. No one would have to press against her body to put cuffs on her hands, touching, inadvertently, something under the transparent negligee that Cy made her keep on. No one would push her head down as she entered the police vehicle. No man-handling would occur.

I thought back to the three of us looking out the fly-specked window a few weeks earlier, wondering why only Daddy saw the danger festering below. But nothing bad would happen to Mother. Not when I was so willing to play the looney daughter. Not when it was clear I'd misunderstood the adult events transpiring in the next room. Got it wrong when I'd come in on a scene, mistaking ardor for violence. Mistaking shrieks of passion for those of fear. It was a nicely fashioned story I told.

CHAPTER
Three

I was eventually ordered to see a court-appointed shrink and that was it from a legal standpoint. There was no trial since I'd pleaded guilty, just a cozy hearing in the judge's chamber. The story never appeared in any newspaper. If it spread at all, it was over the telephone, through whispers in grocery store checkout lines, and over backyard fences in the blocks of row houses of my grandmother's neighborhood.

Jerry Santini was found to be an exceptionally solitary man, someone whose origins weren't ever fully discovered. He'd come to Philly in the fifties following a stint in Korea, worked for a national soda manufacturing company, lived alone in a small apartment in the northeast section of the city. But beyond this scant history—nothing. No family members or friends came forward to ask questions, to demand justice.

Daddy's family was influential in the community; the soda salesman, an almost itinerant salaried worker, was not. Mother chose both the right guy to marry and the right one to kill. And most importantly, she mothered the correct daughter to save her, wrapping me around her crime like the needy girl I was.

The judge gave me some stern admonitions and scolded my parents for keeping a loaded gun in the house. My father assured him the gun hadn't been loaded when he put it in the drawer some weeks earlier; the bullets were in a separate package, the safety on. Possessions in Daddy's control were always maintained as they should be. Except for his former wife.

"I taught Eve how to use it myself," Daddy told the judge. "We went together to a shooting range in northeast Philly. A good shot, too. Steady hand, great eye." For a minute, he sounded boastful, but then he glared at my mother. "And Eve knew damned well not to keep it loaded with a kid in the house."

Your kid, I mouthed silently. Once again, he reminded the judge that his part in all this had been well-executed. It was my mother and me who screwed things up. We made the mess, not he. Not once did Daddy express any doubt about either Mother's story or mine, but he must have questioned its truth. *He must have.* The judge nodded approvingly at every word he said. I wondered if they attended the same private schools and college, belonged to the same fraternity. They were that much alike.

I also couldn't help but wonder exactly *when* Mother *had* loaded the gun since she'd been so dismissive of my father's purchase, shoving it in the drawer with no outward interest. But no one else looked bothered by such facts. In fact, few questions were asked as we went through our rehearsed scene. The notion of a scripted play occurred to me.

But then my mother stepped forward, suddenly denying laying a hand on the weapon. "I don't think I consciously knew the gun was in the drawer. And I certainly never touched it." She waved her arms around as if indicating the gun could have been anywhere in the apartment, anywhere in the world as far as she knew. Cy's eyes fluttered in alarm at this diversion from the script. I could see his hand itching to clamp itself over her mouth.

A forensics report, read aloud by the judge, contradicted what she'd said, announcing her fingerprints had been found on the gun. Thinking quickly when her preservation was at stake, Mother instantly recalled taking it from my shaking hands.

"Christine was nearly paralyzed with horror at what she'd done. I had to pry it loose from her frozen fingers, terrified it'd go off again."

Cy signaled her to stop speaking with a jabbing slash of his hand. She'd already said far more than he'd advised. I could see the indecision in Mother's eyes because she thought her account of the events was going well, and she didn't like ceding her minutes on the stage. But finally she did stop speaking, her mouth closing so quickly you could hear her jawbones protest. A collective sigh drifted across the small room, all of us enervated by what we'd heard, all of us relieved it hadn't gone too badly.

During those moments, I could nearly remember pulling the gun from the drawer. I could feel Mother's hands on mine, prying the gun loose. I watched, transfixed by my imagination, as the revolver fell to the floor emptied of bullets. I think we all saw it her way for a minute; the drama of her account was compelling, convincing.

She grew more persuasive over time since I halfway believed the entire story at some point. Or part of me did. It was always easier to believe Mother, always better to go along with whatever she said or wanted or did. I wondered what my father thought. Did he think he had sired a murderess or married one? Did he care? He avoided my eyes, and I, his.

I also wondered if all of the hearings that took place in the judge's chambers were set pieces like ours. Were there rehearsals to keep things from getting out of hand—insuring the person who'd been coached or coaxed to take the fall was locked away so the book could be closed? Were all court decisions made like this one?

Mother and I shared moments of intense intimacy for years to come, but none would match the neon brilliance of the night she killed Jerry Santini. How could they?

CHAPTER
Four

Mother drove me to Dr. Bailey's office in her cherry-colored Impala (a trade-in and trade-up) each week, and soon every other week, and eventually once a month. We entered his office together: Mother, a flurry of pastel fragrant with Chanel No. 5, her blonde hair poufy, a discreet amount of eye shadow, a touch of lipstick. I was a blander rendition since I lacked both her confidence and figure.

No one but Dr. Bailey monitored my behavior. Children were still ceded some protection from the media glare unless you were Lana Turner's kid. At school, I continued my long-standing role as the too-smart girl who kept to herself. It was safer to play it like that. None of my classmates asked about my summer vacation, but it was a new school and I had few friends. For once I was happy to be one of the anonymous ones in middle school—one of those kids who walked home alone looking at the ground, kicking at the leaves so they appeared occupied in thought rather than lonely. If anyone accompanied me, it was the boy with his glasses held together with tape, the new girl who didn't know anyone yet, a stray dog sniffing at my heels.

Mother and I sat side by side on Dr. B's slightly faded black-and-white checkered loveseat until his door opened. Mother would immediately fix her best evil eye on his, daring him to undermine her. I marched into his office week after week and told him stories of my pre-teenage crushes, my straight As in school, my bouts with insomnia—all material perfected beforehand by Mother, an expert in such details. It was a rare occasion when an uncharted sentence escaped my lips.

Some of the material she invented sent us into giggling fits the night before a session.

"See if he doesn't have a cow over this incident," Mother'd say when she thought of a particularly good idea—a colorful line to sling at him. "I bet he'll do his little cough when he hears it."

I enjoyed the camaraderie these visits necessitated, loved having Mother's attention for hours more than usual each week. Only later would I realize her manipulation of my therapy made it impossible for those sessions to do me any good.

Though I was not a murderer, I badly needed someone's help, someone who might shine a light on my relationship with my mother, tell me it wasn't normal for a mother to see her daughter as someone to manipulate, to use. Such insight from a therapist skilled in breaking through a façade might have saved me years of pain.

But when I told Dr. B something even remotely troubling, he coughed lightly, guiding me, through respiratory cues, to a safer topic. Confronting my mother on any issue inadvertently arising in his office was not in his playbook. His unintentional collusion with Mother in manufacturing a fairly safe neurosis for me might just as well have been deliberate.

"Tell yourself a story," he suggested when I complained

about not sleeping. Or, "Those straight A's will get you into a fine college."

Banalities and set pieces of advice were the only therapeutic tools I saw. It'd been decided at some point I misunderstood what I saw in my living room. And that I was not a murderer. Instead I was a frightened child protecting her mother.

After each session, Mother and I went for a hot-fudge sundae, or a lime rickey, or a cheesesteak and fries. Anything I wanted. And there I'd report on my session more fully.

"I love your father paying for it all," she said once. "Makes the whole thing worthwhile." The haze of cigarette smoke, exhaled unhurriedly from her pink lips, engulfed our table. Those were some of the most intimate moments in my life.

"Worthwhile?"

She shrugged. "Turning dross into gold—something like that."

I wondered, too, if by "the whole thing" she meant Jerry's death or my being thought of as a murderess. But probably it was the burden of driving me to his office and wasting her Saturday mornings. I could've taken a bus by myself, of course, but she wanted to appear the doting mother. And she was, in her own way. Monitoring the sessions became less important as the therapy dragged on for the months the court demanded. Cy had probably recommended such vigilance. He needn't have. Mother always took a healthy interest in protecting herself. It was Dr. B. who was most disturbed by the length of the sentence. It grew progressively harder to think of things to say to each other.

I didn't mention my mother unless prodded, and only then when it felt like *not discussing* her was going to get us into trouble. I always thought of it as "us." It was "we" who were in a fix. "We" who had to improvise a solution. There'd hardly been a moment of my life when Mother was not at its center.

I assumed it was similar for all children: a child's life was not truly her own, nor should she want it to be.

My father was fair game for discussion though and guilty of all the clichés you could list about a former military man: rigid yet indulgent, smart but only in a narrow sense, demanding of perfection, yet pleased when he had to rescue us — before the divorce, at least. I needed to hand someone over to my therapist, and Daddy was the prime candidate. I focused unfairly on Daddy as the "problem" and fired away.

"Daddy doesn't visit me." Or, "Daddy never invites me to stay at his house." Or, "When I showed Daddy my report card, he said I needed to work harder if I wanted the Ivy League." This was all true.

Dr. Bailey raised his eyebrows, and I moved on.

No one else, including my grandparents, much entered into our chats. If this sounds disloyal, remember Daddy saw me less than once a month over the next five years; Mother and I often slept in the same bed. It was not unusual to wake and find my arms wrapped around her in a near stranglehold. My nocturnal grip never woke her.

By the end of my therapy, Dr. Bailey must have known the story I'd told the police, a social worker, a judge — wasn't true. I got vaguer on details, more confused over events since the initial neon clarity had faded. Mother and I hadn't practiced it often enough. She'd avoided a return to that night, perhaps having forgotten her exact lies.

And Dr. Bailey was probably too weary of Mother's presence in his outer sanctum to relive that night. Frightened of the swarm of female hormones rushing across the waiting room toward him each time he opened the door, scared of the spidery arms waving a cigarette around the room despite the "No Smoking" sign, scared too of the deep throaty laugh often erupting at his expense, scared to death of a woman who'd murdered a soda salesman with no known bad habits and let her daughter take the rap. Well, I was too.

He wasn't prepared for me either. His typical, wealthy adolescent patient was one who didn't make friends easily, got into fights at school, or told too many lies. Or perhaps a girl who suffered an eating disorder or sneaked drinks from her parents' liquor cabinet. He hadn't listened to the oddly prosaic rambling of a murderess before. Never one with a mother scarier than her daughter. He stood, mouth open, at the door of his office, his "Whip Inflation Now" coffee cup in hand, and gazed at my mother like you'd gaze at the Sphinx.

"Am I the only mother who waits for her child? Do the rest of your patients find their way here alone?" she demanded one day, holding a pile of children's magazines. "*Jack and Jill? American Miss, Seventeen?* Really?"

The next week, a fresh copy of *Vogue* sat on the table and Mother grabbed it with a squeak of delight. She put it inside her handbag when we left.

"Well, so what? He picked it up for me, right? Who else's going read *Vogue* in this nuthouse?" She glanced at it again, saying, "See his name isn't on the cover. He bought this at a newsstand. Probably afraid to look fruity to the mailman."

"Nothing like this will happen again," my mother assured me throughout my therapy, after it ended, and for years after that. "I'm off men for good, Christine."

It wasn't true. New men would appear with regularity, always bringing us trouble. Or, more often perhaps, she'd bring trouble to them.

Therapy ended, and I mostly regretted it. There were no more cheeseburgers at the Hot Shoppe, no more giggling over what I should say next week. We resumed our life without

Daddy, dreariness set in. The neon colors of the night of the murder, of those Saturday sessions at Dr. Bailey's, began to fade.

Bu before the divorce, even before what happened with Jerry Santini, my mother and I were irrevocably entwined.

CHAPTER
Five

think I was born knowing my mother was different from other mothers: prettier, more fun, more acquisitive—though I didn't know the word. I certainly knew she was more trouble. Not a day went by when I wasn't reminded.

"Your mother always wanted *things*, Christine. We hoped she'd outgrow it." Grandmother's voice was a whisper even though my mother wasn't around.

I was perhaps seven years old and as usual Mother was the topic of conversation. What else was there in our shared world? Also, as usual, Grandmother was defending her parenting more than my mother's behavior.

"It was hard for her to let go of having something once she got in her head. The day the *Sears Catalog* arrived was always a big one. It kept her occupied for weeks. I remember the time she insisted on me calling her "Little Princess." Grandmother laughed nervously. "Luckily Herbert didn't hear it. He would've had a fit. Perhaps it wasn't a *good* idea, but the boy next door wore a bath towel clipped to his collar for six months around that time, always jumping off of porch rails and trash cans. Superman, I guess. After his behavior, calling Evelyn "Little Princess" was pretty tame."

"Maybe she got her ideas from TV."

My grandmother was skeptical. "We didn't have a TV until Evelyn was in high school, and nobody turned it on much. Your grandfather hated the din." She said the word "din" carefully; as if it was the first time she'd used it aloud. "What do you think, Christine? Why does she want so many things? Why didn't she outgrow it?"

By a young age, I had a clear idea of the sort of things Mother wanted and could see the peril in certain objects from across a store.

Sometimes—and this was far worse—I could see desire creeping across her face from across a room in someone's house. I dreaded the occasions when Bucks Country matrons, back in the day when we were still with Daddy, left us alone while they went to get us lemonade and cookies. Mother's eyes would light on various items, and it was easy to imagine her sizing the odds in making off with a glass figurine without getting caught. Would Mrs. Crane remember how many Dresden figurines filled her mahogany cabinet? Maybe the red ceramic fox on the bottom shelf could go missing.

If Mother rose from her chair, I rose with her, shadowing her like a ghost. She didn't pull these tricks on the rare occasions Daddy was along, but if he was absent from the festivities, she regarded me as her ally. Winking at me, as her hand grazed a pretty trinket.

"Maybe it was the movies," I said to my grandmother, still trying to be helpful. "Maybe Mother wanted to be like Liz Taylor or Grace Kelly. Glamorous." I'd seen my mother's old movie magazines on shelves in the basement and those two actresses were often on the covers. In my opinion, Mother's life with Daddy was not so different than theirs. But there was more to Mother's difficulties than a need for glamour. I don't know when this became evident.

My grandmother nodded, but hesitantly. "My mother— your great-grandmother—worshipped movie stars. Lillian Gish, Clara Bow. Frankly, I never saw any sense in admiring someone for her looks. I tried to impress this on Evelyn, but…" She paused, and we each took a thoughtful sip of our hot chocolate.

"Now me, I admire Billy Graham's wife, Ruth," she said with fervor. "She was called to his side at a young age, you know. Following God's plan for her."

An often told tale, Grandmother had gone on the church bus to a Billy Graham Crusade meeting in downtown Philly several years before, coming home struck by his wife rather than Billy.

"Ruth saw her calling as clearly as Billy saw his." Grandmother's face flushed with the memory. "I'd never thought about being a helpmeet before. There's nobility in such service."

One of Billy's books sat proudly on her end table, signed by the great man himself. But it was a photograph of Ruth that held pride of place on their mantel. Grandmother was making her way through the Bible for the third time. If I really wanted to please her, I'd memorize a verse to recite over lunch. An especially long one might earn me a quarter.

Grandfather Hobart was even more at sea with his daughter, and in the years before he died, he often sneaked off to his woodworking projects in the garage once he'd hugged us, asked about what new thing I'd learned in school, Mother's constant headaches, if we needed any money, how the printing business my dad's family owned was doing.

"Evelyn, say the word," Grandfather would say, already edging toward the backdoor, rattling the change in his pocket as if she might demand a quarter for candy. "You too, Christine. Tell me what you need. Learn any verses today?"

Mother seldom took him up on such offers, even after the divorce when money was tighter, knowing the kind of cash she had in mind wouldn't come from his oft-mended pockets. I knew there was some bad blood between them, but nobody had filled me in on what it was.

On the trolley to their house, Mother would pull a worn copy of the New Testament out of her pocket and encourage me to learn a few lines. "Recite this one," she'd say. "For God so loved the world…"

And I'd repeat those lines or some other ones.

"Good," she'd say, sticking it back in her pocket. "No harm in softening him up a bit. He'll give you a quarter at least and look more favorably on me."

Gazing favorably on his daughter seemed pretty remote from what I saw.

"Where'd you get the Bible?"

She shrugged. "He gave me one every birthday. I raised an uneven leg on my vanity table with a stack of them back in high school." I started to say something when she interrupted, saying, "He never came in my room, you know. If he wanted me, he'd call from the hallway. Probably afraid he would spot something sordid. Dried blood on the mattress pad or something like that."

Sordid? I'd have to look up the word. But my grandfather was soured on small talk by the time I came along. We didn't get many words out of him beyond greeting and departing clichés. ("You look so pretty in your dress; still not over your cold, huh; watch out for the traffic crossing Route 211, Evelyn.")

When my grandmother and he were alone, he usually could be found in his garage woodshop. At some point, they'd divided the house. Grandmother Hobart ruled from the kitchen and living room; he, the garage. Neither of them found this partitioned occupation strange; perhaps it was generational. He was dead before my ninth birthday.

"The love of my life," my grandmother wept. She continued to weep for weeks, though I'd never once seen them touch or exchange more than the most prosaic words.

Visits to our house from my grandparents were rarer still, considering their proximity. They always chose a time when Daddy was at work, perhaps fearing recriminations on Mother's upbringing or the introduction of embarrassing information on current misdeeds. They entered our living room in Shelterville with trepidation on their faces. It was hard not to see it.

"My, this is a lovely house," my grandmother would say. "Mrs. Murphy's a wonder. Still cleaning for you? Cooking too?"

"See how I don't get an ounce of praise from her," Mother'd say after they left. "It's Mrs. Murphy, she credits. What about the décor? All my doing."

Both my grandparents probably wondered which items, displayed tastefully, were legitimately purchased and which ones had been brought home through other means. Could they get into trouble, years later, for harboring a criminal, for raising such a daughter? Had it been their duty to report her to the authorities decades ago? To do something about Eve, or Evelyn to them, before it got out of hand.

Even the items purchased legitimately were worrisome to people who lived so frugally. Shouldn't their daughter be tithing or helping missionaries in Africa like they did? Shouldn't we be saving for my college costs or their own old age? Shouldn't Mother put something away in case Daddy got disgusted enough to leave her? What was our bank account like with so many expensive items filling our shelves? Later I wondered why Mother had left such items on display—knowing how they'd react. But house-pride trumped any good sense. And she probably thought she *was* being prudent given the number of things she'd stashed away.

Yes, there were many things to examine in my mother's house, and occasionally my grandparents recognized one.

"Isn't that the cut-glass bowl your Aunt Lillian kept on her buffet?" Grandmother asked one day, her hand going at once to her mouth as if covering an imminent scream. I could tell right away she'd said it without thinking and already regretted her words—especially given the presence of my grandfather. She had a higher level of tolerance for my mother's ways than he did.

All eight eyes shot to the item in question. Grandfather began to shake his head in despair. "I tell you, Dell…"

Mother 's eyes darted around, searching for inspiration. "It's slightly different from hers, Mother." I could see her brain clicking from across the room, the swift invention of a cover story. "When I spotted the bowl in an antiques' store in New Hope, I had to have it—remembering hers so fondly." Her eyes flashed back and forth between her parents. "Dear Aunt Lillian. What good taste she has. She's famous for it. Right, Mother?"

My mother was gaining confidence as her story took shape. I could see a fulsome reminiscence on the horizon. I nodded, trying to provide any support I could.

My grandmother, eyes darting fearfully from her husband, to her daughter, to the bowl in question, voiced her agreement.

"Lillian did the altar at church on Sundays. People remarked on it all the time. Lovely taste—in flowers especially."

My grandfather sighed, pulling out a handkerchief to pat his damp forehead. A low hum began. It was unclear which grandparent used this device as a balm until my grandfather died and with him the hum.

Mother, ignoring the hum, grew more convincing as she began to believe her own lie. "I paid the moon for it too.

Probably too much but..." Her voice was strong now and she looked them straight in the eye. "Had to have it once I saw the likeness—almost a tribute to her."

She proceeded to spin the story of her purchase of the cut-glass bowl into something as fragile as the bowl itself, embellishing it with stories of trips to get its worth assessed, the insurance paid bi-monthly, a mention of registered mail orders to Dublin for special cleaning fluid.

I was on pins and needles—waiting to see what came next and wondering when she'd stolen it. We rarely visited Aunt Lillian so it might've been hidden away for years, perhaps for as much as a decade—long before I was born probably. Why did she decide to display it now? Had she forgotten where it came from or did she like to torment her parents with stories like this one? Did she relish displaying her abilities as both a thief and a liar? Although a regular circulation of Mother's booty took place in our house, she had a pretty good memory about which items were taboo. Was there a part of her wanting to be caught, confronted, and shamed?

As the details about the purchase of the bowl mounted, I was faint with anxiety. Certainly she'd go too far and they'd know the truth. They'd feel obliged to bundle the bowl under their arm and take it to Hackensack, New Jersey where Aunt Lillian lived, admitting to the elderly woman, in some stage of dementia now, that her great-niece was a thief.

What I didn't understand for a long time was my grandparents didn't want to know the truth. They were neck-deep in Mother's lies, and there was no way out. Not for any of us. They'd coddled her instead of taking action. They'd turned their heads.

"Would anyone like some peanuts?" I said.

The bowl for the peanuts was thankfully a tin with a picture of the planter's nut on it. No one would wonder about its provenance. No one acknowledged me or the bowl of nuts, and I sat back down.

Grandfather shook his head and stood, bringing an end to this particular string of lies. But perhaps their daughter, Eve, hadn't stolen it. They wanted to believe her, just as they always had. Over the years, many of Eve's "things" had come into their house with stories much like this one. Elaborate, risky stories, which were never repeated. No one trusted that Mother would fully remember her "origin" stories.

There'd always been a lot of stuff. The Hobarts encouraged it unwittingly by dragging Eve along to church rummage sales where she was given a quarter to spend, and by overlooking the items that regularly turned up in her closet or on her shelves. Items they must have known were not lawfully purchased.

Occasionally wealthier relatives, like Aunt Lillian in Hackensack, would send along trinkets and clothes they were done with. Forgotten Christmas decorations left on the sidewalk for the garbage men found their way home with her. When other kids brought home sick puppies or birds, Eve brought the crepe paper from a May pole or the tinsel from a tree. Hoarding was her real passion, although no one had named it as a disorder yet. She was perfectly willing to acquire things legitimately when the means presented themselves. It didn't always work out though, so she improvised.

Her parents' basement overflowed with such souvenirs in *my* childhood, possessions she'd outgrown but couldn't discard. All of her purchases, gifts, and stolen goods, squirreled away in carefully labeled boxes in cubby holes and cedar closets, were flashy: jewelry, baubles, knick-knacks. Pennies, but only the shiniest ones. She was not indiscriminant.

"I like pretty things. Don't you think this bracelet is pretty?"

she'd ask, showing me a gold circle formed from twined asps.

The gold paint might be chipped and one of the jeweled eyes of the snake long gone, but Mother still loved it, loved the hundreds of similar items stashed there—even after she had possessions at home worth ten or a hundred times the amount of these keepsakes. Years after she became known for her impeccable taste, there was this hidden side.

"If only we had more room at home," she'd sigh, "I'd bundle this up and ship it over. Though it's kinda nice to discover them waiting here for me like buried treasure." She waved a creamy white porcelain swan in my face. "Have you ever seen anything so sweet?"

Our house was filled with newer, more acceptable, bounty, and Daddy put his foot down about incorporating these reminders of her youth.

"It's all trash, Eve, accept it. Adults outgrow a love for dime-store jewelry and carnival prizes." When she didn't accede, he added, "Do you want me to bring my trophies and sports' gear in here too? Should I have saved my baseball cards, my Batman comics?"

I could see Mother didn't equate Daddy's memorabilia with hers, but she let it go. The Hobart basement would do as storage space for now.

Eventually she rented a storage unit in the northeastern section of Philly to handle the overflow. Ultimately she leased units in various parts of the city. She lost track of a few over the years, holding a key quizzically in her hand from time to time.

"Remember what this one opens, Christine? Was it the unit in Germantown? Conshohocken? The tag's disappeared." She smiled. "Probably means it's an older unit. Maybe Flourtown? Oh, I haven't been over to see some of my junk in ages. Let's plan a visit."

"You need to make a filing system for me, Christine. What

a help it'd be."

She often called her booty junk, making its theft or dubious acquisition less criminal perhaps. The joke was that none of it, not the trashiest possession, was junk to her. For me, her fortitude, skill, and wherewithal gave something like a cheap glass snowball some worth. Her delight was contagious. To Mother, each item was beautiful on its own terms, and she needed all of it. Wanted more of it, in fact.

Our visits to my grandparents' row house in Philly were always more about visiting her treasures than seeing her parents. They were the sentry guards to the palace, dealt with in a few minutes. We'd sit in my grandparents' slightly musty basement, unwrapping and examining some new box she'd found in a corner—or behind the furnace or under the steps.

Mother didn't offer any of her treasures to me, not the most insignificant ones, the things destroyed by time, the objects damaged by damp or rust or infestations.

"You look better in silver than gold," she'd say quickly if she saw me eyeing an item. "You prefer a more austere room. Right? None of this silly clutter for you. You're too sensible for my junk. You're more like your father."

Anything to excuse her hand's iron grip on the candlestick, the copper kettle, or the tiara.

"Or maybe I'm more like Grandmother."

She'd eye me suspiciously when I said such things, wondering if I was completely reliable.

But I didn't mind her selfishness. There was no way I could give Mother's treasures the requisite love. My eyes couldn't find the beauty in a necklace missing half its jewels. But I understood Mother's love for these trinkets. I knew to honor it, let it be.

Mother's predilections were nothing new and to understand them, to understand her, it was necessary to start at the beginning.

CHAPTER
Six

My grandparents couldn't figure out what to do with little Evelyn. Neither coveted (a word they often used) material things, craving only God's and each other's love — hoping fervently for a spot in heaven when their earthly ordeal was ended. And a large part of that ordeal centered on little Evie. She descended on their simple Lutheran lives in 1938 like a tsunami.

When Grandmother learned she was pregnant, they'd hoped for a girl, someone to help around the house, accompany them to church, tend to them in their old age. Raising a girl was easier from what they'd observed around them.

I've no doubt Evelyn Hobart was a shock and probably from her earliest days. They marveled at her beauty, her energy, her passion, but by her teenage years tried to steer clear of her. There'd been a few dicey times early in high school, occasions when a teacher called them in about items missing from drawers or locker thefts; Monday mornings when a classmate's parent called to report items lost after a party on the weekend. But none of those incidents were important enough to make a fuss about. Silly things went missing: a pair of cheap hoop earrings, a small porcelain poodle.

"These were not weekly events," Grandmother told me. "We'd forget about it, push it out of our minds."

"It's ridiculous to bring this up," a friend's parent might say to Grandmother in the grocery store or at church, "but it was my mother's favorite broach and it's been missing since Eve spent the night. It could've fallen into some crevice, but I've looked and looked…"

"Can I pay for it?" my grandmother offered quickly, unlatching the clasp on her huge handbag, looking worriedly in her change purse for the spare five. Or would it be more? What if this person demanded a fifty?

"Oh, of course not," the woman said, alarmed at the lightening-quick gesture. "It's a silly trinket—a family remembrance. A worthless thing—probably misplaced. You know teenagers." My grandmother nodded, dispiritedly. "No one would want such junk. But I thought I'd check with the girls' families before calling it a day." The woman sputtered on, any sense of an accusation buried by now.

No one, certainly not her parents, understood Mother's dreams were made of silly worthless trinkets. With the exception of one or two more serious incidents, the years passed. And my grandparents tried to forget about it.

"Dropping her off at college was such a relief," my grandmother confessed. "What a wonderful feeling." Looking at my expression, her eyes dropped.

They sent Evelyn off to college, barely able to afford the fees, but relieved she'd agreed to go despite her complete disinterest in all things academic, ecstatic when her mediocre grades opened the door to one distant, overpriced religious school in New England. They bought her the number of outfits she decreed necessary, filled out the forms, helped her settle into her room, and drove away with a relief seldom experienced by empty-nesters.

"I wonder if she'll take to her roommate," my grandfather said as they headed for the Massachusetts turnpike. "Nice enough family, wasn't it? I liked the look of her too. What was her name, Dell?"

"Gertrude or Trudy, I guess. A perfect roommate for our Evelyn," my grandmother said. "Didn't pluck her eyebrows or wear lipstick." They exchanged glances. "She probably won't have the kind of things Evelyn might take." She paused. "Want to borrow, I mean."

Her husband nodded. "No calls from Trudy's family in the middle of the night."

My grandmother chuckled, a rare thing. "The only thing for Evelyn to take from that girl would be a Bible or her cross."

"Is the cross gold?" Grandfather asked, a rare smile lighting his face.

I imagine they flashed each other a carefree look and stepped on the gas, eager to put distance between their daughter and their future lives.

They drove the two hundred miles home and within days packed away the many possessions of Mother's that had worried them over the years: items with tags still on them, or things clearly costing far more than any allowance she'd been given, belongings looking like gifts from older men — and carried them to the basement, filling the cubbyholes, cedar chest, and shelves in a few hours. In effect, they created a lifelong sanctuary for stolen property without realizing it. Once or twice, something too valuable, too likely to have been stolen, went into the trash.

"Think I'm doing the right thing," Grandfather said, a pink

cashmere scarf in his hand.

"Why wouldn't she have taken something so pretty along to college?" Grandmother wondered aloud. "If it was hers, that is."

"Must belong to the girl who went up there too. Remember the night they filled out their application together."

"Madeleine something. A rich girl, I think." Grandmother fell silent.

They'd forgotten, of course, that Eve would have to return home for holidays and vacations. Or maybe they thought ridding themselves of her belongings was the first step toward ridding themselves of her. Her bedroom was turned into a sewing room, and when Eve returned home, she lay wedged between an ironing board and a sewing machine, both relics from another time, made of iron and cumbersome. Instead of storing her prized possessions, the shelves on the walls in her bedroom now held baskets of thread and fabric, tape measures, balls of wool, packets of needles, extra parts for the sewing machine. It smelled of lubricating oil, new fabric, and the starch my grandmother sprayed on clothing before ironing. Gone too were Eve's delicate scents.

"You can't imagine how quickly they dispatched both me and my things," Mother told me when she wanted sympathy.

I stroked her soft hand.

The shelves, the ironing board, the sewing machine must have loomed over her head at night, casting shadows on the walls and giving her claustrophobia. It reminded Eve she didn't live there anymore. But her booty in the basement still had a secure home.

My grandmother told me stories about Mother's girlhood many times over the years, humbled, embarrassed, and still tearful.

Not confessions about what her daughter had done, probably still did, but at how little love she'd felt for her and, I think, of their inability to seek help. Mother grew up at a time when finding professional help for children was not much discussed. It'd never occurred to the Hobarts' that Evelyn could be "fixed" or "changed" in any way. She was an immutable presence in their life.

"It's good you can overlook your mother's ways," my grandmother told me often. "She needs someone who can. We let her down—got scared of her at some point."

But the real Eve was not their Evelyn and was a woman who needed things, glitzy things. And I didn't overlook her "ways," I abetted them, not finding it odd that I, a child, was supposed to do for her what they hadn't. And Daddy, well Daddy…

Mother met Daddy at a dance during Christmas vacation in her freshmen year of college in 1957. Hank Moran, a former high school football star and straight "A" pupil at Philadelphia's St. Joseph's High School, was a cadet at West Point. His uniform, with its shiny buttons, crisp pleats, and row of insignias, knocked her out. "In a room full of dopey teenagers, he stood out. Our eyes met in an instant and our future was set."

His shoes were polished to a sheen seldom seen in college-age men, his haircut more precise than the ones given by military barbers. Creased, shined, and clipped into perfection. Exactly the sort of man Mother would've selected from a Hollywood casting office.

"You look wonderful," his mother, Sophie Moran, had said with approval earlier, adjusting his tie although it needed no such alteration. "Perhaps you'll find the perfect girl tonight. It would be so nice if you married a local girl, someone who knows our ways—someone eager to settle here, not halfway across the country."

Since Daddy was with men only at West Point, this scenario was unlikely, but still a source of worry for Sophie. She'd no idea what was coming down the pike vis a vis a local girl.

It was one of those crisp December days in Pennsylvania, a hint of snow in the air, and Eve wore a tight, green satin dress with four-inch heels dyed to match. The dress was so snug, she didn't sit once during the evening. A picture of her was featured in the local paper to illustrate the occasion; she showed me it time and again. Her hair was shoulder-length, blonde for the first time, and poker straight in an era when everyone else's was curled and short. No one at the dance approached her level of glamour — in her estimation. Girls still dressed in full-skirts with squared-toed shoes. Stockings only occasionally replaced bobby socks. A bit of plumpness was not uncommon, and ponytails were the rage if your hair was long enough.

"You look lovely," her mother, Adele Hobart, said as she watched her slip on a coat. "But you've probably met more interesting men at college dances than you're likely to meet here."

Rail thin, Eve looked better in clothes than out of them when all of her angles looked potentially painful. Her hair and her makeup followed the trend in Hollywood at the time, lots of pearly pink. There was a legion of young blonde actresses she imitated in the late fifties: Tuesday Weld, Sandra Dee, Carol Lynley and, of course, the new plastic Barbie Doll: small-waisted, high-busted, long-legged, pert-nosed.

She'd been talked into coming along to the dance by an old school friend who assured her some men of distinction would be present.

"If it turns out to be the jokers we went to high school with, I'm leaving," Eve said. "I didn't buy this dress to dance cheek-to-cheek with a bunch of drips."

Actually she hadn't bought the dress at all, but had slipped her street clothes on over it at Filene's Department Store in Boston. The paltry spending money her father gave her would not buy dresses like this one.

"It was ridiculously easy to steal clothes back in the fifties," she told me later. "Especially if you had an air of confidence about you."

There'd been no one worthy of her attention at the Bible College, despite what her mother thought, and she was growing anxious about returning to the Hobart home permanently one day soon. Sleeping wedged between the iron board and sewing machine well into middle-age.

Her father dropped several hints suggesting her college expenses exceeded his expectation. "Wouldn't be such a bad idea to take a year off and find some work. Boston might be a good place to set down roots."

Hank Moran, clearly one of the so-called men of distinction in his cadet uniform, was smitten with Eve Hobart in seconds. He'd been waiting for the "one" too, if only subconsciously. It was an era when people married young, finding no reason to put it off. Birth control was still a chancy thing, and women, even educated ones, often couldn't support themselves. Marrying solved both of those problems. Mother sashayed into his arms, laughing at his jokes, hanging on his every word.

"Eve Hobart," he said, looking into her eyes. "Sounds like a name I was destined to hear."

"Or one I was destined to leave behind," she told him, proud of her clever repartee.

We lit up the room like Scott and Zelda," Mother said later when she was feeling charitable about Daddy. "They all must have felt the electrical charge."

I didn't doubt it for a minute. I'd felt the effects of their vibration all my life.

They took in a play at the Walnut Theater the next night, and had dinner at the Latin Casino in New Jersey the following evening. Hank Moran knew how to treat a girl, bringing a white orchid for each outing. The plain-living Hobarts were impressed. And hopeful. Marriage would be a more permanent solution than college, where the price of Eve's tuition and first semester grades, newly arrived, were worrisome. And Hank was in the service so Eve would have a chance to travel. Perhaps across the country or to Germany, they hoped.

Mother and Daddy returned to their respective educational institutions in January but wrote long, soulful letters, saw each other over breaks, and eloped when Hank graduated a year later, Eve dropping out without hesitation.

Carting her stuff to his parents' home to Bucks County gave Hank a hint of Eve's proclivities. "I brought my stuff home in the trunk of the car," he told her, climbing into the front seat of the truck they'd rented. The back was more than half-full. Several girls in her dorm had apparently stored things for her.

"Oh you, boys," she said. "You've no sentiment." She'd watched incredulously a week earlier when he tossed half of his things before moving out of his room at West Point. For a rich guy, he didn't have much of a wardrobe.

"More room for me," she'd said gaily.

Eve linked her arm through his and put her head on his shoulder as they made the six-hour drive with her loot in a trailer looming inches behind them.

"Didn't you want a big wedding?" I asked her later. A big wedding should have been the perfect centerpiece for her.

She shook her head. "My parents were planning a reception

in our church basement. Can you imagine the Morans and their hoity-toity friends in the basement with the mold, the battered tables and folding chairs, the boxes of extra Bibles and hymnals? Watching the festivities with smiles pasted on their faces as the church ladies carried in chipped trays with bowls of steaming cauliflower and a platter of pot roast. Toasting the happy couple with pineapple juice from a five-quart can placed on each table, a faint circle of rust on its bottom." She made a face. "I preferred eloping to being humiliated. You know, I've never cared so much about being the center of attention."

And it was true in a way. It was her own attention that interested her.

My grandparents were pleased on many counts: she married someone who'd take care of her; there'd be no more college tuition to pay, no more Evelyn creeping up the stairs at two in the morning. And no more Evelyn in their basement, unwrapping and repacking countless items of dubious origin. They waited a few weeks to be sure the marriage *took*, wrapped her mattress in plastic, and took it down to join the rest of her things. They were too frugal to toss it, which turned out to be a good thing.

Daddy was assigned to a base in South Carolina, and the young couple moved into their first home. Mother spent her days traipsing around the new indoor mall and in the shops on Main Street, spending the allowance her husband gave her. Occasionally she dragged a dust cloth across the tables or made some instant coffee or toast. Once in a while, she did a load of wash or put a plant on the window sill where it withered in days.

She always put on a show for Hank's return home at night and especially outdid herself at the officers' parties. Hank liked having men eye her, and as a result, him, with envy.

"You gonna wear the orange number tonight?" he'd ask her, hovering in the hallway outside their room. "I can't believe you found such a dress at the church rummage sale. Who would've tossed such a thing out? Looks brand spanking new."

"I can't imagine," Eve said. She was in the bedroom with the door closed, biting the tags off. "And it's apricot, not orange. For Pete's sake, who wears orange?" A minute later, she threw open the door and stepped out, saying. "You can dress pretty well if you're clever."

"Someone should tell my mother. You wouldn't believe what she spends on clothes."

Hank was years away from the truth. He liked glittery things too, and in some fundamental way, Eve wasn't so different from the other army wives, marking time till their days on a base in a backwater town were over. It wasn't considered decadent in 1960 to be a homemaker. Not that Eve made much of a home. Her sole inspiration had been to splatter paste on the wall behind the couch and throw gold glitter on it.

"You sure we can get it off the wall when we move on," her husband asked her, eyeing the blobs of dried paste nervously. "They don't even like us to make nail holes."

"We can take sandpaper to it," she said, improvising—but certain it would work. He liked the effect a bit more when she turned the lights low and they danced under their own stars. She never held back in such matters. That was the thing with her—she convinced you that you were something special, you were the one.

"I was probably as much in love as I'd ever be," she told me.

They dined at the officer's club nearly every night. Eve hadn't learned to cook, but this habit tightened their belts considerably.

"How about signing up for a cooking class?" Hank suggested

when he saw one offered in an adult education program nearby. "If nothing else, you'll make some friends. Learn a few recipes."

"If my mother couldn't teach me to cook, who can?" Eve shot back, trying for humor. She shrugged. "I've never cared much about food. Don't you like skinny girls?" It didn't occur to her that her husband might have an interest in eating since she didn't share it.

"I don't need anything fancy. Meat and potatoes— the sort of meals my mother served. Open a cookbook. We'd have more money for the clothes you like so much if we dined at home once in a while."

Daddy was probably remembering the German farm woman who cooked and served the dinner back in Bucks County, standing silently at Sophie Moran's elbow until she was dismissed.

Mother had only stayed at the Morans once or twice, but the vision of life there was clear. "Served—with the help of a cook! And you claim plain food is all you want. Look, I don't want it to become a problem between us later. I can hear you already— complaining to your pals about my dull meals. I've heard some of the other fellows tell tales on their wives."

"I wouldn't do such a thing." He grabbed her by the waist and enfolded her in his arms.

I imagine mother placing a hand on his thigh about then so he'd forgot about her cooking for a few hours. Still in her thrall, none of the rest seemed important to Daddy.

"And remember, we've got a perfectly good cafeteria right out the door," Eve said. "I could hardly prepare food for less than they charge."

But the cafeteria wasn't the venue for dinner. It would've been ridiculous for her to dress like she did, look like she did, and go to eat in the mess hall. Carting her still-damp brown tray to a table without a linen cloth, eating on worn Formica with the crumbs from the men who ate there earlier stuck to her elbows. Hank's good looks and precision haircut would be wasted among the proles.

So they dined at the officer's club most nights. Their food and bar bill continued to rise, and her clothing allowance was never enough.

Hank's parents subsidized their years on the base. The financial burden that living on military pay placed on the young couple made a lengthy career in the service unlikely.

"I wasn't about to spend the rest of my life on a godforsaken base," Mother said once. "Those camps are always in two-bit towns where a Friday night movie in the mess hall was the only thing going on. They showed *Bridge On the River Kwai* for months at the local theater. Military service was one of those things you got out of the way early, quickly moving on."

When money grew tight, despite the Moran family's largesse, Eve stole the things she had to have, and most often they were improbable items that nobody needed: a crystal ashtray, a doll with a face made to look like Vivian Leigh, a table lighter shaped like a cannon. Most of these items were brought home, quickly wrapped in tissue paper, and stored in the tiny basement army housing offered. Mother soon worked out a deal with the wife next door, using their basement for the overflow.

"Their basement was empty, Christine. A laundry area, a ping-pong table, and some winter boots. Can you imagine people with so few things? It was homier once I put some of my stuff in there. After I took the ping-pong table down, I had loads of room for my junk."

Mother didn't dare show Daddy the number of things she was accumulating, most of them stolen. "It was easy to pop 'em in my bag. No one expected a woman like me to take things, and I seldom hit the same place twice. Plus, I always made sure to buy goods from their stores when I could afford it, making myself known as a loyal patron. probably spent more than I stole."

She told me this as if it meant she'd played fair — had done what she did only when pushed by circumstances.

"The one or two times someone caught me at it, they were willing to overlook it. Nobody wanted legal problems with an officer's wife. A good-looking military wife could steal the moon right out of the sky, and no one would say a word about the resulting darkness."

When I looked puzzled, she clarified it. "The base kept the town afloat — the soldiers and their families — the things they bought." This arrangement evened things out for her; she would buy what she could afford and take the rest. What more could they expect?

Daddy's family disapproved of Eve Hobart from the start — though they had no specific knowledge of her acquisitive ways. Nouveau-riche country-club people, the Morans' ran a printing business in Philadelphia, then eventually in Bucks County. Sporadic visits from the young couple to their spacious property in Lahaska seldom went well. It wasn't merely a matter of using the right fork or proper grammar either.

"They were always asking me what I was reading, what I thought about the famine in China or wherever it was going on that particular year. Who I voted for in the election, did I think Castro would govern better than Batista? One long test I was certain to fail."

Mother didn't know these were the topics most people talked about — that serious discussions were the norm in some families. Being informed, witty, and quick-thinking was valued in certain sets. She assumed she was at the wrong end of a test, the only one being asked to perform.

These were not the sort of skills passed on at the Hobart

home. The dinner table was a place for chewing, swallowing, breathing, and little else. Both of Mother's parents came from families poorer than they were, families less likely to have something interesting to say, even more religious. Silence at the dinner table was immutable. Any attempt on Mother's part to introduce a discussion was met with...

"Evelyn, don't talk with your mouth full."

"There's nothing in my mouth."

"Your food's going to get cold." Silence. "You'll digest your dinner better if you save your chitchat."

She explained it to me later. "Oh, I know the Moran dinner table talk sounds normal to you, you're used to their ways, used to them putting on a show, but it was a test they knew I'd fail. If I read a book, I wouldn't tell them what it was. They turned up their noses at the kind of books I liked. Snooty bastards. They wanted me to read Steinbeck, Pearl Buck, or Michener, the books they read. Big intellectual doorstops. Nothing by Harold Robbins or Grace Metalious. I never heard them quizzing each other on the political situation. Only me."

Mother pushed a thumb into her chest and frowned, remembering. "They loved making me look bad in front of Hank. It got so I hardly came out of my room when we visited — which was probably what they wanted — to have their precious son to themselves. "Oh, is Eve ill again, Hank? Too bad. Not taking dinner tonight, we'll send her a tray. Doesn't want to go riding today? Tsk, tsk."

After two years on the base in South Carolina and some more time in Texas, Daddy's commission ended, and my parents moved back to Pennsylvania. Daddy began the slow process of taking over the family business. His father, Big Dave Moran, had married and had children late in life and was already entering his sixties with medical conditions that made full-time work difficult. Sophie wanted to travel while they still could. Daddy's sister, Linda, in her late twenties, lived at home, already a companion to both of them.

"Once we moved north, they were in my face all the time. They found us a house about five miles from theirs in Doylestown, a pokey little burg. Not like now, Christine," Mother said. "The whole area was Hicksville in the 1960s. The Morans' and their friends hid out at the clubs, and you know how well I got along with that set, which left me to consort with the hoi-polloi."

"Couldn't we at least live in the city," Eve asked Hank, once she'd seen the 1870s house her mother-in-law had chosen for them — a house with irregular ceilings in every room, bulging walls, tiny windows placed in odd spots, a stove from the nineteen twenties. She stared menacingly at the clawed foot bathtub, the porch with the sagging floor, the water-marred wallpaper with its huge, predatory flowers.

"Philadelphia, Hank," she went on, insistently. "You grew up there. You'd be a lesser man today if you'd lived out here instead. My stuff — our stuff's — not going to look good in this house. We like modern furniture, right, Hank? Not the kind of horse-haired sneeze factories that go well in this dump. Doilies, wicker birdcages, chandeliers with a million crystals to keep clean. Dusty old rugs they call antiques so you can't pitch them."

"The business is located out here now," Hank said. "You'll have to make do with a more rural setting. Join a few clubs and get into the swing of country life. Take up golf or charity work. Horseback riding, tennis, the Ladies' Auxiliary, one of the women's circles at the church, a book group." He was probably already beginning to get the pinched look he'd have for the rest of his life.

It was hard for Mother to feed her need for shiny acquisitions in a place like Doylestown, where local merchants catered to farmers and townspeople, who seldom made the one-hour trek into the city. People who rarely demanded more than canned goods and Sears' catalog merchandise. The rich ordered by phone from New York or made the monthly trip into Philadelphia.

"Maybe you can help out in the office if you get bored," Daddy suggested.

"Can you imagine me answering the phone or typing bills? I didn't go to college to be a secretary."

"What did you go to college for, Eve? How *do* you see yourself spending your days," Daddy asked after several months of her idleness, a year of pleading with him to move. "Register for a few courses, get your teaching certificate. Or maybe learn real estate. The guy running against Joe Clark for the Senate could use your help."

There was no question, Hank's tolerance for her indolence and acquisitiveness had waned. Eve could wear anyone out. She wouldn't find her natural lieutenant till I was born.

Eve puffed up with indignation. "I see myself taking care of your children," she said, cagily. "A boy and a girl." She lowered her eyes. "I already have their names picked out."

"If such a thing happens, you can pick out a house wherever you like." He patted her head, probably assuming such an event was not in the cards since his wife guarded any unprotected entrée to her baby-making parts more carefully than Coca Cola guarded access to its secret formula.

But he was wrong. Eventually.

CHAPTER
Seven

Two detours interrupted Mother's path to reproduction, neither happy events. A few days after Hank asked Eve whether she had any plans for herself, when he was still flush with anticipation, if slight skepticism, at his approaching fatherhood, Eve traveled into the city to do some spring shopping. 1962. Shopping in downtown Philadelphia was still something special. A trip "downtown," rather than to suburban main streets or the mushrooming malls, communicated a message about the seriousness and glamour of the task.

Mother's trip on that particular day was a story told to me many times: by Mother, Daddy, Aunt Linda, Grandmother Hobart, and other Moran family members. Perhaps all families have a story repeated often, but probably one with a less calamitous conclusion. A saga where something noble happened, where someone does a good turn, saves a life. Ours was a different sort of story.

Since it's mostly Mother's story, this is her version and the one I loved to hear her tell. She had no compunctions about spilling the more salacious parts of it and I had none about listening.

Eve put on her new pink linen suit, a pair of black, patent-leather heels, short pink gloves, and a perky Janet Leigh kind of hat. She ordered a taxi to the railroad station and took a train to 30th Street in Philadelphia, and then another train to Market Street, the principal shopping area. The length of the trip worked against it becoming a commonplace event, which may have been Hank Moran's primary reason for choosing Doylestown for their home.

But Eve got herself to center Philly without much fanfare, stepping off the train full of expectation for the day ahead. There were four elegant department stores in which to shop in 1962. Not playing favorites, Eve pocketed an item from each of the stores within an hour of arriving. The "rush" she experienced from impetuous forays into quasi-criminal activity was a feeling she'd subconsciously sought since their return to Pennsylvania. Her life in Doylestown played as flat, monotonous, gray. And yet, she hadn't *planned* on spending the day like this. It simply overtook her more ordinary intentions.

Lit Brothers, the most modestly appointed and priced department store, occupied a city block and appeared to be forged from cast-iron. Its place in the Philadelphia pantheon of stores — its very reputation — rested on being the affordable alternative to the remaining triumvirate. Affordable or not, Eve waltzed in through the Market Street door and stole a bottle of perfume from the first counter she came on. The clerk, busy with a large purchase from an imposing Main Line matron at the other end of the counter, missed both Eve's fleeting appearance and the theft. This customer seemed to inhale all the air in the room with her voluminous baggage and personage. Eve stored this observation for later use.

"It wasn't the scent," Mother admitted. "I've smelled nicer perfume at People's Drugstore. It was the bottle—pink crystal and shaped like a swan. I'd have it still if those security men hadn't seized it as evidence."

Eve exited Lit's and made her way to Strawbridge and Clothier's, across the street. The fourth-floor lingerie department was a quick jaunt up the escalator. In minutes, Eve found the rose, lace-trimmed negligee she'd been dreaming about. She folded it into a square the size of a table napkin, stuffed it in her purse, and moved on. Again, no one gave her a glance. Department stores in 1962 teemed with bored, rich women, especially on a mild spring day. It was nearly lunch hour now. Businessmen often dined here after choosing a necktie to match a shirt or purchasing a gift for the wife at home. Noon was a pleasant hour. It was the after-school and weekend crowd that made store management anxious.

Eve took a ceramic candy dish from a window display near the back of the store at Gimbels. Little more than a prop, but its pattern was perfect for her new modernistic décor: small irregular squares of bright colors, looking like it'd been designed by Paul Klee. The dish would be perfect on the coffee table with a handful of Hershey's silver kisses inside. She'd whip her hideous house into something elegant or else. Into her purse it went.

Wannamaker's: a bit of a walk, but the Queen Bee of Philadelphia stores was the emporium where dreams were made, boasting the largest organ in the world, which hovered over the Grand Court. Through some mysterious mechanics, floral scents wafted over the throngs of shoppers at Easter. Models stalked the floor in spring fashions that time of year, answering customer queries in a hushed tone. Eve ducked to avoid a collision with a model in tennis togs. Lilac was big—

tiny checks, taffeta, cinched waists. Women mirrored Jackie Kennedy and Audrey Hepburn. The number of blondes had decreased since the presidential election two years ago. Suddenly brunettes, willowy thin, were in vogue.

Eve was drawn to a bracelet with chunky gambling charms: dice, a roulette wheel, a horse, a racing form. She had to have that trinket and unobtrusively slid it off the disembodied plastic arm on the counter, admiring her own skill as she dropped it into her pocket.

On her way to the door, a clerk handed her a shopping bag. "We don't like to see our competition's bag so prominently displayed," the woman joked, motioning toward the Gimbel's bag in Eve's hand. The Gimbel's bag held a soft pretzel and two wrapped chocolates purchased from Gimbel's food counters.

After the clerk moved on, Eve stepped into the passage to the restrooms, cleared her handbag of merchandise, popped a chocolate in her mouth and headed for the door. A man in a dark suit grabbed her arm as it reached for the door. It was a firm grip. No way to wiggle out of it.

"Come along this way, Miss," he said in a low tone. Like Paul Winchell, the ventriloquist on TV, his lips hardly moved at all. "Don't want to make a fuss now, do we?"

He swiveled his head, nodding toward the crowd of shoppers threatening to engulf them. Eve reviewed her options, found none, and went along.

In the elevator, his hand continued to grip her elbow. The uniformed operator shot her a sympathetic glance while delivering them to the top floor. She'd probably seen this a hundred times, watched other women or children or men make this wretched trip. The man in control of Eve's arm captured shoplifters and miscreants every day: women who couldn't keep their hands off the merchandise; men who picked pockets; scoundrels of both sexes with stolen charge plates; boys who broke things then ran; girls who sneaked into dressing rooms and came out looking like polar bears, or ones ransacking the makeup counters, dropping tubes down their blouse or into their pockets. There were the new teams of *boosters* too, who made a science out of it according to the newspapers. It was an epidemic and today Eve was part of it.

This man was an expert in methods to defraud his store and felt no pity for her; she could sense it. She was certain to have bruises and a nasty wrinkle or two in her jacket. And this would be the least of her troubles.

No one spoke to them as they passed along narrow hallways and climbed the final flight of uncarpeted steps. He showed her inside a gloomy office minutes later, silently holding the door open. She pushed by him, trying not to brush against his obvious disdain. But she was close enough to smell onions on his breath, garlic, power.

It was more cell than office. Dark, almost windowless, small—a battered walnut table, two chairs, cheap paneled walls. It smelled of smoke, burnt coffee, Dentyne chewing gum, sweat. It was a serious office, not the sort of room where suburban women were coddled, pitied, or forgiven. Not a place where sympathetic gestures were made, not where men in off-the-rack suits overlooked transgressions if a pretty face stared back at them. My mother couldn't think of how to turn this around—of how to make it go away. Her brief detentions with inexperienced clerks in backrooms of tiny shops in South Carolina or Texas were no preparation for the security staff at John D. Wannamaker's. She'd no leverage to use here, no husband wearing bars or stars on his chest on a base a mile away to allude to obliquely.

"I think you may've misunderstood what happened today." It was important to establish herself as a person of character. "My husband runs a printing business…"

"Not a day goes by when someone doesn't say something like that to me," he said, motioning to a chair. "Says they were gonna pay for it all in a minute."

"I'm sure I have the necessary receipts somewhere in my bag." She began to reach for her handbag, but he didn't hand it over.

This man, this security guard looking like military police, had seen and heard it all before. She couldn't think of anything to offer him. Any idea about how to charm him. He seemed far too tired to trade her release for a grope or a kiss. There was some relief in this information though, in knowing she'd been out-maneuvered and could wait for her sentence without discussion. A sort of calm descended.

He gestured again to a wooden chair, and once she was seated, he proceeded to remove the items from her bag, one by one, shaking his head at the variety of store tags, and saying, with a hint of a chuckle, "Don't play favorites, do you? Was it on a dare?" He tossed her hard-won booty on the table. "Half of this is junk, Lady. A dish probably selling for $2.99? Crissake, it has dust in it!" He held up his finger and she blushed. "And this. This," he said, picking up the bracelet from downstairs, "this is something a twelve-year old girl buys. Not a woman like you." He fingered the dice. "Kind of a sign, isn't it? You like taking chances, right? Have to have your souvenirs, don't you? Even though they're worthless ones."

He asked to see her driver's license, wrote a sentence or two on his pad, gathered the stolen goods, and headed for the door. "Part of the kick, huh? Seeing if you can get away with it? Guess what? You can't." He shut the door behind him.

She hadn't uttered another word about her innocence, not a sentence more of denial. No protests or grimaces at her rough handling. And his suggestion that seeing if she could get away with it was part of the kick, was ridiculous. She knew she'd get away with it. Dime-store psychologists were running loose. She sat for a long time wondering if they'd called the police yet. What the fine or punishment might be? Could she cover it herself? How would Hank react if she couldn't? Would she have to tell him? She could already picture his red face, purple when she crossed swords with him. Maybe there'd be some way to avoid his involvement. How much money did she have with her? She hadn't planned on needing more than enough for a quick sandwich at a counter. Money spent on food was wasted money. She reached for her purse.

Something similar to this—an incident where things had spun out of control—had happened to her once before when she was fifteen. She'd taken a lipstick from Woolworth's makeup counter. Well okay, a couple of tubes of lipstick and some eye shadow on the theory "in for a penny in for a pound."

The clerk caught her, grabbing her wrist as she reached for the third tube, making her sit on a stool while she called Herbert Hobart after going through her pocketbook to find his name. The clerk had dumped all the contents on the counter, attracting the attention of a number of shoppers as they rattled on the glass. Her cheap, worn-out possessions were ridiculous on display—a comb needing cleaning, used tissues, bus tokens, a torn makeup case. Shabby. The whole incident might've been forgotten if her purse's interior hadn't branded her as that.

Her father came after her. Grim-faced, stoop-shouldered, scuffed-shoed Herbert Hobart, hat in hand. Leaving his cubicle at the Philadelphia Naval Yard, paying the dime store clerk with nickels and dimes and quarters for her theft as if he didn't have a real bill in his pocket, as if the Hobarts were the poorest mice in the city. The clerk scooped Eve's things from the counter, making a face, returning them to her pocketbook, her pocketbook to her.

Her father didn't speak once on the bus ride home, hadn't

said a word about it since. She didn't know if he'd told her mother. She'd brought shame on him once again. He didn't ask her why she'd done it. Didn't remind her of the eighth commandment.

Somehow there was nothing but a long line of dour-faced men in her life: fathers, husbands, school principals, security guards, cops. Each of them avoiding her eyes, disappointed with her in the end. The episode back in high school hadn't changed her behavior, but it'd made her more careful. No one who counted had caught her — until today.

And no one caught her with a pocketbook full of dross again. She became careful about many things — and one of them was the contents of that bag, which became clear that day was a reflection of herself. Never again would someone empty her purse on a counter and find used tissues, dirty combs, Tampax, worn lipsticks and other makeup, half-eaten boxes of Good & Plenty, stuff she'd taken from other girls' lockers in school, snapshots of movie stars from Hollywood studios autographed by a machine.

"Those little shops near the army base — the stores I was used to — none of them hired security guards, Christine."

The women in such stores, many the wives of GIs making a little pin money, were glad to let it go knowing she'd come back and spend double what she stole. But a store like Wanamaker's...

There was less than fifteen dollars in her purse. She counted it twice to be sure, checked the little pockets, unrolled the white hanky, dug around in her suit jacket pockets. Too little money to pay a fine or bribe the guard if it came to that.

Looking at the spare change made Mother feel like the old Eve Hobart again, paying bills with nickels and dimes, walking across a college campus with no money in her pocket when everyone else had plenty, when the other girls had a new dress for the dance, money to go into Boston to see a play, money for a dinner in town.

She hadn't expected to need much cash today, had no expectations for the day at all. She'd come here in a fog. In fact, she seldom set out to do what she'd done. Some part of her brain must make the plan, lay out the geography of it, and only let her in on it incrementally.

Could she tell this to whoever came into this room? Say she hadn't known any of this would happen—that she didn't mean to take those things, hadn't exactly considered her heart's desire till it was tucked inside her purse. Would they care she'd set out from Doylestown this morning in her pretty pink suit with nothing but a jaunt into the city in mind. Then suddenly—and it always came over her like this—she had to have one or two of the beautiful things she saw, things she'd always wanted— for practically her whole life. It was as if she was in a dream— maybe she was. She did these things like she was sleepwalking. There must be a name for it.

It would be a long time before she heard it though.

She rose, stretched, and glanced out the tiny window, down at the people on the street floors below, people free to walk around, to have lunch, to make a purchase. Only an hour ago, it'd been she who was free and walking these streets without a care. She paced the cell-like room, thinking about the injustice of it. Occasionally a secretary or a uniformed guard opened the door, never saying a word, probably checking on whether she'd disappeared. Making sure she hadn't magically stuffed herself in some bag or box or drawer and found her way out of the office, out of the store, much like the stuff she'd tried to take. But there was no escape, only long, sinewy hallways lined with the offices of people who'd spot her should she try to run: her captors.

She couldn't make herself disappear or she'd have done it long ago. Certainly done it back at Woolworth's. Or on that bus ride home with her father. The Hobart family always used public transportation for travel to work and school, and her theft was not deemed reason enough to change this. Cars were for church and shopping trips, where carrying so many packages was out of the question, where the trip was too long. Not for prosaic destinations like the dime store. She still remembered the tired faces of the people getting on and off the bus as her father's nose pressed hard against the window, his breath fogging it up, his faint reflection in the dirty glass a rebuke.

She'd waited years for him to bring the day up, to ask why she took those ridiculous things, to slap her, punish her, or banish her. Instead the incident festered between them, one more thing to hold against her.

Hank suddenly stood in the doorway on Wanamaker's top floor, looking more tired than angry. His face was ashen.

"Come on," he said, offering his hand. "Let's get it over with."

Although the gesture implied some feeling for her — some pity — his voice was cold. Holding her hand firmly, he led her out of the room. No one stood in their way in the hallway; no one peeked from drawn blinds or through open doors. Mother was in a fog still, absolutely terrified at ending her days at Eastern State Penitentiary. Horrified at the thought of being in a room the size of the one she'd left, or a smaller one, for years perhaps. Would this be her fate? Get what over with? What had Hank meant by that phrase?

Her husband led her to a larger, brighter office in the famous Wanamaker's Department Store, the mother ship of emporiums in Philadelphia. It was too bad she hadn't been caught at Lit's, she thought, as she followed him. Lit Brothers, or even Strawbridges, or Gimbels didn't have such an exalted notion of itself. She'd have been able to bluff her way out—their security wouldn't have made so much of it.

The room Hank led her to was carpeted with a richly-colored, thick rug. A slight odor of stale cigars—but better ones— also hung in the air. Maybe the odor of a fine whiskey and perfume perhaps? She wasn't going to be put in the Eastern State Penitentiary, she realized. Hank had seen to it. People charged with a crime didn't get ushered into offices like this one. Somewhere along the way, her fortune had changed. Someone realized her circumstances. Hank had probably given them a deal on their printing needs for the next fifty years. Men like him didn't have wives incarcerated in the Eastern State Penitentiary. It was unthinkable—unallowable no matter what the cost.

The store manager came in, Bill Something, a fellow St. Joseph's graduate though ten years earlier. Hank abandoned his silence for loquaciousness. A rush of glad-handing followed; jocular remembrances of St. Joe's; memories about which priests were still teaching in Hank's day; talk of cafeteria food; of theatricals with all-male casts; the punishments dispensed by the principal; a few common friends. This took five minutes, during which my mother said she stood like a convicted felon awaiting sentence.

"Those were the worst minutes in my life," she said.

The two men eventually ran out of high school remembrances, agreeing Eve would get professional help.

"I've something in mind already," Hank told the store manager. "A place for Eve. I've heard good things about this facility. Talked to the administrator today—right after your call." (Mother didn't get upset at these words, assuming it was a lie meant to extricate her.)

"It's a sickness," the store manager said, nodding his approval at Daddy's solution. "We see it all the time here—as you can imagine." He looked obliquely at Mrs. Hank Moran and shook his head. "Can't help herself, you know. And she'll keep doing it until she gets some counseling. Or goes to jail."

My mother, with great effort, controlled the urge to whack him with her purse. Did he think she was deaf or mentally deficient? Speaking to Hank like she wasn't in the room. And Hank had done it, too, not once glancing at her. Ashamed of her like her father was all those years ago but better at hiding it. Some boys' school behavior he'd learned at his costly Catholic high school, where girls were seen only as suitable for childbearing or dance partners.

The men talked over her head—literally. Why had no one spoken to her for the entire two hours she'd sat in that dark office? Why had her husband been brought here? Why must he speak for her, take care of her? If it'd made sense when she was fifteen, it didn't now. There was a woman in the Senate, for god's sake. It was the 1960s. Her gynecologist was a woman, the vet who tended the Morans' horses too.

"Won't do you a bit of good to smack her around either," the security manager added, snapping her out of her stupor. "It's a compulsion she's got." A bead of sweat suddenly mustached his lip. "A disorder or something." Hadn't he said this minutes before? "You'll have to ask the men in white coats what to call it. I see it all the time. Itchy fingers."

The store manager's desire to both align himself with Hank and demonstrate his power over them was making him babble. The heat in the office rose. Hank must have seen the dangerous look in Eve's eyes because he began edging her toward the door.

"Well, thanks for giving—us—another chance," he told Bill Something. "There won't be another incident, I can assure you. She'll stay away from Wanamaker's in the future. Right, Eve?"

He didn't look at her. No one was looking at her. She nodded anyway.

"Forget about it," the man said, released from the need to dominate the room. "I know you'll take care of the little lady. Make sure she gets the kind of help she needs." He looked at my mother directly for the first time. "Our upbringing, you know. The Church. Made us responsible men. We take care of our women."

Eve didn't hear his last name—this responsible man with good upbringing from fine schools, who now was a department store cop. He was still talking.

"I've expunged the record, Hank. You can forget about it."

She felt something coming off this Bill. Some sort of stench at the thought of hitting her, hurting her, having her sexually probably. His eyes seemed unfocused in some insidious way. His hands clenched and unclenched at the sudden flood of power moving through them. If he hadn't discovered Hank Moran was her husband, would he have come alone to that other dank office and done something foul to her?

She'd stay away from downtown Wanamaker's. Frequent one of their smaller, more anonymous stores.

"To say I'd never cross their foyer again was too great of a promise," Mother told me. "But not any time soon."

Not with the chance of this guy bringing her to his office without Hank's protective arm—an arm she needed but resented. She wondered if he'd inform the other stores of her activity and decided no. He'd have to admit he let her go, that he was bought off.

Like her father, ten years earlier, her husband didn't speak on the ride home. It was a Buick LeSabre rather than a bus, but that was the only difference. The silence was the same: scorching and horrible. There were always grim-faced men in charge of her, she thought again. Men who guided her around by the elbow, steering her like an unwieldy ship into port. Men whose faces would crack if they tried to smile. Men who were ashamed of what she'd done—at their association with her.

When they pulled up to the Moran family home, Hank turned to her and said, "I thought your thieving would stop once we left those army bases. Once we had enough money."

She was shocked. So he'd known of her thefts. Probably paid people off, did things like he'd done today to keep her out of jail. And she'd believed those women—those shopkeepers—had let it go. She believed she had conned them.

Daddy deposited her in her old room at the Morans' house, where she could be more easily watched, and went downstairs to do battle with his family. She listened at the heating grate—like she always did.

If I had written Daddy's version of the day, it'd be about shame, about meeting with a lummox he hadn't known at all but been forced to bargain with. To play the beta male to an idiot's alpha. Being humiliated again for his wife's petty thefts, having a stranger assume he was surprised at his wife's need to steal baubles he could easily pay for.

The Terraces was a progressive sanitarium, created to satisfy the needs of the area's wealthy. Less fortunate people in southeastern Pennsylvania needing a "rest" went to Norristown State Hospital. The Moran family voted to send Mother to Norristown, claiming The Terraces was more a gift than a punishment. But Daddy overruled them, coughing up the dough without their help for the campus-like feel of The Terraces: for the large, well-appointed single rooms, for the naturalized swimming pool, the game room, for the horses, three-hole golf course, and tennis courts. And, of course, it was chockfull of psychiatrists with progressive ideas.

Hank had visited an aunt at Norristown State Hospital years ago and still remembered the pleas for deliverance coming from each door he passed. It'd been like a prison. It was a prison. "It's not about gifts or punishments. We want Eve to get well," he told the gathered Moran clan. "Which place has the better doctors?"

"Isn't prison what your wife deserves? Isn't prison where she'd be if you hadn't paid the fool off? It's not like she's weepy or talks to herself," his mother said. "She's hardly likely to throw herself out a window. She's a troublemaker and a thief."

Hank stuck by Mother, despite the Morans' machinations, although he didn't tell his parents what she'd actually done — the entire scope of it at least.

"Can you blame me?" he asked me when I was old enough to understand.

He made it sound like she'd forgotten to pay for the bracelet, leaving out the other thefts entirely. The full story about Eve's frontal assault on Philadelphia's big four department stores would've become family legend (as it eventually did) had he spilled the entire sordid story, and Daddy wasn't going to be the starting point for what would soon drift beyond the family circle and into Bucks County lore. It could easily turn up on the back page of the town paper — the rag listing local break-ins and car thefts.

Hank loved Eve and still believed they could work things out. But he also wanted to impress his parents with his decisiveness, with his ability to handle a situation — especially his wife. It was important to act quickly to deal with Eve's addiction, obsession, or whatever it was, to show he was on top of things, ready for the task of running the family business.

"An observation period," the doctors at The Terraces told

him, "Forty-five days. Truthfully, Mr. Moran, a stunt like this is a cry for help."

The doctors at The Terraces expressed confidence in a quick and complete cure.

The two doctors he spoke with acted self-assured in their starched white coats, the sort of men Daddy was used to dealing with in both the military and in business. He was immediately convinced by both their demeanor and words.

"You think she might be well enough to return home after the forty-five days?"

The doctors nodded without hesitation.

"I'll have her here tomorrow."

He hurried back to Doylestown, packed her bags, and escorted her to the car. The family doctor had given Mother a prescription for Valium to ease the move. At twice the usual dose, it produced an immediate torpor.

Later, Mother claimed to remember nothing between exiting the Buick after her mischief at John D. Wanamaker's and finding herself standing in the rather grand entrance hall at The Terraces. She also forgot Hank had known about some of her misadventures in South Carolina, had paid people off there.

CHAPTER

Eight

The Regimen. It was the cusp of a new era of treatment for the mentally ill. No more lobotomies or electric or insulin shock treatments. No more straight-jackets or wrapping patients in wet cloths. Instead it was the era of talk therapy.

Patients in 1962 at an institution like The Terraces talked to their therapist on a daily basis, like it or not. There were group meetings, sessions with residents, chats with the interns. A weekly conference on the patient's individual recovery process was de rigueur. Patients had to talk their head off to be released, remembering or inventing dreams, thoughts, fixations, grievances, childhood traumas — all of this to feed the doctors' need to probe their minds.

"Tell me how you feel," employees of The Terraces demanded. "What did you dream about last night? How do you feel about your mother, your father, your fourth-grade teacher? When you hear the word "tree" what's the first word you think of? Do you believe in God? Do you have evil thoughts? Ever contemplated killing yourself? Anyone else? Has anyone beaten you? Made you stay in the cellar? Sent you to bed hungry? Did your father come into your room at night and touch you? Ask you to touch him?"

The last questions, ones to which Mother's doctors constantly returned, were laughable. Her father never touched her — period. No hugs, kisses, no sitting on his lap — as far back as she could remember.

"We weren't a terribly physical family," she told them.

And as her daughter, I can vouch for it.

When she told a therapist this after several weeks at The Terraces, he'd nodded sagely as if they'd finally arrived at the truth.

"Repressed desire on the part of your father," he murmured aloud, noting it on her chart. "Afraid to touch you, which is just as lethal as sexual desire acted upon. Either way, the child senses himself at fault for a parent's actions or inactions. Is he still alive?"

Eve nodded.

They sat quietly for a moment, contemplating this piece of information. The doctor raised his head, smiling. "How about your mother? Adele, is it?" He looked at this chart. "Kiss you, hug you?"

Eve shrugged, unwilling to disclose any more information.

"Did my mother kiss me?" Mother wondered aloud years later. She remembered stiff little embraces, a peck on the cheek, but nothing more.

"Did your parents' religion advise such treatment?" the doctor at The Terraces had wanted to know. "What sect were they in?"

At first, she though he'd said sex, and this idea shook her out of her inertia for a moment. No, sect. Did their horrid little church with its clear glass windows and hard wooden pews set her on this course? Was it the responsibility of that unbearably thin minister, Mr. Peeley, who'd refused to wear a collar or any adornment and sauntered up and down the aisle to yell at them at close hand? Had he been significant? Had their barren church and bleak life led to a need for adornment?"

"It wasn't a regular church," she told the doctor. "Nothing like Episcopalian, I mean."

Yes, a patient had to talk herself hoarse to be released from The Terraces. Had to find some way to gain the upper hand through a pretense of cooperation, gratitude, trust.

"Mrs. Moran, wouldn't you like to join our little group?" a nurse or doctor or social worker might say. It took Mother some time to learn such an invitation wasn't optional. Refusals only lengthened the stay. Eve Moran's chart was soon peppered with words like "unresponsive," "uncooperative," "negative." Oh yes, she sneaked a look more than once.

Talk therapy wasn't the preferred treatment for a case like Mother's. Freud said "talking" worked best on garden-variety neurotics, and there were plenty of those to practice on at The Terraces. Rich older women, running wild on the huge boost of adrenaline accompanying menopause loved to talk, and they sustained The Terraces. In the afternoon, it was hard to differentiate the group chattering enthusiastically on the back patio from a Bucks County gardening club.

The "talking cure" continued to be highly thought of at The Terraces although it was losing popularity elsewhere as a new generation of drugs came along. The Terraces was meant to function like the expensive spa of a generation later, or the tuberculosis sanatorium of a generation earlier, not as a dispenser of quick-fix medication. Doctors hired by the management were slow to make any changes depriving them of their greatest strength. What were those doctors to do once their patients were jerked or smoothed into normalcy by pharmaceuticals?

Talking's efficacy at The Terraces was also somewhat negatively affected by the sanitarium's continuing reliance on the one drug they liberally dispensed to the least cooperative patients—Thorazine. An antipsychotic drug of the time, it stifled its partakers more effectively than a gag. The only thing coming out of their mouths was drool. So the principal drug and the principal philosophy were at cross-purposes, but the drug still got prescribed. Residents on Thorazine were often sequestered when visitors arrived. A scare—such as seeing a loved one or even a stranger on Thorazine—was to be avoided at all costs.

Talk. The rest of a patient's day was spent outdoors when possible, taking exercise, doing the array of activities (volleyball, badminton, swimming) one would do on a restful retreat. Walking was especially prized as a therapeutic tool, and the grounds were lovely. Stay on the gravel path and you were neurotic; drift from it and you were manic. Someone was always taking notes, filming the patients at play with their large, obtrusive movie cameras, recording individual and group sessions.

Eventually The Terraces existed only in a documentary film, hours long—which was shown as amusement for students at medical schools half a century later. The patients often waved to the camera man, making it clear the footage couldn't be taken as credible. It was similar to the newsreels shown of the royal family at leisure.

Visitors, especially those viewing the facility briefly or those viewing patients not on Thorazine, went away thinking that spending some time there—perhaps a few weeks—wasn't such a bad idea. And what if their loved one complained about his treatment? Well, they weren't to be trusted, were they? This was why Aunt Mildred, Cousin Arthur, or Eve Moran was at The

Terraces. Because their words and impressions were cockeyed, their analysis of a situation, unreliable.

"Hank, you got to get me out of this place," Mother told him the first time he visited, her teeth chattering like a gag gift.

Some staff member had chosen her clothes — and badly. Her hair was scraped back with barrettes — like a fifth grader.

"Be patient, Eve," Daddy said, patting her. "The good people here are going to get you back on track."

Daddy's clichés, his bon vivant speech, wasn't convincing, Mother later said. Wouldn't they see easy compliance as a superficial solution to her problems?

"I've seen a sample of that *track*, Hank — the way people walk on it. In lock-step." She gazed meaningfully around the terrace, where most of the residents had the same flattened-out look on their faces.

Despite Mother's harsh assessment, institutional life turned out to be pleasant for many residents. Constant comments on their little oddities came to a halt; no worrisome access to the weapons available in the average house; someone handy to make sure they were out of bed and dressed; a kindly hand to adjust the water temperature in the shower; a hand on the elbow should they begin to slip (the affect again of Thorazine) when walking the hills; if requested, a goodnight kiss on the forehead. Nothing untoward, but a level of care no longer — if ever — received at the hands of their loved ones. Touch and talk. This was the way to treat mental illness.

Eve shunned much of this regime. Giving the staff the idea she was going to be difficult. A hostile patient — no scratch that — a hostile resident who might make life hard would need certain handling. Information like this snaked down the hallways within hours.

Hobbies were encouraged at The Terraces: music, painting, dance, writing poetry to read aloud to other residents, after-dinner, skits. Walk, eat, talk—what's so terrible about that? Mother had no interest in spending time on these pursuits. Once she shook off her initial torpor, she was usually engaged in active revolt toward attempts to include her.

"I was a regular activist. Someone needed to remind the patients they were being handled, not treated."

A few centuries earlier, "residents" at a facility like The Terraces, eager to be free of the awfulness of their lives, would have gone to a nunnery or the army instead. The Terraces was quite a bit nicer and demanded no fealty to God or Country. It was the Self which needed elevating, developing, defending, exalting. Love Thy Self and the rest would follow.

My mother believed in this credo on some level, or would have if she'd given it any thought. She wasn't at The Terraces for more than a week of her forty-five-day observation period when she began placing telephone orders to various stores for "the sort of things I needed to make my room homey. I hate an institutional look."

She had a stack of fat catalogs sitting on her lap. No theory about where such catalogs came from was ever voiced.

Eve was now occupied—had found a way to tolerate if not enjoy life at The Terraces. No more would she roam the halls, bitching about this or that. By then, no one would give too much thought to what had sated her. The people "in charge of her" were relieved the period of wrestling over various issues had ended, happy her incitement of dissatisfaction in other patients was done.

The cavalcade of incoming merchandise kept the attendants busy, and Mrs. Hank Moran soon had a personal Candy Striper. Her doctors didn't like to admit to Hank, or themselves, that the "daily talks" and the "group activities" and the "incessant walking outdoors" wasn't making a dent in Eve's acquisitive ways. So the influx of goods continued for some time before my father found out.

Most of the medical staff openly or secretly disapproved of her shopping—knowing acquisitiveness was the principal manifestation of Eve's mental illness, the reason she was being treated at The Terraces. But when deprived of the excitement of opening the newest purchase, she could turn ugly. Sending her goods into storage was much like depositing money in a bank for her.

An occasional shopping spree was a small price to pay for tranquility, and The Terraces wasn't footing the bill for her purchases: Daddy was. The nurses and attendants frankly enjoyed opening the packages with her. She never gave a single item away but was willing to share the excitement of seeing what was inside with her staff. Sometimes she let them choose the colored tissue paper to wrap it in. It made for a break from finding vases for flowers, the only gift most patients received.

Normally, Daddy met Mother on the lawn or sunroom at preordained times, but one day, he unexpectedly swept into her room, charge plate and invoices in hand, and found stacks of purchases on every surface, some still unopened.

"Is this it?" he asked the flummoxed nurse by his side, waving his hand. She stood mute, her stockinged legs crinkling unhappily. "Is this all of it?" He turned toward Mother, who was in the midst of wrapping a bud vase in yellow tissue paper. She'd taken to color-coding her merchandise. Yellow for household goods, pink for personal items, blue for the rest.

Eve gave him a measured smile. She hadn't stolen any of the merchandise filling her room and couldn't see why he was so angry. He could easily afford a few trifles to make her stay bearable. It was he who'd put her in here after all. Committed her. She hated that word. Hank needed to be taught the price of her imprisonment.

And she, well, she needed these things. Did he expect her to live like Mrs. Rochester in her lonely attic, stalking the floors at night, weeping and wailing? She wasn't athletic or crafty. She couldn't act in their little shows. Couldn't sing. Didn't read newspapers or play cards. She had to do something. Flirting with the better-looking aides and saner male residents wasn't enough for a healthy young woman.

"Really, Hank, you take all the fun out of life. There's a lot of your mother in you — and it isn't a good thing. Hey, could someone put their finger right here?" She was trying to tie a knot on her wrapped article.

"I think there might be more items in the storage rooms," the nurse admitted. "We assign each patient a unit when they arrive. A place to put gifts they haven't the space for, out-of-season clothes, you know. Furniture they don't care to have around," she continued, evoking an increasingly angrier gaze from the resident. "Some of our guests stay for longer periods." Silence. The nurse glanced around the room for help, but there was only the three of them. Daddy drew himself up and charged out the door — Mother and the nurse following mutely.

The three descended to the basement, the nurse leading the way to one of the lettered storage rooms. Inside Room C was a series of surprisingly large individual storage units. Eve Moran's was half-filled after only seven weeks at The Terraces.

"For god's sake," Daddy said, rattling the door like a monkey trying to escape. "Why do you allow such a thing?" He whipped around and confronted the nurse. "You're feeding her sickness. When you carry a box down here, you're abetting her. A shopping compulsion brought her here and you're allowing her to shop — encouraging her even by giving her a room to fill. Filling rooms is her specialty. Does her doctor know about this?" He gestured to Mother's unit, shaking the metal harder. Both women blanched at the noise and force of his actions.

The nurse shook her head. "Not the precise extent."

She looked to Mother for help—but found none in her patient's immobile face. "I might as well tell you, Mr. Moran. We sent some of the more perishable items to a children's home in the City. Candy, fruit, a few baked items."

Her voice tailed off. Clearly the ridiculous nature of the entire venture had become clear to her. Had she thought about it earlier, everyone might have been saved this scene.

Mother was grateful the turncoat had forgotten a thing or two. "Those were gifts silly people sent me," she said prissily, after a few seconds. "Not things I bought myself. Stuff from members of my parents' church—people who don't know me at all. I don't know why my parents told people I was... here."

"There's no disgrace in needing a rest, Eve," Daddy said, calmer suddenly. "I hope you've kept some kind of record of the gifts so we can thank the folks who remembered you."

"It's nothing worth writing a thank you card for. Cans of Planter's Peanuts—like you can buy at the A & P, small jars of Pennsylvania Dutch stuff."

"Chow-chow?" the nurse said. "Apple butter?"

"See what I mean," Mother said.

"And a few boxes of out-of-season clothing and accessories went to her parents' house," the nurse added. "I spoke with Mrs. Hobart before sending them. She said it was quite all right." Her voice had tapered off to a whisper. "She had some extra space. Not much but a bit..."

"Of course, it's all right. I told you not to bother asking her." Mother's voice was a whiplash, and the nurse's neck jerked accordingly. "I've always stored things there. Items I wasn't using. Off-season goods."

Her husband was already marching back to the elevator, preparing to confront her doctors on their decision to look the other way, getting ready to remind them what fees were being handed over to The Terraces each month, asking how Eve's enterprise fit in with the therapy they'd discussed.

Mother didn't feel guilty. That was the thing about her — the characteristic it was difficult to understand. If she'd felt guilty, how would it change things? She'd still have made her purchases but perhaps not enjoyed them as much.

"Do you get it?" she asked me. "Does anyone understand?"

Eve Moran was released from The Terraces three months later. Once the ability to shop was taken away, she bore down and did what was needed, talking to the therapists, seeking out groups who'd help her appear compliant, involved, sane. There were so many women like Mother there — the bored wives of rich men, the aging wives of rich men, the drug-addicted wives of rich men.

The rich men themselves saw their therapists after work in the city. Few men were guests at The Terraces because they needed to earn the money necessary to keep their wives, or sometimes children, inside, out of harm's way they might've said.

The lack of such males at The Terraces was a contributing factor in Mother's rush toward release. Women rarely found her charming and, second only to the shopping, she needed the boost being found charming and desirable gave her. She hadn't gone without sex since her early teens. She could sense herself dehydrating, day by day.

Mother saw what was needed to escape from The Terraces. There was no reason for her to remain there once her room returned to the dull four walls the institution and her husband deemed acceptable. No reason to hang around the billiards table, the screening room, the indoor bowling alley. She didn't dance, paint, write poetry, or act in skits. She only liked to shop.

So she came home. She came home to shop.

CHAPTER
Nine

Things weren't the same for a long time between Mother and Daddy after her vigil at The Terraces. He was embarrassed their problems had become town gossip in Doylestown despite his precautions, spreading well beyond the tight circle of the Moran clan.

If her parents' little enclave in Philly knew about her breakdown, so be it. But if someone Hank played golf or did business with found out, it was another issue. Nervous breakdowns, compulsions, or whatever it was Eve suffered from, were not publicly spoken of in 1962. Her absence had already got him strange looks at the country club, and the family doctor probed more than his throat when he went in with a fever.

"Eve seeing another doctor?"

"Of course not. She's the picture of health this spring. Put on a pound or two." A large harrumph followed this statement, leading Daddy to believe someone advised the doctor otherwise.

"Doylestown's a small town. The idea your mother's

months in a sanitarium would go unnoticed was foolish," Daddy admitted later.

Mother continued to be bitter about her incarceration. Aside from the curtailment of her shopping, not one family member visited her after the first two weeks. Her father hadn't come to see her at all.

"You know your father," my grandmother tried to explain to her. "A place like that—well, you know."

Eve came home to find Hank's sister, Linda, waiting on the front porch when they pulled up, waving limply at the couple with a lace handkerchief.

"Welcome, home," Linda said, stationed in the rocking chair with the best view. Her voice was high-pitched, reminding me when I came along later, of Helen Keller.

"What am I supposed to do with her around all day?" Eve asked as soon as it was clear Linda was ensconced for an undetermined period of time in their spare bedroom. She stood at the door of the room, looking menacingly at the homey touches Linda had already made: crocheted quilts, lace doilies, a large porcelain doll that hid her nightgown under its profuse skirt on the bed.

"The plaid bedspread has to go. I can't bear to pass the room." She took Linda's vase of plastic flowers and overturned it into the wastepaper basket, letting the cheap dime store vase fall in, too. "She'll have to keep the door closed. It disrupts the entire décor."

"None of this is permanent," Hank said. "You have to expect Linda to make herself comfortable. She's doing us a favor."

"Ha! Doing you a favor."

He retrieved the flowers and vase from the wastepaper basket and reinstalled them on the bureau top. "Is this handful of silk daisies so offensive? You have crates of stuff like this, don't you?"

"Which goes to show how much attention you pay to my taste."

The boxes filled with this sort of accessories—remnants of earlier days—were taped shut in the Hobart basement; she hadn't opened them in months. Eve moved with the times. Her taste was not immutable.

"Yes, but this is Linda's room for now."

"Temporary houseguests don't usually get to redecorate." Eve flung open the closet door, doubtlessly wincing at both the number and choice of clothes inside. "You can hardly close the door." The closet already reeked of some flowery scent. She held her nose. "She wears the same perfume as your mother."

Linda Moran, Hank's younger sister, was short, squat, sedentary—a throwback in a family of tall, energetic people. When I came to know her a few years later, she'd already arrived at spinsterhood—feet first and with little resentment.

"We don't have a damned thing to say to each other," Mother said, continuing the discussion over the next few days. "And it's not like she *does* anything to help. Linda can't cook any better than me. She talks on the phone to your mother most of the day. Never-ending conferences about the most minute details of their lives. 'What shall I wear to the ladies' tea, Mother?'" Eve mimicked her sister-in-law's voice. "Do you think my lavender shirtwaist will do? Shall I wear my pearls or the gold cross?"

Eve had her elbow propped on the window sill and was watching her sister-in-law on the porch below. Linda was gazing at the street traffic from the aqua glider, her foot making it move every few seconds, a glass of lemonade beside her. "Look at her, Hanky—already out there at eight-thirty in the morning. She's twenty-eight years old and acts ninety."

"She's here to make sure your convalescence goes smoothly," Hank said, trying to soothe his wife. "The sanitarium didn't want to release you. I assured Dr. Doakes we'd have someone here with you. Would you rather spend another month or two at The Terraces?"

"You could've signed me out of the loony bin any time you wanted. Don't try to pin it on them. Your role in my incarceration is considerable. Don't think I'll forget that."

Nearly all of the residents at The Terraces had a story like Eve's to tell—some husband or father or brother or mother who'd signed the commitment papers with impunity. Long evenings there had been whiled away listening to such stories. "Committal tales" someone had named them.

"I had to rely on the doctors' evaluations, Eve," Daddy said. "Isn't it better coming home early, even if Linda has to stick around for a few weeks?"

"A close call," Eve said, smiling slightly. "Doakes wanted to keep me there forever. Bleeding you dry while I did jigsaw puzzles with my drippy O.T. guy. Waiting on pins and needles to see how soon he'd slide his hand up my dress again." She made a face.

"You invented that, Evelyn Moran."

Ignoring him, she went on. "And using the word 'companion' implies Linda and I do things together. Me and Tubbylinda." She sat on the bed, contemplating another hour of sleep. What else was there to do?

"Look, bear with me till things get straightened out. I have a lot on my plate."

"But not as much as your sister has on hers."

Hank was working a dab of Brill Cream into his hair. He raked both sides of his head a final time and wiped his hands.

"Don't call her Tubbylinda again," he said, choking back a laugh. "I'll slip and call her that myself." His face became a mask at he looked critically in the mirror. "I wonder how I'd look with a mustache."

"Hideous. Only Clark Gable got away with a moustache when they were out of style." She stretched." Straightened out how?"

Mother was probably feeling headachy was, in fact, hungover. Lately, they'd both been drinking too much. Hank had come home the night before with an orange liqueur a client gave him, and they put a good dent in it after the red wine they'd had with dinner and the martini still earlier. Since alcoholism was not deemed one of Eve's problems, no prohibition had been placed on her social drinking.

"Boredom drinking," she often told me.

She only drank when Hank was home. Although if he worked late, she often began without him. And mostly, he did stay at the office fairly late. She'd discovered it was surprisingly easy to make your own cocktail and to drink it alone. Easy also to have a second one when Hank was out even later.

Linda had not joined them in their alcohol consumption the night before, of course, looking on with disapproval and a strawberry ice cream soda in her hand. Hank brought it home from the Doylestown soda shop, flourishing it like flowers. She actually blushed. "Oh Hank," she started to say.

"You know those calories go right on your hips," Eve said, jutting out a boney one.

Hank sighed loudly, and Linda walked into her bedroom. The sound of her blaring TV was a reminder of her presence though. She liked the sort of goofy shows my mother couldn't tolerate.

"*The Beverly Hillbillies, McHale's Navy.* You can imagine her favorites, Christine."

Eve could sleep as long as she wanted. Eleven or twelve hours a night was not unheard of. Sleeping in became a habit in the nuthouse where rest was considered therapeutic. And it gave the staff time to put up their feet.

But if she returned to bed now, she remembered, she'd have to get up all over again, waking once more to the long and boring day ahead, the hours to wait until cocktails. An endless sentence of shopping-free days or else she'd be booted back from whence she came. I imagine none of this was particularly palatable to my mother.

"Why do you have to be gone such long hours," she'd asked her husband. "You're the boss, right?"

"You know what I mean, Eve." Hank's voice now was low, and she turned to him with surprise. What he meant about what? Was she missing bits and pieces of what people said? Had the few times she'd taken Thorazine done some damage. She'd entirely forgotten the subject under discussion.

"She'll stay until things are back on an even keel."

He was still talking about Linda. Good grief! Maybe he was obsessed with his sister. This hadn't occurred to her before. Obsessed with Tubbylinda? What had their childhood been like? Was she being crazy? Too much time spent with shrinks and you started thinking like them. Something sexual, a deviant act, explained everything. No one completed childhood unscathed according to them.

Hank began knotting his tie. "We became used to having things a certain way around here: Mrs. Murphy, Linda, and me. Our days went smoothly, and I'm not inclined to make any big changes right now. We'll ease you in…"

"Linda stayed here while I was gone?" Eve was appalled, more suspicious now of some sort of incestuous liaison. "I thought she'd moved in right before I came home."

He shook his head, his eyes averted.

So Linda had insinuated herself here weeks ago, perhaps taking her place in his life if not his bed.

"Well, a fine scene you paint, Hank. An even keel? They wouldn't have released me if I wasn't fit for society. Ease me in indeed!" Her eyes glittered. "You've destroyed all the charge plates, hid the checkbooks. What could I possibly do to embarrass you now that I'm a prisoner in your house? It's two miles into town, and this hillbilly place has no bus system." She pressed her handkerchief to her mouth. "Life went smoothly with you and Linda, huh? It's me that turns things topsy-turvy."

"Take it easy, will you." A band of sweat stretched across his forehead. "Linda's only here for a week or two." He frowned and undid his tie. "She's a good-hearted girl. Not a mean bone in her body. She can be on the lookout for trouble."

"Trouble? You keep saying that word. Do you think I'm about to kill myself, Hank? Is it my health that concerns you or my spending money? Maybe I'll smuggle in the Cartier diamond? Is that what this is really about? I can guarantee you I won't do either." She crossed the room and stood behind him. "I'll wear tattered old nightgowns like this one," she gestured to her flawless blue silk gown, "for the rest of my life if you send your sister home. I won't shop at all. I swear to God, she gives me the creeps. She and your mother watch *Edge of Night* together, playing out every scene over the phone. It's ridiculous she's minding me. She's a nutcase herself."

"Linda's bored, Eve. She's never known what to do with herself. Not when she was a kid nor later. Dad should've worked her into the business—given her a position." He said this under his breath, giving Eve a sidelong glance, finally getting the knot in his tie done properly. "Have some sympathy. She doesn't have your looks or brains. Linda may not ever have a life of her own. We have an aunt who's lived with her sister and her family her whole life."

I could well imagine my mother shriveling at that remark.

"Christ! Some sort of Moran family custom? Linda can't have *my* life or live with *us* forever if that's what she's expecting." She was probably shouting by then, confirming his idea she needed a companion. "Having a ton of money won't hurt her chances of finding a man. If she'd get a handle on her weight, she'd be the catch of the season. Some man will eventually see past the fat to her bankbook anyway. I can help her out. Give her some advice." She paused. "But from a distance, Hank. Not from under my feet."

"Did that happen with us? Did you get the catch of the season?"

"Don't be ridiculous. You're handsome, fun, smart. I fell for you before I knew you were anything more than the average neighborhood hoodlum."

Hank smiled. "Who's to say I wasn't?"

Eve had handed out her allotment of compliments for the morning and let his comment drop, returning to the subject of Linda. "What will we talk about today? Give me an idea, at least." There was real panic in her voice. "The dinner menu? What Sissie Burt is up to at the Country Club?"

She flounced over to her mirror and began running a brush through her hair. It was a heavy silver brush she'd picked up in Charleston. She'd actually paid for this item—she told me that when I admired it years later. The bristles were thick and soft on her scalp. Good quality was worth the price. There'd be no going back to bed now. Her hair was brushed and she was fully awake.

"I wonder if Mrs. Murphy has my breakfast ready." She smelled only coffee, but Linda looked well-fed. Maybe there'd be French toast. That was the best thing about breakfast. Desserts counted as an entrée.

"Goodness knows, you could both take some interest in managing this household." Hank was still going on. "Cooking, cleaning, making a home. With two healthy adult women with nothing to do all day, why am I paying a housekeeper?"

"Because Mrs. Murphy's a good cook and keeps the house

immaculately clean. And your sister hasn't held a dust cloth in her fat hands in her life. If you take Mrs. Murphy away from me, I swear I'll leave," Eve said tearfully. "At least she's someone to talk to. Why can't she look after me if that's what we're going to call it?"

Yesterday, she'd convinced Mrs. Murphy to pick up a few things for her in town. "I'll reimburse you when I get my allowance," she told the older woman, their eyes locked.

"Oh, of course, she can stay. I couldn't go long without her potato pancakes," Hank said, slipping his jacket on. It was a pinstriped suit he rarely wore. He didn't usually put on a suit to go to the plant, preferring to seem to fit in with his workers. "I like to eat as much as the next man."

"A meeting today?" She brushed some imaginary lint from his shoulder.

He glanced down at his shoulder, nodding. "Princeton. The University, in fact. I may pick up some new business if things go well. Can you imagine the increase in revenue if we get our foot in their door?"

He was ready to leave, shaking her and her troubles off, his mind on his future sales pitch. This would always be my father's tactics, work made his troubles at home seem minor.

"Such ambition so early in the morning." Mother yawned. "Go ahead," she said, dismissing him. "It would've been nice if you'd let me sleep in though. What a long day I'll have now. And with your sister and this heat…"

Cocktail hour was a long way off.

Mother only "shopped" once or twice in those first few weeks. She'd call a store in town, ask them to send something out to the house, and bill the item to Hank's account.

"I misplaced my card," she told the clerk on the phone, "and

I need a new pair of short, beige kidskin gloves. Could you send me out a pair in size seven?"

Sounding authoritative—like she did this sort of thing all the time—probably greased the transaction. The Moran family was too well regarded to refuse her. My father hadn't thought to call the stores and warn them off. He hadn't thought beyond her previous activities, probably assuming she was only capable of repeating herself. Hardships spurred my mother on, led to creativity and innovation.

"Don't you want to try them on first?" the woman on the phone asked. "Sometimes the length isn't right. Or the color. Beige can be kind of peculiar. It can be tan or ochre or…"

"Look, I'm not particular. Plus, I'm not well at the moment," Mother said, cutting her off.

And Mother wasn't fussy. She liked the excitement of having nice things arrive, of stowing them away, having them as protection against—well, Mother wasn't sure what. Excess was what did her in at The Terraces, and she wouldn't repeat her mistake. When the gloves arrived in a darling box with mauve ribbon two days later, Linda watched enviously as Eve opened the box, allowing the ribbon to fall on the floor.

"I could wear this ribbon in my hair," Linda said, swooping to retrieve it and draping it across her head. "What do you think?"

Her sister-in-law didn't dignify her suggestion with a response. Linda already gave the impression she was a character from a children's book—the barnyard pig dressed in human clothes. The mauve ribbon accentuated it.

"Oh, isn't it nice of someone to send me these gloves," Eve lied. "Beige is an unusual color choice, but I do have a beaver coat." She handed the gloves over to Linda to admire, recovering the ribbon in one swift movement.

"When will you wear them?" Linda asked, stroking the

leather enviously. "It's still summer. It'll be months before you need leather gloves." She made as if to pull them on her chubby hands.

"Oh, that's not the point, Linda," Eve said, grabbing them. "It's nice to think someone thought of me. Wanted me to have something pretty."

She stared at the box, probably wondering who that someone might be — not having thought ahead to the probability of Linda being on the spot to witness the packages' arrival. That an explanation would be in order.

"My mother, I guess." There was no card, of course.

"Of course," Linda said agreeably. "I didn't see a card, did you?" She scrambled through the tissue paper. "What a lovely present to receive out of the blue. Certainly brightens the day."

Linda actually seemed pleased. It was like The Terraces again. People taking pleasure in someone else's gift. She didn't get it herself.

Later she told me, "And for a moment, I liked my sister-in-law because it honestly seemed like that to me too. Like maybe my fairy godmother sent the gloves. Do you see how I felt, Christine? Of course, my real mother would never have done such a thing."

The arrival of the jaunty little truck with the store's name in gilt letters was enough to raise Eve's spirits. She loved watching the uniformed men trot to her door and ring the bell, loved signing the slip with her ornate initials.

A leather handbag arrived two days later ("my best friend from college") and a set of demitasse cups a week later ("Mother again, she shouldn't have.") Eve realized at some point how few people might send her gifts, which must have made her all the sorrier for herself and led to another round of purchases.

"I can't imagine someone I haven't seen for years sending me a handbag that must have cost fifty dollars," Linda had said, eyeing the soft brown leather envyingly. "How did she know you were hospitalized? It's an odd present for convalescence. You could use something to do with yourself. Like a crossword puzzle book or a jigsaw puzzle. Maybe a good novel."

Mother let pass the irony of a woman who did nothing telling her this, saying, "Oh, she can afford it. And we were close in college." She gave her sister-in-law the evil eye, adding, "And there's the difference between us, Linda. I have friends who want to cheer me up, not give me a headache."

After the delivery, an enervating heat wave moved into southeastern Pennsylvania, and the two women spent much of the day on the porch, staring at each other from pitched outposts: Linda on the aqua glider, Eve in a cushioned wicker chair. They took turns filling their glasses with lemonade and iced tea, both of which Mrs. Murphy kept ready in the fridge. Eve was engrossed in a current work of Harold Robbins. Linda listened to *Art Linkletter's House Party* and similar fare, the sound turned low after frequent requests from Eve.

"You do know that show is also on TV now," she told Linda repeatedly.

There was only one air-conditioning unit in the house — and that was in the bedroom. "Your brother's a tightwad," Mother told Linda. "Lots of people have air-conditioning throughout their entire house now. My goodness, it's 1962. They don't have to make do with a lousy, dripping, belching machine that makes the bedroom dark and dank. Last night I could hardly sleep over its grinding motor. He's got air-conditioning at the office."

"Clients need to be comfortable to conduct business. And there's only the one window in Hank's office," Linda said. "No cross-ventilation. Daddy insisted on air-conditioning when they built the new offices. A delivery man had a stroke in there last year."

"You've certainly given it some thought."

"Father sends me into the office now and then, with papers to sign."

"Nice they provide their hourly workers with more comfort than their wives and sisters."

"This house isn't one of those Levittown ranches or bi-levels or a one-story office building. The heat comes from radiators. You'd have to tear the house apart, Eve." Linda caught her breath. "Anyway sitting on the porch is nice. There's a certain smell…"

"If you're eighty-five years old maybe," Mother said, looking around for further proof. "I feel like I'm living in the nineteenth century. Sitting on porches, fanning myself, drinking iced tea all day long. I took three showers yesterday. My skin's going to peel off." She waved her hand fan vigorously, killing a passing bee midair. "I'm going to go stark-raving mad if I don't get out of here." She must've realized the meaning of her last words and amended it. "Maybe I need a vacation."

"Hank's too busy for vacations," Linda said authoritatively, not sensing the subject was winding down. "Trying to line up the Princeton job, and then, maybe Rutgers. It'll bring in hundreds of thousands of dollars over the next decade." She drained her latest glass of iced tea. "Maybe in the fall, you can go to the shore for the weekend. Hank might make a reservation at the huge hotel on the boardwalk in Ocean City. Flanders, isn't it?" She blinked twice. "Anyway, wasn't The Terraces like a vacation?"

"Oh, sure. A vacation spot where they jolt you to life when things get a tad dull."

"Hank said they never did that—jolted you."

Mother looked at her sister-in-law carefully. "You certainly monitor our lives closely, Linda. Maybe it's you who needs a companion."

"I've been here several months," Linda said. "You can't help but notice things."

"Well, keep those "things you notice" to yourself," Eve told her. "And I'll do the same."

"Why don't you pay your parents a visit?" Daddy said, when Mother mentioned her need for a vacation.

"They don't even have a window unit."

It was seven o'clock and the temperature was still in the mid-nineties. The thought of her parent's tiny row house, with the pathetic box fan propped on the coffee table with a bowl of melting ice cubes in front of it, was appalling. Her father'd be watching the Phillies game or listening to it on the radio, the only program he turned on. Her mother would be darning, inches out of his sight line.

"Take a taxi into town tomorrow and take in a movie," her husband suggested. "You'll get out of the heat for a couple hours. Linda can go along too."

The movie showing was *A Touch of Mink* with Doris Day and Cary Grant. Eve came out of the dark theater into the enervating heat steaming. *A Touch of Mink* was the story of her life. It was the tale of man who nearly turns a woman into a harlot because she wants some nice things in her life.

"I wonder if Doris Day is as pleasant as she seems in the movies," Linda said. "I prefer to see Rock Hudson in the lead though—like in *Pillow Talk*. It's easy to imagine them making a life together. Cary Grant always acts kind of fruity. Do you think he's a homosexual?"

Mother glanced at Linda in surprise. She wouldn't have guessed her to know about such things.

Then Mother got pregnant.

She left the diaphragm she'd secretly worn for years in the drawer one night and a few weeks later she was throwing up.

"Aren't you glad we have Linda here to help you now?" Hank asked once she'd been to the doctor.

"I've already packed her bags," Eve told him, eating one of the endless apples her new condition dictated. Small, tart apples — the kind nobody else but the horses on the Moran farm liked. "I can't be made upset by endless quarrels with Linda with the baby coming. It wouldn't be good for me to be angry all the time." Hank finally nodded. "When can we start looking for a house in the city? I've been looking at the ads for houses in the Society Hill area."

"Moving now wouldn't be a good idea, Honey. I'm sure your doctor agrees. Can't we wait until the baby comes and we're back on our feet?"

"Back on our feet! I'm not falling for that line again. You said I could choose where to live once I was pregnant. We might as well get ourselves into place beforehand. Things will only get more confusing with a baby to care for."

"Bucks County's a lovely area. People can't wait to get away from the dirty, crime-infested city and live out here. Can you see its beauty?"

He was rubbing her shoulders, but she squirmed away. Acquiescence to sexual invitations came at a price with my mother.

"I can't see anything but animals. Dowdy clothes, diners instead of restaurants, a drive-in-movie with heaters for the cold weather, the church choir instead of the Philadelphia Orchestra, Kiwanis square dances instead of a night club. The whole town smells like manure when it doesn't smell of skunk. Do you want your son to go to school with farmers?"

When Hank started to suggest there was nothing wrong

with the local schools, she reminded him he hadn't been a pupil in a rural school.

"Philly was different in the late forties and early fifties." He walked over and dug around in his desk, coming over with a pamphlet from The Templeton School, which he handed to her. "I play golf with a fellow who sends his kids here. You know, Pete Weideman?" She shrugged. "Or, if you like, we can move nearer the city when our child reaches school age. Meanwhile he can roam the countryside like a boy should: fish, ice-skate on a pond, run through the woods."

She always hated it when he was so well-prepared for her arguments.

"How about this?" she said to her husband. "Let's look for a spot between Doylestown and the city. You won't have such a long commute, and I can be nearer cultural institutions, fine schools, fine restaurants…decent shopping."

"And the last shall be first."

"What?" She paused. "See there's a good example of your fine education. I bet you learned that line in school. Shakespeare, the Bible?"

"Never mind." He sighed. "Sure, find a suburb you like. I can live with it." He paused. "Between here and the city though. I don't want to spend all day on the road with a new baby to bounce on my knee." He smiled. "Or his mother."

CHAPTER
Ten

Shelterville was ten minutes outside the city limits and only forty-five minutes from Daddy's office. A leafy suburb with good schools, it boasted several parks, good city services and a nice shopping area. Unlike Doylestown, chic stores abounded — whereas ones carrying canning supplies, farming equipment, yarn, and sturdy overalls were scarce. Trains traveled from Shelterville to downtown, Philadelphia, New York, and other parts of Pennsylvania on a regular basis.

My parents needed a bigger house with a baby on the way and found a nineteenth century colonial with a stone façade. Pale blue shutters framed the windows and the door was a royal blue with a fetching stencil of an oak tree. Although it was nearly as old as the house in Doylestown, it'd been modernized in the mid-fifties. It was equipped with central air when such things were uncommon.

With a baby coming, there was a lot of shopping to do.

"Maybe you should wait until after the baby showers," Daddy suggested, looking at the boxes piling up in the nursery and elsewhere. "Mother's invited everyone in town."

Mother winced. "I can imagine the sort of gifts your mother's friends will buy." The only smart shop in Doylestown—the one where she'd bought the gloves and handbag—didn't carry children's things.

"My only hope was the Doylestown matrons would send items I could easily return, Christine," she told me later. "Or order stylish presents from New York or downtown Philadelphia stores."

My mother was able to satisfy her immediate need with sterling silver baby cups, plush stuffed toys, darling dresses with smocking and lace trim. She knew it was a girl despite her words to Daddy.

Daddy probably didn't mind that the nursery was well outfitted. He clung to the hope motherhood would change his wife, satisfying the restive thing inside her, the part of her needing to be fed by possessions. Though he must have shaken his head when the bills came in, he didn't say a word.

My birth was an easy one, but Daddy dutifully paced the floor in a waiting room, the last generation of men to be excluded from the delivery room. If he was disappointed in my sex, he never said so, and in three days, Mother and daughter went home. Mother recovered under the care of a nurse—a gift from her in-laws. I had my own nurse for six weeks longer.

Instead of a post-partum depression, Mother slipped into a new phase, one no one had seen before. She became a Supermom, keeping the house spotlessly clean with only the occasional help, entertaining Daddy's associates at home and at the club, pushing the pram to the Curtis Hall park, learning to heat prepared foods. She joined theater groups, bridge groups, golf groups, and a church. Everything was hunky-dory.

"A nice time, it was," Aunt Linda said later. "We were certain your mother's troubles were behind her. Convinced she'd only needed to have a baby to keep her mind off of buying things. Or taking things, Christine. Another theory discussed was that her hormones straightened themselves out after your birth. 'Course what did we know?'" Aunt Linda paused to catch her breath. "Oh, I'm not saying you didn't have more dresses than you would have occasion to wear. Or that Eve didn't shop more often than she should, but compared to what came before... and later..." Aunt Linda shook her head

If the Jesuits were right, those four Supermom years anchored my fealty solely with my mother. Her presence was like that of the sun, she blocked everything else from my view. She focused on making each day special. I'd wake from a nap to find my stuffed animals seated at the dining room table, ready for a tea party. She let me order any item that caught my fancy on a restaurant menu: the most improbable and expensive dishes—like oysters or vichyssoise were mine.

"She encouraged you to try new things," Aunt Linda said, "even if she ended up eating it herself. Even if the entree was left untouched on the plate." She stared out the window as if summoning back those days. "She was gay, always gay, but we shouldn't have trusted the manic quality. We should've seen the desperation lying beneath." Aunt Linda blushed. "Anyway, that's what they said at the hospital when she fell apart."

Mother and I dressed in outlandish costumes and paraded down the streets. Bedtime came whenever I liked. In fact, she encouraged me to stay up late, to sleep with her, to take a bubble bath whenever I felt like it, to try on her clothes, her makeup. She did my nails in the most improbable colors—before Goth girls inured us to such things. We bought a dozen pink-iced donuts once and ate them without pause.

One December, when I told her I missed splashing in my

plastic swimming pool, she dragged it out of the garage, blew it up, set it on the kitchen floor, and filled it with water doused with bubble bath.

We watched old movies, westerns, and Johnny Carson, despite the hour it came on. We indulged in themed shopping day, filled the house with balloons, flowers, bubbles, painted a mural of jungle animals on the dining room wall, covering it with white paint before Daddy saw it. We hung crepe paper from the chandelier, pretending it was a maypole.

I adored her. No one had such a mother. I was her confidante long before I knew the word. "The bad days are behind me, Christine," she said repeatedly.

I smiled hopefully when she said this, but not having the slightest idea of what she meant.

Where was my father? Working constantly or at least gone from the house. He probably had a mistress. Perhaps a second or third. A manic Eve was not much better than the other ones he'd known. He spent a lot of time with his parents in Bucks County, something Mother never wanted to do. When he was home, he was often poring over bills, watching sports on TV, getting ready to leave. He was glad to have a child, but didn't find me very interesting. Perhaps later we'd spend more time together, I heard him say. When we could play tennis or golf or ride horses. Perhaps if I ever had something interesting to say, we'd grow close. He'd listen to me.

If Mother's behavior during these years sounds like a manic phase of mental illness, well, that's what it was. There were little peaks and valleys along the way, a day here and there when she didn't get out of bed; made a quick visit to the local GP for a B12 shot or some Valium; spent a weekend at home with her parents from time to time, but on the whole, it was a good period.

When I was nearly five, she crashed. Couldn't get out of her

bed, wash, dress, care for me. I went to sleep with the sound of
Daddy's feet pacing the hallway. I'd wake to hear him begging
her to get up, pleading with her to try and pull herself together.

"I can't pull you out of this hole alone," he said, his eyes
glittering as I huddled with her under the blanket. "Dig yourself
in far enough and you'll have to go away again."

Go away again. I didn't know what he meant. They'd all
managed to keep her period at The Terraces from me. If she
went away, would I go too? How could I possibly get along
without her?

She couldn't respond, continued to stare out the window,
clutching one of her shiny things, her eyes black holes. I was
sure it was my fault. Only yesterday, we'd gone to the circus, the
zoo, the ballet. What had I done? Had I twined myself around
her too tightly? But still I clung tight. Or did she cling to me?

Aunt Linda or one of my grandmothers showed up most
mornings. They stood outside her bedroom door wringing
their hands, softly asking if she'd like some tea, soup, a glass of
ginger ale. How about a new book from the library? Maybe the
minister should come by? Maybe her GP? The Morans didn't
like Mother much, but they hated to see her like this, hated to
think Daddy might be pushed to his limits again. That he might
have to spend a fortune to whip her into shape. Grandmother
Hobart was still less inclined to interfere, perhaps intuiting the
blame for this creature was on her head—perhaps she set Eve
on this course.

Mother refused to see anyone or ask for anything. There
was only me, swaddling with her under the covers. Trying to
crawl, or perhaps, claw my way inside her again. I had no faith
I could exist on my own. Was I was anything at all without her?

The Terraces had closed its doors during Mother's period of sanity, the new drug regimen its undoing. It was now a golf club where many of the same people cavorted. Mental institutions had dramatically changed with the influx of new drugs. Daddy chose a different sort of hospital this time, one which sanctioned both drugs and administering judicious shock therapy to patients no drugs or therapy could reach.

Mother was one of those patients. They weren't called residents or guests at this facility. There wasn't much talking, no large green lawns, no tennis courts or swimming pool. No one strolled the grounds; patients were hardly outside at all. The idea was to get the patient on her feet as quickly as possible, even if she had to be jolted back to a vertical position. No one would attempt to get inside Mother's head this time; her mind was an unfathomable place—a place only drugs or electricity could reach.

And the patients looked dazed, according to Daddy.

"Either they're recovering from the shocks or the drugs," Daddy told Aunt Linda wearily. "There's a kind of murmuring when you walk the hall, a low hum of despair."

"You tried the other route," the doctor told Daddy in defense of their techniques. "Now let's assume her brain, rather than her mind, needs stimulation."

Before Mother was shown to her Spartan room, she had her first dose of electric shock. They shocked her three times a week over the eight weeks she was there. She forgot Daddy's name for days at a time. Mine too. Once or twice, Aunt Linda handed me the phone and I'd listen to Mother babble and try not to cry.

She'd forgotten her own name by the third or fourth week. I listened to Daddy tell Grandmother Moran this in the hallway.

"Shocked senseless—that's what it means," she told him. "I never thought of it till now."

"What else can I do?" Daddy asked.

"You don't have to persuade me." Taking pity on her son,

she added, "You've tried everything else."

I wasn't sure what she meant by this, but it was bound to be bad for my mother, and I stuck my tongue out at her. I didn't waver in support of Mother.

Aunt Linda moved in while Mother was gone. In her own more benign way, she was as unbalanced as my mother. Our days were spent in languid contemplation of the offerings on the television schedule, the ebb and flow of street traffic, the grocery aisles at the A & P, the local candy store's showcases. I didn't mind spending time with Aunt Linda nearly as much as my mother did. I found her restful. Especially since, unlike the rest or her family, she never said a bad word about Mother. After a few days, we hardly mentioned her at all.

"So do you think we should have the beef or the chicken Hungry Man?" she'd say contemplatively, peering into the freezer, cold air rushing into her red face. Such decisions merited the same degree of thought as the question of what we'd watch on TV; answers to such questions were not to be rushed.

We were well-stocked with every frozen entrée of the era as well as the entire line of Pepperidge Farm desserts. Aunt Linda could finish off an entire cheesecake in fifteen minutes, not bothering to cut it into slices, forking into one side and eating her way across. She made it feel like the proper way to have dessert—whoever heard of saving some for later? Sometimes she'd ice a cheesecake with some jam or colored sugar, upping the sweetness a bit.

"I learned this trick at the women's circle at church," she told me.

Aunt Linda'd gone from plump to fat in the six years since she'd chaperoned Mother in Doylestown. It didn't bother her in the least. I never knew a person more at ease with herself, and

I soon began to look like Aunt Linda's child. Little rolls of fat ribboned my thighs in only a few weeks.

"I told your daddy we could get by on our own," she said, explaining the absence of Mrs. Murphy. "I've learned a bit about cooking since I last lived with your parents."

She *had* learned a few things; she could defrost and heat anything she found in the freezer. She was quite adept at shopping for sauces to "jazz up" duller dishes.

"Whoever heard of chicken without milk gravy?" she'd say, peppering the frozen fried chicken with heavy canned gravy. There were also powdered sauces should we get bored with the canned selections. Convenience trumped taste or nutrition in the late sixties, and Aunt Linda served few dishes that weren't covered with some sort of sauce.

"Nothing worse than a dried-up piece of meat," she'd say, lathering on béchamel, Hollandaise, or sweet and sour.

After lunch, we'd walk the three blocks to the main thoroughfare and buy an ice cream cone or a sundae. "A little exercise can't hurt us."

Linda would stretch out on the too-flimsy bench outside of the ice-cream shop, dipping her bright pink tongue into the pink or green or peach ice cream. The bench undulated with her weight, and I watched, partly worried and partly fascinated as she constantly adjusted her position to keep all four legs of the bench grounded. The proprietor peeked out the window, probably worried about actionable accidents or the demise of his bench. But since we were his most loyal customers, his only ones some days, he was forced to accept it. Aunt Linda didn't notice his fretfulness, completely engrossed in the sweet before her.

She went through their entire menu of flavors and choices during the months she stayed with me. I always chose something with chocolate.

"You need to branch out, Christine. You're missing some of life's greatest pleasures. Try pistachio or cherry vanilla."

If life with Mother had been exciting and unpredictable, life with Aunt Linda was quiet and held no nasty surprises. She was completely satisfied with being what she was—a spinster aunt, the unmarried daughter of a rich man, a gourmand of epic proportions. I liked this about her. Where Mother exhaled her dissatisfaction, Aunt Linda inhaled stasis with content. She was as indulgent with me as my mother had been, but without the fits or tempers. It was a time of serenity, and I breathed it in. We might not engage in exciting adventures but life with her had its pleasures.

Physical contact was problematic though. Climbing into bed with Aunt Linda was out of the question. She needed every inch of space the double bed provided, so I was forced to sleep alone. Sitting in her lap was a battle between quickly finding a valley or tumbling to the floor.

"Whoops," she'd say, scooping me up. "You're a slippery little girl."

Despite my love of Aunt Linda, some of the shine did go out of my life during Mother's hospitalization. The sparkly things were gone. Daddy was away more than ever. Neither Aunt Linda nor I knew what to do with him when he *was* around. He interrupted the schedule we'd worked out by wanting to eat sensible meals and take exercise. He expected us to talk about more important things than what scheme Samantha had in mind to foil Darren or Endora on *Bewitched*. There was more on his mind than what ice cream flavor Aunt Linda should try next. More to think about than what Cissy Burt was up to at the Country Club wearing a bare-midriff dress to dinner. He disapproved of the pile of gossipy magazines always next to Aunt Linda's chair, of the empty dishes filling the tabletops in the mornings, the endless wailing of the TV.

I'm sure he wondered if Mother had been right about Linda. Yet the peace and my contentedness convinced him she should stay. We got by. Perhaps there were no women who could satisfy Daddy, as Mother often said.

When Mother returned home after nearly three months in *Shock Corridor*, she was different: no longer interested in keeping a perfect house, not as manic, nor much fun. She was perfectly quiet for the first few weeks. Probably her brain needed time to unfurl itself from the fetal position it'd taken throughout her treatment. Her interest in being a CEO's wife was completely gone. We didn't drive to Ocean City, New Jersey to eat cotton candy and French fries on the boardwalk for breakfast. We didn't make crazy costumes from the remnant table at The Sewing Bee. She wasn't nearly as much fun as she'd been a year ago, but was certainly in better shape than three months earlier.

What did arise was her need to shop. But how to do it without getting caught? This was when Mother, with a grim determination and an innate inventiveness, came up with the "return" business.

CHAPTER
Eleven

t began at Grandmother Hobart's house. It was someone's birthday, but I can't remember whose. Mother punished Grandmother those first few weeks after her return, not answering the telephone, blaming Grandmother Hobart for allowing Daddy to commit her to such a place, for not visiting her, for letting Aunt Linda take care of me. Her list of grievances was enormous and her subdued demeanor off-putting.

I crept around the house, avoiding her whenever I could, careful not to do anything to annoy her, although what that might be remained mysterious. She was a new person and I'd no idea how to handle her. After the weeks with Aunt Linda and the peace I'd grown used to, her behavior was especially scary. Aunt Linda had planned our day around food and joint activities. Mother never ate, mostly stayed in her room, and scowled at those she deemed responsible for her incarceration. Apparently at six, I wasn't completely immune.

"You were practically in a coma the times I did come, Eve," Grandmother Hobart said in defense. "I came home completely in despair, unable to do my housekeeping or care for your father—and well—he refused to even speak of it." Mother rolled her eyes. She had yet to accuse her mother of anything specific, but it hung in the air.

My eyes went to Grandfather's place at the table. It was already set for his dinner. He loomed over this household: his was the only padded seat, the only chair with arms. No one could sit there even in his absence.

But things between my mother and grandmother had slowly returned to normal, whatever normal was in our family, and we were sitting at the kitchen table digging into the same lemon cake with coconut icing Grandmother Hobart made for every birthday or special occasion. It was an exceedingly dry cake, a piece of pastry crying out for a scoop of ice cream, but my grandmother thought such additions excessive. I'd proposed ice cream earlier and been promptly told ice cream would make it too rich for a girl of my size.

"I put less icing on your side of the cake too," Grandmother said, eyeing my burgeoning bulk. "Doesn't do to give into a love for sugary treats at your age. It'll dog you your whole life."

She looked at me sternly, and I tucked myself further under the table. I was still coming off the Aunt Linda regime, and her words fell on me like hammers from the sky. My grandmother felt little need to endear herself to me through compliments and favorite treats. Children needed a firm hand. It might not have worked with my mother, but I was a difference case.

"That's what comes from having a self-indulgent woman care for you."

I looked at Mother, ready to watch her mount a defense, but then I realized Grandmother meant Aunt Linda.

"I didn't notice you stepping in to help out while I was away," Mother said finally, getting it out into the open and bringing an abrupt end to her period of unspoken recriminations.

Grandmother was not used to hearing herself publicly criticized. Her mouth opened once or twice as if a defense was forthcoming, but it never did.

I spent a lot of time at their house over the next few years. When I was there, I could easily imagine where my mother's need to hoard came from. It was a cheerless house, and Mother had had to invent a way to overcome it. I passively accepted the dullness, using her role model to keep me in check.

My mother was slightly allergic to the coconut in the cake and a light rash broke out around her mouth as she continued to eat her paper-thin slice. She never turned down sweets the only food she cared about. So she persevered, her throat slightly raspy after a few minutes.

"Did you put vanilla extract in here?" she asked her mother. "Tastes more like nuts."

"Very good, Evelyn," Grandmother said. "Almonds. You're developing a palate. Perhaps you'll become a cook yet."

"Why did you use almond?" Mother sniffed at her piece. "Almond would be more for a spice cake. Right?"

I was impressed by how much my mother knew about baking considering she hadn't so much as baked me a brownie. "What's a bakery for?" she'd say if anyone suggested such a thing. Or, "you can't beat a good old Tastykake."

Grandmother's bravado broke down a little here. "You've certainly become quite an expert in pastry ingredients." She sat a bit straighter in her chair, playing with her slice of cake rather than eating it, looking at it more critically.

I began to eat quickly, fearing the cake might be whisked away any second. It *was* odd-tasting, but there was nothing wrong with its sugar content.

Grandmother sighed, rose suddenly, and walked to the cabinet over the sink. She pulled out a little box, withdrawing the bottle of vanilla inside.

"I can't get the cap off the vanilla. I think it's off the track." She yanked at it, nearly elbowing herself in the process.

"Let me see." Mother grabbed the jar and twisted the top fruitlessly for several seconds before passing it back. "You'll have to take it back to the A & P and demand a refund."

"Oh, you would make a big fuss over such a small purchase. What did it cost? Pennies."

"You deserve a refund." Mother reached over and slid her finger across the top of the cake. Grandmother didn't say a word, but Mother, not expecting silence, defended her iced finger. "Oh, the cake's ruined anyway. Where's the harm?"

"They'll tell me it's a manufacturing problem or something I did wrong," Grandmother said, ignoring Mother's finger. "And if I want reimbursement, I'll have to write the company. The store won't admit any fault." Grandmother peered farsightedly at the bottle. "I've been through things like this before."

"Which is why you have to take action at once. I'll write the letter."

Mother reached for her purse and took out a pen and an old deposit slip from the bank to scratch out a rough version. "You've gotta give 'em hell. I know how it's done." And she did apparently.

Two weeks later, Grandmother was hammering at our door, an unusual occurrence. "You're not going to believe the nice note I got from Meadow Fresh," she said, breathless with excitement. "Remember Meadow Fresh—that faulty bottle of vanilla? Writing was a good idea, Evelyn." The note of respect in her voice made me smile.

"Just a note?" Mother said. "Didn't they give you a coupon? Or a refund check?"

"You're not going to believe this, but they sent me an entire case of vanilla extract! Did you ever hear of such a thing? A whole case! I'll have to give it away at church or something. They'll think I've gone senile, carting vanilla extract around. Isn't it the stuff alcoholics drink? I don't guess you'll be needing any?"

Mother declined her offer and went off to sit in her favorite chair in the living room to think.

At first, Mother actually bought the merchandise. Knowing one returned can of hairspray might possibly net a carton of twelve cans, it felt like small potatoes to purchase a can. And that familiar red can was her first return: Aquanet hairspray, which she took a pair of pliers to, bending the nozzle slightly. She packaged it, including a sweet, slightly apologetic note.

> *Dear Sir:*
> *I have been a lifelong admirer and purchaser of your excellent product, which has kept my hair tidy through thick and thin. Imagine my disappointment today when I tried to press the nozzle on a brand new can and it didn't work. It was actually bent. I thought I should advise you of this flaw in your product.*
>
> *Yours truly,*
> *Mrs. Eve Moran*

She included the receipt for the item. Two weeks later, a case of Aquanet arrived. Twelve cans to be stockpiled for future use. Aquanet Hairspray was not the kind of thing my mother craved, but the less money spent on household items, the more money that could be given over to sparkly things. Over the next months, dozens of cartons arrived with beauty products, kitchen products, bathroom products, and the various odd things Mother took a fancy to. Some people might say six dozen boxes of swizzle sticks was overkill, but when Mother wrote the manufacturer that a chipped stick had cut a guest's tongue, what could they do? I was able to use some of them on projects for school.

It was exciting, if worrisome, to see Mother reinvent herself. She'd gone from a mental patient to an entrepreneur practically overnight. The color in her cheeks rose, her posture improved, and I watched with only a small degree of trepidation. Her newly minted control persuaded me.

Not all of the manufacturers fell into line. Some ignored her letter; others sent an apology with a small coupon; some, a paltry refund check for the exact amount. And when she made the mistake of hitting the same company twice, she received a threatening letter instead of the expected window cleaner. After that, she decided a filing system was required.

"This is a damned good way for you to learn the alphabet," Mother said as she sat me at the table with a box of manila file folders.

I was six perhaps and knew the alphabet, of course.

"Find the file folder with the letter the company's name begins with. Tuck the letter inside. See, A for Aquanet."

After only a few months of this enterprise, she'd amassed a pile of paperwork. Soon she was making copies of her letters at the nearest branch of the library. "No sense forgetting what I said to them." She turned out to have significant organizational skills, which had never been tapped.

And I was good at numbers. My future as a low-level office worker was assured. I didn't mind the business' prosaic nature; it was nearly as good as my time with Aunt Linda or my early days with Mother. She grew happier with each delivery, and I enjoyed my new status as a member of her gang: anything winning Mother's approval was gravy to me.

"Daddy doesn't need to know about this," she said as she tried to shove another carton in a closet.

Our house in Shelterville, with its three-car garage in the rear, was testing Mother's ability to store her goods. "Let's have a little yard sale," she decided one day and hung out a sign.

Daddy was playing golf probably. Even on Saturdays he was seldom available to us before dinnertime, claiming he made important contacts on the green.

Mother didn't want to be caught in yet another scheme to accrue merchandise, and an ad in the paper would do just that. Daddy read the local gazette from front to back, having a contract with the company to supply its paper. But she quickly found she could attract a fair number of customers by merely sitting outside in a pink two-piece bathing suit—not a common sight in an upscale suburb.

"It's so darn hot today," she said to her first customer, fanning her damp chest. "Can I pour you some lemonade?"

It was a middle-aged man who'd braked with a squeal when he spotted her.

"I bet we have loads of stuff your wife would find useful." Mother handed him a glass of lemonade as he stood open-mouthed at the table. "There are so many items it's foolish to pay retail prices for." She waved her hand over the table top. "You'll net quite a savings here."

He shook his stupor off, saying, "Helen could probably use some scouring powder. Or maybe a package of vacuum bags. Helen's my wife," he explained, looking around hungrily. "Always running out of Ajax, my Helen."

"I'm sure Helen could use vacuum bags and Ajax," Mother said, stuffing both items into a bag, "but wouldn't she love it if you came home with some bath salts—something just for her."

She laughed her most womanly laugh and handed him a

jar. His eyes filled with doubt. Mother had cut the prices, if only slightly, from what was asked for in stores, but these were pricey bath salts. She seldom bothered with the low-end beauty products.

"I have three scents," she told him. "But I bet she's a lilac girl."

The man watched slack-jawed as she bent over and retrieved a larger jar from under the table.

"You look like a fellow who'd marry a girl who smells of lilacs," she said, adding it to his bag. "I'm one myself. That'll be four dollars."

Robotically, he gave me a five and waved the change away, hanging around for ten minutes and watching Mother make another sale or two.

At the end of our first yard sale, my mother had netted a tidy sum without expending more than our time. But nothing was half as interesting as watching Mother in action. If we were no longer going to eat iced donuts, or drive to the beach to watch the sunset, or dress like fairies and sashay down the streets, this was the best I could hope for.

And that was how Mother's business operated for a long time. If Daddy knew what Mother was doing—why the closets had filled, what went on most Saturdays, where those delivery trucks came from—he didn't let on. It probably would've looked a lot more innocent than some of her past stunts. Their bills tumbled, looking better than they'd been for years. There were no complaints from stores about thefts, no irate phone calls. It was a serene period although the volume of goods stashed away continue to mount. Mother couldn't part with any of her nicer possessions. It was strictly the more ordinary products that found their way to the sales table. But there were quite a lot of those. Quite a lot of everything.

The yard sales became a regular event in our neighborhood.

I wonder now why they continued for so long with no one asking her where all her products came from. And if the police noticed anything, they never asked for a permit. Mother was behind the eight ball for once. She was good at giving the impression of being sure of herself.

The final blow came a year or so later, when she was finally forced to cut a couple of nosy neighbors in on the scheme along with the mailman. It'd become too big an enterprise to ignore, too many fingers wiggling in the pie. It was one of my mother's last fairly innocuous schemes.

CHAPTER

"**D**o you know what your grandmother said to me on the last day of her life," Grandmother asked my mother, adjusting the tablecloth so each side had a twelve-inch drop. "Wait a sec," she said, straightening up with a hand on her back. "I'm sure I've told you this before."

Her tone was faintly accusatory—as if Mother solicited the story. She'd dragged the tablecloth out of a buffet drawer an hour earlier. It was one of the few decorative items Adele Hobart took any joy in. She smoothed a nonexistent wrinkle from the starched linen and waited. I was playing with my dolls under the very table: forgotten.

"Maybe, but I don't remember it." Mother lay on the sofa waiting for the phone to ring, watching her mother walk from one end of the table to the other.

Since our return to the Hobart house, only a week or so after Daddy had been forced to pay extortion money, we'd regretted our quick decision.

"But the words he hurled at me for days couldn't be ignored, Christine. Do you see what I mean? We had to go home."

Home! Did Mother see this place as home? But where else would we go? Who else would take us in until things got sorted out? That she would give us a home wasn't at all certain either. And since our arrival at Grandmother's, things had become even iffier. The silence between Mother and Daddy had gone from a crack to a chasm.

If our house in Shelterville had turned into a warfront, this one had its own set of hurdles. Sometimes, it was small things like my grandmother's repetition of stories that drove Mother crazy. Other times, it was as if Grandmother absorbed her husband's more disapproving attitude after his death and redoubled her attempts to control Mother's behavior in memory of him. Control of me became an impediment to peace too.

One thing was certain, Mother would have to behave herself here because there was nowhere else to camp out. From under the table, I could see Mother's fingers clench and unclench as she listened to Grandmother's feet moving from one end of the table to the other, to the sound of her creaking knees, the little clicks her dentures made, and her story now going into full swing. From under the table, it was all pretty scary.

("She has us where she wants us, Christine. She'd been waiting for that day.")

"I haven't told you this before?" Grandmother continued. "Your grandmother was in the hospital and I came in bringing a few drugstore items: a packet of bobby pins, Woodbury soap, Spearmint gum, and the latest issue of *Photoplay*. I never cared much for movie magazines or movies themselves, but my mother loved them. She's like you, Evelyn. Me, I couldn't get past the fact that movies were made up stories. None of it real."

"And why is that a problem?"

"Well, because it feels like a waste of time. Like someone telling you about their dreams all day long. Anyway, Mother was sleeping, but she woke when I opened the drawer to put her things away. That's when she said it."

Grandmother's feet stopped abruptly as she placed a pair of blue and white candlesticks in the center of the table, inching back to check their placement. "Don't the candlesticks look nice on the white? I know these are only from Woolworth's, but they look genuine on my grandmother's linen tablecloth. Delft-like, aren't they? You have to remember, I'm not like you—keeping such a fancy house, squirreling away more place-settings than there are places. But I have a few good things." She stood back far enough for me to see her fully as she admired her table. Her eyes lit up. "But I bet you have something better in the cellar, Evelyn. Do you want to go down and look?"

"Look, tonight's nothing special." Mother sat up suddenly, glancing at the phone as if he—Roy Tyson—might be listening. "It's just…"

I could tell she didn't want to talk about Roy.

"Okay, then back to my story. Suddenly your grandmother looked me right in the eyes and said, 'Dell, you look like hell.'" Grandmother moistened her fingers, straightening the wick on one of the candles. "Make sure you have a book of matches handy tonight, Evelyn. I don't think the table lighter has a drop of fluid in it. No one around here smokes since the Surgeon General's report. I suppose it's a good thing, but I miss the smell of a rich pipe tobacco, of watching a man fill his pipe and light it."

"Everyone I know still smokes. Roy does, for instance," Mother said triumphantly, putting her feet on the arm of the couch and pushing off. "Smokes, drinks, swears. He's a devil, all right."

I wondered why she was bragging about this.

Grandmother laughed weakly. "I'm not sure I like the sound of this—Roy."

"You couldn't stand Hank either," Mother reminded her.

"You made that perfectly clear."

"Well, I never said it—at least not in so many words. I always thought he saw us as hicks, I guess."

"Too true. Hey, maybe your mother was making a poem," Mother suggested, lying down again. "Dell, you look like hell rhymes, doesn't it?"

"What? Oh, you mean Mother, no, she wasn't making a poem. And now I do remember telling you this before because you said the same thing then." Grandmother was lost in thought for a second or two. "She may not have said Dell. It might have been just, 'You look like hell.'"

"You *always* put the Dell in. Plus, it's more memorable as a poem. Doesn't come off as mean."

"She was *mean*. I could tell you stories... Anyway, I was taken by surprise," Grandmother continued, "and said, 'Look, Mother, as it happens, I'm on my way to the beauty parlor this minute. I was dropping these things off first so you'd have them.'"

She pulled out a chair abruptly and checked the seat for crumbs. "Anyway, she closed her eyes, and then...died." Aggrieved, she pushed the chair back under the table a bit too roughly and then patted the back in apology. "These chairs are antiques. Not that I put store in such things. I can't remember where we found them." Grandmother hesitated. "I'd rather if you didn't use your father's chair. I know it's silly..."

Mother interrupted. "I'm sure Grandmother didn't realize what it was she was saying. No one can be at the top of their game under those circumstances. In the middle of dying, I mean."

"She knew all right," Grandmother said, bitter again. "I did look like hell, although I'd never use the word. Oh, my mother was different from me—very different. She was always turned out well, even on her death bed. More like you," she said, semi-accusingly. "Whereas my hair tied up in a bandana, ready to do battle…"

I could see her lips draw into the familiar knot from my hiding place, and she wrung her reddened hands as if preparing to stick them in a tub of ammonia—an item always sitting somewhere in Adele Hobart's house.

"Did you know right away she was dead?" Mother asked.

"I thought she'd only drifted off at first. I've always wondered if she had any notion those would be her last words. She always said mean things to me—though I was the most obedient child you could imagine. A mealy-mouthed pussycat. Now my brother, Carleton, well, he could do no wrong in her mind, and he was a demon." Grandmother shook her head. "She was blind to his faults. Completely blind. I had to track him down at a bar to give him the news. I remember taking the #23 trolley car along Germantown Avenue, hopping off at his favorite watering holes, places I never went into before or since. Oh, remember those dear old trolleys. I miss the sound of…"

She was standing over my mother now, as upright as a flagpole, her hands clasped in remembrance. It was hard to imagine her young. But even from my supine position, I could feel some strange strength pulsing through her body, heaving in her chest, making her hands tremble with energy. It threatened to well up and run right out of my grandmother like a bolt of electricity. I could see several long hairs sprouting from her chin. Was she turning into a witch like Mother always said?

If we stayed in my grandmother's house much longer, we'd be invalids. Each day was a little more exhausting than the last. We had left Shelterville so precipitously, we hadn't had time to get ourselves together. Now, months later, Mother still hadn't had the energy to examine her junk in the basement; she hadn't been to a shop in weeks. Unheard of. Grandmother had driven the spirit out of her. Why had this return to her childhood home seemed like a good idea? I went over it again, fingering the nearest edge of the tablecloth. Because she'd no other place to go. Not with a child in tow. I watched as Mother rubbed the hands on the chair arms agitatedly. Was it a myth thieves had itchy fingers?

"I wish you wouldn't do that," Grandmother said immediately. "Makes little grease stains and I can't afford to have it cleaned constantly. And please stop pushing on the arm with your feet. There's no money in the budget for a new couch."

With an air of satisfaction at having said her piece, Grandmother continued dusting, going over the top of the buffet with her dust cloth for the third time, moving each item as if it hadn't been thoroughly dusted five minutes before. She was a spinning top of vitality. It was dizzying.

"Rheumatic fever, huh?" Mother asked.

For a minute, I'd forgotten their conversation.

Grandmother nodded. "She came down with it as a child and after that she was never strong." Her voice sounded spent; she was running out of words like a top about to turn on its side.

Mother rose and checked her hair in the wall-sized mirror over the sofa, fluffing it up where lying down had flattened it. Grandmother had long accused her daughter of being obsessed with her looks, but actually, according to Mother, it was all because of the mirror's placement, reminding her of her face each time she passed through the room. The mirror also spawned the habit of addressing the image rather than the person you were speaking to.

I wasn't tall enough to make use of it unless I stood on the steps.

"I'm going to take a bath before Christine gets home from school," Eve told her mother — the mirror version — and walked into our bedroom.

They'd both actually forgotten I had the day off. I wondered what I should do now—try to sneak out or hold my ground. I could still monitor their behavior, so I stayed put. It was always better to know what they were up to.

Wiggling to the other end of the table for a better view, I watched Mother take off her clothes, cramming them into the pink hamper separating our two single beds. Gone from our shared bedroom were the ironing board and sewing machine. My addition to the household had necessitated moving certain domestic activity to the basement. Mother claimed she almost missed the smell of damp fabric being steamed into submission by the ancient iron.

She walked naked down the hallway. Through the open bathroom door, I watched as she poured a generous amount of bath salts into the tub and turned on the tap. There was no shower in my grandmother's house. Water splashing on the walls and floor was a no-no: moisture, mildew, mold. The progression was inevitable. And only six inches of water was allowed in the tub. Mother told me in her childhood, her father actually inspected the water level while she waited in the hallway, still clothed. No nudity in his household.

"It was always cold by the time I got in," Mother told me. "He kept the water heater turned low to save money."

I bet she would fill it to the top as a bonus for listening to that story again.

Over the sound of the running water, I could hear my grandmother running the vacuum in her bedroom, diligently crashing into a wall every few seconds, pushing the old Hoover with such fervor it made the floorboards groan.

"Anyone else would play the radio while they cleaned, but she prefers the sound of her own efforts," Mother told me once.

"Can't concentrate with that noise," she'd say if anyone

attempted to play a record. Concentrate on what? Perhaps grandmother prayed as she worked. Recited the Bible verses she favored.

The phone rang. A shrill ring making all of us jump. The Hobarts didn't encourage phone calls and got few, so when one came it was always a shock. The vacuum stopped in a split second. Nothing wrong with my grandmother's hearing. I watched as Mother paused in the bathroom too, listening to what her mother said to the caller.

"It's him," Grandmother said a second later, outside the still semi-open door. "What's his name? Can you take it?"

"Tell him I'm in the bath." I could tell Mother was angry.

"That's not a genteel thing for a mother to say to a strange man," Adele said, fretting, poised at enough of an angle *not* to see my mother's naked body. "Can't I say you're out shopping or at the dentist?"

"For God's sake, Mother. He takes baths, too. *Roy*," Mother had suddenly remembered his name, I realized, and she turned the tap hard enough to make the pipes squeal. "Never mind, I'll take it." She stood and dried her wet hand on the towel.

Grandmother sighed with relief and quickly stepped away as her daughter came barreling past her naked. I could see the small smile on Mother's face.

"I'll get out of your way."

Grandmother turned away from the flash of Eve's pink-gold skin and tiptoed into the kitchen where I knew she'd be listening. Apparently my spot under the dining room table was not visible from any room. It was Mother who claimed her mother's attention—everyone's attention.

It was nothing new for Mother to be watched. At least grandfather's days of evoking guilt had ended with his death. We could never have returned to his house. He'd never put himself in the position of coming to a store to retrieve Mother again, or to answer a phone call from a cop or an irate parent whose earrings had gone missing, or dole out hush money to keep her out of jail. These facts didn't come to me until later, of course.

Our first day back.

It was hard to reconstruct the exact events: the vitriolic words hurled hurtfully across rooms in Shelterville, the slammed doors, the shoves, pinches, slaps and name-calling, the broken glass, broken coffee table, broken promises, Daddy's secretive phone calls to lawyers, his girlfriend, his parents. Oh, it was nasty. I tried to stay out of the line of fire as much as possible. But her need for a confidante, a nine-year old one if no one else was available, trumped good sense. She filled me in on anything I might have missed.

"What harm did we do having our little garage sales?" she asked me.

The call to grandmother was humiliating. "It'll only be till I get on my feet," she told Grandmother. When was the last time she'd been on her feet? We stood in the doorway of the infamous bedroom/sewing room a few days later. Bright pink curtains with white bunnies fluttered in the faint summer breeze, a surprising new touch but something I was long past at nine. I heard Mother sniffing, probably detecting a familiar odor from her childhood—ammonia? She put a hand on the doorframe for support. Who'd rescue us this time? How would we escape? Was Mother too old to attract the sort of men she desired? For certainly only a man could save us. I would have to help.

Grandmother didn't notice my mother's apprehension. She was too busy fussing over me. I was tearful at our swift move and sitting fretfully on my new bed. My bed in Shelterville had a canopy, a ruffled bed skirt, crisp pink sheets Mrs. Murphy ironed. It smelled good, and I didn't share it with anyone. My closet was filled with expensive dresses my grandmother Moran purchased at stores in New York, toys from all over the world. Although I was not a spoiled child, I was a well-equipped one. We'd brought few things with us. Basically we came looking like the paupers we'd now be so as not to incur my grandmother's rage at our lifestyle.

"We'll only take the clothes on our back," Mother said, her voice full of rage. "We'll show your father how little we really care for material things."

At grandmother's house, my bed, and Mother's too, were little more than thin mattresses covered with thin white sheets. The box springs seem to shiver. No bedspreads — another dust collector. No attempt to make it cozy. Clean, simple, clinical. Typical Hobart décor.

"Give her the stuffed cat," Mother said, motioning to the toy peeking out of her purse, which sat next to my grandmother. "Give her Beloved. Then she'll go to sleep."

I put out my hands expectantly. Beloved had been the only toy I'd managed to grab in our flight.

Grandmother snorted. "Beloved? Who came up with that? Sounds like something — well — something romantic. I'm surprised Hank Moran would allow his child to sleep with a thing like this." She dangled it a foot in front of her.

"You think he notices such things."

"Christine can't touch it until I have a chance to sterilize it. It looks like it was left outside in the rain. Probably full of mold. And she's nearly nine years old." She turned to me. "Christine, do you absolutely need this — cat — to get to sleep?"

I began to shake my head, but Mother stepped in.

"She won't go to sleep without it," she said, flopping onto her old bed and giving a start as the sharp springs poked her.

"Of course, she'll go to sleep. She's too old to drag such a thing around, soil her bedclothes with it. I put you to bed every night with nothing to distract you from your sleep. But that's me. Maybe you know something different. Have some modern ideas about bedtime." Grandmother waited for a comment, and when none came, said, "Well, I'll leave you to settle in. Beloved!" she repeated, shaking her head.

A minute later, I started to cry and Mother handed me the cat. I was a bit of a crybaby and missed Daddy. He'd always put me to bed. Well, nearly always. Well, sometimes. I also missed Mrs. Murphy, the most likely person to be there at bedtime. And the thing *did* smell; I hadn't noticed it before. Its fur was matted, one eye missing. Why had I grabbed this toy instead of one of the nicer ones Grandmother Hobart might approve of? I put a thumb in my mouth, wrapped both arms around the cat, and fell asleep instantly.

Beloved had disappeared by morning. A new toy— a horse made of a washable brown plastic—took its place. My grandmother threw the nameless horse into the washing machine once a week so it never smelled of anything other than plastic or detergent. I didn't take to it but felt it useless to complain. Mother was more than enough for Grandmother to cope with. And Grandmother was more than enough for Mother. I trod carefully around their jousting matches. Learned how to be even quieter. I'd adjusted to living with Aunt Linda; I could adjust to Adele Hobart.

Ready to look for something? A job, I mean." Grandmother had asked Mother a few days after our return. Daddy was refusing to give Mother money until she signed the papers his attorney drew up.

"I hear the Woolworth's in center city's hiring girls to work cosmetics." Grandmother folded a dishtowel and put it aside. It was one of the few items she didn't iron. "God knows, you know all there is to know about makeup."

"I filled out an application there already," Mother lied.

"And what kind of job is working behind the notions counter for a college graduate." She unrolled a curler from her hair. It was still a bit damp, but it would have to do.

"I don't remember your graduation, Evelyn. Maybe you didn't invite me." Silence. "Your father's pension wasn't meant to stretch to three people," Grandmother said with a sniff. "What if Christine needs orthopedic shoes or braces—like you did?"

It felt like an accusation and I shut my mouth and shoved my feet under the chair.

Mother snorted. "Hank'll take care of things like corrective shoes. He wouldn't let his kid go without anything important."

"I think you'll be surprised. Men can start a new family in no time at all."

"I'm thinking of going back to school." Mother tucked the roller into its net bag, but it rolled right back out and dropped onto the floor.

I made a swipe for it, but Grandmother grabbed it first, handing it to her with a grimace. "Sticky, aren't they? You use too much hairspray. Could you run them through the dishwasher?" Finally dropping the issue of the curlers, she asked, " Beauty school?"

"No, I meant real school. Well, secretarial, at least."

"With your looks, you could probably get a job as a receptionist right now," my grandmother said, brightening. "I could watch Christine after school and over vacations."

I smiled wanly, hoping it wouldn't happen. Some of the nicest times with my mother were after school when she could justify pouring herself the first drink of the day from the bottle she kept in her shoe bag. Mother was likely to turn her full attention on me between drink number one and two. Sometimes she'd set the table and put out all sorts of nice food. I'd drink Coca Cola with a cherry in it. Or strawberry Kool- Aid in a pinch.

I prayed. Oh, please God, don't let Mother take a job.

I needn't have worried.

Eve wasn't sure why she didn't want a job. In high school, she'd stood behind the cash register at a drugstore one summer, hating every minute.

"People were always handing me an odd coin or two along with their dollar as if I was supposed to know what to do with it. Standing at a counter was unbearable in heels, and I didn't like the way my legs looked in flats. You're good with money, Christine. You'd have no problems."

She was certain she could think of a way to make some money if Grandmother would let her alone for a minute. She needed to think and her mother's screechy voice prevented it.

"Did he back out?" Grandmother asked Eve after she'd finished talking to Roy. Adele stepped out of the kitchen and handed her daughter a towel. "You must be freezing."

"It's nearly summer, Mother, and no, he didn't *back out!*" Mother wrapped the towel around her waist like a man would, her breasts in full view. "You sound like you wish he had."

"Where did you meet this fellow anyway?" Grandmother asked, obviously trying to avoid her daughter's chest as her eyes darted around. I was in the room with them now, out from under the table, but still nobody noticed.

"There's something about his voice. Unsavory, I think you'd

call it. Like Raymond Burr in *Rear Window*. Raymond Burr was so comforting as Perry Mason and on *Ironside* and yet..."

She'd watched *Rear Window* on *The Late Show* with us a few weeks earlier, a rare concession to my mother's love of old movies. "Eve, listen, only the other day, Mrs. Brewer told me her nephew was looking for a nice girl. I've seen his photograph and..."

"For Pete's sake, Mother, I don't need you to find dates for me. He—Roy—wanted to go out to a restaurant, but I told him I already had dinner in the oven."

Grandmother laughed. "That'll be the day."

Mother paused. "Listen, I don't have the time to go into this stuff right now. I need to look good tonight."

She hurried off, knowing my grandmother would put out the best spread she could and let her take credit. The farther Mother was from the kitchen, the better things would go. While they were occupied, I went outside and rang the bell. It took a long time for anyone to answer.

"Oh, Christine," Mother said. "Here you are. You shouldn't stay out so long. We were getting worried."

Making dinner for my mother and her date was apparently the kind of strange thing Grandmother did on her quest for a new husband for her daughter. She was positive the marriage was over. Before Mother had time to digest Daddy's defection, her mother accepted it and had set out to replace him. Having us with her was clearly a temporary situation although our departure seemed more unlikely all the time. Mother was thirty-four, a number many men would think of as middle aged. Plus she was used goods—with a kid to boot.

Roy was scheduled to come at eight-thirty—after I was in bed. Grandmother had arranged to visit her friend, Dottie, down the block—an unusual concession as she didn't like to be out at night. A pan of lasagna sat in the oven; a salad awaited a dressing, both made by my grandmother.

"What if he asks about it?" Mother asked, hovering over her mother's final touches. "I can never keep all those cheeses straight."

I saw the worry lines creep across her face and, sensing it, she smoothed her forehead with her hand.

"He won't ask," Adele told her, buttoning a cardigan despite the heat. "No man gives a thought to where his food comes from if a woman's involved. Turn it on about fifteen minutes before he's due to come and it will be done half an hour after he arrives. You'll be in bed, Christine."

I nodded, knowing who was boss.

Lasagna was the fanciest and most fattening meal Grandmother made so tonight was important to her too. She left with only the familiar smell of her Jean Nate cologne wafting behind.

Mother stood in the kitchen for a minute, panicking. "How will I get the lasagna out of the pan, Christine."

It seemed to be impenetrable with the oozing cheeses and tomato sauce. Thankfully, we remembered the pie-shaped utensil. You could slice it — like pie. Mother turned the oven on, running into the bathroom for a final check.

"How do I look, kiddo?"

I beamed at her.

I was hustled off to bed when the doorbell rang and went gladly. Maybe this would be the end to our imprisonment with Grandmother. I'd do what I could to aid my mother. I would make him like us, make him think I was adorable.

I could hear him from my bedroom and peeked out to see what kind of guy Mother had landed. He wore a light-colored pinstriped suit with an open-collared, starched white shirt and was definitely the type of man who attracted her: tall, well-dressed, at ease in his body and not afraid to show it. The men Grandmother pointed out on the street or in stores were more like elementary school principals or ministers. They were sweaty, paunchy, and poorly-dressed. Not like my father at all.

Mother gave a quick glance at the bedroom door, jerked her head for me to go, and let him kiss her. It looked like he was trying to pour himself into her mouth. She staggered a little afterward, as if he'd sucked all the oxygen out of her. There was no doubt this Roy took kissing seriously.

There had been only one man so far — for a few dates — after Hank and before Roy. Don was a cheese monger at the Reading Terminal Market and smelled faintly of Limburger when he came to get her. He wore a Bavarian outfit to work inside his minuscule booth at the marketplace, a buxom blonde woman named Dora or Norah dispensing hunks of cheese beside him, irritating German music playing in the background, a row of sausages hanging from the ceiling of the booth like party decorations.

Once we went downtown to see Don in his shop, things deteriorated at a fast clip, much to my grandmother's regret.

Roy came up for air now and took a seat on the sofa. "Sheesh, you keep a clean house," he said, looking around. "I should wash my hands or something."

"Make yourself at home," Mother told him, sounding like she was already regretting the evening. She glanced around for a magazine to hand him. "I need to check on your dinner," she finally said and fled.

It was years before I heard the full story of what happened next.

Eve, sounding like the waitress at Littleton's Diner on Ogontz Avenue, rushed into the kitchen and opened the oven. Things were surprisingly cool for an appliance cooking their dinner. Did the thing turn off by itself when the meal was done? Except it wasn't done, she discovered, when she poked a finger inside the noodles. Not even close. The oven was set at 350, what could be wrong? Should she smuggle Christine in here, she wondered? Calling on a nine-year old for help wouldn't look right.

Did she do something wrong? Forget something Adele had told her?

When these failures occurred, she wondered if such incidents were the result of the shock therapy. Had certain passages in her brain been jumbled? Or had she always been this way? Would Roy know what was wrong with the stove and be able to fix it or would bringing him into the kitchen only give her ignorance away? She could call her mother, but the phone was in the living room and he'd hear the call, perhaps hear Adele chiding her. Maybe she should dash down the street and ask her mother in person? In moments like this, she reverted to a totally dependent child. They had talked about this at The Terraces, the discrepancy between how she felt shopping and how she felt growing up in the Hobart house. And, all of her dazzling ideas flew from her head when confronted with any domestic task.

"I need to borrow some salt—from next door," she said, popping into the living room. "I'll just be a minute."

Roy, who'd discovered the TV and was already watching some comedy, nodded. "Take your time, honey. I never eat this early."

She hurried down the block, and after battering uselessly on Dottie's front door, realized the women were probably in the back. With row houses, getting to the rear meant circling the entire block, and she took the longer route, not wanting to cross Roy's field of vision.

The two older women were heading into the house, folded chairs under their arms, when she arrived.

"For god's sake, you have to light it! It's gas." Adele said once she'd told her the problem. "Haven't you been married for years? What did poor Hank do for his dinner? Never mind, I know the answer."

"Is this really the best time to go over my failings?" Eve felt completely depleted by this turn of events and wondered if she had the energy to go through with the evening.

Adele gave a dramatic sigh, looking meaningfully at her friend so Eve couldn't help but know the subject of her ineptitude had been discussed at length—probably for years. Dottie was Adele's only friend and confidant. "Look, I'll show you how to do it on Dottie's stove."

"Ooh, mine's electric, Dell," Dottie said apologetically. "Turn mine on and you're ready to go."

Adele looked at Dottie as if she were being difficult on purpose. "Well, I can tell you how to do it, Eve—or draw a picture, I guess. You need to hold a match to the pilot—down in the broiler. Or maybe I should come home with you." She sighed again. "He might not think anything of it. Knows it's my house, right? You can tell him I don't let anyone into the kitchen." Adele sounded proud of her quick-thinking.

Before Eve could respond, Dottie cut in. "Oh, I just remembered. My neighbor has a gas oven. Mrs. Mackin—right next door."

"Well, let's be quick about it," Adele said with a sigh. The three women hurried over to the Mackins' house.

"You know, I don't like having a strange man alone in my house. My best gold earrings—the ones I wear to church—are right on the tray on my bureau. What do you know about this man anyway? She met him at the hairdresser's, Dottie. What kind of man has his hair cut in a beauty parlor? And I didn't care for his voice on the telephone. Not at all. What was the word I used to describe it?" Eve shook her head, lips tight. "Whatever it was, it caught it perfectly." Adele glared at her daughter. "Come on. You remember, Eve."

"I *don't* remember," Eve said. "It wasn't that memorable."

"We usually eat at six," Celie Mackin said, waving them into the tiny kitchen when they arrived. Her girth took most of the available space and her three visitors huddled by the door. The Mackin family was wedged hip to hip around the kitchen table, eating peach shortcake on a red-checked tablecloth. "I can't think why we're eating so late tonight. Oh, look, I forgot to turn the oven off when I took out the meatloaf. It won't relight now—has to cool off first. It's a funny old thing that came with the house."

Eve was about to make a break for it, putting an end to this agony, when Mr. Mackin, a burly gray-haired man, rose from the table suddenly, nearly lifting it off the floor. His napkin waved from his collar.

"Do you want me to light it for you, Eve?" When she didn't answer, he added, "Or I can probably show you how to do it on paper?" He hiked his pants up and threw his napkin on the table as if he were accepting a challenge.

"He's an engineer at the phone company," Celie Mackin said. "He can draw a diagram of anything mechanical. But don't ask him to draw a bird or flower!" Husband and wife chuckled simultaneously, obviously a family joke.

In Eve's family, the jokes were almost always hurtful anecdotes about her thievery, incompetence, or acquisitiveness, so the Mackins' camaraderie was refreshing. She smiled wanly, listening patiently as the four adults offered tips on how to light a gas stove. Feeling more confident, she sailed out the door, wondering whether Roy had given up on dinner and gone home. She'd bet anything he hadn't touched her mother's dime-store jewelry. He probably hadn't left the orbit of the television set.

When she got back to the house, Roy was sitting in the living room with Christine, wearing a pair of lavender shorty pajamas, perched on his lap. A bony leg draped each side of his thighs. Her head, sweaty from sleep, nestled in Roy's neck.

It was disturbing, though Eve couldn't say why. He did look a bit like Raymond Burr, for one thing. A name for certain men—what was it—played hide and seek in her head.

"She came rushing out of her room," Roy said, placing Christine carefully on the floor and rising. "Bad dream, I guess."

"Did you have a bad dream?"

I remembered shrugging, noncommittal, unsure how to play this. I'd thought I was helping my mother by cuddling with Roy, but it was turning out badly.

"Christine doesn't usually take to strangers," Mother said, still sounding uncomfortable. "Christine, you go back to bed now. I'll be in to check on you in a minute. I'm sorry I was gone so long, Roy. I meant to come right back but…"

"I didn't know you had a daughter that age."

"She's only nine. I don't know what she said, but I'm sor—"

"I have a niece about ten, but she's a bigger girl. Stocky. I could fit Christine's foot in the palm of my hand. Delicate."

Could Christine be flirtatious with strange men? Eve wondered. Roy was still talking. Saying something about girls thinking they were adults before they were.

"So when she flounced into the room like a junior Scarlett O'Hara, I had to laugh." He laughed now as if to show her.

Why was he still talking about Christine? Five minutes had passed and still he went on. A lone drop of perspiration made its way down the middle of Eve's back. She looked at Roy closely. As he spotted her inspection, a guarded look crept over his face.

"She's a kid and I'm not around kids much—I probably

don't know how to compliment them. What to say to their mothers."

Eve could think of a lot of things, but none of them were the sentiments she just heard expressed. Roy stood in front of her, slumping and damp. He'd never appeared so unattractive. Maybe she should check the tray on Adele's bureau, but she had the sense it wasn't jewelry that interested Roy. A sharp needle pierced her brain with little stabbing pricks. He'd hardly laid a hand on her in the three weeks they dated. Only the preliminary and impressive kiss each time. Not a finger on her breast, a hand on her thigh. Not once. Had he asked about Christine before? Had he tried to get inside the house?

"Roy, I was about to tell you. Our oven's broken so I won't be able to cook dinner after all." The words came out of her mouth fluidly. "I was hoping the oven could be fixed but…"

"We can go out, Eve" he offered. "I know a great spot—"

"I don't have a babysitter tonight. You know—I thought we were staying in and wouldn't need one." Her voice had grown narrow, constricted. It was hard to get the words out.

"Well, let's take the little doll with us. She's wide awake."

He was trying hard for the charm and confidence of ten minutes ago, but it was gone—for her at least. Did she imagine it or did he perk up, looking eagerly toward the bedroom door? His hands clenched and unclenched. Hers did too. He also had the slightly unfocused look men got after several drinks. Had he been drinking? He only smelled of cologne. And a little like some sort of animal—musky and wet-furred.

He leaned in for a kiss at the door, but she nudged him away. His face registering the brush-off as he turned to go.

"I think I hear Christine," she said easing the door closed. "Coming, Honey."

She pressed her back against the door until she heard his car start.

"*I like* your new boyfriend, Mommy," I said as soon as the door opened. "He laughed at the show—like Daddy used to. He's got a funny laugh."

I was still trying to stick my landing, as perky as I could pull off. I wasn't the least bit tired, probably too old to be put to bed so early. Eight o'clock had been my grandmother's idea of a suitable bedtime.

"Christine, you know better than to sit on a strange man's lap. Whose idea was that?"

Did I know better? I didn't remember being given this information. "Mine, I guess."

"Are you sure?"

"Sort of. He was sitting on the sofa where I usually sit. I think he might have patted his knee," I added suddenly. "Like with a horsy ride." I was sweating now myself. I shouldn't have tried this stunt. I was in way over my head.

Mother swallowed visibly. "A horsy ride? What did he do when you were sitting on his lap?"

"We watched the show." I frowned, working hard to give Mother the right answer—the one that would end the questioning and make the tight look on her face go away.

"Nothing else?"

"Well, he bumped me up and down a couple times, like his leg was a bucking bronco. I'm too old for that, but I didn't say it." I paused, remembering. "It kind of hurt." I pointed to the place it had hurt, and Mother's face fell. I wasn't sure whose fault this all was, but I wasn't gonna take the blame. I'd tried my best.

"Do you want me to read to you?" she asked a few seconds later, either not willing or not able to ask the next question: the questions she'd raise with me a few years later, ask me when I was long past remembering.

Did you tell him it hurt? What did he do after that? Did

he do it more? Did he offer to rub the sore place? Instead, that night my mother thought this: Roy may not have known nine-year olds don't play horsy. It was possible.

"I'm too old to be read to. I like hearing the story in my head. Telling it to myself. I'm used to it now."

"You are growing up, aren't you? Well, don't read too long. You're up way past your bedtime already."

"*Mother?*" *Eve* said softly into the receiver a minute later.

"Oven still won't light?" Adele sounded tired.

"What? No, no, it's not the oven. I sent him home anyway."

Adele sighed. "He did do something awful, didn't he? Grabbed you? Broke something?" Her voice was growing shrill. "If you'd let me find…"

Eve could picture her mother shaking her head, the downward turn of her mouth, the droop of her shoulders.

"Could you please come home?" she asked, breaking off a piece of the French bread on the counter and sticking it in her mouth. "I don't want to be alone."

"Is Christine okay?" The annoyance in her mother's voice gave way to edginess.

"Fine. It's me. I got the heebie-jeebies."

"The heebie-jeebies! For Pete's sake, Evelyn. You're supposed to be an adult." Adele sighed. "Heebie-jeebies. I'll be along when we're done this hand of rummy. I don't like to disappoint Dottie. She planned her evening around me. I thought you could get along without me for a few hours. I guess you need a babysitter as much as your daughter."

Eve couldn't dispute this charge. "Come as soon as you can."

She hung up and sat there quietly. The light under the bedroom door had gone out and the house was completely silent. Outside she could hear the sound of someone walking down the street. Someone with cleats on his shoes. Despite knowing in her heart it wasn't Roy, she rose, pushed the heaviest chair in the room in front of the door and sat down on it. The cleats had receded before she was seated.

The next morning, she called Hank and they made a deal.

CHAPTER
Thirteen

M y parents had split more over mother's refusal to agree to twice-weekly sessions with a therapist than the extortion money Daddy paid to the mailman. He went to considerable trouble to find a psychiatrist specializing in "acquisitive women."

That's what the mental health professionals labeled women like Mother back in the early seventies. Bored, rich women who compulsively shopped and shoplifted were endemic. And as stores began to step up their specialization in apprehending shoplifters, the psychiatric profession embraced sufferers of the newly named disorder. Mother's "hoarding" obsession, her most basic problem, would not be recognized for years. And after it was labeled, unlike other obsessive-compulsive disorders, it was difficult to treat, being more tied to childhood trauma and less to brain chemistry malfunctions. Like the yo-yo I would be for several more years, I followed her home, brown plastic horse in hand.

"*Haven't we* been down this rabbit hole enough times?" Eve asked her first morning back. She'd already agreed to his demands in principle but for the moment, no plans had been made. "No one can cure me because there's nothing to cure. I just like my junk."

She stretched lazily, taking her first and only bite of egg. It'd been good to sleep in her own bed last night—no springs prodding her in the back, no odor of detergent, enough space in the bed to turn over. Another smell had greeted her in the bedroom, however—one she'd yet to identify. She decided to let the matter rest for the present.

Seeing me tucked into my own canopied bed also reassured her that things would quickly return to normal—even if her definition of normal was skewed.

Daddy read me a story—the first time I'd allowed it in months. The story was far too young for a nine-year old, but what did he know?

"Some of your junk's pretty costly, Eve. Few would call Delftware junk." Eve was jolted back to the present and the examination of her "problems" once again. Hank motioned toward a cabinet of shepherdesses and dogs. "This fellow at the club says this doctor's been successful with other...collectors."

"Clever word choice, Hank. I'm sure it's a lucrative specialty. Avaricious women often have rich husbands—ones who can afford to pay the bills." She looked at him smugly. "Acquisitive women must rank at the top of the list of faddish psychiatric disorders." She blinked her eyes twice. "You only have to think of how many synonyms there are for greedy to get the gist."

"You're one sharp tack for a college dropout, Eve. Your insight into your condition is especially impressive. Except you don't know how to stop wanting things—or taking them if the checkbook balance is low or you left your pocketbook at home. As long as you have to bring home every shiny thing your eyes light on, you need help."

His fingers played obsessively with the crease in his slacks. He could step out of the house and into a magazine shoot, Eve thought with annoyance. Once, this attention to his appearance was a good thing. Now Eve wondered who it was requiring it.

The sharp crease especially irked her. Did he steam it in again at midday, perhaps hopping over to the drycleaners to revive it at lunch time? Because the crease never disappeared despite the soft material of the slacks.

"You need to lay every shiny woman your eyes light on, and nobody sends you off to the loony bin, Hank. Let's compare notes on the costs of our activities. I'm sure the women you court don't come cheap."

Hank shook his head, but he didn't deny it.

The smell in their bedroom: whose was it? Faint but not stale. Definitely expensive.

Those long months of exile at my grandmother's house came about when my father found out how extensive the "return" business was too. He must've had an inkling of what was going on before the lid blew, but chose to look the other way—as he so often did. He wasn't able to adhere to the notion that early intervention was important with his wife. Daddy was mostly relieved for a few months' grace from time to time—more than happy to look the other way, hoping the problem would resolve itself.

It all came to a head when a new postman on our route proved unreasonably greedy on what his share of the take should be and blew the whistle—in Hank's direction.

"I've found it necessary to see a chiropractor and get special arch supports," he told Hank prissily in a registered letter—a doctor's bill and a picture of the supports in question from the

Sears Catalog enclosed. "I haven't looked into the cost of spinal surgery, but it's a definite possibility." He made no specific demands in his first letter. Later he tossed out some pretty hefty numbers.

It would've been difficult to prosecute Mother though. Meticulous in her record-keeping (thanks to me) no single company had been badly scammed by her scheme. Who'd hire an attorney to seek a legal settlement for the return of twelve boxes of Rice-A-Roni? Only a class action suit from a large number of retailers would merit the legal fees necessary to claim a court's time.

The eventual "homecoming" after the debacle with Roy, the pedophile (if that's what he was), came with the proviso that Mother see a Dr. Richard Cox on Tuesdays and Fridays. Friday's visit, in particular, tuned her up for the weekend. Maybe with Dr. Cox's help, it'd be possible for her to attend some club functions or entertain Hank's clients as she had a few years' before. Maybe there was a way to find a way back to the time of my birth—the days of the gay and perfect wife and mother. The hostess with the mostest as was said of women like my mother.

"*People still* ask for you," Hank said. "You were a favorite at the Christmas Cotillion in '64."

Eve didn't remind him 1964 was many years ago now. She had little memory of that person, doubted she'd really existed.

"If that's true, it was a side effect of the increased (or was it decreased?) estrogen levels after birth," she told me.

Gynecological research, always a backwater science, was at a standstill on which.

Whereas a few years *later*, a more psychiatrically wised up, Eve would accompany me on trips to Dr. B, manipulating my treatment with great finesse, she went to these sessions alone — Hank insisting family counseling wasn't required.

"His surname fits him to a tee," she told Hank after her first visit. "Hell, his first name too. His parents must have been imbeciles, which brings his intelligence into question. Dick Cox, really. At least he could use the name Rick." She was pacing the room.

"Unfortunate choice," Hank agreed. "Perhaps in his day..."

"Well, it certainly suits him. He rarely gets off the subject of sex." Eve lowered her voice slightly. "Gets off *on* it, I should say."

"Shun the pun," her husband reminded her.

I sat in the backseat of the car, listening to their back and forth for several minutes before we pulled into the driveway. When Mother said something lewd, Daddy threatened to send me upstairs.

"I'm almost ten," I reminded them as we entered the foyer, and they briefly relented, although no conversation between my parents was PG-rated for long.

In my grandmother's house, I'd been treated like an infant and acted accordingly by sitting on strange men's laps to win Mother a beau. But back home now, I was nearly an adult — or as much of one as necessary to hold onto my father. I'd pulled up my socks, as Daddy often suggested, and taken on the role of caretaker again. Who else would do it?

"What does sex have to do with you being a thief?" Daddy asked, pulling the *New York Times* out of his briefcase and tossing it on his favorite chair. "You're in therapy to discuss your stealing, not your libido."

Mother shrugged. "Haven't you heard therapists believe all problems stem from harm done in childhood and its effect on future sexuality? There's an article in some magazine about it every month. Subscribing to *Psychology Today* keeps me abreast of such things." She spun around the room, looking for a recent copy. "You're the one who heard about this dope — at your *club*." She said the word derisively. "Don't blame me if he's more interested in what's between my legs than what's between my ears."

"You were stealing things long before that flower bloomed."

Looking longingly at the newspaper on his chair, Daddy stroked his chin where an early seventies beard was making its first appearance. It would be a short-lived experiment since the beard turned gray within months. He wasn't even forty.

"Did you fill him in on your early career? The juicy stuff from elementary school?"

"Elementary school? I never stole..." Mother blushed. "Look, I don't volunteer anything with shrinks. I let them take the lead. If I learned anything at those last two snake pits, it was that. Otherwise, you get sent for a little electric pick-me-up or a sugar boost." She waved the latest issue of the *Psychology Today* in the air and then tossed it to him. "A conversation can get tragically sidetracked by some silly thing you only said to lighten the mood, to be entertaining when the silence lasted too long. Words they'll throw back at you when you least expect it. Oh, it's quite a juggling act."

Mother's knowledge of the psychiatric process, its ins and outs, would prove invaluable when my turn came, and that night was growing closer.

"So you're manipulating him," Daddy said, his eyes blazing. "It's always a game for you, isn't it?" He flopped down, opened the magazine, and pretended to read the table of contents page.

"Shouldn't the good doctor be used to it by now? Know how to get past it? Isn't it typical patient behavior? The guy must be sixty — at least. He graduated from the best schools. I saw a degree from University of Pennsylvania Medical School hanging on his wall. He should have learned some useful techniques for probing the reluctant or stage-managing patient during his studies."

Mother was busy mixing a drink though it wasn't close to cocktail hour. Mrs. Murphy had become adept at always having ice in the bucket, clean glasses on hand, a variety of whiskeys.

"Give him a chance, Eve. Stop trying to outfox him. Answer his questions." Daddy sighed and flung the magazine aside. "Have you ever understood you really need help? Do you think other women — other people — spend their days acquiring so much stuff that no house can contain it. Things not even removed from their packaging on occasion. I recently found a — "

"Oh, give it a rest." Mother took a long swallow. "I agree my troubles don't stem from my libido. Or, lack thereof, to hear him tell it."

"That'll be the day."

They both laughed suddenly, explosively. It was one of the few areas of their marriage that didn't dog them apparently.

Daddy grew serious. "But maybe the two things *are* related, Eve. Maybe my penis *is* a glitter stick to you. One more toy in your box." They both burst into laughter again at his inadvertent pun.

Mother looked over at me quickly, batting her eyes. I climbed the stairs reluctantly.

"*Most shrinks* think there's a connection," Eve continued as soon as they heard me climbing the stairs. I stopped midway up, hoping to overhear what I could.

"Perhaps women shoplift more than men because they don't have the gold between their legs." She breathed deeply. "Want a drink?'

"It's not four." He shrugged. "Yes."

She mixed him a Scotch and water. "Oh, I've heard all the theories. 'My father didn't love me so I am trying to get attention through glitzy purchases, through sex.' Trouble is he's dead now, so I'll never get his attention."

The memory of Herbert Hobart making his way down the narrow aisle at Woolworth's Dime Store would never fade. She could still remember the smell of parakeets and pet food as they marched through the store. Still remember eyes following them from behind every counter. Had some alarm gone off alerting them to the procession? She never sought her father's attention — before or after. There may have been triumph on his face. He'd been proven right about his daughter."

"Doesn't matter to your ID, Eve. Or ego — whatever it is. Part of you is still trying to please your father. Even if he is dead." Hank was stroking his chin again. Or what must have been his chin under that fuzz.

"Watching you play with the hair on your chin is making me itch," Eve made a face and wiggled. "I wonder if they had sex at all. My parents. Can you imagine them doing it as uptight as they were? I never saw either of them naked, was never permitted to be undressed outside of my bedroom. The sight of me naked today is more than my mother can bear. My father's only interest in my bath, for instance, was the amount of water in the bathtub, and my mother didn't bathe me after age four, only inspecting me for missed areas when I was fully dressed. And mostly it was my ears — as if they harbored truckloads of dirt."

"It's not so remarkable. Their generation is — was — prudish. Anyway, no children can imagine their parents having sex. Ask Christine. I bet she'd be shocked to know we have sex." He paused. "That's always been all right with us. Right? The sex part of it."

"Christine doesn't know enough about sex to think about

quantity. She's immature in certain ways. Kids think adults do it only to have babies. In my parents' case it was probably true." Eve put the glass down and looked him right in the eye. "If you're home, we have a lot of it, Hank. If we're speaking to each other, if I'm not in the nuthouse or at my mother's." She felt generous giving him this. And what did she know about quantity or quality after only one man? She was almost embarrassed at that, in fact, knowing he surely had outdone her there.

"Still, it's a healthy amount."

Let him have this, she thought again. She hated that beard though. It'd have to come off. She could imagine the scratches on various areas of her body from the idiotic thing. But she couldn't say anything right now. Reacquiring the upper hand would take some time.

Dr. Cox thought it'd be a good idea for Mother to get a job.

"What I could do?" she asked Daddy and me across the table at the Oak Ridge Country Club. "I didn't finish college and can't type worth a damn."

Dressed entirely in white, she was drinking champagne and eating lobster and a hearts of palm salad, both dripping with butter. It was nerve-wracking watching her eat greasy food in a white dress, but she was unconcerned—never doubting her ability to remain pristine. I kept my eye on the bottle of club soda on the waiters' station but, as usual, she ate only a bite or two before putting down her fork. Just a taste to keep the waist, I remembered her saying once. I dug in.

It was important to Daddy that we look nice. He'd approved my outfit grudgingly. I was skinny again, thanks to my months with Grandmother Hobart, but my exposed knees were scabbed from a fall off my new bike, and the dress Grandmother Moran sent over was too babyish for me. It looked like something Heidi might wear in the Alps.

"Why don't you come and work at the new stationery shop in Hatboro?" Daddy said smoothly. "A job there will keep you busy."

The Moran family had decided owning a shop where ordinary people could buy their new lines of lovely stationery, paper products, and wedding invitations was a good idea. Now was the right time for the family business to become more than an anonymous, if successful, factory operation in the backwoods of Bucks County. Retail was sexier in the new economy. Chic shops were replacing the pedestrian businesses of an earlier era. The new store had replaced one fixing irons, percolators, and toasters. Now people threw broken items away.

"A fire hazard," more than one advertisement warned. "Don't risk electric shocks."

Even if our new shop didn't turn a big profit, the Moran name would become more familiar to the general public. Daddy's team of salesmen would have an easier time of it when they showed up on doorsteps. People would recognize the name before a salesman held out a business card.

"You mean stand at a counter all day long ringing up sales. A saleswoman?"

"Well, you'd be more like a designer. A decorator. Make recommendations on what items might look nice at a party. What weight and color of paper would be a good choice for a wedding invitation. What sort of font to use. You'd be terrific at it—with your great taste." Daddy's charm was turned on high, and I could feel its warmth; we were suffused with it within seconds. It was a rare demonstration of his salesmanship abilities, and it took us both by surprise.

Mother looked more enthusiastic. "You don't have a fulltime job in mind? I still have Christine—and other things."

I nodded quickly, always willing to back the myth she took care of me—that I was a fulltime job, a bit of a pest. It felt like little to ask, these small subterfuges. When had Daddy stuck by me? I put my fork down in alliance.

He shook his head. "Nah. I was thinking of three afternoons a week. The girl I hired—Debbie—recently had a baby and wants to work part-time. It'll work out all around." He smile grew a little brighter—if such a thing was possible. I basked in the light, waiting for Mother to protest.

"I might give it a try."

I was horrified. How could I possibly monitor her behavior from that distance? What new shenanigans would she introduce while I was stuck behind a desk at school? Or sitting and eating cookies at the kitchen table with Mrs. Murphy. Disasters had come about in such circumstances before. My grandmother's watchful eye had not been enough. Strange men had tried to have their way with both of us.

Mother, for her part, was probably already thinking about the personal fulfillment derived from offering advice to the ordinary town folks of Hatboro, setting a smart tone, being a style-maker. And having money in her pocket she didn't have to beg from Daddy wouldn't be half-bad. She didn't give a thought to the cost her job would have on me. When had either of them stuck by me? I was alone.

Eve's employment at Moran's in Hatboro began the next week. She saw Dr. Cox Tuesdays and Fridays, working afternoons the other days. The shop was not expected to generate huge revenues, so there was little pressure to make a lot of sales. As Daddy spelled out repeatedly, Moran's Stationers was primarily to remind area businessmen that the family ran a successful printing business not ten miles away, a business that could take care of all their paper and printing needs — large or small.

The shop was small but nicely appointed with cherry cabinetry and ceiling moldings and highly-glossed, wide-planked flooring. The name was inscribed in a wrought-iron font over the front door. A jaunty awning, in the same color as the logo on the letterhead, hung above. Shops hadn't begun to pay much attention to their façades in Hatboro so Moran's Stationer was a scene-stealer.

"People will want to stop in if only to see the decor," Hank told his wife with confidence.

He'd come into his own as a businessman now, sitting on various planning commissions, foundations, and boards. It was his damned wife's behavior that tripped him up. He must've wondered again, as he saw her hands gliding over the merchandise, whether employing his wife was a wise move.

But things started out on a high note. Eve enjoyed giving advice to the newly engaged, to matrons planning parties, to anyone who asked for her help. She quickly became known in town and began to function as an early version of an event planner.

All went well until she realized, inadvertently, she later said, that sales rung up as "no sale" could put pennies in her pocket. She was in the shop alone for hours at a time and if she wanted to pocket the odd five dollar bill, no one would know. If the inventory didn't disappear too quickly, who would figure it out? It didn't occur to her, or so she later claimed, she was robbing her husband and his family. It didn't seem very different from taking an odd twenty from his wallet. More than fair when you considered the paltry salary he paid her. Actually, he was paying Debbie Knotts, a twenty-five-year old, more than his own wife.

"When you're the proprietor, you don't take a big paycheck," he explained more than once. "We are the recipients of the shop's profits."

"Give me a seat on the board and perhaps I'll think differently."

Eve's past inability to understand the mechanics of making change had faded over the years. She understood the mechanics of money better now that an incentive for mastering it had been presented. High finance wouldn't be her forte, but this sort of finagling was within her grasp.

As she grew bolder, she'd sometimes write a large order for a prospective bride or a ladies' group affair and pocket the entire payment, crumbling any trace of the paperwork once the job was complete. She didn't do this often, understanding it would come to light if it was anything more than an infrequent stunt. As in the past, it was the little thefts she could most easily justify and live with. She didn't crave a Cadillac, just crystal goblets.

At home, things were going well. No strange men were fondling her child, Adele was temporarily out of their daily lives, and Hank was coming home for dinner more often since Mrs. Murphy had returned. Eve's "work" necessitated it. She was able to integrate a few of her nicer purchases, paid for by her inventive bookkeeping at Morans, into the household decor without Hank noticing. The rest went into storage.

The boxes in the basement and garage continued to accumulate. A new storage unit on the edge of the city was secured and another of the little keys found itself onto her key ring. She took me along to stow the first load of boxes. It was impossible to believe she'd fill the unit, but she succeeded in less than two years. She'd brought a dolly with her and we struggled to unload the orange and white VW camper she'd borrowed from a neighbor.

"Cute little place," she said, on opening the door to the unit. She yanked a string and a sixty-watt bulb illuminated the room. "We could practically live in here, Christine."

There'd come a time when we spent a few days in such a storage unit in Burlington, New Jersey. We heard noises from other units there too. Apparently storage units actually hosted the multiple uses the brochure promised. The unit was made of aluminum and clattered as we tossed in her bounty.

CHAPTER
Fourteen

I t's hard to believe my father wouldn't have known what would happen when he installed Mother in the Hatboro store. Maybe he thought she'd take some loose change from the cash register on occasion. Figured it'd be no worse than what happened with any unsupervised employee with access to the money. No worse than the sort of tricks she pulled at home. It'd keep her busy, and if her paycheck was small enough, it might all even out.

It was Debbie Knotts who figured out such thefts were taking place and squealed. And because Mrs. Moran, Senior, happened to stop in the shop to pick up some stationery for a friend, it was she who was the recipient of the bad news.

"I don't like to tattle on Mrs. Moran, but I couldn't take the chance I'd be blamed," Debbie told Sophie Moran. "I can't sleep at nights for worrying over it."

"She'd been gunning for me since Day One, Christine. I'd actually expected the old biddy to go through the books. I was so damned careful with the accounts but didn't give Debbie

Knotts a thought. From all signs, she was too preoccupied with her baby to pay much attention to me or the stock."

"*Do you* have any idea how much her thefts might amount to?" Sophie Moran finally asked the shaking stationery store clerk.

Debbie shook her head. "Eve has kept track of the inventory for months." She took a gulp of air. "The big printing job we did last month for the Harbisons never showed up on the books. I only noticed 'cause—"

"How much was the order?" My grandmother couldn't wait to get to the point.

"Nearly two hundred dollars. Invitations, place cards, cocktail napkins, some other stuff. I noticed another job from a few weeks earlier wasn't on the books either. An order for the Southampton Garden Club—a small one for paper for their program and such—under twenty-five dollars. But it wasn't entered in the books." Debbie was wringing her hands with anxiety. "I feel awful. Eve being the boss's wife and all."

Yes, Debbie was completely undone at this point, according to my grandmother, probably unsure about how this information would play out. Would she get in trouble for either squealing on Eve or for not noticing it earlier? Oh, it was fraught with dire possibilities. Debbie looked so white with terror my grandmother made her sit down. They both sat down, in fact, and went through the books together. Nothing stood out. But mother hadn't doctored the books. She'd merely omitted an item here or there.

"Have you noticed a loss of inventory?"

Debbie shrugged. "Once or twice. An item I had my eye on as a gift once. Or something I was planning to recommend to a customer. But with the both of us selling things separately, it's hard to know when something's missing. The store's not big, but it's well-stocked."

My grandmother told Debbie she'd done the right thing and a big bonus would appear in her next paycheck.

"That's not necessary," Debbie said sheepishly.

"You're going to find out how a loyal employee is treated by the Morans," Sophie said. "You can advance in the business, you know. We have a growing operation…"

"Three days a week works fine for me — with the baby and all," Debbie said. "My mother can only look after the baby that often. I'm really a housewife. I don't really want to — advance — right now." She shook her head at the thought.

Of course, Daddy went crazy when his mother, breathless with excitement, flew into his office and told him about his wife's thefts.

"Nobody thought having Eve at the shop would work out for long, Hank, but we didn't imagine this. We should probably notify the bunko squad. Is that what they call it? But, of course, we can't. It makes us look foolish — once again."

Still breathing hard, his mother sank into a chair, pretending or perhaps experiencing real grief at the circumstances. Certainly its consequences on the family disturbed her. She took a pocket fan from her pocketbook and began to fan her face.

"We're going to have to find a way to keep Debbie Knotts' mouth shut."

She told him about Debbie's refusal of a better job. "I think I handled it as well as I could. Linked it to her loyalty rather than the fact we wanted a lid kept on Eve's activities."

"Deb's twenty-five years old and wants a job for pin money," he said. "But her husband's a mechanic at the Sunoco station so things are probably tight." He paused, thinking hard. "Maybe we can hire him to work in the factory. I'm sure I can beat whatever the station pays him." They smiled simultaneously.

Hank drove home immediately. Obviously it was not one of Eve's days in the shop. The house was quiet as he opened the back door—Mrs. Murphy was out shopping perhaps. He took the back stairs two at a time and pushed open the door of his bedroom, wondering if his wife was still in bed.

Eve was in bed all right. An ecru negligee lay crumpled on the floor. Mother was having her regular Tuesday session with Dr. Cox, and for the first time, it was between her much-disheveled robin's egg blue sheets.

Hank stood at the door silently for a few seconds before turning on his heel. He was not quiet enough, however, to avoid his wife's ears.

"Damn," Eve said, nimbly hopping out of bed. "You never come home unexpectedly. It's a goddamned thirty-minute drive. Hey, did you hear me?"

She was yelling by now, hopping around with one slipper on as she looked for the other. Dr. Cox shrugged and rose wearily, the smell of sweat, sperm, deodorant, cologne, booze, and Eve hanging pungently in the air around him.

"What's up, Hank?" Eve shouted, still naked. "What brought you home? Look, it's not what you think—" she said, ricocheting between which strategy to try. "What's going on here with me and Dr. Cox." She didn't glance at her bedmate. "Is it something to do with Christine? Did the school call?" Hank had already fled down the steps. "Truly, this is unheard of," Eve said, turning back to Dr. Cox. "I could count on one hand the times—"

"Are you sure you hadn't planned on this, Eve?" Doctor Cox broke in, calm, cold and reasonable as always. "Research suggests there are few true accidents in life. Only expressions

of unconscious desires that appear to be accidents. I haven't
bought into Freud's idea on this completely, but in this case…"

He stood, his spent penis looking sticky and atrophied.

She gave it an unavoidable look. "Keep your insights for our
sessions," she said, throwing the ecru negligee in his direction.
But its light weight made reaching its target impossible, and it
fell to the floor. They both dressed hurriedly.

"You know it's not at all unusual, Mr. Moran—or can I call
you Hank," Dr. Cox said, once Eve and he were dressed and
in the kitchen. Hank had a bottle of Dewar's in front of him.
"Sexual activity between a doctor and a patient. Many therapists
speak to the efficacy of 'overt transference' or the utilization of
'sex' in their treatment of patients. I warned Eve my role in the
so-called 'sexual relationship' she sought would be in keeping
with the acting out of 'transference love' rather than 'romantic
love.'"Eve snorted from her corner.

"How considerate, Dr. Cox," Hank said from his chair at the
table. He hammered his fist on the table lightly and said, "So far
I have been repeatedly unimpressed with the ethics and skill of
your profession despite the necessity of using psychiatry again
and again with poor Eve here."

"Fuck you," Eve said softly.

"I'm sorry you feel that way, Mr. Moran. It would've
certainly been preferable to keep this interlude between doctor
and patient a private affair." He glanced over at his patient.
"Eve assured me you rarely made trips home midday, so I
assumed…"

"He told me it meant nothing to him, Hank. And it meant
less still to me."

Eve didn't know why this information was relevant, but a
workable strategy for calming Hank down had yet to occur to
her. She looked over at Dick Cox, hoping for a way out of this

"I guess you think you're pretty funny, Eve," Hank said,

holding a half-empty glass of Scotch. "Imagining you could defuse the situation by denying it had any meaning?" His hand shook and some of the Scotch sloshed out. "Wait until I sue the pants off this bastard. We'll see exactly how funny it all is. You didn't sign anything, did you?" He glanced at Dr. Cox. "You didn't make her put her request for sexual favors in writing, did you? And what about your part in this... escapade, Cox? Did you sign a waiver of some sort and file it with your attorney? Do you maintain a file on patients who sleep with you? Do you offer a discount or do you charge more?" He took a large sip of the Scotch and winced.

Eve let out an enormous sigh. "Of course not, Hank. Neither of those things. And I didn't have an orgasm if that's any consolation. You are much livelier in the sack than the doctor here."

Eve, who'd never said the word "orgasm" in public before, opened the refrigerator, took out an apple and offered it to Dr. Cox. When the doctor shook his head, Eve took a bite. "I'm starving," she explained. "Sex makes me hungry."

"I know," Hank said. "But usually it's pastry. Quite an appropriate item of food, Eve. An apple? Practically a cliché." Eve looked at the apple and shrugged. "Now me, I like to drink when I see things like—like what I saw. How long has this been going on?"

"Nobody doubts it," Eve said, nodding toward the glass in his hand. Her mouth full of apple, she asked, "Does Mrs. Murphy wash the fruit before putting it in the fridge? I suddenly can't remember."

She stuck the apple under the faucet and turned it on hard. The water hit the apple and splattered the counter. Absentmindedly, Eve slid her forearm across it.

Hank finished his drink, slammed the glass down, and reached for the bottle. "Things started out badly and have only gotten worse here. And you've splashed water all over the backsplash as well, Eve. Can your arm sop that up, too?" When his wife didn't blink, he repeated it. "Eve, you're making a mess, and Mrs. Murphy isn't here to help you out." When his wife looked confused, he added, "A mess with the water. Turn the goddamned water off."

"Well, isn't that the point of a backsplash? Where the name comes from?"

Eve turned the tap hard enough to make the pipes scream. The three of them stood frozen, having lost any sense of who should speak next or what should be said.

"I'm not in the mood for cleaning up after you today." Hank took a large sip of his second glass of Scotch in ten minutes. "And it's not Mrs. Murphy's day, as I said."

"Like you once did such a thing! Cleaned up after me or anyone else."

The apple was sour. She remembered liking sour apples when she was pregnant with Christine. Well, she wasn't pregnant now, would probably never be pregnant again. Hopefully. She tossed the apple in the trashcan.

"I've done nothing but mop your messes for the last fifteen years."

Hank's eyes were venomous, making her even angrier. When you considered what she'd put up with in the matter of his sexual liaisons, it was infuriating. He had had ten women to her one man. And what a man to choose for her first foray into an affair. She felt deeply embarrassed she hadn't taken the care to find a man worth the resulting situation.

"You're not here often enough to comment, Hank. This is the first time I've seen you in days."

They stood like warriors on a battlefield, their words fired across linoleum instead of bare earth.

"Excuse me," Dr. Cox interrupted. "Let's get back to

the subject at hand. As for our recent sexual encounter," he continued. "I deliberately kept things low-keyed. During the sex, I mean," he added, looking at their confused faces. "We needed to get past it—this need of Eve's to have sex—before moving on to the real issues. It'd become a real impediment to any meaningful therapy. This wish to get naked and fuck—a situation female patients sometimes experience with a male doctor—it gets in the way. But it'll never happen again." He looked at Hank as if the matter was resolved. "With Eve, that is. We're ready to move on." He repeated it more forcefully, in case the pair had been unfocused the first time he said it. "Ready to buckle down to the hard work necessary to make Eve a functioning wife and mother."

"You are a colossal ass," Hank said. "Really a world-class idiot. And you're damned right it won't happen again. I have half a mind to slug you right now." He paused for a second. "Hey, I wonder if you bedded ole' Jeff's wife too."

"Now you can see what I mean about him always wanting to talk about sex?" Eve told Hank. "You probably thought I was exaggerating and here I wasn't telling you the half of it. I didn't mention the constant invitations to disrobe in his office for one thing. Strike the word invitations and make that demand. He demanded it."

"You screw my wife and expect me to keep paying your bills?" Ignoring Eve, Hank shook his head and took another swallow of his Scotch, wincing. "You're finished screwing my wife or probing her head unless Eve can afford pay your fees out of the money she's stolen at my store. Did you charge for the sex or merely the therapy?"

Eve stared at him in alarm. So this was what sent him home midday. He'd found out about the paltry money she'd taken and was going to make a big deal about it. It'd be like the brouhaha over the payoffs to the mailman all over. She began working on her story, regretting she hadn't given it more thought earlier. Planning ahead for situations like this was not her forte. It just never occurred to her she'd get caught. Either with her hand in the till or at having sex with Dr. Cox.

Dr. Cox responded at once. "Jung slept with a patient, you know. It's not unusual. And in my case, I did it only to be able to put the issue behind us. So long as Eve was fixating on the possibility of a romance…"

"Oh, give me a break. Not romance, Dick. Sex. For god's sake, you're no romantic figure." Eve wiped her hands on a towel and opened the fridge door again. Maybe there was something sweet in the back. "But that's true, too, Hank. Now I've slept with Dick once, I won't need to do it again. It was nothing special. Switching to some new doctor is too much trouble at this point."

She'd grown sick of her doctor's intimations she'd begged for sex and remembering what had transpired upstairs, she realized again, it hadn't been so hot. And she hadn't begged for it. At least, not at first. And the other situation—the more important one—had that damned Debbie ratted her out? This was where her mind wanted to go, but there was this thing at home to deal with first.

CHAPTER
Fifteen

ifteen minutes into her first visit some weeks earlier, Dr. Cox said, "Nothing's off-limits in my office, Mrs. Moran. If you want to take off your clothes, for instance, and sit naked on my couch, I'm okay with it."

He punctuated this statement with a little smirk of a smile she'd come to know well. Was this guy kidding? She could imagine making embarrassing sounds whenever she moved. Leather furniture in public spaces seemed designed to assert control. It was slippery, noisy, sweaty, cold. Not a good spot for a naked body. Not that she had the least interest in fulfilling his fantasy.

He had to be well over sixty. Bushy hair sprouted from his nose and ears. The hair on his head was steely gray, and he wore a gray suit. A portrait of his family sat on his bookshelf. The children were teenagers, but one wore an "I Like Ike" button, dating the photograph back at least fifteen years.

"Maybe later—when we know each other better. If at all."

"The thing is," he continued, ignoring her sarcasm, "we

want an uninhibited workplace here. And yes, I do consider this office a workplace." He waited for a response and when he got none, continued, "You can cry, you can sit silently, you can do whatever you like. It's the establishment of trust I'm interested in. We need to form a bond. Until such a thing happens, no progress will occur." He linked his fingers and put his hands behind his head, stretching. His fingers were chubby but nicely groomed, perhaps professionally manicured. "We can't begin efficacious therapy until we reach a plateau of trust."

Eve nodded, having heard all of this before. Well, maybe not the bit about getting naked, but the rest of it: the stuff about trust and bonds and progress. The bit about workplaces and plateaus. The lingo of modern psychiatry. It was total shit. Crappola—except for the electric shocks. That delivered an incontestable message.

After the initial surprise, the first session continued much like the ones at The Terraces, the place using *talking* rather than *shocking* to solve problems. She felt in control, knew she hadn't given him anything to use against her—yet. Session Two and Three went smoothly, too. The words "get naked" continued to run in her head along with fantasies about sitting on his couch with nothing on but her heels. She wasn't exactly attracted to him. But she wasn't exactly not. She *was* one complicated broad, she thought.

Session Four. Another surprise attack. He met her at the door and kissed her passionately, sticking his tongue down her throat, rubbing himself against her. It both turned on and repulsed her. His tongue was shockingly cold and she wondered if he'd iced it.

"Do you have a refrigerator in here?"

Nodding, he gestured to it like she was asking for a Coke or a Popsicle, and then took his usual spot, notebook in hand. Had it happened? Was he a predator? She'd heard of such doctors at The Terraces. Doctors who preyed on patients too undone by drugs or shock or their illness to defend themselves, too witless to register a protest, too flattered to see the onslaught as inappropriate behavior.

The hair in his nose, on display as she gazed up at him, kept her grounded. So she pursued it.

"What about the kiss? You know. What just happened?"

He shrugged—acting like it'd been nothing more than a handshake.

"Have you had any difficulty with frigidity?" he asked her a few minutes later. "Do you get wet when you think of sex?" He was eyeing her crotch openly.

"I've been married thirteen years, so I've been around the block." She sounded like a hooker on Broad Street. She was losing ground now. The tips of her fingers were hanging onto an increasingly unstable spur.

"And you haven't been with another man in all that time?" She didn't answer. "Never wanted to try something—someone—new?"

"Newness is overrated."

He had a point though. Why all this fidelity when Hank was a cheater? Had she been too busy accumulating possessions to have other men? Was junk her sublimation?

It went on like this: sexual moves, embarrassing questions, subsequent denials that anything unusual took place. He put a hand on her breast and when she squirmed away, he asked her a humiliating question, bound to provoke hurt.

"So your husband bags a new woman every few months. Does he make sure you find out?"

Did Hank leave hints? She wasn't sure but shook her head. Hank was not about confrontations. He'd be delighted to assume she'd never questioned his faithfulness—proud that he had been clever.

The overall effect of Dr. Cox's therapeutic style was she quickly wanted to sleep with him. He gave every indication of being someone who'd sweep her away. Someone who knew the intricacies of sex better than Hank. He was a medical doctor after all—not just a shrink. He'd spent years studying the body before he moved onto the mind.

Despite all the shrinks she'd talked to, no one had ever spoken about sex quite this openly before—never put a move on her. No one gave her signs she was attractive. No one had tried to seduce her since Hank, in fact. The one or two men she dated during her recent banishment hadn't meant a thing to her. And before them —nothing. Why didn't men hit on her more often? Had she neglected her looks in pursuit of her junk?

She began to think about little else. Standing behind the counter at the shop in Hatboro, lying in bed alone most nights, watching TV, fixing Christine a snack, it was all she could think about. So she made a tentative move.

"I'm not sure if that's a good idea," Dr. Cox said when she put her mouth on his one day. His lips were drier than a snake's would be if a snake had lips.

"Come on. You've been pushing me in this direction for weeks."

She was both outraged and embarrassed. But for some reason, she *wasn't* surprised. Perhaps it *was* her. Maybe she'd invented his seduction—his hand up her skirt, his breath on her neck, his tongue down her throat. Were these actual incidents or fantasies? "If you think it's a bad idea…"

"Let me think about it," he said hurriedly, splaying a hand across his chin in contemplation. One finger caressed his lips.

So Eve had become the predator. Was this his plan?

Half-an-hour later when their session was finished, he edged her onto the sofa, pushed up her skirt, jerked down her panties, and entered her, one knee on the floor. It was rather how she'd imagined her parents making love, without prelude or romantic gestures. It was rather painful. He appeared satisfied, however, and walked into the bathroom.

"Can we try this again?" she asked when he returned. It'd happened too quickly to take it in. "I don't think I was at my best."

"The cleaning woman will be coming in," he said, reassembling himself quickly.

"A hotel?"

He put a finger to his lips again. "What about your house? You said your husband's not home much." She nodded. He cleared his throat. "You do understand such an act would be part of your therapy and not a romantic overture."

"I need to get it out of the way," she said, licking her lips. "So I can stop thinking about it. Fixating on it."

"I see. Well, as your therapist, I won't think of it as having sex with you, Eve." He rubbed his chin again. "I do think such an encounter... perhaps two... may deepen the level of our relationship, the level of trust. Do you think you're ready to go there? Explore that area of your sexuality?"

"Whatever," Eve said, already planning it in her head. And, of course, it turned out to be the disaster you'd expect.

Between my tenth and twelfth birthday, my parents split three more times. We stayed in a motel in Atlantic City for a summer. Mother landed a job at the first casino there, Resorts International. Nothing to do with the gambling operation, however. They would've looked into her past too closely if she'd applied for that type of position. Nothing glamorous or well-paying. She may have been a waitress or a hostess. She didn't talk about it much. The hours were few; the pay bad.

We stayed with my grandmother several times. We rented

cheap rooms from time to time, and spent three nights in one of those storage units. Once we found ourselves on Aunt Linda's steps. She had a place of her own by then. Mother used the interlude to disappear, figuring I'd be happy with Linda for a few weeks. And I was.

Later I found Mother spent some time in jail over those months. She'd forged a check, got caught with her hand in the till. She was always able to talk her way out of it, to make it look like it was more trouble than it was worth to prosecute. It was too cruel to trouble a single mother over trivial matters. Cy Granholm made his first brief appearances, always skilled at framing a defense on the spot. A night or two in jail certainly. Perhaps thirty days once.

Despite the fact these were hard times, Mother held herself together pretty well. She always denied it, wouldn't believe it when I told her this later, but she functioned best without a man in her life. Looking for a man, holding on to one, hiding things from one, all of this was a lot of work. A new man introduced new desires, schemes, risks. Still, she found it hard to be without one for long. One night she even murdered Jerry Santini but that's a story you already know.

When I had the patently incorrect idea her romantic life was behind her, Mickey came on the scene.

CHAPTER
Sixteen

M other and I sat facing each other across a tiny kitchen
table. Space was so tight our knees touched, making little
kissing sounds from time to time. Although my legs were
skinny, my knees had excessively large knobs that tapped on
hers every few seconds. Mother's legs, on the other hand, were
tan and shapely enough to draw the eyes of men. Her legs,
and similarly attractive features, earned her a second husband:
Mickey DiSantis.

The great, and still-to-be answered, question was why she
wanted him; why we were stuck in a tiny house in the Mt.
Airy section of Philadelphia with this guy—this man quite a
bit like Jerry Santini—the one she'd knocked off. We no longer
talked about that incident, and I'm sure Mickey never hear a
word about it. Sometimes I wondered if I'd imagined it all—
if those visits to Dr. Bailey hadn't been a sort of fever dream.
Whole sections of my life—our lives—were forbidden topics.
No, more than forbidden. They'd virtually disappeared once
we moved into Mickey's. There was no one in my current life

who wanted to hear about my past. There was no past; we lived in the moment. Mother had reinvented us time and again. And would forever, I feared.

Things had taken a less glamorous turn with the current reinvention, and I couldn't make sense of it. It was as if Mickey DiSantis had put a spell on her. My grandmother, so anxious to have us settled with a respectable man, disapproved of him on sight and more so in the weeks following their first meeting. She'd begged us to stay put when we'd moved out of her house nine or ten months before.

"Quite a step down from Hank," she said repeatedly. "Used cars. Couldn't he at least sell new ones? What kind of people buy used cars?"

This was a bit of a stretch as a criticism—Grandmother was driving a car from the late fifties—when she drove at all. I could've given her more information to use against him, but I was biding my time, waiting to see what happened next.

Mother refused to discuss Mickey's faults. Some form of blackmail must be involved. What did he have on her? What had he seen her do in the foyer of Gimbel's?

With a little effort, she could've gotten my father back, but instead, here we were stuck with Mickey. I was beginning to lose respect for my mother. My awe of her was declining and would never resurface in full bloom again. With the possible exception of my father, she'd chosen a motley assortment of men.

Mother's fake capezios were aqua, which she claimed was one of the better colors for showing off a tan. I watched her feet under the table, as she slid the shoes off and on. Mother's feet were at least a size seven, too big for her tastes. So she bought a six or six-and-a-half and suffered. The shoes revealed a half-inch of swollen toe flesh, which she claimed drove men wild. Too-small shoes pumped out more toe décolletage than the proper size would.

"It brings to mind a higher cleavage," she explained.

I was with her when she made the purchase, when she labored long and hard over the choice between aqua and peach. With Daddy, she could've had them both and the real deal.

I was wearing the sturdy sandals that began making an appearance in the seventies, shoes making feet look twice as wide as they were. It was a shoe to climb a mountain and probably expressly designed to prevent a woman's foot from appearing small, delicate, sexual. You couldn't bend those sandals with a surgical instrument.

"It'll take a few weeks to break them in," Grandmother said, pulling them out of the box. "Your arch has to get used to it."

It was some time before I realized how ugly they were. And my arch didn't get used to it. Instead I developed a permanent cramp in the instep of my right foot. Other than my footwear though, I was a carbon copy of my mother, wearing my hair in styles unflattering to a teenager, not suited to my face at all. What did I know? I didn't spend any time with kids. I had no more insight into teenage society than Pat Boone.

"You see what I mean about your grandmother," Mother said, looking pointedly at my feet when I came in the door. "She'll try to dress you like someone from *Petticoat Junction* if you let her. Next it'll be overalls and gingham. Mickey says..."

On principle, I stopped listening. Mickey's pronouncements were aired incessantly despite him exhibiting no discernible signs of intelligence. How could my mother be so clever about some things and so blind about others?

We were eating scrambled eggs and toast. The jam or jam-like substance was in one of those little packets filched from the corner diner, not the expensive kind of peach preserves Mickey liked. Mickey. It was bizarre how a man so completely unknown to me last summer now dominated our lives. Had there ever been a man named Mickey you could take seriously? Someone who didn't hold a baseball bat or speak in a squeaky voice? Why didn't he use the name Mike like any normal guy?

"His brother was called Mike," my mother said when I pressed her.

Did the DiSantis' name both their sons Michael? If so what happened to Mike? I didn't ask. It was a piece of the Mickey folklore I could live without.

Mother met Mickey DiSantis when she traded in her '66 Cutlass for a newer model. Mickey sauntered out of the showroom, selling her a low-mileage two-year old model in minutes. The car was black. He told her *only* black was classy enough for her. Was there ever a person who used the word classy and was? Certainly not my stepfather.

This would be the first in a long line of pronouncements from Mickey on subjects as varied as clothing styles, refrigeration, NATO, digging for clams on the New Jersey beach, methods of burial, President Kennedy, Vietnam, the proper temperature for red wine, the proper maintenance of the bowels, how to bluff in poker, and dog racing. His mind was wide-ranging in subject if narrow in comprehension. This all occurred to me later. At the time I classified him as weird, icky, a dope, a dork—who still wore his hair in a slicked-back pompadour in 1978.

Mother was hungry for compliments—so the "classy" car comment worked brilliantly, giving her hope for a brighter future, possibly with Mickey. Her current job, spritzing people with perfume at Gimbel's Department Stores, was poor-paying and hard on the back since she insisted on wearing high heels. She decided the foyer of a department store was as good a spot to meet potential beaus. Daddy had found the job for her himself, telling her she'd get a store discount for her trouble as well as a small salary. He still pumped in the majority of our upkeep.

"Should Hank put you in harm's way," my grandmother asked worriedly. "We all know your history with department stores."

"That's all behind me now," my mother promised. Behind her perhaps — but also in front of her.

Gimbels' Cheltenham's store manager played golf with Daddy on Saturdays, and the feeling was Mother wouldn't have the nerve to try something with him circuiting the floor twice a day. She was tightly reined between the entrance and the cosmetic counters. The scents, delightful at first, permeated her clothes, our house, her. I've never been able to wear perfume since her short stint at Gimbels.

There were an amazing number of things that had soured for me. Eating evoked guilt; friends were not to be trusted; books produced eye-strain; the medical profession — all frauds; Daddy was a cheat; his family — snobs; my grandmother, Hobart, a scold. I was beginning to wonder if sex would be another tarnished subject. Sex had yet to be discussed despite my age.

Mickey DiSantis didn't approve of women working.

"God made women to look good, give birth, and shop," he told her on their first date. "I can see why Gimbels wants you standing at their entrance though," he said. "You probably account for a huge increase in traffic — people drawn in from the mall. You're magnetic." And so were his words.

Mickey and Mother's romance took off like a rocket, the building blocks being a mutual adoration of Mickey. Okay, he *was* good-looking in a Vic Damone kind of way. But before I knew it, I was stuck at the tiny kitchen table, brushing up against their new found love until it hurt.

"A long courtship doesn't make sense at our age," Mother told me when I questioned the speedy union.

When Mickey wasn't home, I was lucky to get much of

anything for dinner, but too many complaints put a tense look on Mother's face. I'd thought the strained look would disappear once she married, but instead it grew worse. She was like a juggler with all her balls in the air, waiting to see which one would fall first, where it would land. Cooking was still problematic, but Mickey's salary didn't stretch to household help and he couldn't be manipulated as easily my father.

Mickey was world-weary at forty-five. He'd seen it all sometime in the past, maybe in the Marines in Korea. Or perhaps with his first wife, Racine.

"A little house like this practically takes care of itself," he told us repeatedly. "And feeding me is child's play. What else would you do all day now that you're not spritzing?"

Mother swallowed any complaints. She'd finally rid herself of the smell of Obsession and wasn't going back.

Finishing my eggs in two mouthfuls, I looked desolately at my dessert—an apple. It was May and the apple was pulpy and tasteless. Didn't my mother know it'd probably been sitting in a bin somewhere since October? You were supposed to buy strawberries in May. Or apricots. I started to tell my mother this, but her eyes had gone slit-like as she stared at her almost empty plate.

Mother was definitely in one of her moods, and it was useless to expect much thought about food. It was hard to remember the Eve of the tea parties and trips to the shore for cotton candy. The mother who was glib, sassy, and fun. It was easier to recall the mother who'd repeatedly fucked things up. Was this another example of a screw up or a smart move? A fuck-up or a step-up? The only reason I could come up with for Mickey's presence in our lives was she was playing it safe somehow. Hiding out in this lower middleclass neighborhood where no one would know her, far out of the reach of Daddy's country clubs and cotillions. Out of her mother's house and orbit as well—in a different section of the city. Choosing a domineering fellow like Mickey to keep her in line perhaps? Although he'd claimed to like women to shop, it hadn't worked out that way. He had a skill for sniffing out money spent, could sense something new in the house in minutes. Mother's time with Mickey would refine her survival skills for the years ahead. No way would this marriage last, or so I hoped.

If Mickey had been home for dinner, there would've been pastry. Yesterday Mother had run over to Hansen's Bakery on Ogontz Avenue, a twenty-minute trip each way, for éclairs. She hadn't trusted me to perform this errand since the time I'd come home with a stale angel food cake.

"Couldn't you tell it was old by the puckered look?" my mother said, tossing it in the trashcan. She might not know how to bake a cake, but she had a keen eye for a deficient one. Cakes, she understood.

"They don't give their best stuff to kids."

I didn't like angel food cake anyway—it reminded me of cotton, but it was the only sweet Mother ate nowadays. She'd slice the smallest piece imaginable with a razor-bladed cake cutter and eat it standing at the sink; there was no joy in pastry for my mother anymore. The bathroom scale was the enemy because Mickey liked skinny women. Skinnier than she'd ever been and she'd always been thin. His eyes followed women in restaurants or on the street, ones who looked like Audrey Hepburn or Faye Dunaway. Mother, though thin, had curves. Now she struggled to flatten them.

"You're not a *kid*," she'd reminded me as we stared sadly into the trashcan. "Put on a little eyes shadow and you could pass for eighteen." Was that what she wanted?

Mother pushed her egg around on her plate until it dissolved into runny white goo; her toast sat untouched. I could see the effort such fasting took as she nervously fingered the flowery oilcloth. Her nails were polished sherbet-pink. I wondered if she'd bought the lipstick to match. We spotted the new color in the latest issue of *Glamour*, which we thumbed through quietly at the corner drugstore. According to Mickey, subscriptions were a waste when you could read magazines free at the library.

"It costs me half the price of the magazine to get to the library," Mother told me but not him.

"Any éclairs left?" I was frantic with hunger.

Mother shook her head. Dispirited, I took another bite of the apple. Had I eaten enough? My grandmother always scolded me if I didn't eat a proper meal. Aunt Linda, years before, had also emphasized the importance of eating well. Their definitions of *well* might differ, but here I was becoming skeletal without an anorexic instinct in my body. All because of — you know who. I ached for a real dinner. Pot roast, roasted potatoes, and corn on the cob. Peach cobbler, for dessert. I was desperate enough to consider moving back in with my grandmother. Or better yet, Aunt Linda.

"There's always room here for you, Christine," she'd said last time I visited. I often fantasized what life with Aunt Linda might be like. No angel food cakes in her house. She was particularly partial to Red Velvet cake, a creation revealed to her on recent trip to Savannah.

"Boys don't make passes at girls with big asses," Mother told me whenever she caught me reaching for a cookie.

Not true, and these were strange assertions coming from someone who wouldn't let me date or even do homework with a boy. Sometimes it made me dizzy, figuring my mother out. Looking good was something I should do only for *her* apparently. Or was it Mickey? I was almost fifteen after all, my child-murderess days long behind me. I was ready for boys or at least a friend. The ties binding us had been loosened considerable by Mickey's sudden appearance on the scene. I slipped effortlessly into the wallpaper as soon as he entered the house. But an existence on the perimeter of my parents' lives was something I'd learned years before.

As far as having a friend, there had always been a reason to avoid close relationships. We were on the run half the time—from what I didn't usually know—and things like friends were dangerous. People too close asked questions, demanded confidences shared over Coca Cola or old episodes of *The Brady Bunch*. They tricked information out of you, ratted you out to principals, store detectives, cops, fathers, husbands. This was my mother's assessment, her history, and girlfriends I brought home were disparaged.

"She certainly is a plain one." Or, "I found her going through your closet while you were downstairs." Any mention of an unfamiliar name evoked such responses from my mother.

"Your mother couldn't possibly object to me," Neil Burbage, a guy at school, had said disbelievingly only the week before. He was a tall, gawky boy with acne despite the new medications on the market. His jeans were always too new, too pressed. But I knew she'd object to him—and strenuously. Mother didn't even like me to go with a friend to Luther League at St. Paul's Church.

"The minister's wife's always there," I told her.

She continued to shake her head. Why? Sometime I felt like I lived in a house of secrets. It was like *Imitation of Life*, my favorite old movie. Maybe I'd turn out to be black like Susan Kohner. Maybe Hank Moran wasn't my real father and I might bump into my actual dad on the streets if she let me wander them. Why was she keeping me under wraps? Was I the secret weapon? Hadn't I already done enough?

Mother began clearing the table. "Want to fix my hair, kiddo? Mickey'll be home soon, and I'm a mess." This was untrue; on her worst day, she looked better than anyone. At forty, she was still a peach.

Their bedroom had been two separate rooms until Mickey, gleefully swinging a sledgehammer, removed the offending wall. Now, it was a shrine to Mother's beauty products and rituals. A wall-length closet housed her clothing, each piece hung on wooden hangers in vinyl sleeves; fourteen foot maple shelves held her makeup, wigs, hair products, and assorted beauty aids. Mickey installed a fan so the air was always fresh. This was his single act of generosity: making Mother gorgeous.

"You'll thank me for it when your clothes smell as sweet as the day you bought them." He threw us both the slimy smile I'd quickly grown to hate.

There wasn't much room for Mickey and Mother in the room and the improvements had cost my stepfather a lot. But having a wife who took her looks seriously pleased him. I dreaded watching his eyes go wide and soft when he came home to find his wife dolled up, his dinner waiting. I could tell he wanted to do "it" as soon as possible. Doing it had become an obsession with me since their marriage. I imagined I heard them "doing it" every night—all night long. He looked like Robert Mitchum watching Marilyn Monroe in *River of No Return*, which I'd seen on television recently.

Entering Mother's marital bedroom was risky. The bed mustn't be sat on, nor should I wear street shoes on the fluffy white carpeting. No fingerprints could mar the white walls or woodwork. I was not to use her comb or brush. Mother was repulsed, or was it terrified, the one time I forgot this dictum and idly pulled her best brush through my hair. I watched mutely as she grabbed the brush, removed a fistful of hair from it, and threw it into an ammonia bath.

"You're a pug— like my father," my mother said with a degree of affection once when she saw me in the mirror behind her. "Herbert Hobart lives on."

A pug? I examined my face closely, looking for the squashed-in features of the breed. I didn't see it, but maybe I was kidding myself. I could hardly remember my mysterious grandfather by now, and we certainly kept no pictures of him around. Neither did my grandmother. No dust collectors in her house. If you wanted to see him, you had to pull her one slim volume of photographs off the top shelf in the bedroom closet, and this activity was not encouraged.

"Now, what do you want to go and make a mess for, Christine," my grandmother would say. "Those little black corners are losing their glue." The album was out of my hands in seconds.

I was meant to forget Herbert Hobart, and I had.

Mother didn't realize she was being mean when she compared me to a pug. Or at least that's what I told myself.

"In her mind, she's being honest—about other people, at least," my grandmother said. "And she's not exactly statuesque herself." Grandmother puffed herself up. "Your grandfather was considered a handsome man in his day—a real catch for me."

Mickey's possessions were entirely off-limits. Mother had found a husband who took his belongings as seriously as she did. His black velvet robe and soft leather slippers waited for him now on his mahogany valet. At night, these items were replaced with a dark suit, white shirt, subdued tie, and highly buffed black shoes. An expensive mother-of-pearl brush and comb set, an inlaid wooden box for his cufflinks and watch, and a black onyx dish for his change rested on his bureau.

Except there were never any coins in the dish. Mickey deposited his loose change into a coin counter he'd found in a notions store in New York City. Money was dirty and Mickey didn't like to handle it. Often he'd tell a surprised clerk to keep the change rather than put his soft, manicured hands on the few coins owed to him.

"Never mind," he'd say, turning his back if the clerks tried to give it to him. "Don't you have a Lion's Club jar? A crippled kid's fund?"

The gilt and walnut mirror above Mickey's bureau was especially valuable. The glass was old and didn't reflect properly, but such trivial things apparently didn't matter with an antique. It was regularly polished with a special cleaner purchased from a mail order shop in Toronto. Mickey's things must cost a lot of money, I thought. He must have been rich once, had possibly gambled it all away. But Mother said his stuff was mostly bought at pawn shops or flea markets.

"Rich people don't grow up in row houses in Philadelphia; they live in Bryn Mawr or Bucks County." The name Bucks County brought a strained look to her face. She was probably thinking about Daddy out there in a big house. "So don't get any ideas about Mickey being able to support us like your father did," she added. "The days of Hank's largesse are gone. I've returned to my roots."

It took me a minute to realize she meant she'd returned to a life much like the one she'd known in the Hobart house. Why had she done this? It was better when we were on our own. I still hoped she'd reform, that she'd ditch Mickey, that my father might take us back. Return us to our rightful home in Shelterville. It was growing less and less likely though. Mickey wasn't about to give her the necessary divorce after knocking down a wall. It'd be hard to sell the place with only two bedrooms. And mine was teensy, more a nursery than a proper room.

After six months of studying their bedroom, I was still fascinated with its excess. For the two years before, we'd often shared a room and my mother's things had been carelessly stuffed in a cardboard bureau, sometimes even a box. For all Mother's eccentricities, being overly fastidious was not one

of them. She did not care about the stuff in this room. Those
things, the ones she truly loved, were wrapped in tissue paper
in Grandmother's basement or in her storage units. Those were
her secret possessions, ones no one, including me, could ever
hope to understand.

Most of her clothes had hung from doorknobs or hooks in
Grandmother's house. Loose buttons and fraying hems were
repaired by my grandmother. Only Mother's shoes retained the
glamour of her bygone days in Bucks County and Shelterville.
Our toothbrushes had mingled along with combs and brushes
in the tiny bathroom all three of us used. What had changed?

Was Mickey demanding hyper-attention to housekeeping
and personal hygiene? Did he inspect their bedroom for telltale
curly hairs and dandruff? All I had to go by was his ex-wife,
Racine, who enjoyed a similar setup. Or that's what Mickey told
us. We'd never been there. And she could do her own hair since
she wore it in a pixie cut Mother claimed was long out of style.

"A woman's hair should neither be too long or too short."
She seemed angry about Racine's disregard for the current
styles. As if such apathy was letting Mickey down—even in her
position as former wife.

"If you can comb your hair with your fingers, it's too short.
Men like to watch women brush their hair. That's what they call
allure. Only Claudette Colbert and Jane Wyman got away with
short hair."

Oh yes, I thought about Mickey and my mother a lot. About
what they saw in each other, what they did in their bedroom,
if they ever considered my position as an onlooker to their
romance. I was certain there'd be no more babies because
Mother complained about what carrying me for nine months
did to her figure. Mickey didn't want any more kids either. He
already had a daughter, Mary Theresa, who lived with Racine.

Mary Theresa wore her parochial school uniform with the

dedication of a novice nun. It was a navy jumper topping a white, long-sleeved blouse. On a cold day, she was permitted to add a white or navy sweater. Her knee socks never slumped, her black Mary-Janes were polished to a high glint.

"Snap out of it, kiddo," Mother demanded now.

Seated at the mirror, she was stroking her face. She was especially enamored with her cheekbones, imagining them to be her best feature. Once, I mistakenly voiced the opinion that men seemed more interested in other areas of a woman's body in movies and books.

"Shows how much you know, Christine. Hips and cheekbones hold it all together. Nothing would sit right without them." She gazed into the mirror as if she were going to say something important, something profound, and I held my breath. "I couldn't live with a man who didn't respect cheekbones," she said. "Mickey noticed mine right away." She paused and made a face. "Hank — not so much. Maybe because his are imperceptible."

The perfect union despoiled by cheekbones.

I picked up the comb. (God knows why I'd become proficient in hair styling — perhaps Mother willed it into being.) "How do you want it?" I asked, stroking her honey-colored hair upward. Her eyelids quivered with pleasure.

Truthfully, it gave me pleasure too, handling my mother's hair. Usually we did it up — in twists, knots or buns. Such hairdos were out of style, but she was convinced upswept hair pulled her skin taut. There *was* the slightest suggestion of slackness in her chin, I'd noticed with horror. No hairdo would tighten skin under a chin. Mother'd have to go to high-necked dresses and scarves like older soap opera stars wore.

"Instant plastic surgery," she told me now, gathering her hair in her hands, still oblivious to what lurked — like the shark in *Jaws* — beneath. "How about like Grace's?" she suggested, referring to the new way Princess Grace was wearing her hair in *Ladies Home Journal*. Jackie Onassis, our former source of inspiration, had been replaced when Mickey turned out to be a rabid Republican rather than a temperate one like Daddy. Because Mickey wore a white shirt and dark suit to work, he identified with his employers. Or his oppressors, as a future boyfriend would note.

Eve's hair had faded rapidly in the first months of dating Mickey, paling from the rich chestnut she'd favored in the mid-seventies to nearly platinum now. Her makeup and nail color had also been altered.

"As long as he doesn't expect me to look like Pat Nixon."

I was struck dumb. Perhaps I'd have to copy Tricia or Julie's styles—those plastered big bobs they favored. But nobody knew how they wore their hair anymore. They'd all disappeared from the public eye after getting on the plane on the White House lawn some years before.

"Tell her to get off her boney backside and spend some of his money at a hairdresser," my grandmother said on the subject of her daughter's hair.

But most of the time, I didn't mind. It was one of the few times I emerged from the background and took center stage—or at least the part of the stage behind her. "Isn't it nice being together like this?" she'd say to me as I stood there, comb in hand. But it was her face she sought out in the mirror, her eyes she watched.

Information came pouring out of her during these sessions. Most of it was about Mickey. Why hadn't my father held her interest the way Mickey did? If Mother had treated him this well, we'd be in Shelterville, sitting pretty, Mrs. Murphy fixing our meals, cleaning our house. It didn't occur to me till years later she'd learned something with the failure of her first marriage and was applying the knowledge.

"Do a twist tonight—so he doesn't see the roots. He won't say anything because he's too worried about his damned angelfish to notice me. It's got some fish funk and he's talking about bringing a fish expert out here to look at it." She shook her head. "When I had the flu last month, I dragged myself to the doctor's office on the H bus, but the fish gets a house visit." Mother's dislike of Mickey's hobby was a rare source of friction between them—and something I would've liked to exploit.

"Does the house smell of fish food?" I routinely asked, sending her into paroxysms of cleaning. "Don't you hate sticking your hands in that water?" This remark necessitated her donning two pairs of rubber gloves.

Mickey had lined our miniscule living room with wall-to-wall fish tanks as he was fond of the room lit by aquarium lights. Mother wasn't supposed to open the curtains even in the daytime. She went along with the tank decor, thinking the humidity was probably good for her skin, reading her trashy romance novels in the dim light when she wasn't scouring the kitchen floor or working on her tan.

Only a few of her most prized pieces were interspersed here and there among the tanks. I doubted Mickey had any idea about the true magnitude of her junk.

"What's this doing here?" Mickey had asked the other night, pulling a pewter candlestick off a corner chest. "Were you gonna light a candle near my tanks? Christ!"

"It was just an accessory," Eve said, taking it out of his hands. Her tone was soothing. "I'd never light it. The wax, you know."

"You'd better believe it, Babe. Hey, it left a mark."

Outraged, he reached in his pocket and polished the sullied spot with his handkerchief, looking at her with disdain. "Didn't you see the care sheet for this chest? You can't put anything on it that sweats."

On the return from their honeymoon, he'd presented Mother with a list on how to care for every item in this house, neatly typed by Racine. Her handoff to Mother had been flawless.

The idea for this marine decor had come to Mickey in a restaurant in Miami on their honeymoon. An event I missed, although Mother promised I could accompany them to the Hotel Fontainebleau next year. I couldn't wait to choose a lobster from one of the tanks, even if it was kind of icky to pick one when you knew the chef would drop the poor thing into scalding water moments later.

"They don't feel a thing," Mother said when I mentioned it. "It's why they have those hard shells. The shells absorb all the heat and turn red. Totally painless." Her sharp red nails mimed the fall into scalding water.

Since the Miami trip, Mickey had fallen hard for the fish. Hook, line, and stinker—Mother complained. He spent hours poring through thick books he checked out of the children's room at the library. We couldn't get over how many books were written about aquariums. Caring for fish, it turned out, was more time consuming than raising a child.

"I guess it's because there so many different kinds," I said.

"Well, they're all fish to me." Mother stared at an orange and blue one that never emerged from its hole in a rock. "What the heck do you think that one's afraid of? He kind of reminds me of you, Christine."

She looked at me with a frown—as if I had spawned such a deviant. I was always startled to hear my name in her conversation—shocked to hear any pronouncements or observations about me. If I hid inside rocks, it was because of her. I wondered what kind of mother the fish had had.

Mickey was glued to the counter at the Woolworth's fish department on Saturday afternoons, discussing which neon tetra might make the best adjustment to his habitat. The entire setup cost more than the honeymoon that spawned the idea. One tiny diver in the Mediterranean tank was more expensive than the rarest fish since its arm could wave and the scuba gear he wore emitted real bubbles. It was made from pure silver or some precious metal so it wouldn't rot or turn green.

"For Pete's sake," Mother said, once she was out of his hearing, "how much time can he spend on them? Don't they pretty much take care of themselves in the ocean?"

Minutes (and money) spent on the fish meant minutes not spent on Mother. She couldn't survive another defection, my grandmother told me, shaking her head. Though Hank had been a womanizer, he was her daughter's first love.

"If she'd treated Hank better, you'd still be living inside that lovely house in Shelterville," Grandmother reminded me constantly.

It'd been weeks since Daddy asked me to spend the night or even have dinner with him. His occasional call was always rushed — and most of our conversation was about what Mother was up to.

"Need anything, Christine," he'd say at the end of each call, reminding me of Grandfather Hobart's half-hearted offers ten years earlier. It was clear he'd no expectation I might take him up on it. Never imagined I'd ask for a new dress or a larger allowance. And I didn't. My father believed me to be a murderer. Surely it was this fact, and not some innate dislike of me, that put a wedge between us. Would there come a day when I could tell him the truth?

So now it was Mickey on Mother's tanned, toned arm, escorting her like Prince Rainier out to their *classy* dark sedan. If the evening's entertainment was more likely to take place in a closet-sized bar owned by a bookie on Washington Lane instead of the dining room of the Oak Ridge Country Club, so be it. A Saturday night out was the goal and Mickey was more inclined to supply it than Hank had been. Mickey didn't play golf, had no business associates, and believed in Saturday night dates.

Mickey came in at nine-thirty, right after the showroom closed and I stayed in my room. Sometimes my mother practically threw herself at him when he came through the door. Once I saw Mickey's hand slide down my mother's tight slacks, fondling her bony backside before he remembered I was watching.

"Whoops," he said, throwing his hands up like someone caught robbing the bank in a western.

Mother laughed hysterically, with her new, hard, fake laugh. Since that incident, I'd kept my distance during these nightly reunions, waiting until the cooing and shrieking stopped.

If too much time passed, as it did that night, Mother made an appearance. "Don't you want to come and see Mickey, Sweetie? He gets kinda hurt when you stay in your room." She waited impatiently at the door while I put on my slippers. "Don't you want to comb your hair first? And a little lipstick wouldn't hurt." You'd think she was setting us up.

It wasn't enough that *she* was gorgeous, I was expected to do the best I could with what limited assets I had. All of Mickey's women were made to do their best—just like with Daddy. Mickey's ancient mother, who I'd met only once, still tottered around on high heels and wore false eyelashes at the age of seventy-five.

Downstairs, I found Mickey eating his nightly lemon at the dining room table. Yes, lemon. He asked for the same dinner every night: a salted lemon, a small steak cooked well, a small potato, no butter-just pepper and Tabasco, and a salad of lettuce and tomato dressed with red wine vinegar. No coffee—just tomato juice. He also took a handful of vitamins in the morning and did a Jack LaLanne workout on a record album at six-thirty a.m. in the basement. He glued pictures of Jack in the correct positions on the wall, facing the photos as he struck each pose. Doing my homework, I had the eerie feeling Jack was doing sit-ups right behind me. Mother told me Mickey's father had died of a heart attack at forty-three, and it scared him.

My mother could talk about Mickey forever. It was hard to believe a man, rather than *things*, could capture her attention to this degree. And a poor man to boot—by Moran family standards. Mickey's Achilles' heel was a sweet tooth. That night, the extra éclair was waiting at his elbow. I gave my mother the evil eye, and she shrugged, throwing her arms around Mickey's shoulders. He went on eating with Mother draped around him like an evening wrap. With her heavy tan and sharp features, she resembled a fox like the one on those stoles women had worn twenty years earlier. The ones where the clasp was the fox's mouth biting its own tail. She mouthed something across the table to me, gesturing with her head, batting her eyes.

"So what's up, Christine," Mickey asked, pushing his plate aside.

Mother winced when he pushed his plate back, a sign of poor table manners in the Moran family. Mother, schooled by my father, had often told me that eating silently at the dinner table was rude. You were supposed to talk pleasantly about interesting subjects while enjoying your meal.

My grandmother said when Evelyn said *rude*, she meant lower-class. Apparently, none of these rules applied to Mickey. He took no interest in talking as long as there was food on his plate and could damned well shove his plate wherever he pleased. I could easily imagine him saying such a thing. I often considered what awful things he might say once he was done biding his time. I toyed with the idea of dropping a hint that I was more lethal than he might expect. Actually, I might take him out without a second thought.

"Can I babysit for the Martins on Friday night?"

The request came out in one long hiss. Mother wanted Mickey to begin thinking of me like a daughter. She'd gotten the idea from one of the numerous advice columns she consulted — all read with the goal of reigning Mickey in more tightly than his first wife had, by not repeating Racine's mistakes — though neither of us knew what they'd been. Not repeating Mother's blunders with Hank Moran either — a fresh start.

"He's a dirty wop," Grandmother said bitterly. "He can wash those greasy hands ten times a day, but it won't fool me. Hank Moran had clean nails."

Mickey's nails were never dirty — he was overly meticulous if anything — but I kept quiet. Because of her unfortunate and obvious attitude toward Mickey, visits with my grandmother had declined. He could sense her animosity. If he came in and found Mother on the phone with her, he immediately bristled.

"Plotting against me?" he'd said only last week. Oh my, it was a house full of suspicions all right. And all of them festering within eight-hundred square feet.

"Babysit, huh? Mary Theresa didn't babysit."

"Christine wants to earn her own spending money."

He thought about it for a minute. "What would you do if the Martins' house caught on fire?"

"Get the kids out of there and call the fire department from the neighbor's house."

"Pretty good thinking. All righty. Babysit away. Pocket money's a good idea."

The three of us watched as a large, flat translucent fish devoured a tiny, bright blue one. "Damn," Mickey said. "The guy at the store said they could cohabit."

CHAPTER
Seventeen

O ne of Mother's economies in the lean years before Mickey appeared had been the "return" of her "return business," although on a smaller scale than the earlier version due to various irksome constraints. She now knew no postal worker was going to deliver a constant stream of goods without getting a cut or turning her in. She knew, too, a surplus of garage sales, though they'd grown in popularity in the intervening years, made her too visible to a variety of overseers. She'd soon be accused of running a business without a license. Especially in the tightly configured neighborhoods we'd lived in since leaving Shelterville. But a temperate use of the scheme seemed feasible, especially given our economic status in the pre-Mickey days. Although I knew about it, she mostly ran it herself this time, perhaps wanting no witness available to be quizzed.

After their marriage, Mother worried Mickey might find out and call a halt. She was addicted to the free merchandise as well as to the excitement of pulling it off. She needn't have been concerned; Mickey thought she was a genius. He was sorry, he said chuckling, that she couldn't think of a way to get a few products from the U.S.Treasury. I didn't get the joke until my mother explained it, but it never failed to send my mother into gales of laughter. If Mickey gave any clue that he was making a joke, however feeble, she was quick to supply the laughs. Although on her own, Mother had a poor sense of humor.

Coming home from school, I spotted Mother sunning herself on a chaise on the front walk. She did a half-hour on each side with large applications of cream in between, wearing a tiny yellow plastic eye protector that made her look meaner than usual and a swimsuit designed to garner a perfect tan. She'd decided to ignore new information about the effects of sun-tanning, reasoning the ozone layer had been intact during her formative years.

"I read it's the bad burns you get as a kid that give you cancer."

"Hand me the lotion, Christine," she said now, her eyes slowly opening. "No, no, the pink stuff!"

I watched while she slathered it on, and then went into the kitchen and poured some milk, grabbing one of Mickey's expensive peanut butter cookies to go with it.

My babysitting job wasn't until six so I went to the basement and turned on *The Mike Douglas Show* where Kristy McNichol was singing "He's so Fine" to Burt Reynolds. Over Kristy's wall of sound, I could still hear my mother on the phone with her new friend, Fran. Fran disappeared from our lives quickly as most women did since mother was never long interested in the company of females. But on that day, lots of giggling followed, probably about Mother's newest returns.

Mother was running out of room. Only last month, she donated three boxes of merchandise to the Salvation Army, something that went against her scruples. The woman acted surprised to receive so many unused beauty products, but listened attentively as Mother assured her that paying more attention to improving one's looks would help the poor secure jobs.

"And help yourself, of course," she told the open-mouthed woman. "You get first dibs."

The Martins left for their dinner party at eight, their two toddlers already fast asleep. Neil Burbage arrived at nine. He lived alone with his mother, which gave us something in common—an absentee father. Neil's father had died in the early days of the Vietnam War, and he barely remembered him.

Although I wasn't allowed to have a boyfriend, no one could stop me from talking to Neil at school. We weren't exactly dating but had kissed three times. The last time, in a back row of a movie theater downtown, he'd put a shaky hand on my breast. It sat there twitching for several seconds before I brushed it off. If I was supposed to feel sexy—like I might suddenly want to do *it*—something was wrong. Mostly I'd felt embarrassed, weird. My breasts, small and covered by layers of white cotton: bra, slip, blouse, sweater, hardly merited such attention. They seemed no more sexual than my ankle or ear. But maybe Neil wasn't doing it right.

Kissing, I could get; there was something for both of us to do. If you were to rate Neil as a desirable boyfriend—like they did practically each month in my mother's magazines— he'd rank near the bottom. But so would Mickey. My father would also rate as a bust, based on his history of cheating and being out of the house so often. The "absentee father," one of the quizzes labeled him. Neither Mother nor I had ever met the kind of men who topped those lists. If there was a list rating women in *Esquire Magazine*, where would we be on it? What was our claim to a high number? So for the present, Neil was nice enough and a pretty good kisser.

We were getting to the point where we might begin kissing when I heard a cautious knock at the door. Jumping up, I grabbed Neil's hand. He was a bit dazed and slow to move; his feet were too big and clumsy to make a hasty escape. It always surprised me how large most men's feet were in shoes. At the swimming pool, they always seemed to be a normal size, but something happened once they slid into shoes.

"Come on," I hissed, tugging at him. Seconds later, I practically shoved him down the basement steps. "You can come back up once whoever it is goes," I hissed.

I pressed the door closed, sensing him standing there at the top of the steps, thinking the situation over. I listened to his heavy footsteps as he slowly descended.

"Mother," I said a second later, back at the door. She stood in the doorway looking wan and worried, her eyes blinking blindly in the blast of light. I held the door open and she stepped inside. Did she really think I needed her help? That woman who couldn't raise me?

"Bet you didn't expect me." She laughed raggedly and grabbed my hand. "Don't worry, Baby. Nobody died." She quickly sank into the nearest chair, but immediately rose, examining the seat like something on it had stung her. "Look, I think I made a mistake tonight. A pretty big one actually."

It was hard to concentrate on what she was saying because I could hear Neil walking around in the basement, sounding like a huge animal moving through the brush. I heard a ping pong ball drop and bounce a few times, a racquet clattered to the floor. Did he have to entertain himself with the sports' equipment? Mother appeared oblivious to the noise though she might have thought it was the children playing.

"What kind of mistake?" I asked, wondering if Neil had managed to turn on a light before his descent. Perhaps he was in the dark?

"Look, I took—I took something a little while ago. She told me it'd do the trick, but now I'm sort of sick." Mother put her hand on her stomach and made a face. "You know—nauseated."

"You took something for what? Cramps?"

The sudden and reassuring silence below allowed me to concentrate now. My mother did look sort of green; she wore two different shoes too. Unheard of.

"Where's Mickey?" There was no way this didn't involve him. "And who's she? The one who said it would do the trick?"

She chose the question to answer. "Plays poker tonight. You know that!"

My stepfather played poker on second Friday nights. On the nights when it was at our house, Mother went crazy fixing packaged treats. Mickey had to practically drag her out of the kitchen when the other men came. Or "the boys" as she referred to them.

"The boys love my California dip."

"Sure, Baby," Mickey said, grinning crazy-eyed at the men sitting behind her. "You're some great cook."

I felt like dumping the platter in his lap. She was trying so hard for the first time in her life, and this was her reward. I always wondered if Racine had done any better.

"So what did'ya take, Mom? What kind of pill?" Hadn't I already asked her? She had an unnatural fear of doctors and had been known to medicate herself with anything available. "Who's she?" I repeated.

"A kind of potion, I guess you'd call it. Brewer's yeast and pennyroyal tea."

I'd never heard of either. She made a face, and then busied herself with examining the framed photos on the mantel.

"Cute kids. They look exactly like their father. I've seen him mowing the lawn once or twice. Muscular guy, blonde?"

I nodded and she turned away suddenly, a fist to her mouth.

"What's pennyroyal?" I asked, pretending not to notice her unusual gesture.

"It's an herb, I think." Seeing my blank look, she added, "A weed. Oh god, I might as well tell you. I think I might be pregnant." She waited for my reaction, which was slow to come, so she went on with the story. "Someone told me pennyroyal tea mixed with brewer's yeast would do the trick. Can you imagine — having a kid — at my age? You know, I actually tried to get pregnant a few years back. With Hank, that is. When it might have been a good idea. But now..."

"You mean kill the baby?" I was shocked. This was something out of a Danielle Steele novel. I knew young girls had abortions but not married women. Not my mother. "You think you might be pregnant or you know you are?" I wasn't too sure about the mechanics. Were there signs other than the obvious one? Did a rabbit actually have to die?

"Oh, it's the same as when I was pregnant with you. The same feeling. If Mickey finds out, he'll make me go through with it though he won't want another kid. Catholics, you know." Mother swished around the room, examining the knick-knacks and not looking me in the eye. "Every piece in this room was purchased around 1965. Must have been the year they got married. The Martins." She fingered a porcelain figurine of a shepherd girl. "I bet they bought this at Kresge's — even if it looks expensive. With little kids around, you aren't going to spend money on stuff like this. You put your valuables away somewhere. Probably in the basement."

She looked vaguely in the direction of the basement door. Would she insist on going to look? Thinking there were boxes of junk for her to investigate? Maybe a thing or two to take? Was there some other place Neil could hide?

I took the shepherdess out of her hands, steering her back to what brought her here. "Mom, listen, what's the stuff you took supposed to do?"

"She said it'd start me cramping in a few hours, and I'd go on to miscarry within a day or two. I took it about an hour ago. So far I only feel sick to my stomach." She paused, considering her state. "Maybe its nerves. I'm as jittery as a canary." She started prowling the room again, and I followed close behind.

"Why don't you go back to *her*, Mom. Or at least call."

I heard Neil moving around again, but Mother didn't flinch. Why had she come to me anyway? Wouldn't my grandmother have been a better choice? Probably not, given her hatred of Mickey. And she'd certainly not support Mother in an abortion. She was one of those women who put crosses on her church lawn. But what could I do? Fixing her hair hadn't prepared me for this. Taking the rap for a murder too was poor preparation for assisting in an abortion. Would there be no end to supporting her? Was there ever going to be an escape?

"She's out playing bridge tonight. Does everyone in this city play cards on Friday nights?" She ran a hand through her hair. "Told me to wait till tomorrow, but I wanted to get it out of the way—take it while Mickey was out. You too. I thought I could handle it. She made it sound like I could." Mother put a hand over her stomach again. "I don't think anything's happening, Christine. They're not cramps—mostly I'm kind of nauseous." She checked her watch. "What time do you expect the Martins home?"

"They didn't say."

"I guess I'll go on home. No sense running into them." She started toward the door. "I think I'm a little better. Not that that's a good thing. Nothing's going to happen now except I'm going to have a baby at age forty-two. Can you imagine? If I wasn't married to a Catholic, I could get a legal abortion. Why did I hook up with a Catholic?" The tears started. "Mickey will blame it all on me." She took a tissue from her pocket and blew her nose. "Maybe it'll be a boy. Most men want a son, don't they?"

I couldn't picture Mickey surrounded by baby gear: cribs, high-chairs, bassinets. Would he sacrifice his fish tanks to make room for a kid?

"I bet that stuff—the penny royal—takes time to work." I patted her shoulder. "Call me if something happens."

I wasn't sure how I felt about any of this. Should I help her murder my little brother or sister? If discovered, what would the punishment be? More visits to a shrink? Jail? I doubted I could avoid jail with another suspicious death on my record. But abortion was legal. But this kind? Self-induced. I wasn't sure.

And wasn't I too old to have a sibling? Given what I knew about my mother, I'd be more like a teenaged mother than a sister.

"Are you sure you'll be okay alone?" The words were perfunctory since my head was spinning with the possible outcomes.

"Sure, sure. I've been in worse fixes than this."

As she started out the door, we both noticed the Martins' blue Torino pulling up. "Oh boy, they're home earlier than you thought," Mother said brightly. "Now you can come home and take care of me."

The Martins weren't surprised to find my mother there and within a few minutes, we were home again with Neil left behind. It was hard to keep his dilemma in my head over the next few hours, which were mostly spent turning Mother's problem over and over. I drew her two hot baths, made tea, rubbed her feet, found a heating pad, did her hair. "Thanks. It always makes things better—to look like myself." We waited expectantly—forgive the word.

Nothing happened.

Neil ended up spending the night in the Martins' basement. The phone rang at seven-thirty the next morning. "I think we have something of yours," Mrs. Martin told me icily.

"Hi, Christine." Neil sounded dopey, either from lack of sleep or embarrassment. Or maybe he *was* a dope. Why had I chosen so poorly — was it a family curse? Was I on the road to a Mickey already?

"Why didn't you go home?" I hissed into the phone. He started to answer when I interrupted. "No, never mind. We'll talk about it later."

I hung up quietly and then heard a snuffling sound, only partially muffled, and remembered too late Mother'd be awake and was probably listening in.

Downstairs, she sat at the kitchen table clicking her nails, now platinum, on the vinyl. Even after the night she'd spent, the troubles she had, Mother was prepped for the day ahead. Her negligee was apricot and her bare shoulders were peachy in the morning light. Her hair, loose for once, was well-brushed. She wore light makeup. A light scent carried on the breeze coming in the tiny kitchen window. I couldn't help but stare at her; after the night we'd spent, she was ready for action whereas I was my usually soggy mess.

Mickey never rose before ten on Saturdays so there'd be plenty of time to discuss recent events. I sat down. Nobody said anything for a long time.

"Well, I don't know what to do with you," she finally said. She jerked her head suddenly. "After what I already have to tell Mickey, you bring me this? Was this Neil person hiding in the basement the whole time, making a fool of me? When I was pouring out my heart to you? Were you planning a little escapade of your own?" She paused. "Hey, is that Mickey getting up?"

"I didn't hear anything."

"Well, I can't talk about this now, Christine. If Mickey finds out what you did, he'll probably send us back to your grandmother's. Or if he finds out about what I tried to do. He takes his orders from Rome, you know." Tears streamed down her face suddenly, and I started crying, too. "I can only hope we aren't both pregnant," she said as a parting shot.

This took me by surprise; the idea she wouldn't know whether I was having sex. I thought she knew everything about me. I was years away from such an episode—how could she not know it? She'd made me fearful of anything sexual. Afraid of close relationships. How could she not know the price I'd paid for *her* choices?

She began to water the African violets that sat on the kitchen windowsill. Each one had to be placed individually in a pan of water where it bobbled unevenly like a sail-less boat on a lake. The leaves didn't like to be wet, she told me, making it sound like the plants had confided this tidbit to her. Mary Theresa, Mickey's daughter, brought a plant with her whenever she visited. This almost ceremonial gift giving had the air of a religious act since Mary Theresa always wore her school uniform, holding the plant out to Mother like a communion wafer or a religious relic.

Racine, Mickey's ex, had a miniature greenhouse in a knocked-out kitchen window where she raised the violets from cuttings. My mother lived in deep fear that one of the possibly rarer plants might die and she'd be unable to replace it, though I voiced the opinion that none of the violets were rare, repeatedly assuring her of this. But she regarded the ritual as a test—one she was bound to fail.

So far we'd had to buy eight replacements at the Kresge plant department. The supposed *gifts* put an enormous pressure on Mother, who'd never had to raise anything other than me before this year.

I felt sorry for my mother. Wasn't there a single thing in her life that was easy or normal? There was our impossible-to-keep-clean white house, the finicky fish with their funky diseases, the oversensitive plants, the bookkeeping duties of the return business, her health-conscious husband, her delinquent child, her hair and skin requirements, her scornful mother across town, her ex-husband in Bucks County who'd recently become engaged to the heiress to a chocolate fortune—all of these things preying on her mind, requiring an output of her limited resources.

But why did she marry Mickey? How many of these problems emanated from his presence in our lives? More than half by my calculation. I could have kept her happier were we alone—when had I once let her down. But she'd preferred having a consort.

I crept up to my room and stayed there all day. Maybe I wasn't convinced I wanted Mickey for a stepfather, having him tell me what I could do as if he had a right to it, being forced to witness the million quirky things that were part of him, watching Mother alternately drool and grovel in his presence. But sending Mother back to her previous life was too cruel. Another defeat could be her undoing and she'd be back in an institution, trying out the latest therapy for whatever ailed her. Or spritizing innocent women who entered a store.

On Monday, Neil was waiting at the bus stop. "Why didn't you get out of there when they went to bed on Friday night?" I asked, swiping at him with my lab book.

"The old man threw the lock on the kitchen door before they went to bed. The basement door was locked, too. Dead bolted."

"Did your mother go crazy?"

He nodded. "I'm not allowed to see you anymore. She called the Martins and apologized Sunday morning. They were laughing about it by then." He scratched his head. "But they didn't think it was so funny when I knocked on their basement door Saturday morning. The old man opened the door with a Louisville Slugger in his hand."

I shuddered. "What if he kept a gun?"

I knew this scenario all too well. Being involved, in any way, in a second shooting would probably send me to jail and examples of how it might happen threatened me from every corner. Would I have to tread carefully forever?

Neil nodded, "Don't think I didn't give it some thought before I knocked at the door. I kept yelling I was Christine's boyfriend."

Boyfriend? Was this how he saw himself? Well, it was over now. I wouldn't take a chance like this again—not for a long time.

The bus came and we climbed on, finding seats as far apart as possible. Neil faded into the advertisement for Noxzema medication pasted behind him on the bus and ceased to exist. Having a *boyfriend*, or any friend at all, was too much trouble with my mother around. She was right to warn me off friendships. It was better to keep other people out of it. Perhaps someday the situation would change, but I wasn't hopeful.

Days turned into weeks as I waited for Mother to tell Mickey about her condition. The tension continued to mount as day after day passed. I spent much of those weeks alone, staring at the fish tanks, throwing darts at the board in the basement. I pushed the ping pong table against the wall and played against myself. I cleaned out my bureau drawers though they were already perfectly fine. Mickey floated above or below me, making his demands, eating his lemons, spending time with fish, working on his pecs. I avoided him as much as possible, waiting for the explosion to come.

She managed to get to the fifth month before showing. I

came home from the library and found Mickey sitting on the front steps, a beer in hand at noon. He looked at me, frowning. "I suppose you knew."

I slid around him. Mother was in the kitchen, polishing the burners on the stove wearing rubber gloves. "I can't go back to the way things were before, Christine. Hank's out of the picture. I can't depend on my mother's help or our return business. Or working at the makeup counter in Woolworth's like a teenager, spritzing people with perfume. On my feet all day. I'm thirty-six old, Christine!" Her voice died away. She hated to talk about her age. Even when she was taking off many years as she was now. It took all the life out of her.

If Mickey leaves me, I don't know what I'll do." Mother dabbed daintily at her eyes. "He means the world to me, Christine. To us! I bet a son will turn things around."

Russell was born four months later and our lives changed profoundly.

CHAPTER
Eighteen

ary Theresa and I stood on one side of the hospital bed, Mickey on the other. Mother held the sleeping baby—as yet unnamed—in her arms. Frankly I'd never heard them discuss a name or anything else related to the coming child. Mother's swelling middle was a topic nobody wanted to take on—and Mickey's enmity simmered just beneath the cracking veneer of our family life.

Even though Eve was *my* mother, it was hard to imagine her taking care of a baby, hard to picture her changing a diaper or breast-feeding an infant, giving over a part of her body to someone else if only temporarily. Now that the kid was on the scene, it was even more improbable.

Our small living room was already crammed with stuff my grandmother had sneaked in, nearly crowding out Mickey's fish. Knocking the wall down added to the difficulties. It'd be a tight fit in other ways with Mary Theresa wanting her share of Mickey too. Mother's late announcement gave Mickey very little time to adjust. An uneasy and unnatural silence had held in the household until Mother's first scream, and unsurprisingly it was me escorting her to the hospital, sitting with her in the delivery room, present for the birth.

Now Mickey was looking grimly at his offspring.

"A boy, huh?" He sounded neither pleased nor overly interested. "Don't suppose you got a name in mind."

Before she could open her mouth, Mickey said, "Well, let's name the kid after my father. Russell John DiSantis. Russ, for short. What d'ya think, Mary Theresa?" he asked his daughter — as if her opinion counted for anything — as if it were solely a DiSantis family decision. "You remember him, don't you? Your grandad? Always had a pipe sticking out of his mouth. Looked kinda like Popeye." He turned toward his wife. "Smelled like a walking ashtray, Eve. Funny how smoke clings to some people and not others. Him — you could smell fifty feet away." Then back to Mary Theresa, smiling like it was a grand joke. "Still, he was my dad, God love him."

Popeye? It would be hard to wipe that name from my mind. Popeye DiSantis? Why would you want to name a baby after a man who stunk of smoke? Or resembled a cartoon figure?

"I think I remember him," Mary Theresa said, cautious as always.

She was probably calculating the odds in the name being a joke before she spoke. No daughter was more eager to please her parent — except me, perhaps — though I thought I hid it better. The intensity of paternal love I saw in her eyes had faded in mine. It was more about risk management and self-preservation; more about keeping the harm to a minimum. The beads of perspiration on her face as she tried to please him were unlikely to pepper mine again.

I was certainly wrong there, although my forced involvement in the death of Jerry Santini had started the process of separation. What came later hardened me more. Mary Theresa wouldn't be as cool under fire. Her hands, clutching at her skirt until she'd made a horizontal pleat, always got my attention because she'd no idea what real stress was.

"Popeye, Daddy?"

I groaned inwardly. This was bound to be the kid's nickname after this lengthy discussion.

"Well, he wasn't a sailor. Didn't wear a sailor uniform. Kind of bandy-legged though." Was he treating this discussion as serious? Mother and I flashed each other a look.

"Racine remembers him. He had a thing for her near the end. Wouldn't let anyone else feed him. Always looking for an excuse to put his paws on her. Rub up against those boobs." He laughed.

So Racine was big-breasted? I'd only seen her once and hadn't noticed. It wasn't an era for tight knit tops revealing such things.

"You wanna name him Russell?" Mother said. Apparently the name had taken a while to sink in or she was still under the influence of the drugs she'd insisted on. "I don't know, Mickey. Sounds like an old man. Who'd want to name an itsy bitsy baby Russell?"

She said the last words in baby talk, looking at her swaddled offspring. Russell—and he didn't look like a Russell, but who would—was silent. He'd always be able to sleep through tight situations. A stoic. I felt something stir inside me, in a place unknown until that moment.

"I was thinking of something like Jason. Or Joshua. Maybe Ryan." Mother paused a second. "I thought you hated your dad, Mick? Didn't he used to whip you with his belt? Accuse you of doing things he'd done? Beat your mother? Drink till he passed out?"

Jeez, and she'd married his son?

"Sissy names," Mickey said, ignoring her questions. "Racine

wanted to name Mary Theresa something goofy—Cheyenne, I think—and I hadda put my foot down."

"Was it really Cheyenne, Daddy?" Mary Theresa asked, perking up.

It was rare when any piece of information about Mary Theresa entered his conversation. Mostly she served as his prop or ally. Even I was better at grabbing the spotlight. I could see her lips forming the name that might have been hers.

He thought for a moment. "I don't know. Coulda been Cody. Or maybe it was something like Gigi or Gidget. After some movie or TV show she liked. Ridiculous. A name for a poodle not a person. Gidget!" he repeated, looking at Mary Theresa as if she had suggested it.

"Oh, I don't know," my stepsister said, eager to hold onto his attention for a few more seconds. "I kind of like those names. Mary Theresa's such a dull name."

She put her hands under her thick hair and lifted it. We all watched spellbound as several pounds of heaviness disappeared from her face. I noticed for the first time she had long eyelashes and her chin was pert. Maybe the name Gigi would've made a difference. A girl named Gigi wouldn't wear a uniform all the time. Or if she did, it'd be seen as fashion statement instead of stodginess. Gidget would've given a father like Mickey the cold shoulder, would've spoken French, and smoked black cigarettes. Maybe had affairs. We could've been close friends. I yearned for Gigi too.

"Stodgy?" Mickey started to say. But he too was captivated by Mary Theresa's transformation. "Hey, don't wear your hair like to school," he said, after a minute. "We got enough trouble around here." He looked over at his new son and all of our eyes followed.

"Look, what's done is done as far as Mary Theresa's name goes," Mother put in, reclaiming the spotlight. "It's this kid who needs a name. *My kid.* Let's focus on him."

Mary Theresa visibly wilted. Any chance at a name change to something like Gigi or Cheyenne disappeared. She let her hair drop back to its rightful position.

The name Russell sounded funny to me already, the way words sometimes do when they're repeated too often. Mickey continued to stare at his baby dispassionately.

"Russell. Solid name. Not too common, not too unusual."

I got the idea he was seeing a future used car dealer. Or perhaps a future used car buyer.

He took a step closer to the baby. "Little Russ doesn't look a thing like my father though. Looks a little like—well like Christine." Mary Theresa stifled a laugh. "Why does he look like Christine, Eve?" Mickey continued. "Hank come around when I was out?" Mickey's voice had a nasty edge in it. He laughed after a few seconds, and it dissolved. "Old habits die hard, right?" I peered at my brother, trying to see a pug nose—and all of the other less than desirable features I'd been saddled with. But he was perfect.

"Don't be ridiculous." Mother adjusted Russell's blanket. "All babies look like Christine. She's got that kinda face."

I glared at Mother, but she was still looking at Russ with a beatific look on her face.

"It takes a while before you find out who a baby looks like. All their eyes are blue, for instance, but I think his will change to brown. Like yours, Mick." When he didn't respond to the coo in her voice, she added, "I thought Christine looked like her grandmother Moran the first few weeks. Thank god, it didn't last."

Pow! Another hit. My mind flew to my paternal grandmother. I never did understand how people saw a baby in the face of a senior citizen. How did they push away the wrinkles, the sagging flesh and fat, to find a baby's features?

"Can I hold him?"

They all stared at me in surprise. Ignoring their somewhat hostile expressions, I put my arms out.

"You want to hold him?" Mother said, cuddling him closer. "Well, I don't know."

Never any good at sharing, Russell was the nearest thing to a possession in Mother's hospital room. I wondered again if she'd be able to give her milk away—a nipple even. I could picture her pumping milk into little bottles she'd store in a fridge in one of her storage units. Stock-piling breast milk for future use.

"I've held babies before," I reminded her.

"Not babies a few hours old, Christine." Mother shrugged. "Oh, well. I guess it'll be okay."

Reluctantly, she held my brother out to me and I took him in my arms. Instantly, I knew Russell, or whatever his name turned out to be, belonged to me. He may have come from Mother's uterus, but he'd be mine soon enough. Her interest in him would fade over time, very little time. Especially if he didn't make himself useful, which he was unlikely to do for years. (I was wrong about this.) But my devotion to my brother would never diminish, and he'd quickly grow to depend on my unwavering loyalty. I gulped this knowledge down, held him for a minute, and reluctantly passed my brother on to Mary Theresa so as not to tip my hand. Being overly interested in my brother would alert all three of them. It was a tough group to play poker with.

My stepsister barely glanced at the baby, even more uninterested in him than Mickey was. So the intensity I'd experienced minutes ago wasn't typical of all girls my age— or of all female relatives. He was her half-brother too, but she could've been holding anything. Probably she saw the baby as another distraction for her father. Perhaps I needed to watch her carefully for signs of her harboring a murderous rage toward Russell. Immediately I pictured her wielding a knife over his sleeping body, her school uniform merely adding a grotesque element to the image.

If my father remarried, as he threatened to do occasionally, how would I react to a new stepbrother or sister? Probably somewhat indifferently since I'd see the kid so rarely. But Mary Theresa had a close relationship with Mickey. She adored him, visiting twice a week at least, bringing him little presents, calling him most nights. If my presence in her father's house had been difficult to get used to, Russell's would be thornier still, and he'd take more of Mickey's limited time. Although I hadn't wished my stepsister any ill will before, and had grown to somewhat like her, I wrote her off. Love me, love my brother. Her face betrayed her feelings. You could sense her fingers itching to hand him off to someone.

"Your turn, Mick," Mother said, sensing it too. She gestured to him with her head. It was like the two DiSantis' were passing the offering plate at church, a necessary if annoying task foisted on them. Neither wanted to throw in the fiver.

Mary Theresa stepped closer to her father quickly, preparing to give him the bundle. "Here, Daddy, our little Russ."

The father-son introduction didn't go well. All of our arms twitched as we wondered if she'd drop the baby in her rush to be rid of him. Only Russell slept on, unconcerned.

"Maybe later. Never been much good around infants. You know that."

How would any of us know that, I wondered? Had I said it aloud?

"Wait till he can throw a ball," Mickey said. "We'll be big buddies."

So neither DiSantis liked my new brother. It was good to know this from the outset. Good to know I'd have to protect him from what was to come. He wouldn't know the hurt of their indifference because I'd take their places in his life. Be everything to him. I knew how to devote myself to one person. I learned fealty at the master's knees. I'd merely transfer it. I swelled inside, feeling like I might burst with emotion. Instantly, he became the love of my life.

"I've never seen you throw a ball, Mick," Mother said icily, taking the baby back. "Is there even a ball in the house?" She clutched Russell to her chest as if some harm had already been done to him. "Maybe if he learns to play poker, you'll take to him. Or if he gets interested in tropical fish."

Mickey groaned. "You know what I mean, Eve. Look, I didn't hold Mary Theresa much either. These hands," he said, looking at them, "are clumsy mitts. But Racine didn't push me. Didn't expect a man to know much about babies. And in time, we were as close as any father and daughter. Right, Baby."

Mary Theresa nodded happily, eager to accept this myth. Having Mother say such a thing to someone would've seduced me once.

Here it was again though—the idea Racine was wise and wonderful. She got everything right where Mickey was concerned, and I wondered why he left her. Why did he desert two devoted women who so clearly worshipped him? For all her bluster, I knew Mother didn't love Mickey. She was using him for something—just what I hadn't figured out.

Maybe Mickey couldn't take so much devotion. He liked being tolerated rather than loved. He'd done some horrible thing in the past and couldn't accept such adulation.

I'd tried on many occasions to get my stepsister to fill me in on their final days as a family, what went wrong. But Mary Theresa was silent, perhaps regarding any answer as potentially disloyal. I got the idea it was some sexual thing though. Racine was certainly attractive, but maybe over time she saw things my mother hadn't seen yet—such as Mickey resembling a rodent, for instance. Perhaps the exact one he took his name from. Maybe he'd demanded weird and demeaning things from her. Nothing would surprise me.

Mickey fled when the nurse came to administer some topical ointment, Mary Theresa following at his heels. Perhaps he was worried his fish had jumped ship. Used his absence to make their escape upstream.

"Those fish are probably up to no good," Mother said as if she'd read my mind. Neither of us smiled at her wan attempt at humor. Things were not going well. We could both feel the change in the climate and wondered what new trouble would blow in.

Soon it'd be the three of us. I wondered if Mother knew this too. I hovered over my brother until another nurse came into the room and sent me home. I had to take two buses to get there, but Mickey had never thought about my situation when he took off with his blood child. What did he care if someone abducted me on the street?

The next day, Mother and Russell came home and the situation grew worse. There was nowhere for Russell to sleep except in their room, and Mickey hated having him there.

"The room smells like baby poop and breast milk," he complained. "I made this room into something special for you, Eve. Something glamorous and romantic." He waved his arms around as if Mother had committed an act of treachery. "Can't we put him somewhere else? I've heard a baby shouldn't sleep with his parents anyway."

Mother had already packed her beauty products and moved them to the basement, and her clothing now occupied most of my closet. My stuff, pushed to the far end, was too pathetic in comparison with her wardrobe to complain. Why did corduroy skirts and cotton blouses need much room?

"Where do you expect Russell to sleep? In the basement with Jack LaLanne? The air isn't good enough with a furnace five feet away. Probably there's mold growing too. The dryer isn't vented right."

"How about in Christine's room?" Mickey suggested. "Couldn't Russ sleep in there? We could stick his crib in the little alcove."

"Sure," I said, without hesitation.

Within a few hours, Russell was dozing next to my bed. I heard every nocturnal breath my brother took for the next few years, although only a few months of those breaths would be in that house. I'm sure he thought of me as his mother— almost from the start. I certainly thought of him as my child. Virgin I might be—but a mother too. Others had done it.

"You're telling me, you never married him? Never married Mickey?"

My grandmother was shouting when I came in from school. I'd never heard her shout so loudly before so I was taken aback.

"What about the honeymoon in Florida? Was any of it true?"

I was flabbergasted by this news. Flabbergasted but delighted. The reign of Mr. Fishstick was coming to an end.

My mother sighed. "Look, the whole thing got away from me. First, we were going to see a Justice of the Peace before we left for Miami. Some judge Mickey knows."

Probably one in traffic court, I thought to myself. Mother was fluttering around the living room, avoiding eye contact, indicating she expected to tell some pretty big lies along the way. She didn't stop moving when she fibbed.

"But it was one thing after another getting ready for the trip.

We didn't have the right luggage for a nice resort so I had to go into town to the luggage store. Twice. And clothes! You can't imagine the things I needed. I'd been dressing like a pauper for years." She glanced at her mother's face, saw no incredulity, and so continued. "Miami was a whirl of activity. We played golf every day, a little tennis too, met some dealers, car dealers, that is," she explained when she saw my grandmother's face. "And we had reservations for dinner or a show most nights."

"Sounds great," my grandmother said, fanning her face. "Wish I'd been there. I could've stood up for you at least. At the ceremony, I mean."

Ignoring her sarcasm, Mother continued, "Turned out we didn't have the proper licenses to get married in Florida. We didn't understand the legalities — the fact we needed a specific state license. We were back here before we knew what hit us."

"And there's been no time to rectify this state in the last year, Evelyn. You've been so occupied with household chores, and Mickey with his fish, you couldn't find the time? You're truly a fool if you believe it was accidental. That he didn't know exactly what he was doing. I don't think you were together long enough to qualify as a common-law wife. You've been had. "

"He meant to marry me. I'm sure of it."

Mother sounded quite credible, and I believed her. Believed she thought they'd get married at some point. I'm sure her perfect behavior over the last year was partly to seal the deal. Her interest in my being the ideal daughter was meant to help lure him in. He'd be unlikely to marry her if she brought a troublesome daughter into the mix. We were being tested, undergoing a probationary period. And we'd failed. Hurray!

"So this is why you got pregnant? Thinking he'd marry you if you had a kid? Do you understand he's Catholic? The church still sees him as married to — what was her name? Ravine?"

"Racine." Mother shook her head. "No, no, the pregnancy

just happened. I knew he wouldn't go for an abortion. Catholic, you know. It'd be a real mess. Is a real mess," she amended. "There was no good way out of it. I turned it over in my head a million times."

"Oh, I know about those Catholics." Grandmother shook her head. "Not that I'd condone an abortion either, of course. Poor little Russell. Can you imagine not having him with us? Poor little tyke."

My mind went back to the night Mother'd tried to abort him with herbal preparations, and how I aided and abetted her.

"My church is against murder," Grandmother continued. "Have you seen the field of crosses? Brings cars to a halt on Old York Road."

"Your church is against everything, Mother, and look, call the baby Ryan from now on, please. If Mickey's out of the picture, I'm not going to be stuck with a name like Russell for the rest of his life." She paused for a minute. "You know from the moment Mickey chose his name I knew he was leaving. I never heard him say a single good word about his old man. And then to insist we name our little Ryan after him?"

Unbelievably, Mother already had her figure back and was wearing tight black pants. Her boobs were big now too; she was already hot stuff again and would probably have a new man in days if the Mickey thing had truly ended. She might outdo Racine in that department as long as she breastfed. Actually, she rarely breastfed; she mostly pumped milk into bottles and handed them to me. It worked out well for all three of us.

"Is there anything that doesn't 'just happen' to you, Eve? Do you ever have a conscious plan for your life? Goals you set. Do you ever think to pray on it?"

"Goals? Well, now you sound like one of my shrinks."

Grandmother walked over to the baby and shook her head. "There's three of you now. You'll have to get a job this time.

Hank's child support money won't keep you all. And I've done my time and then some."

Mother was too defeated to respond. It was true, I thought. She didn't have a plan. Or a goal beyond getting her hands on more junk. She equated success with the number of storage unit keys on her ring.

CHAPTER
Nineteen

I looked around the room we'd just cleaned. The broken glass from the fish tanks had been swept away, but a pale salmon-colored fish of some sort was stuck to the top of the table, moving, in what was probably its death throes, in a puddle of sorts. I picked him up by his tail, depositing him in the trashcan. I wasn't heartless, but nothing remained available for a fish requiring salt water and extravagant care. The saltwater from its former tank had flowed out the door or down the drain. We'd be gone soon ourselves. The only question was where.

Perfect behavior from Mother and me probably wouldn't have made a difference. Had I contributed to the demise of the union of Mickey and my mother? I'd yet to give up on the notion all bad things emanated from me, but there were plenty of candidates should I look.

My grandmother had told Mother, with vehemence, we'd have to make it on our own this time. She'd said it several times, in fact, and was unlikely to change her mind and yank her ironing board out of the spare bedroom again. There were three of us now too. Ryan could only sleep in a bassinet for so long.

If Grandmother's house was no longer an alternative, she'd still probably agree to help care for Ryan should my mother land a job. What kind of job could Mother get? She was getting too old for some of the ones in her past. Spritzing perfume? Did women in their forties still get hired to spritz? And she certainly was not going to be invited to stand behind the counter at the stationery store in Hatboro. Was there anything else she could do? Legal things, I mean.

The carpet beneath my feet was sodden with water, and I wondered if the floor would give way. Ten large fish tanks in a twelve-by-eighteen foot room—all deep-sixed by my mother—made for quite a tidal wave. The amount of water still in the room was a serious issue. Armed with mops, we attempted to push it out the door and onto the lawn but much of it lay trapped in the carpet fiber, puddling on furniture, cascading down the basement steps until Mother slammed the door.

Mother's romance novels floated by until the weight of the water finally sunk them. Her collection of *Cosmo* magazines had turned the water blue and red. Pieces of seaweed from the tanks embroidered most of the furniture and thousands of colored pebbles clustered in spots where the soaked rug had created boulders and dams. The smell of fish food, fish waste, and wet sand hung in the air. I wore knee-boots, but water still sloshed inside them and there was nasty stuff between my toes. Luckily, Ryan's crib, one floor up, had saved him from all of this. He slept on, oblivious to the family he'd been born into. He'd find out soon enough.

"I'd cry if I wasn't so damned tired," Mother said, standing, hands on hips, on a carpet soggy enough to suggest the room was undersea. Although she'd wrought the scene we looked on, she seemed as surprised as me.

"I think we have enough water," I told her.

We exchanged a tired smile. There was no point in berating her for her performance now. The anger had built over a period of days, finally erupting a few hours earlier. I felt like destroying one or two of Mickey's things myself and wondered if he'd removed his clothing from the wooden valet upstairs. Had he gathered his precious accouterments. Looking around, I pocketed the silver deep sea diver, perched now on the fake Eames chair, desperate for my own revenge. Maybe it could be hocked.

The kitchen floor, another spectacle, was ankle deep in dirt. Mother had swung at the sill full of African violets once she was done with the fish. Mary Theresa was in there now sweeping the remnants into a dustpan.

"Maybe my mother can save a few," she said, a chewed-up pink-striped plant in her hand. Water and dirt had mingled, making mud everywhere. I'd called my step-sister, not knowing how to deal with the plants or if any could be saved. She was one of the few people I could call on for help. Why did we have such a paucity of friends? When I had the time to think about it the answer was clear — we were a freak show and witnesses were unwise.

The only thing I knew about the plants was that Mary Theresa and her mother put a high premium on them, had a house full of them, implying some sort of expertise.

"My mother didn't deserve this — this wanton destruction of her gifts. She had nothing to do with the trouble between Eve and Mickey." Mary Theresa nodded toward the plants. "She was trying to make your house a home." Looking mournfully at the African violet in her hand, she said, "Poor innocent things."

I thought she was talking about us for a moment and started to nod. But it was the plants she cooed to. She swept around the room with despair, stooping to fetch an intact root ball.

"I thought about bringing my mother with me today, but seeing this, I'm glad I didn't. She'd have been heartbroken. I'd no idea it was this bad." Mary Theresa flung out a desperate arm. "You know, you could've invited her over for coffee and dessert before this happened. She'd have enjoyed seeing her plants in Daddy's new house." I rolled my eyes, but Mary Theresa was going too strong to catch it. "She'd nothing against Eve, you know. She was happy Daddy found someone to take care of him."

I found this information surprising and, although I didn't say anything, I thought it strange the death of dozens of fish held no trauma for my stepsister, but those African violets brought her to tears. It was Mother's trip with Mick to Florida that spawned his interest in fish. Maybe she saw the fish the same way she saw Russell/Ryan. Maybe both were too much a part of Mickey's new life—a life only including her peripherally.

Having only seen Racine once and from afar, I wished we'd invited her over too. I never did get a good idea of why Mickey'd left her, didn't discover what sexual problem she might've suffered.

"I imagine they're shell-shocked," I said, looking at the plants she'd recovered. "I've heard plants can sense things."

"Mother swears to it." The white blouse of her uniform was streaked brown. I didn't have the heart to tell her, but she probably knew. "She can feel vibrations in a plant's roots when she takes a cutting."

Did I sound this obsequious when I spoke about my mother? Of course, I tried not to mention her outside the family. Who'd believe it beyond the few who already knew?

"Look, why don't you go on home, Mary Theresa. We can take care of the rest of it. Those plants probably need to be replanted quickly."

All of her grousing and fretting was getting on my nerves.

Normally a competent girl, she was undone by the actions of her stepmother, a situation I was not unaccustomed to. But still, suck it up, I wanted to say. Who asked you to take the fall for murder? How have you suffered? You don't know what a life not lived is like. Or did she?

She'd nearly fainted when she first walked through the door, probably thinking some sort of rogue storm had hit us.

"Did Daddy do this?" she asked after a minute.

I shook my head, wondering momentarily if he'd done something similar in the past. But it was probably natural to assume actions like this were the work of a man. Mother could surprise anyone.

"Eve?" she asked unbelievingly.

I nodded. Her mouth formed the word, "why" but no sound came out. I couldn't have told her the exact precipitating event anyway. It was mostly over by the time I'd arrived. Mickey was gone, and my mother was sitting on the steps, exhausted. "I think I'm having chest pains."

"It's no wonder."

"Could you give me a hand," she said, nodding toward a mop. We worked silently and with little effect until I called Mary Theresa in for the second shift.

My earlier attempt to lure Grandmother over hadn't worked. "Don't you think I'm a little old for all the bending and lifting?" she asked when I described the battle scene. "Maybe Hank will help out again." She snickered unbecomingly.

Looking grimmer, Mary Theresa said now, "I guess this is the end of us being sisters." She searched for her jacket. "Hey, Christine, I always meant to tell you to call me Terry," she said, finding her coat under a layer of newspapers and shaking it out. "Everyone but Daddy does. I never got around to telling you."

Terry. Suddenly I remembered her lifting the hair of her neck back in the hospital. Maybe *Terry*, away from her father, was a different creature.

"That's okay," I said. "We weren't really, were we? Sisters, I mean."

And I felt some miasma of regret. We'd never once gone anywhere together, not even to buy an ice cream cone or to shop at the mall. I wondered why. We might've worked together to make this family work. But then she summed it up—perhaps having the necessary distance to recognize it.

"It's hard to have friends—with the way it is. The way they are."

I nodded. So Racine was like Eve in some ways. "My parents—they can suck the life out of me," she said, sounding bitter. With Mickey gone, she could let her hair down—or in her case, put it up.

I wished it wasn't too late to ask "Terry" if she could tell me how the women were alike. Had she confessed to some terrible crime to save Racine years ago too? Had she hurried home from school each day to see what trouble her mother had gotten herself into? I think Racine's behavior was probably of a more normal ilk. But there was no sense rubbing it in.

Mary Theresa closed the front door quietly, the plastic bag of damaged plants in her hand. I wondered if she'd always known Eve and Mickey weren't married or if the information was recent to her too. I'd bet on the former and wished she hadn't been too polite to tell me. It would've saved me a lot of anxiety.

I never saw Mary Theresa DiSantis again. I always imagined she'd gone into a convent but probably Racine couldn't have gotten along without her. Certainly I couldn't get away from Mother by pleading a calling from God.

Mother, Ryan, and I rented a small apartment near Grandmother's house on Cooke Street, and Mother took her most humiliating job yet—a chambermaid in a downtown hotel.

"Eve, you know this is not the right job for you given your predilections," Daddy told her, shaking his head. "I can't think of a worse fit, in fact."

Unlike Mickey, Daddy took to Ryan immediately, confirming my idea he'd always wanted a son, a future cadet at West Point, a junior partner at the firm.

Or maybe he did have his own son in his arms that day, although it was hard to believe my parents could put their bickering aside long enough to make another baby. Still Mother's behavior at the time of her pregnancy had been strange.

Daddy began to pace, jiggling Ryan as he walked. I wondered if he held me so tenderly. He wasn't the father my mother described Herbert Hobart as being, but he wasn't John Walton either. How easy it was to settle in with the *The Waltons*, the antidote to what I found in my life. Only the grandmother on the show reminded me of mine.

Grandmother and I had fretted about Mother's job choice from the moment she came home, paperwork in hand. "Don't look at me like that," she told both of us. "Do you want a steady paycheck or not?"

She'd applied for jobs all over the city. The Philadelphia House, a downtown hotel catering mostly to medium-income tourists rather than flush businessmen, was the only place to respond. I supposed the turnover in hotel maids was significant, large enough for the hotel to take a chance on Mother's scant job history. It was still a time when a short job history was not unusual for a woman.

Dad was able to bury most of her peccadilloes, including her stays at mental institutions, her nights in the slammer, her run-ins with the post office and various other officials. He composed a sterling recommendation for her to brandish, especially glowing about her time spent at the stationary store in Hatboro, her business acumen, her creativity. Someone else signed it. He wanted her to find work badly. The fear his child support might now extend to Ryan for the next eighteen years was probably gnawing at him. Eve, at work, might do less harm than Eve, at home. Maybe. This was probably the same thinking that led to the job in the stationary store earlier.

Now he'd heard what his letter wrought, I expected him to comment on Mother's ineptitude at housework or the on impropriety of the mother of his child cleaning hotel rooms, but it was another aspect worrying him.

"You're not going to be able to resist taking things you see in those rooms, Eve. It's like an alcoholic working in a bar." He paced the floor smoothly now, careful not to jolt Ryan awake. "There must be some other line of work that'd suit you better." He paused, clearly at a loss for what it might be. We all were.

"I'm waiting for your ideas on the subject," she said, tapping her foot. "Maybe you'd like to send me back to school so I could train for something."

I could see she was already imagining her new co-ed wardrobe.

"She hasn't taken anything from a store in years," I said.

Perhaps her time with Mickey had been a sort of penance period. Mother flashed me a look it was impossible to decipher-part grateful but partly annoyed her child had to stick up for her—maybe annoyed too that I knew as much as I did about her past peccadilloes. I was sitting in judgment somehow. She could never get it into her head that the murder of Jerry Santini and its cover-up laid her open to my probe. She was indebted if only she could see it.

But instead she was unashamed, contemptuous of Daddy's remarks.

"Nobody's made me a better offer, Hank. And I haven't

taken anything from a store, much less a hotel room, in years. That part of my life is long past. And now, with little Ryan here," she gestured toward the crib, not noticing Daddy held him, "I've an incentive to leave it all behind me. *Us*," she corrected herself. She glanced fondly toward the crib again, *still* not seeing it was empty. "I'm looking forward to supporting my little family."

When Mother spoke like that, with an overblown vocabulary and too much virtue in her voice, it made me worry. Did she already have some plan in the works? Had she pocketed an item from the human resources office of the hotel on her way out the door? Whether I liked him or not, Mickey had kept her in check, confining her to the low-stakes return business.

Daddy shook his head, handing me my brother. "I don't believe you can do it. I'd like to think so, but I don't." He paced the floor. "It's some sort of sickness you have. I used to think it was about the thrill involved in taking stuff, but now I'm not so sure. I read an article somewhere about people who hoard. Maybe you've got such a disorder: hoarding. Still have the storage unit? Or is it more than one unit by now?" He fired this question at my grandmother who'd been silent. "Is your basement still a flea market, Adele?"

Nobody said anything. The apartment we stood in was curiously empty. Mother had pretty much destroyed the things she'd had in the house with Mickey. Our home was Spartan, for once: no fish, no glitter, no African violets, no hula dancers on the wall.

"You'd think you'd have some interest in finding out what your problem is and solving it." He whipped around. "Or that *you*'d want to know what's wrong with her, Adele. You must be up to your eyeballs in her crap."

"I..." my grandmother started to say, but Mother interrupted.

"I'm done with it, Hank. Give me a break." Mother paced the floor, a cigarette hanging from her lips. "What do you care? It's not on your head anymore. Last time I was in trouble, my one call wasn't to you."

"Look, it's none of my damned business what job you take on, but if you go to jail again—even for a night—I'll ask for, and get, custody of Christine. She can spend her final year at home in my house. It'd probably be the best year of her life—free of you and your shenanigans. My tolerance is running out." He laughed. "That's not true. It ran out years ago. But…"

This was a startling statement. Never once had I heard him express the slightest interest in taking me in. Was it really me who'd stood in the way of his complete desertion of Eve Moran? I'd always wondered if I reminded him too much of my mother. Did he see me as her willing accomplice in crime?

He confirmed my idea at once. "Christine's out of it soon enough, but I don't know what will happen to Ryan. Poor little fellow."

I looked at my brother, vowing nothing bad would happen to him. And Daddy couldn't have him. I might not be sure about who his father was, but his mother was definitively mine. Ryan was ours until he declared otherwise himself.

"Don't you think I know all this?" Mother stubbed out her cigarette. "What kind a job did you think I'd get with my experience? Model, actress, editor of *Cosmo*." I waved the smoke away, wondering why she'd taken to smoking again when the rest of the world had quit. "I've no real employment record and several smirches needing explaining. You couldn't erase all of it apparently."

"You think you can control the thieving?" Daddy sounded weary but almost ready to believe her. This was their pattern after all. Pretend it's okay and maybe it will be. "You never have yet."

"I know I can. I managed to stop completely—this last year or two." Her eyelids fluttered.

I could tell when she was lying about seventy-five percent of the time. Mostly when it wasn't my eyes she was looking into. At those times, a sort of hypnosis took place.

"With Mickey," she unnecessarily explained. "I tried."

Was she counting the return to the return business? Was that what was lurking in her eyes?

Daddy sighed. "I've half-a-mind to call The Philadelphia House and tell them about you. Stop it before it starts—before you wind up in jail. Disgracing us all yet again."

"Then bump up the little bit of money you send us. If you do, I'll call the hotel and quit. I'd certainly prefer to stay home with my children. Be a mother—"

Daddy waved his hand. "Please, Eve. Have a little pride. I'll increase your support somewhat if you promise you won't take anything out of those hotel rooms. Not even a discarded magazine. If you get the urge to steal something, quit immediately and get the hell out of Dodge. Right? Promise? Isn't Mickey kicking in some support for Ryan?" Mother shrugged.

Daddy didn't have to do this. Perhaps custody of me was such a turnoff he was willing to put some dough on the line to head it off. "Deal?"

"I'll quit the first time I'm tempted."

She said it too quickly, and we all avoided looking at one another. But there were only so many places to look.

She kept her word though. Five days a week for the next two months, she dropped Ryan off at Grandmother's house at five-thirty a.m. and took the train downtown. I got myself off to school an hour later. When I got home from school, she and Ryan were already back home— takeout, or something my grandmother made, on the table. It might work out—despite her daily litany of complaints.

"The nicest couples you can imagine, Christine, community pillars, elders at the church, presidents of the ladies circle—all of them check into a respectable hotel like The Philadelphia House, and proceed to do strange, sometimes unspeakable, things," she'd say, and start out with mild stories about bodily and other fluids she found every day: "urine, mucus, saliva, semen, coffee, blood, breast milk, booze— stuff I can't identify."

I'd grit my teeth as she continued. "An elderly couple from the Midwest, I think, ripped their sheets to shreds last night." Or, "I found toenail clippings in the bed sheets this morning, nearly cut my hand on them." Or, "I walked in on two naked boys passed out on the bathroom floor. A gagged girl was in their bathtub. When I helped her out, she laughed and said this would teach her not to drink tequila." Another time. "There were four of them, crammed into the one bed with another bed not two feet away. They'd torn the curtains from the rod for some reason, had the air set at fifty-five degrees. I thought they were dead for a minute. A mass-suicide pact. Can you imagine calling it in to the front desk?" She giggled. "'Only on my floor,' the damned man I work for would say. He's convinced I'm a bad luck charm."

"And oddest of all," she began, making me shiver, "are the couples who leave no signs of their occupancy. They remake the bed, clean the bathroom, polish every surface. What're they hiding beneath the cleanliness?" She shrugged. "I get one every week or two, and I turn on the TV and take a good rest when I walk into the room. Sometimes they even leave a big tip. Probably they're harmless neurotics, but you never know."

"Sounds interesting."

I could easily imagine a finicky guest not trusting the cleaning techniques of the average hotel maid, who'd been taught speed was most important. Mistrust of hotel cleanliness must be especially common since the Legionnaire's Disease.

"Oh, yeah, real interesting. The job is like a college education. Last week, I did fourteen rooms in one day. Including two suites. At least, I'm catching up on the soaps. That's how most of them learn English, you know."

"Them?"

"The chambermaids I work with. I'm the only native English speaker on the staff. So patrons always look for me in the hallway to tell me their light bulb needs changing or their pillow isn't fluffy enough. I'm thinking of saying, 'Hola' to conceal it. Some of them are from the islands. Poorer countries. Speaking English is probably what gave me a leg up on getting this job. Oh, I'm talented all right."

We were in her bed with Ryan between us, watching Mike Douglas on TV. She fluffed her pillow, saying, "I'd think twice before staying in a hotel after this job. Especially the cheaper chains. You should hear the stories the girls tell. Lots of 'em have worked at place like the Bates Motel."

"But you get good tips, right?" I stroked Ryan's cheek, and he turned his head as if to find a breast waiting. Mother noticed and laughed. "That's one thing he still has to come to me for, Christine." Ryan was over a year old and I wondered why she still breastfed.

If she pumped though, he didn't know the difference. He liked me to feed him. I eyed the two enviously as they snuggled. She held a certain allure for him, I couldn't quite match. "And the tips?" I repeated.

Mother generally didn't discuss money with me, but her ire at this injustice opened her mouth. "I'm lucky to get twenty dollars a night and I do twelve rooms most days. Sometimes more."

I wasn't sure what her salary was. "Still, with your salary

and what Daddy gives us we can make it, right? It's not so bad. I've been filling out college applications…"

"I can't do it forever, Christine. My back aches and my shoulders are nearly paralyzed by the end of the shift from holding up the mattress to get those sheets tucked tight." To prove her point, she lifted her arm as if a twenty-pound weight rested on it. "We have a protocol on bed making and square corners are a must. They actually do sporadic checks. There's gotta be some easier way to make a living." My heart sank. I could think of some easier ways and knew she could too.

Mother never went long without male companionship. She met Bud Pelgrave in the Philadelphia House's hotel bar a few weeks later.

CHAPTER
Twenty

"Can I buy you a drink?" he asked, minutes after she slid onto the red leatherette stool two seats away. He was tall, skinny, and had thinning salt and pepper hair worn in a pony tail. No exactly her usual type, but he had a way about him. Cocky, glib. He'd do in a pinch. He was wearing blue scrubs, but they didn't look like a doctor's. Lab tech?

She'd decided to get a drink at the bar after an unusually hard day. The hotel was shorthanded and didn't maintain much of a list of backup help. Adele wouldn't mind watching Ryan a little longer. Half the time, Eve arrived at her mother's house in the middle of his nap and was made to cool her heels while Ryan finished sleeping. Déjà vu from the days when Christine'd been in her care. And now Christine was trying to horn in too. Her kid didn't fool her.

Eve thought she deserved a drink, and the first drink for hotel employees was often free if the right bartender was working. He was.

"Got it covered," Tom, the barkeep, told her skinny

companion when he saw him pulling out a billfold. His voice was brusque. It was obvious Tom didn't like the fellow. Eve wondered whether there was a reason for it.

"Know each other?" she asked, her eyes sweeping back and forth.

Each man had the same clenched-jawed look, the same twitchy eyes. Both shook their head. Perhaps Tom had a crush on her. She hadn't considered this before. He had to be under thirty, and his shoes were scuffed when he walked over to a table to clear it.

When Tom went to attend to another customer, she took a careful sip of the gin and tonic, looking the new guy over more openly. She winced; Tom had apparently decided to impress her with the strongest drink he could make. She set it down carefully, pacing herself but remembering, somewhat fondly, when she drank like this all the time. Lesson learned. The smell of the lime was the nicest thing about it.

The guy with the ponytail noticed her sniffing. "Best smell in the world, isn't it?"

"The booze or the lime?"

"Well, what's one without the other?" They both laughed. Click.

"Second best smell anyway," she said.

"And the first?"

"Cut grass."

"Gasoline. But grass isn't bad either. And if you cut it with a power motor, well, you get both. Like a gin and tonic." He took a swig of his beer. "Bud Pelgrave." He didn't smile or hold out a hand, and she didn't offer hers.

"Eve... Moran." She'd used Mickey's name for more than two years despite having no legal claim to it, but returning to Moran was easier than she'd expected.

"You don't act too sure of your moniker. Have a purse full

of fake IDs there?" His eyes shot to her lap where her handbag nestled. "Hey, you're not trouble, are you?" He said it like he was hoping she was.

"Not lately," she said sadly. Recently all she did was clean hotel rooms and dream about her yesterdays. No need to tell him this though. Not yet, at least. She carried herself like a hotel patron and would act like one. She put on her best smile.

And so it began. Bud Pelgrave entered her life.

CHAPTER
Twenty-One

"**I** can get you a job as a personal housekeeper, secretary. Something cushy," Bud Pelgrave told her a few weeks later. "It'd be lot easier than this gig. This job's for wetbacks." He was lying on a guest bed on the 10th floor of The Philadelphia House, watching her go through her routine. "You already dusted the phone, honey."

"It's grimy. And you're distracting me, Bud. I told you to come over at four and it's not three-thirty. You shouldn't be here..."

She looked around warily, wondering if the room might be bugged. Examples of her inadequacies as a chambermaid kept coming up when she ran into her boss punching out. Maybe there was a video device somewhere. On her cart? Or, more likely, inside the TV. It'd be like Mr. Duggan to install expensive surveillance equipment at the same time he claimed poverty if anyone asked for a fifty-cent an hour raise.

Bud glanced at his watch. "Place is deserted, Babe. Let up a little. The room is clean." He struggled to sit, putting another pillow behind him. "Look, here's the thing I came early to tell you—just occurred to me today. I run into old guys who need help all the time at work. They're completely lost once their wives go—one way or the other. I can introduce you to one of 'em. They'll probably pay you more than you earn here if only to listen to their life story, flash a pretty smile." He paused. "Mostly that's what I do—just listen. Lots of 'em seem more lonely than sick." He closed his eyes and settled back into the pillows. "This mattress stinks. Sleep on this bed a few nights and I'll be needing my own services. Maybe I can make a deal with the hotel. Or stick a card under the doors."

"This room's scheduled for refurbishing so a new mattress is on the way. Whole floor is. They'll bump the rates to pay for it. Same rooms on Floors 1-5 are ten dollars more a night." She stopped what she was doing. "Don't you do exercises to prevent back pain? Leaning over a massage table all day long must be murder." She knew because she did this herself—leaned over beds half the day. "Isn't there some reciprocal arrangement with one of your pals?"

Bud was an acupuncturist and ran a practice touting the benefits of vitamin therapy, acupuncture, relaxation tapes, massage—all the stuff beginning to flood the market. Lots of stressed-out people turned up at his practice once they'd exhausted everything else, or when their medical plan wouldn't cough up the dough for a legitimate orthopedist. Bud didn't have a degree in anything requiring state licensing, but it didn't stop him from hanging a vaguely worded sign above his office on a side street in Manayunk. A mail-order degree in one of the new-age procedures from a non-disclosed school permitted him to call himself Doctor. His greatest talent was in the art of persuasion.

Sometimes his clients or patients did get better, mostly due to either the passage of time or the placebo effect. He was careful not to fool with someone genuinely ill. Careful not to charge too much or make too many promises. His disposition could be quite pleasing when he set his mind to it. He was a good listener — or knew how to appear so.

Sometimes he fooled her until he was forced by some circumstance or other to admit he hadn't heard a word she'd said.

"Learned how to listen as a kid. My mother never stopped talking. She was a hairdresser, and I used to clean the place after she closed. Sweep the floor, clean the combs, untangle cords. And all the time, gab, gab, gab as she sat in her chair and drank a six-pack."

Eve saw through the snake oil pitch immediately but liked Bud for other reasons. Most of the men she knew were like Bud. Even Hank, to some extent. Had Hank not had access to his parents' money, he'd probably been forced into something dicey. Certainly Mickey DiSantis was similar to Bud, selling used cars where the speedometers were turned back and the damage carefully masked. Mickey's boss had a process to temporarily hide rust, for instance. It bled through within weeks, especially in wet weather, but the legal papers the customer blindly signed took care of things. She pushed thoughts of Mickey out of her head.

"Gonna smooth that out before we go?" she asked, emptying the wastepaper basket and shooting him a look. "The bedspread, I mean." He sighed. "And watch out for your shoes, Buddy. It's hard to get scuff marks off the fabric." She shook her head. "The world's still bonkers for polyester. They haven't caught on yet. You should see how nasty cigarette burns look on that sheen. I bet the place goes up like a torch some night."

"You sound like a regular little hausfrau, Eve. Dispensing housekeeping information like Erma Bombeck." Bud jumped up and gave the spread a swipe. "See, no wrinkles at all. *It's magic.*"

He sang it like the old Sinatra song. Most of the men in her life were Sinatra fans. Maybe she was attracted to this one type of guy and would choose him over and over again until one of them murdered her. Or she killed him. Whoops, no, she'd done that already. What had his name been?

"That's its one asset. Polyester," she said when he looked blankly at her.

"You could drive a car over it and not make a crease."

"So why you buggin' me?"

"I don't know. It makes me tense having you in here. Like it or not, I need this damned job. The doofus, Duggan, shows and finds you here, I'm toast."

"Duggan's probably nailin' one of the Latinas in a room down the hall."

"Hardly. His wife has him on a six-inch leash."

"You'd be surprised how much wiggle room six inches gives you."

"Very funny."

Bud stalked around the room, picking things, examining them, and putting them back in the wrong spot. "Come on, old girl. This room was clean ten minutes ago." He raised and lowered his shoulders impatiently. "I'm getting the idea you're trying to avoid me."

She wiped the wastepaper basket off, placing it under the desk. If it were up to her, they'd put plastic bags in those trash baskets. There was always a coating of dust or grime or sticky stuff inside from the crap people pitched. God, she was beginning to think like her mother. Spend too much time on wifely duties and shit happened.

"Looks tacky," Mr. Duggan told her when she mentioned her idea about bag inserts. "Plus an added cost. Just wipe 'em down." He demonstrated the proper method on a trashcan already pristine, his eyes narrowing with attention. "Hotel's already paying you, right?" He shook his head like she'd suggested something crazy.

Duggan had trained her himself, going through the room with unrepressed pleasure, showing her the mistakes often made by newbies. He dusted the light bulbs, for instance, and vacuumed the inside of the closet.

"Course you'll have to complete each room in a timely manner," he said. "If it's been trashed, these niceties will need to be dispensed with." The room he chose had already been cleaned so he could accomplish the task in about fifteen minutes. "Not saying fifteen minutes should be your benchmark at first," he said, running a hand along the windowsill and wincing as his hand came away coated with grime. "Like to nail these damned windows shut. Look at it out there. Why do they need to open the window? Cities are filthy places." He turned to glare at her. "Think of thirty for dirty." When she didn't show she understood him, he added, "Minutes. Thirty minutes a room."

She'd like to see Duggan take on the typical trashcan she handled. More days than not, she'd find a used condom inside, although she'd rather find them there than in the bed. Often she'd miss one, yank the sheet off, and send a rubber flying through the air. God, she hated this job. Oh, and gum—gum was bad. No one would believe how many people tossed chewed gum, opened cans of soda, half-filled coffee containers, lit cigarettes, and drug paraphernalia into those little, brown, fake-leather cans. It was amazing the number of guests who assumed she wouldn't rat them out for their drug usage. Wouldn't call a cop in to see what the Browns' had been up to in Room 1014. Did they think she took a secrecy oath as a maid? A confidentiality pact? Did they think two bucks on the desktop was a fitting recompense for fishing needles and assorted drug paraphernalia out of the trash can? For having to flush unflushed toilets. For crawling around on her hands and knees retrieving things from under the sink because they couldn't be bothered to aim better. And speaking of a better aim...

She'd also suggested wearing gloves to Mr. Duggan, but he said gloves implied their guests were riddled with germs. "People see you coming out of a room in gloves and they'll think we have Legionnaires Disease in here. Remember that disaster a few years ago. Right around the corner too."

A precaution such as gloves might have prevented Legionnaires Disease, she wanted to say. Eve regretted Adele's hygiene standards had permeated her brain, but what could she do? She could attest to the germ issue by the sheer number of tissues, swabs, and medications lining the guests' rooms, from the bandages, bottles of antiseptic ointments, and heating pads, from the odors of decay hanging in the air when she walked in. Most people were a walking medicine chest. And they had no compunctions about expecting her to clean their mess.

"Look, I know this guy who needs one right now." Bud was still talking but she had no idea what he was talking about. "He's practically begging me to help him out." His mouth was inches from her ear.

"What? Help who out?" Was Bud asking her to service a client? Give someone a blow job?

"A housekeeper, Eve! What did you think I meant. This old dude I know needs a housekeeper." Bud shook his head. "Ever listen to what I'm saying? Anyway, his wife croaked recently, and he's damn near helpless. She took care of everything, I guess. He's coming in to see me for neck pain. Stress probably. Or grief. Grief can make you physically ache."

His fingers absentmindedly massaged the air. It was kind of sensual. Bud had nice fingers, and she wished they were on her right now, sliding up her thigh, her stomach, her breasts, her back.

"Keep his accounts? Stuff like that?" she said, shaking off the image of Bud's fingers, getting the gist of what he meant. "Or cleaning and cooking duties? I'm not the greatest cook on the block if that's what he's after."

She flashed back to the time, nearly a decade ago now, when she couldn't light her mother's oven. Probably still couldn't. Mickey'd been pretty undemanding with his steak and potato, night after night. Why couldn't she get that lout out of her head?

Damn, it'd been a nice life for a while. She was never in over her head with Mickey. She knew his world—had been raised in it. This was his biggest appeal. His primary demands were sexual and she could handle that, especially after his first wife, who'd apparently limited their sex to Saturday nights, the missionary position, and nightgowns buttoning to her clavicle. She'd been a hot number for Mick after Racine.

Yes, it'd been nice hiding out with the tropical fish in her little row house, nothing more to do than keep eight-hundred square feet clean and broil a steak. She managed to buy a trinket now and then, stole one or two items when the clerk looked away, but on the whole she behaved herself. Yes, she had things well under control until she got knocked up.

But Mickey went crazy once Ryan came along. Racine had planted the idea in his head that his fathering days were over, that his low sperm count was the reason she couldn't have another kid. So it had to be someone else's baby—probably Hank's. He was convinced a kid would take over the house too, make it smell, make it dirty. And make her fat, saggy, unattractive.

She missed those African violets, the tidy eight-hundred feet, the distinctive odor of the water in the tanks. Her skin had never looked so good. It was like living in a tropical rain forest. She should open a cosmetics business making use of what she'd learned. She had some business skills from her days at that stationary shop and her return business. That was the way to go. She was sick of working for men. Christine was showing signs of being a whiz at math, taking calculus this year. At least, the kid might make herself useful.

"The guy's not after anything, Eve. The idea of a housekeeper hasn't occurred to him. That's where I come in. Oh, and you can easily take care of this guy's cooking needs. Kowalski'll be so thrilled to have a good-looking woman in his house, he won't notice what's on his plate. And who knows what you'll come across. Looks rich to me—maybe something in it for us. Something beyond a weekly check." Bud walked across the room and put his arms around her waist. "Watching you bend over in that shiny, black polyester number got me going. What're you gonna do about it?"

Eve could tell as much as he pushed up against her. This was the thing about the two of them; they were in sync physically. Hank Moran had seen that she was financially secure, and Mickey DiSantis provided a locked-down stability. But she felt a link with Bud—and not just sexually.

But she could never play her hand that openly, and so she said, "Pretty much *anything* gets you going, Bud." She shrugged him off anyway and squirted the mirror with glass cleaner."I certainly don't feel sexy in a uniform I've been cleaning in all day. Do my feelings count for anything?" She lifted her arm and sniffed. "Not pretty, Bud." "Does it count for anything?" she repeated, "that I'd rather *not*—at least not here. That I'd like to be in the mood myself, feel sexy, too."

She was lying, of course. She was as turned on as he was, but it didn't do to show it. They'd done it in hotel rooms she'd been cleaning before, but she'd lose her job if someone walked in on them. Or if there was a recording device somewhere…

"So take a shower. We can both take a shower. Those little hotel soaps are sexy as hell. Slipping over your boobs, your thighs. They fit inside the nicest places."

She whirled around, her uniform crinkling loudly. "You'd like that, wouldn't you? Then I'd have to scrub the tub again. No thanks. Take me dirty or not at all."

She was beginning to sound like Adele, with her shower-less bathroom, her antiseptic approach to life. Adele only had to clean one bathroom a day though. All day long to clean an eight-hundred square foot house—nothing else to do. That life had been hers too—for a little while. That's what no one understood. How hard this job was! Taking something on like this at her age.

She *was* beginning to feel like doing it. Having sex. Using those little soaps, maybe not in the shower though. Women were programmed to be turned on by erections, by images of strong fingers. Where had she read that? *Cosmo*? She couldn't help it. Bud's fingers aroused her.

"I like your attitude."

Now he was pressing up against her hard enough to make strong contact without removing a garment. She pretended to shake him off, not wanting to make things too easy. He'd be here all the time if she was too easy. Being his own boss, he could schedule her in. Slip up here as her two o'clock appointment. And soon dinner at a nice restaurant might not be necessary. And sooner or later, she'd get caught.

Eve wasn't supposed to close the door to the hotel room and shouldn't have a man in here at all. Ever. It was in the hotel service manual in bold writing:

> **Hotels rooms are not to be used for any form of fraternization. Hotel rooms should be treated as if they belonged to the guest. The guest's privacy and possessions are inviolate. The guestroom door must remain open when staff is inside the room for any purpose.**

There were at least a dozen more rules about guestroom behavior and she'd broken most of them. She walked over and kicked the doorstop away. No one would be checking into this room for another two hours—the entire hallway had emptied out after a dentists' conference ended that morning. Maria, scheduled to clean the other end of the floor, had sneaked out fifteen minutes earlier to meet her boyfriend for lunch. She wouldn't be back until tomorrow probably.

"Not our finest performance," Bud said, buttoning his shirt fifteen minutes later. "You were thinking about remaking the bed the whole time—admit it. Wondering if any hairs had gotten loose. Any bodily fluid."

He didn't offer her a hand in remaking the bed. She'd never known a man willing to lift a finger with household tasks. Wasn't sure she'd respect a man with a dishtowel in his hands.

"I'll have to make it over from scratch," she said, examining the sheets. "Something got away." He shrugged. She sprayed it with a can from her cart and waited for the spot to dry.

"So tell me more about this guy," she said, "the one who needs a housekeeper. How needy is he? Not in diapers, is he? Not some randy old goat? I wouldn't have to read to him, change his diapers or his dressings?"

"You're gonna like Charlie," Bud promised. "He's in great shape. Only lonely, a little lost." He paused. "And rich, I think."

She spent one more week working in the hotel. Having behaved herself for several months, she took advantage of a farewell tour and came home with bags of junk. Stuff she took from rooms she'd never cleaned, items left in the restaurant, a few things from the coat stand in the ladies room. None were worth reporting by their owners, she hoped. They were the sort of objects a guest wondered about later and couldn't remember whether it was left on the vanity, on the back of the door, or under the bed in Philadelphia. Maybe it was forgotten on the airplane. The kind of stuff a person meant to call or write the hotel about but didn't get around to. Glitzy but cheap. Hotel gift shop merchandise. Items from the souvenir shop at the Liberty Bell or in Independence Hall. No one but Eve would miss such things, want them badly enough to pursue it. It made her feel good for a change. Like she'd shown the The Philadelphia House something.

Things started to take shape in her new place after that. It didn't look so bare. She placed the new tin of bath powder on the bathroom shelf, her new traveling clock on the table in the living room. The box of candy, she put under her bed. No sense letting Ryan develop a sweet tooth. The rest of the stuff, she stashed.

CHAPTER
Twenty-Two

M r. Kowalski had lost his wife three months earlier from the ubiquitous protracted illness that sapped the spirit of devoted spouses like Charlie. Months of appointments, horrific treatment, nausea, bed trays, hospital stays.

He answered the door Eve's first day of work looking like a soldier who'd spent years on a scarred battlefield. He was neat, soft-spoken, ramrod straight. His house, outside Philly, was a virtual time capsule of the early nineteen forties.

"Carol redecorated when we moved out here," he told Eve as he showed her around. "It was her lifelong dream to have a stone house in Jenkintown."

He was seventy-two but seemed older. Certainly older than Adele Hobart, who flitted around her house like someone in the prime of life. Eve immediately thought about setting the two up, but Charlie Kowalski was a Catholic. Her mother was biased and would never go for it. As far as Eve knew, Adele hadn't had a single date in the nine years since Herbert died. She wasn't about to start with a Catholic.

Anyway, it was far too soon for Charlie Kowalski to look at another woman. He spent most of the day following Eve around, telling her about his wife.

"I met her coming out of a bakery on Ogontz Avenue," he told her. "She had half a loaf of rye tucked under her arm. It was right in the middle of the depression. They sold half-loaves in those days." His eyes got watery. "I don't know why they don't do it now. A single person can't eat a whole loaf before it goes stale, and freezing it—well, it's not the same."

"I used to shop there," Eve told him, ignoring everything he'd said about Carol. She'd already learned how to head off these weepy interludes. "At Hansens right? I got my ex his éclairs there." Christ, had she really schlepped there on a bus to get Mickey pastry? What an idiot she'd been.

He smiled. "They make the best Charlotte Russe."

"The dessert with lady fingers?"

He nodded.

The two of them hit it off right away. You couldn't help but like Charlie. He was a basset hound who'd lost the object he was meant to track. It was the easiest job she'd ever had. With a little effort, she probably could get *him* to make *her* lunch.

"Look, I'm not much of a cook," she'd warned him the first day on the job. "If some kind of gourmet meal is important..."

"I'm not much of an eater," he said. "Food allergies—and I just don't have much of an appetite." He gave her a long list of the foods he couldn't eat. "It's probably better to work out two or three dinners and rotate them. I get my own cereal for breakfast and have a ham sandwich on rye and some Charlie's Chips for lunch. So if you can come up with two or three dinners, we're in business." He paused. "Food's not so important—not anymore."

She knew this was an invitation for her to ask him what *was* important, or *why not* anymore, but she let it pass. How much sympathy did this guy expect? She could tell *him* some pretty sad tales. Much sadder than his probably. She'd bet anything he'd never been in a nuthouse or in a courtroom. And definitely not in jail.

"Food makes you fat, costs money, and takes too much effort between the shopping, cooking, and cleaning. Better to skip meals whenever you can. I can make a meal or three out of an angel food ..."

"Now my wife," he interrupted, "was a full-figured woman."

And he was off on a lengthy tribute to his wife again—what a marvel she'd been in the kitchen. Much the same kind of food Adele had made for Herbert Hobart—rib-sticking meat, plenty of carbs.

Eve took his list of forbidden foods to her mother, and Adele worked out a menu. "Most men like their meals simple. You can put any of these meals in a Pyrex dish in the oven before you leave. Surely, taking it out of the oven half-an-hour later is not too much for him. What did you say was wrong with him?"

"Some vision problems, diabetes, and god, he's so frail. A stick figure. His wife died a few months back. It knocked the shit out of him."

"Eve! The stuffing knocked out of him sounds so much nicer." Adele shook her head. "Poor man. If he was my sort of person I'd go over there myself. Lend him a hand."

It sounded like her mother was talking about someone from a different species rather than a different religion. She was glad she wasn't filled with prejudice. What would her mother have done if she'd been surrounded by those wetbacks at the hotel? Probably quit the first day. Whereas Eve had put some effort into getting along, learned a little Spanish, shared those messy burritos that gave her diarrhea for lunch.

She shook her head. "You should put that sort of thinking

aside and go over. It'd be the Christian thing to do."

Setting Adele up with Charlie might work. He didn't have any financial problems from what she saw — much like Bud had guessed. Having a wealthy stepfather could take her out of the hole. But Adele had conveniently moved out of earshot, not liking to hear she was imperfect in any way. With Ryan to care for, she probably had no need for another man in her life.

Cleaning Mr. Kowalski's house was a snap since he was the neatest man Eve had ever known. Mickey had been fastidious but had several little peccadilloes she'd rather not think about. (What man pees sitting down?) She drove Charlie to his appointments, did some basic shopping, cleaned a little. Most of the day, they watched the soap operas his wife had watched, some she'd gotten into herself at The Philadelphia House. It made the day pass. She wasn't sure if he liked them too or it was more out of some loyalty to his dead wife.

"Erica is some handful," he said every day. "I think I'm a little in love with Jenny Gardner. Carol liked the stories about Phoebe Tyler and the Martin family. But I like the ones about their kids. Didn't have any of our own, you know."

The guy could get teary-eyed over the craziest things. Stuff that happened a million years ago was something to be mulled over every day. They'd been through this issue before — being childless. Something about clogged fallopian tubes.

"Yeah, well kids can be plenty of trouble," Eve said. "My teenager can get herself into some pretty tight spots. And my little one, well, he's a handful."

"Christine's her name, right? And Ryan?"

Charlie always remembered the details of her life. She nodded, happily thinking he was growing fonder of her — and, by extension, her children.

"I do my best, Charlie. All on my own, you know." Her voice sounded pitiful to her own ears. But you couldn't overdo it with Charlie. His wife must have broken him in good.

"I wish you'd bring them over here sometime. I'd like to meet them."

She nodded. Ryan would destroy the place without Adele or Christine to watch him. She looked nervously at the shelves of ceramic angels. No thanks. She had her eye on them. What did a man want with such things? They were three-deep in spots. If she remembered correctly, she had a box of them over in the Flourtown unit. They didn't have the charm for her they once had, but she wouldn't turn one away should he offer.

"*Do you* think you should show me how to keep your books?" Eve asked him after a few weeks. "I could probably take care of your bills if I knew the system. I helped my ex with his. Bet it's a strain on your eyes."

"Mickey?" he asked. "You kept Mickey's books. I didn't realize he was self-employed."

"No, not Mick. Hank. Hank's books. He has his own printing business in Bucks County. I practically ran the office. Back in the early days before Christine came along. Once she was in school. I ran a little shop in Hatboro."

"I didn't know that, Eve. You're quite accomplished. I hope I'm not taking advantage of your time."

"I love coming here, Charlie. You know that. And with your eyesight and all, learning your books could come in handy," she said again, in case he hadn't heard her the first time. "I help Bud. He says I have a knack for it."

Charlie nodded. "I can show you how to do it. Nothing to it. In January, an accountant comes in and looks things over," he added.

January was a long way off.

"What's this all about?" she asked him one day, poking a

piece of paper with her rubber finger.

She was sitting at his desk, wearing the reading glasses she suddenly needed. She'd found a section in one of his loose-leaf books listing automobiles. Maybe a dream list for the old coot? She paged through it. There were a lot of notations about servicing, car parts, fees, licenses renewals, inspections twice a year. Some guy—she couldn't make out the name—signed off on the purchases for him. Maybe a nephew? So Kowalski owned these vehicles? It wasn't a fantasy? Or were they some sort of model cars—like hobby shop things? But at these prices, it couldn't be.

Charlie walked across the room and peered over her shoulder. He blushed. "Guess I haven't told you about my bad habit," he said. "I'm a bit of a hoarder."

"What do you hoard?" Eve asked with interest, forgetting the vintage cars she saw listed and picturing storage units filled with junk. Clearly the bill in her hand now was for storage of some kind. Higher than any bill she'd paid though—and she had a bunch of units. Certainly too high for model cars—even a platoon of them.

"I buy automobiles. Or I used to. Haven't bought one in years though. Since the wife—well—you know."

"Cars? Carol and you bought cars?"

"Yeah, instead of taking vacations. Carol never wanted to take vacations because she loved this house too much to leave it—always worried about her plants, and she had a little cat. Teeny was a—"

"The cars, Charlie," Eve interrupted.

"Oh, right. So instead of buying gold or stocks with the extra cash, we bought cars. Every two or three years—the fancy kind." He walked across the room and returned with a steel box. "I got pictures of most of 'em in here. We had a professional photographer take them. Oh, those cars were our

babies, all right." He was red-faced. "Seems kind of silly now —
buying all those cars. Some barely driven." He handed her the
box. "But we took them out to a car show now and then. There's
a great one in Bucks County, matter of fact. Probably near your
old stomping grounds."

She opened the lid and found a stack of photos. "And you
still have all of them? All of these cars?" There must have been
a dozen or more. "That's what's in the storage units?"

He nodded, still pink with embarrassment. "Sixteen. The
sweet sixteen." He smiled. "Sixteen felt like the right number to
end on. And they're in garages. Not storage units."

"What's that one?" she asked, pointing to a bright red one.
She'd never seen cars like these. Maybe they were foreign.

"A 1969 Alfa Romeo Spider. You've got good taste, Eve. One
of my favorites." He picked up the box and thumbed through it.
"And this one is a 1958 Ace Bristol. And the yellow baby is a '55
Triumph." In each picture, a small woman, who gradually or
not so gradually aged, stood next to the passenger's door with
a chirpy smile on her face. Carol?

"Your wife?" Eve asked. There were no pictures of his wife
around the house. No photographs at all.

He nodded. "This is my Carol." He sighed. "It's hard
looking at her. I put all of our photographs away so I wouldn't
have to—"

"Very pretty." Actually, Carol *was* an attractive woman. Or
had been at the beginning of their automobile purchases. You
could pinpoint the exact year her illness began.

"It got to be a routine," he said. "Carol always standing
in the same spot. I picked out the automobile, after months of
research and hunting for a good price, but Carol usually picked
the color—if we were buying it new." He shook his head. "Lots
of times, it was an older model, one exceptionally valuable." He
sighed. "Now it's just depressing. How Carol grew more and

more sick, marching toward her death, while I bought those cars, trying to hold onto our hobby. That's why I housecleaned all the photos away around here." He waved his arm. "Lucky I didn't buy any cars after '76." He blinked like an owl. "She got terribly sick that year. The three worst years…"

Eve nodded. She'd heard the story several times. "You mean those cars are sitting in a garage somewhere — to this day? All sixteen?"

What kind of shape would they be in by now? She pictured them as dusty relics.

"And in excellent condition," he said, answering her unvoiced question. "Have a fellow who tends to them. Gus Atkins. He drives them enough to keep them sprightly, rotates tires, washes and waxes them, takes them in for special maintenance, orders parts from European suppliers, that sort of thing. Been doing it for years." He grabbed an invoice from the pile. "Here's his monthly charges."

"Wow!" Could the numbers be right? "You don't drive them anymore? Never take them out on the road?"

The numbers on the invoice were ridiculous. None of her junk needed to be cared for to the tune of… She nearly gasped when she added it up.

Mr. Kowalski looked shocked at the idea of driving them. "Oh, no. Not with my eyes. Haven't been able to drive a car in six years. It became a real problem back when Carol…"

Eve butted in again. "Have you thought about selling them? You could probably put the money to use in some other way. Especially if you don't drive. What's the point, Charlie? Do you go look at them at least?"

He shook his head. "Hard to get there without a car. Ironic, huh? Oh, I don't know, Eve. Those cars were like our children. Each one has its own story. Like the Triumph there," he began to flip through the photos. "Carol saw one at the airport —"

"But children grow up and go away," she interrupted. "You could take a vacation with the profits. Go around the world — twice at least."

He laughed. "I've never wanted to travel — even when I physically could. And Carol — well, you know." He paused. "It was enough for me to travel through the car magazines — to purchase automobiles from Italy, Germany, France. When we could take them out ourselves, it was as good as being there. Each year, we took one or two to a car show or to road rallies. Not too far away, but enough to make it a trip. It was exciting. Something we enjoyed doing together. I have a scrapbook somewhere…"

"Still, the profits from your investment will go to the State of Pennsylvania if you let them sit in those garages."

It was making her angry thinking of it. No children to leave the money to — nobody to profit from this collection — when she'd so many needs herself. Who took care of him after all? She was the only person who came through the door most weeks. One or two old goats stopped by, mostly to watch a 76ers or Flyers' game.

"I never really saw the cars as an investment. I mean, sure, I know they're worth money, but it was something to do together. Carol and me," he repeated. He began to warm to the story. "It was fun deciding which one we'd buy next…"

"When was the last time you went out to see those cars?"

He screwed up his eyes, thinking, "Couple of years probably."

"How can you be sure they're still there? Maybe the guy who tends to them — this Ace fellow — sold them all years ago."

A look of alarm widened Mr. Kowalski's eyes, but then faded. "No, *Gus* wouldn't do anything like that. It's not in him. And anyway, I'd have to sign the title papers over to the new owner. Gus couldn't sell them without my signature."

"I bet he could forge your signature after all these years."

Eve thought she could pull it off. She'd seen his signature enough, and it still looked like the handwriting of a schoolboy from two generations ago. Grade school teachers in his time didn't brook any deviation. She could still picture those flowing cursive letters on a chart above the blackboard.

"You have a real knack for figuring this sort of thing out, Eve. None of this ever occurred to me. But if you knew Gus, you'd see why. He's crazy about those cars. Probably thinks of my babies as his by now—you're right there. But there's not a streak of larceny in him. I could go out there today and all sixteen would be sitting in their spots in perfect condition. I trust him the same as I trust you."

"I'm sure he does think of them as his, which is exactly why we should go over and see them someday," she said. "Make sure they're in tiptop shape. Could be they're rusting away. Bud can come along. He'll get a kick out of it. Loves cars."

Or she assumed he did. Didn't all men? Anyway, it wasn't about the cars.

"Let's do it," he said. "The garage is in Southampton."

"I'll get Bud to drive us out. It'll be a nice outing. We need to get out more."

It took the two of them several months to separate Charlie Kowalski from his cars. The first two months were spent talking Mr. Kowalski into selling the first one. After that the dominoes fell more easily.

"I don't see what harm comes from leaving things as they are," he'd say each time Eve brought the subject up. "I got enough money for my few needs without selling my cars. Carol wouldn't like it." A worried look furrowed his brow.

"You have no heirs," she reminded him. "You might as well

get some pleasure out of the money while you still can."

"I do have heirs," he said stubbornly. "I've left the cars to a few local charities."

"Those charity people — well, they won't take the time to get a good price for them. What does the Red Cross or Salvation Army know about cars anyway? I imagine they'll hand them over to some service who will sell them in bulk." Bud had thought of this argument only the night before. "You can leave those charities more money if Bud helps you. He can make sure you get the best prices. We can also make sure the cars go to people who will love them, too." Sometimes it felt like they were talking about dogs or horses. But this sort of argument eventually won him over, although Gus, his mechanic, was none too happy about it.

"You know," Gus, a stocky fellow with muscular arms and short, thin legs, told her bluntly one day, "you're taking away the one thing he has left. He don't care about money. He's got no place to go — nothing he wants to buy."

But Gus was eventually worn down by the deal's inevitability, and the promise of a fair share. He wasn't getting any younger himself and hadn't had the nerve to tell Mr. Kowalski his salary had needed to be raised for years. No harm in putting a little something in the bank. Not if the cars were going to be sold out from under him.

After both men saw the light, things went quickly. With Bud charging a fee for his role in locating buyers, and a cooked sales slip, they made a tidy sum. Mr. Kowalski didn't realize their share in the profits was nearly equal to his. He was sad — it was bringing back memories of a happier time, and Eve had to buck him up. Gus settled for a flat sum equaling his salary for the next year or so.

"Kowalski could be dead tomorrow and then where would you be," Bud reminded him.

"Carol would've wanted you to have this little nest egg," Eve told Mr. Kowalski. "Those cars make you sad anyway. Right? I can see it when you talk about them. You never once pulled out the scrapbook until I asked about it. Didn't go out to see them either." She was trying to buck herself up as much as him. She'd grown fond of the old coot.

And soon Charlie Kowalski trusted Eve and Bud to invest his profits wisely, which they did. A month or two later, Eve quit her job as his housekeeper, citing her desire to spend more time with her toddler. She had her nest-egg now and would never hold a regular job again.

CHAPTER
Twenty-Three

I began to see my mother more clearly after Ryan's birth—and what I saw wasn't reassuring. Now it wasn't just *me* getting pushed, pulled, and manipulated by whatever mood struck her, whatever scam she was putting into place. It was my helpless baby brother on the rack.

Her relationship with Bud Pelgrave really worried me. As bad as Mickey had been, and he'd been a first-class jerk, Bud had the smell of a possible felon about him. He was also a quack. I worried he was pulling Mother into schemes that might land her in jail. Bigger schemes than she'd come up with on her own. Her money-making methods of the past were small-time, and perhaps Bud had more grandiose ideas. If only I had someone to talk with about it. But, like always, I was pretty much on my own in dealing with my mother. I careened back and forth between hoping she'd get caught before things went too far and dreading it.

If Mother went to jail, Ryan might go into foster care since my grandmother would probably be considered too old to raise a small child. I was eighteen but still in high school with no way to support us. I crossed my fingers and began to look at college brochures. Mother would have to do for now. Despite my concern for Ryan, other things began to draw my interest.

Daddy began paying attention to me. I'd reached an age when we could have discussions about adult topics. And since I was no longer my mother's biggest ally, he could criticize her openly. I might confide my concern about Bud if he approached me the right way — if he gave me an opening.

"I'll pay for any school you can get into, Christine," Daddy said. "What about a school in New England? I bet you could get into Harvard or Yale. They take girls now, right? What were those SAT scores again?"

We were out at his house in Bucks County, a place I'd visited no more than a couple times a year since their divorce. But now I was getting to be a regular. Making friends with the people my mother so feared. I was able to handle them too. I found things to laugh about with my grandmother Moran, and especially enjoyed reviving my relationship with Aunt Linda. We had a history, one mostly based on Mother's absences, but still a history. I went to a dance at the country club, lunched in some of the ritzy New Hope restaurants. The food was spectacular, and Daddy had bought me several of the nicest dresses I'd ever owned. It's not that this new life, with its intimations of luxury, its hanging with the swells, was all that important to me — it wasn't. But I loved being close to someone finally and the Morans filled the bill. Having a grown daughter was easier for Daddy than having one dependent on him. Our new relationship assuaged his guilt for the past.

I looked around his place constantly for a sign of a female presence but found none. No extras toothbrushes, no female products. If Mother was the soul of indiscretion, Daddy was not. He must've had serious relationships — I knew he almost married once or twice—but he was mum with me. His house, decorated without Mother's help, was sleek and masculine. He had a single, huge canvass on the living room wall and not a knick-knack of any kind on a table top. The window faced a horse farm next door. Maybe I could get into country life. But there was Ryan to consider. Mother wouldn't let him come along when I visited Daddy, claiming it was too long a trip.

He poured me a glass of iced tea and passed the sugar and lemon. I took a slice of lemon, shaking my head. "I want to live at home. Ryan's too young."

I didn't have to explain why. Turning Ryan's complete care over to my mother was impossible. Only last week, she ran out to pick up a package at the post office while he was taking a nap.

"I wasn't gone ten minutes," she said, waving a book of stamps in my face when I came home unexpectedly. Did other mothers do this? Had she done this with me? Of course, she had.

"You should go away—you've earned it. Ryan's not your responsibility, Christine" my father said. "Adele will look out for him—she'll spell your mother when necessary." He paused and said quietly, half-believingly. "For all her faults, Eve's not exactly a negligent mother. Or is she?"

But it was too late for these sorts of accusations, so I shook my head.

"No, she's mostly okay."

"She's probably crazy about him. Just like you when you were a tyke."

I said nothing. Somehow I still had a need to protect her. Or was I protecting myself? Was I unwilling to fess up to the role of her accomplice—the one I'd played for so long? Admit to the times I looked the other way, kept mum.

Eve had little interest in Ryan—didn't Daddy know that? It

was me who lavished love on him. It was me he came to when he fell or was sick. But he'd never experienced the manic-mother side of her — the Eve of the Supermom years. She hadn't tried to seduce him as she had me. I came along when she needed such a helpmate. Ryan came after she had one — me. And perhaps Bud too. She could probably be honest with Bud in a way she hadn't been with either Daddy or Mickey. Was that good or bad?

It was possible when Ryan got older and could be of some help to Mother, her feelings for him would change — intensify. If I left home at some point, his value to her would increase. But I didn't intend for such a thing to happen — I was glad there was some distance between them — that he was not completely in her thrall. My brother wasn't going to end up in some courtroom telling a judge some one-night stand had tried to strangle his mother so he had to shoot him. He wouldn't lie so often he forgot what the truth was. He would have friends, be normal.

I wondered for the hundredth time why my father had never asked me outright what actually went on in our apartment on the night Jerry Santini died? Not once in the six years since had he questioned my story, indicated there were some disturbing holes in it, said he was surprised his daughter would have fired six bullets into a breathing person. Didn't it occurred to him murder was something Eve might do, but not me? Didn't he remember her acuity on the gun range.

I was sure my mother now believed the lie we invented — that I shot Jerry Santini to save her — was the truth. The "saving her" part of it *was* God's truth. I hadn't saved her from Jerry but from jail.

"Don't sell yourself short, Christine," Daddy said, drawing me back to the present. "At least go to Penn. You can commute there as easily as Temple or a Penn State campus." He drained his glass. "If Ryan's your primary concern, get an education that will enable you to support him. Sooner or later, your mother's going to do something—well, you know." I nodded. "So far, I've been able to protect her from serious trouble, but she may up the ante on her hi-jinks. This Bud fellow..." Daddy shook his head. "I've no idea what he's up to."

"Me either."

"He's a creep."

I nodded.

Mother was interested in my future too.

"It might pay off if you study business," she'd said only last week. "I could use some help with the new company Bud and me are starting. You could advise me where to invest money. Things are starting to take off. "

"What new business?"

My stomach clenched. Did I truly want to hear it? Wouldn't a deeper knowledge of her schemes make me her accomplice again? Would she suck me in like she had in the past? But she'd grown nearly as mistrustful of me as I had of her. She felt the growing chasm too.

"I don't want to jinx it by talking about it too soon," she'd said. "The start-up money's there. Those cars earned us a tidy fee."

I'd only the vaguest idea of what she meant and didn't ask for clarification.

"Jinx it, jinx it," Ryan said from the floor. He was playing with a Fisher Price farm set. He said it five more times, creating a little song.

Mother stared at him. "Isn't repetition a sign of something bad? Some kind of mental retardation?"

Shooting her a lethal look, I turned to my brother. "It *is* a funny word, Ryan." I crouched to give him a hug. "That's what he means. Right, Mother." I demanded confirmation. "It sounds like music, right."

"You could talk in complete sentences by two."

I felt like strangling her. "He does speak in complete sentences if you bothered to listen."

He was watching us with a worried look on his face. A two-year old shouldn't have to worry, but I remembered worrying at two. Did he already know what his mother was? What was it like when the two of them were alone? Did she pay any attention to him at all?

"I still say something's not quite right with the kid," Mother continued. "He's like a parrot."

"He's supposed to do that," I practically shouted. "He's two. That's how he learns new words. And don't tell me what things I did at two. You were a nutcase, so I can't rely on your observations."

Now it was her turn to steam. "I was fine when you were two," she said. "And I thought we had an agreement about reminding me of those awful times. I'm the one who suffered. You've no idea what those places were like."

"Your life has been nothing but awful times—but mostly because of things you did. I was there. Remember? I was the one who had to watch you when I wasn't actively participating in your shenanigans."

"Watch me? That'll be the day."

But she knew she had me by the throat, drawing my attention to Ryan's presence whenever a college catalog for a school more than a few miles away arrived in the mail.

"Ryan would probably grieve if he couldn't see his big sister. You've let yourself become too important to him."

I couldn't believe the things she was capable of saying. She made it sound like he was my kid. That I was considering abandoning my own child—like she'd abandoned me.

I enrolled at Penn the following fall, living at home. Between my grandmother and me, Ryan was taken care of. Grandmother had mellowed through the years and was as approving with Ryan as she'd been disapproving with Mother and, to a lesser extent, me. Perhaps she favored boys. But I was glad for it. Mother was increasingly preoccupied with Bud and the schemes he'd dreamed up. I didn't ask; she didn't tell—knowing my fealty was weaker than it once was. It was not a good time for her to murder a soda pop salesman. I wasn't sure she could count on me and she wasn't either.

Other than my brief friendship with Neil in high school, I'd yet to have a boyfriend. Or any kind of friend. It was complicated. My mother had demanded most of my attention for sixteen years, and then Ryan came along. Bringing anyone home had always been fraught with problems, and Mother was jealous or suspicious of any activity taking me away from her. At an early age, I got used to it, got used to spending my time with Mother.

Mother: "Do you think that girl's attractive?" She was looking out the window at a friend who was waiting for me. "Hang around with someone who's not good-looking and they'll pull you right down to their level."

Me: "What do her looks have to do with it? She's nice and we both like the same books and movies. We can talk."

Mother: "Talk? She looks sort of sneaky. Like the kind of person who'd tell your deepest secrets to anyone who asked." (This meant Mother's deepest secrets.)

Me: "I never tell her any of our secrets. I'd be too embarrassed. Do you think you're our only topic of conversation?"

This was what it was about: the possibility I might squeal. Tell someone that she'd killed, stolen, and lied her way through life.

And that's how it went, the sort of conversation we had about anyone I mentioned. Better just to keep them away. Keep everything from her.

And it went the other way too. I couldn't depend on Mother to be discreet or appear sane around friends. Nor could I count on which activity she might allude to. Driving outsiders away with a few choice tidbits, true or false, but doled out in some warped way was worth it to her. She was not above mentioning shock therapy or the tactics for catching shoplifters stores employed. I'd already come in on her rolling out a description of The Terraces and the reactions she'd had to various drugs — some poor girl backed against the wall or being spoon fed marshmallow fluff as she regaled her with the story of her strong-arming at Wanamakers when she was a girl, as she put it. She always took a few years off her age, making it appear as if she were a teenager on a bad-hair day who'd run amok. After stories like these, the girl would look at me warily or, on one occasion, with too much interest.

It was all calculated to control me. And the atmosphere she presented to guests generally led to brief relationships. I couldn't be relied on by friends to show up where and when I'd promised. Getting past Mother required more fortitude and imagination than I had, and she wasn't above using Ryan in whatever way she needed.

"I guess he'll be okay over with old Hattie next door. Go ahead with your plans."

Our neighbor was eighty-six, nearly blind, and totally deaf.

But, like any girl of eighteen, I was not impervious to the advances of a male and at Penn I finally, yes, finally, met a boy I really liked: Jason Dobbs. He was pre-med, reasonably goodlooking, and interested in me. And although I'd never be anywhere near as pretty as my mother, I was okay.

"Did you get what Professor Paulson said about Shylock?"

Jason asked me one day after class. Having grown up around money borrowers and lenders, I was able to shed some light on it.

"Literature isn't my strong suit," he added. His eyes were a crazy mix of blue, green, and gray. "If I read novels, I like plain talkers — like Hemingway or Graham Greene. Mysteries or spy stories. Jack London's great too."

Eventually, even I could see Jason was interested in me. Sorting out the reason for his interest was harder. He must want something, I reasoned. Was it my tutoring? Was it sex? Could he spot a potential felon?

He began to wait for me after class, walking with me to the library or to a place to eat lunch. I went home with him a couple of times too — to his parents' house in the Frankfort section of Philly. Their house was chaotic with various half-finished projects, half-finished books, food, lots of food, and a fair share of squabbling, but the Dobbs' were fun to be with. They asked me more questions about my courses and my family than I was used to and, at first, I thought they were overly curious. Did they know about Mother?

But when they asked Jason questions too — I realized this behavior was normal. It was normal for children to take center stage some of the time. It was customary for a mother to want to feed her family, dote on them.

And so that autumn, my life became about me some of the time. I got a taste of counting for something with someone my age. I liked my classes — the work was challenging — and despite Mother's insistence on a business major, I was taking an art history class, a psychology class, and a course on Shakespeare. And actually, I *was* good at math, especially the more esoteric aspects of it. I immersed myself in my classes, and when I had a free moment during the day, I spent it with Jason. It took me eighteen years to discover I had talents, tastes, and needs of my own. Often hours would pass when I didn't give my mother a thought.

Her influence over me continued to decline, growing more strained, more tenuous. I suddenly saw flashes of something I had only vaguely understood before—I had a mother who was greedy, a narcissist, coarse, selfish. In psychology class, I learned the words to describe her.

Few students come home from college and view even the most normal parents in the same light. In my case, my enhanced vision was blinding. The unease I'd begun to experience a year or two earlier with Ryan's birth and Mickey's defection, came careening back at me. Daddy's blunt words, Grandmother's expressed worries, and Aunt Linda's veiled warnings began to take hold.

Spending any extended time with Mother allowed a new seduction to begin. When she put her mind to it, she was hard to resist. She was funny, sharp, still a bright star in the sky. But being away from her shone a spotlight on her flaws.

Although I could've chosen to live in a dorm, an expense Daddy would have paid for, I continued to live with Mother and Ryan. Would she line up my brother as the patsy in her next big scam if I wasn't there? Would he alibi her in some evil activity? Would he be left alone for hours if some opportunity arose? Would he be asked to lie for her in court? To sully his name in order to clear hers? I raced home sooner than I wanted more than once, overcome with fear, asking worriedly,

"What did you two do today?"

"Nothing special," she'd say.

I never believed her and was always looking for signs of criminal activity.

Mother's expectations were I would babysit Ryan weekend nights so she could spend time with Bud Pelgrave, staying overnight at his place, and only returning home if necessity required it. She considered it a fair trade for my unavailability on weeknights when I was studying, writing papers, or taking classes — selfish activities in her mind — anything not centering on her needs was viewed as self-indulgent.

"If you're going to be an accountant, I don't know why you needed to go to Penn," she told me bluntly. "Temple would've done. How can you stand hanging around with those snots? Or those math nerds with the pen protectors in their pockets?"

"It was your idea to be an accountant, not mine."

"But you're so good at math," she said in a wheedling tone.

"Maybe I'll be a math professor."

She looked puzzled. "Why would you want to teach when you can make more money in business? Professors don't make a dime."

At this point our conversation always broke down. She only understood financial goals. Luckily, Jason didn't mind the weekend limitations on our romance. He was a scholarship student and short on cash most of the time, taking part-time jobs wherever he found them. Hanging out at my house was better than sitting in his dorm room, or getting drunk with his dorm-mates, all of whom were younger than he was and consequently not terribly interesting. His parents' house was crowded, boisterous, and he claimed he could get nothing done there. Mother knew he came over but what could she say. She was unwilling to make an issue of it if it meant I might move out.

They met once or twice on her way in or his way in, circling each other apprehensively.

"So you like this Justin, do you? Looks as poor as a church mouse to me."

"He's going to be a doctor," I told her for the tenth time. I didn't bother to correct his name, knowing she'd get it wrong again only to irk me. She trivialized people by forgetting their name, I thought, thinking back to Jerry Santini. She never remembered his name either.

"What is he, a sophomore? Early days yet. Who's gonna cough up the money for med school?"

"He's a vet."

"A dog doctor?"

"A veteran, Mother. Served four years in Germany."

"That war's been over for years," she said, thinking she was shrewd. "I think he's conning you. And the G.I. bill buys him a doctor's degree? How old is he, anyway?"

"Twenty-four."

"A little old for you, isn't he?" I rolled my eyes. Long ago, my mother made it certain any boy my own age would seem immature.

Most of the kids at Penn had money—lots of it—which separated me from them. Daddy paid for my tuition and bought me some nice clothes, but hadn't thought to give me much spending money and certainly not a car. He wasn't used to being generous with us, knowing where any money was likely to go. A job would've helped out, but my real job waited at home—unpaid servitude. Jason led a similarly frugal life.

"You don't want to get too involved with someone who finds poverty and the lifestyle that comes with it so much to his liking," Mother said, after he refused two free tickets to a concert Bud Pelgrave offered us. "Too much pride isn't a good thing."

"He's nice. I like him."

It was always better to speak in simplistic terms with my mother. I didn't want her to think of me as a worthy adversary until I was.

"Nice! Sleeping with him yet?"

When I gave no indication I was going to answer her question, she added, "Make sure you're taking precautions,

Christine. You don't want to get knocked up. You're too smart to let that happen."

She saw no irony in the fact she'd gotten knocked up a few years earlier. And maybe earlier still with me. I wasn't sure. I couldn't imagine her choosing to have a baby. I couldn't imagine my mother wanting a kid — only finding a use for one when I came along.

CHAPTER
Twenty-Four

"I've managed to get along fine without getting tangled up with Wanamaker's again," Eve told Bud. "So I don't like this idea at all." She stretched. "Department stores are pretty sharp at catching shoplifters."

They were at Bud's place, his last client had left minutes earlier. He was wiping the massage table, disposing of the various tools of his trade.

"Must be expensive tossing out all those needles after one use," she said, watching him. "Can't you autoclave them?"

"I did until a friend of mine passed TB on to two patients and got sued for a bundle. Now I get rid of them." He put down the towel. "Look Eve, this little plan has nothing to do with shoplifting. Do you understand the way it works or do I need to go over it again?"

"Forget it. I got a kid at home who needs his mother. I'm not gonna get thrown in the clink. I messed with department stores one time too many."

"Like you're home with Ryan now?" Bud paused a second.

"Hey, forget I said that, baby." He walked over and massaged her neck. "I'm just cranky. Must've walked ten miles with my fingers today." He examined his hands and shook his head. "Can you hand me the moisturizer?" He gestured with his head toward the cabinet, his ponytail slapping his neck. "Washing my hands a dozen times a day is taking the skin off." He held them out and she nodded. She felt them on her body often enough.

"You probably need some subscription stuff for those mitts." She handed him the cream, sighing. "Okay. Explain it to me again."

The plan or scam was simple, provided you had a guy who could make counterfeit IDs, counterfeit checks, counterfeit handicap permits, licenses.

Bud had such a guy: Willie Bishop. "We'll have to give Willie a bundle, but it'll be worth it. I've stolen checks from mailboxes once or twice, but you have to be too damn quick. Passing a check from a fictitious person is much easier than passing off a stolen one. You're never sure how quickly someone will discover one's missing. So you have another adversary to deal with."

Eve looked blank.

"Beside the store. That's what I mean, Eve." He shook his head. "Now I know you're going to understand this once we put it into play. You're too damned smart to let a simple little job like this one trip you up. It's going to be easy-peasy. You'll see."

It turned out he was right. She was adept at it within days. Her favorite stores to hit quickly became Bloomingdales and Lord and Taylor. The ones from twenty years earlier were disappearing, one after the other. She preferred those two stores to JC Penney or Sterns or any of the smaller or more modest stores because looking like the customer that store personnel expected to find at the counter was more than half the challenge. It was hard for her to dress like a Penney's patron. It made her feel bad about herself to put on a polyester pantsuit and cheap shoes. If she stormed into Lord and Taylor's dressed like a rich woman in a hurry, the clerks accommodated her. They scrambled to serve her.

She'd buy some expensive items with a counterfeit check and return the goods an hour or two later for cash. Thanks to Bud's pal, she carried a wallet full of fraudulent IDs. She had to be quick though. Sometimes she and Bud altered the date on the receipt, too. It felt great to get something back from the kind of establishments that had sent her to the "country club" all those years ago. Once, on a dare from Bud, she stole a crocodile handbag from Wanamaker's. Her heart raced as she headed for the door, but nobody gave her a second glance. Nobody expected that a well-dressed woman pushing an expensive stroller with an adorable child in it was up to no good. Profiling was a long way off.

I didn't know about any of this.

"Where are all these clothes coming from?" I asked her, looking in horror as the piles on her bureau and hangers in her closet grew in number. She'd resumed her old methods of housekeeping once Mickey fled the scene and the tabletops were spilling over with new stuff.

She had a shitty, shifty look on her face that always meant trouble.

"Bud's hired me as an associate." She was looking everywhere in the room but at me. "I told you about this already—about how we had a business starting up. I'm gonna pay visits to doctors' offices and hand out brochures. Maybe try a few rehab centers—that sort of thing. I have to look professional. "

This was a complete lie, but it would be a while before I knew it. Before Jason, when my attention was fixed on her like a spotlight, I might have realized the unlikelihood of her spending her days passing out brochures for a boyfriend.

"And you're going to wear this?" I said, holding up a negligee.

"Bud said to get a few things for myself. I do get paid for my work."

I felt like asking her what kind of work she was getting paid to do in negligees, but bit my tongue as I'd done a thousand times before.

"Who's going to watch Ryan while you're…selling Bud's services?" My brother was now too active for my grandmother to watch for any length of time. But Mother would never admit this.

"Oh, I can take him along. I only drive to a few offices at a time. Ryan actually helps me out—being such a cutie pie." She crinkled her face, and I struggled not to barf.

But that part *was* true. He was the lynchpin in Mother's new scheme. But the venue for her endeavors was not doctors' offices.

Eve dressed Ryan more carefully than she dressed herself, buying him little sailor outfits, baseball uniforms—anything drawing attention away from the bogus IDs she offered stores, away from the fraudulent amounts on a receipt she handed over for a refund. He was her greatest diversion, thwarting, through his charm, the possibility that too much attention would be focused on her transactions. She learned quickly how welcoming department stores were to attractive women with cute babies, women who appeared to have plenty of money to spend and the will to spend it. In other words, her.

"What a darling child," the person in line in front of her at the cash register might say, drawing the eyes and attention of the clerk and other customers away. "What a sweet outfit."

Within weeks, Eve began to test the boundaries of their little scam. She'd pick an expensive item off a store rack—something like a silk blouse or a cashmere scarf—and surreptitiously rip off the alarm tags with a tool Bud gave her. Next, she'd push Ryan over to the service desk, seemingly overwhelmed by her child, her shopping bags, coats, his toys, and ask for a refund. She usually had a number of legitimate purchases she piled on the counter, creating a certain amount of chaos for the clerk. Most of the time, the clerks, taken aback by the atmosphere surrounding her, handed her a refund without asking for a receipt. She often chose an hour when the clerks were likely to be busy and anxious to send her on her way: Saturday afternoon was the best time. If she couldn't remove the tag with her tool, she slipped it inside a foil bag and exited the store and had Bud remove it later.

One of her favorite schemes operated like this. She'd purchase an appliance at Strawbridge's or even Korvettes. She'd take the receipt to a Xerox machine—most libraries had them—and make a copy. Next she'd show up at the same chain, but a different location, take the same item from the shelves, and return it using the Xeroxed receipt. When this went well, after the first time or two, she made ten receipts and pulled this stunt at ten different branches of the store over a few days' time—the more quickly the better.

"My, God, this is child's play," she told Bud. "And it serves them right with the prices they charge." What she really thought about was the money. What kind of junk she could buy with it.

Just sashaying through these elegant stores day after day had lit the fire.

But buying too many things soon became a problem. "You can't draw attention to yourself," Bud told her. It was better to act like nothing had changed. So she put the desire to buy things on hold mostly and satisfied herself with piling up the dough and pleasing Bud.

"Baby, you're a natural," he'd say, counting the cash.

She beamed, picturing what she'd soon be able to buy. It was like burying the money in the desert in the old westerns or crime movies. The dollars might not be marked, but they were flags when too much was spent.

Soon driving to New Jersey or Delaware became commonplace. An overnight trip to New York netted many thousands of dollars.

"We can't stuff all of this in a drawer anymore," Bud said. They both eyed the money sitting in neat piles on Bud's kitchen table. "And we certainly can't put too much of it in our bank accounts."

"So what then?" Eve asked. "What do we do?"

I was not so infatuated with Jason nor so preoccupied with my schoolwork that I did not begin to intuit something bigger than usual was going on with my mother. It began to occur to me that what I thought was paste might be the real thing. She was often humming when I came into the house, was often on the phone with Bud.

Bud. He knew what I thought of him and avoided me as much as possible. When we ran in to each other, we exchanged wary glances. If my mother was intent on choosing men like this, I didn't have to please them any longer. No sitting on laps, no asking his permission to babysit, no taking the fall.

Mother still kept all her junk. Nothing got tossed — even the most trivial item was stored away. I began to wonder if she also kept records of her various "purchases." Was there a box somewhere with the records I had childishly written for her during the days of her return business? Was there a record of her court dates, her psychiatric visits, the various things she'd stored in all of those units? What schemes with Bud Pelham had allowed her to increase her wardrobe purchases, buy a new car, and all the new things at home. And this was only the stuff I knew about. What else had she been up to in the hours I was at school or away? If she couldn't toss her junk, could she toss her records? Did a hoarder hold onto paperwork as tightly as product?

It seemed like a good idea to bring myself up to speed on Mother's various purchases, thefts, incidents. At sometime in the near future, I might need to lay my hands on such information. If my priority now was Ryan, in preventing him from being used as I'd been, I needed to be ruthless in bringing my mother down.

CHAPTER
Twenty-Five

started at my grandmother's house. "You really want to go through all her stuff," my grandmother said. "You'll be in that cellar for a year." Grandmother was wearing rubber gloves and scrubbing a trash can. The water coming out of it was as clean as what went into it.

"You know there are probably a hundred or more boxes. Half of 'em haven't been opened in a decade. More."

"I'm working on a project for my social anthropology class," I said. "We're supposed to record the things family members have collected over time. A kind of social history of the last century."

This sounded ridiculous and my grandmother seemed doubtful — but only for a second. I remember her incredulity when I told her I was able to identify hundreds of famous paintings on slides. She was as pragmatic as my mother in what she thought worth studying.

"When will you need to identify all those pictures? In real life, I mean," she'd asked me. "You'd be better off learning shorthand or nursing." She'd given me a book on shorthand at Christmas, advising me to learn it on my own.

"I'm pretty sure shorthand's on its way out," I told her.

"Well, don't make a mess down there, Christine," she told me today. "It's taken me years to get Eve's things boxed and correctly labeled. She had things packed away willy-nilly. I labeled each and every box, though she'd probably kill me if she knew it. But I couldn't bear the thought of passing away and someone thinking the chaos was mine."

I nodded sympathetically. If things turned out the way I expected, a cop or two might find their way down there.

Grandmother's basement was organized like an extremely tidy warehouse. All of the windows in her basement shone as brightly as the ones a floor above. There was not a cobweb or a dust ball to be found. She was right behind me then, turning on lights as we crossed the room.

"Now don't trip over anything," she said, worriedly. "I only have forty-watt bulbs here. Maybe I should change one or two."

"When you were organizing Mother's things, did you run across any paperwork; you know—boxes with records in them." Seeing the skepticism on her face, I quickly added, "Our professor would like us to include any documentation we can locate. He says people who keep records of their hobbies or pursuits provide society with an invaluable history." My years with Mother had apparently taught me to how to lie.

And I was starting to believe in this professor and his assignment myself. Perhaps when this was over with, I would embark on such a study—maybe writing a book about Mother and her sickness. Save other children from living the life of a scapegoat.

"I think there are also boxes with papers in them. Not sure exactly what. Divorce papers, that sort of thing. Your mother added a box or two in the last six months. I glanced through it briefly. Records about antique cars. Maybe for the guy she kept house for." She put a finger to her lips. "You mustn't tell her I check the boxes, Christine. She wouldn't like it at all. No sir." A light bulb in hand now, she changed the one over my head, walking over to a group of red-striped boxes. "Still if I'm going to keep her things for her, I need to know what I'm getting myself into." She paused. "Never know when I'll be hauled into court." She sighed. "You might as well start here."

"We'll keep my project between us," I said, cementing our relationship as co-conspirators. "I'll make sure things are on the up and up while I'm at it." Little likelihood of that happening, I thought, taking the lid off the first box.

Anyway, finding a noose to hang her would be better than hanging her myself.

"*Do you* really mean it?" Jason asked when I let that idea slip. The notion I might have to kill her. "You shouldn't joke about it."

"I suppose not," I said. But I knew I would go pretty far to put an end to it.

"Think about Ryan," he'd said. "What would happen to him without a mother or a sister? Do you want him living with Mickey? Or in foster care?"

I waited until Grandmother climbed the stairs, gripping the railing till her knuckles turned white. In her late sixties now, but she was beginning to wear out. Being Eve's mother probably hadn't helped. Her husband hadn't been the easiest man either from what I remembered. He skittered out of my head as readily as he'd skittered out of any room Eve and, by extension, me, were in.

There was no way Grandmother could take care of Ryan fulltime.

How long would it be before I looked years older than my age. Daddy certainly did. He was as tidy as ever but he had a bend in his back, deep lines in his face, and his hair was mostly gray. He was not fifty. He'd probably never marry again. How could he take such a chance? Who knew where another Eve lurked?

I began going through the boxes with resolve.

CHAPTER
Twenty-Six

"**D**o you think Christine might have any idea of how to deal with this? The money I'm forking over to that school should buy me something useful."

Bud and Eve were driving home from Wilmington in a stinging rain, trying to make their nine o'clock deadline. Adele had told Eve flatly she wouldn't keep Ryan past nine.

"Why can't he spend the night?" Eve asked. "He loves to sleep over."

Her mother refused, saying she needed some time to herself. "He's always awake once or twice a night. You forget how old I am. It's not like it was with Christine. And where is it you go three or four times a week, Eve? Why does a masseuse need to travel so much? And overnight trips?" The pipes howled as she turned on the kitchen tap to fill the kettle. "I know you're up to no good."

"He's not a masseuse, Mother," Eve snapped. "He's a physical therapist, a holistic consultant. He gets referrals throughout the tri-state area now. His out-of-state patients pay for his gas and time, you know."

Adele shook her head. "And why is it you have to go along with him? What exactly do you do on these trips?"

"Oh, it's hard to explain, Mother." When her mother continued to stare at her, she added. "He likes to have company on the drive. Narcolepsy, I think it's called." Her mother was stymied by the word. "He falls asleep at the wheel."

"Oh, for heaven's sake, Evelyn. You'd better drive."

Eve had no idea how she came up with that one. "For the love of God, don't speed, Bud. Especially not in this weather. All we need is for some cop to pull us over and go through the car."

She glanced back at the rear seat where various folders and a few unreturned items sat. They'd have to return them at the King of Prussia Mall or something. It was always easiest to return merchandise at the store where you purchased it, but sometimes it didn't work out.

He slowed down. "You know what they convicted Al Capone for, don't you?"

"What the hell are you talking about? Speeding?"

He gave her a look of disgust. "They convicted Capone of tax evasion when they figured out how much money was sitting in his bank account. He couldn't account for it. That's the thing. You have to show where money came from. Keep records"

"Why would anyone think to look at our bank accounts? And we have a few dummy ones, right? Your guy set them up? It's not all in two accounts?"

Bud shook his head. "We need someone smarter than Willie Bishop. He's okay for making fake IDs, stuff like that. But not for this kind of thing. We need someone smart enough to hide it good."

"I don't think Christine knows enough about such things

to "hide it good" if that's what you have in mind. It's not something they teach in an introductory business course. Plus I don't trust her anymore. She's moody. And this boyfriend of hers…"

"You don't trust her? After all the stuff you told me? She took the rap for you with the beverage salesman, right? The one who put the moves on you?"

Is that what she'd told him? She couldn't remember exactly. Pillow talk. When she thought back on her life, there was a gauzy curtain over parts of it. Maybe the haziness was a result of the drugs she'd taken. Or the shocks. Hank and his bevy of doctors had made her loopy. Burned through essential circuits in her brain, clogged them up. Something.

Bud reached over and fiddled with the radio. "Disco might be over, but damn it ruined music. Will you listen to this shit?" A wailing voice filled the car. "Who the hell are *Jack and Diane?*"

Eve shrugged. "Find an oldies station. Yeah, Christine helped me out back then. It was shoes, wasn't it? He sold shoes. How ridiculous."

"I think you said you met him in a shoe store."

"Oh, right. Soda, he sold soda. Anyway, recently Christine's turned into a —daddy's girl. The two of them hover over her course selections, spend time together every weekend. It figures Hank would take an interest in her now she's an adult—after I put in all the hard years—supported her all this time." She brushed his hand away from the dial as another song began. "Hey I love that song—*Private Eyes*. Leave it on."

"Those two are the biggest fags I've ever laid eyes on."

"You don't know that. And so what if they are. It's a cool song."

They crossed into Pennsylvania, a sign announcing it. The rain had tapered off and Eve finally relaxed, listening more intently as Bud said, "Anyway, we're getting off the subject here. We need to deposit this money in banks. Lots of banks, lots of accounts. I heard some guy in Florida refer to it as smurfing."

"You mean like those little blue squirts on TV."

She guessed giving each one of those Smurfs an occupation was the only way to tell them apart, to sell more than one to kids. She remembered one with a hockey stick, another on a bike. A mushroom hut to live in. What the hell were they anyway? Smurfs?

He nodded. "That's where the term came from. For our purposes, you get a lot of little squirts or Smurfs to head out to a lot of little banks, open accounts, and deposit small sums. I'm talking a dozen or more. Two dozen even. Spread the wealth around." He thought for a minute. "You don't want more than a hundred bucks or so in each account at first. You don't want to attract attention. Smurfs are the kind of people you get to deposit small change. They get a little cut."

She shook her head. "No way am I gonna bring a dozen people into this. Remember what happened with my return business. I was practically a wage slave of the postal carriers union by the time I pulled the plug. Let's find something else. Some other way of hiding the dough."

He continued patiently. "Don't you have a few friends from your days at the hotel? They'd probably do it for some phony IDs, green cards—something easy to get."

"Maybe. But in the meantime, maybe we can do it ourselves. We're not big-time yet. We can open accounts in banks around here using various names and disguises." A frown came over her face. "Let's leave things alone for now. The more people, the more worries."

"You're thinking too small, Eve. Leave it to me. I'll work it out." He jerked the wheel suddenly as they almost missed Roosevelt Boulevard.

"Geez, I hate this drive. Let's shop in New Jersey next time."

CHAPTER
Twenty-Seven

got to Box#74 before I came on something interesting.
Woolworth's Five and Dime had sent my grandfather,
Herbert Hobart, a letter in 1954, outlining certain conditions
to be met to avoid the prosecution of his daughter for theft of
several objects. This was a duplicate of the original, which he'd
apparently signed and returned. My mother would've been
sixteen. It was not one of Mother's boxes, I noticed, looking at
the top where it read Hobart. It was my grandfather's records
and included mostly tax information, social security paperwork.
It was a miracle I went through it.

So Mother's thieving had begun in high school. Not so
unusual. Had she told me this story? Over the years, I had heard
many tales but perhaps not this one. Did my grandfather's
antipathy for her begin with this?

The most unusual thing about her behavior was that it
continued, unabated, for the next twenty-seven years.

More than a dozen boxes held the records of the return
business, much of it in my childish handwriting. Along with the

records, I found copies of letters various businesses had sent to Mother, some threatening her with prosecution for attempting to extort goods and/or money, some shaking a finger at her but nothing more.

I found the remnants of other endeavors, too: things I'd never heard about. Dummy receipts for items customers purchased at Morans Stationery Store in Hatboro in the early seventies. Receipts for more recent purchases of expensive items. I had only the faintest memory of Mother working at Daddy's store. I found box after box of cheap jewelry, the tags still on them, things that looked like gold but weren't. And finally, I found the box of transactions for the cars. Mr. Kowlaski's antique cars. I assembled my own box of things and managed to get out of the house without too many questions from my grandmother.

"Find what you need?" my grandmother asked me, looking over the top of her glasses as she sewed a small tear in a terrycloth dishtowel. I nodded. "Hope your report gets a good mark," she said as I left. "You're a much better student than your mother. Can't remember her once writing a report."

"Oh, Christine," she said as I headed for the door. I turned around. "You did leave it tidy, right? Just like you found it?"

Nodding, I left, wondering what her reaction would be if she knew what was really in my red-striped cardboard box.

I had no precise plan for these records, but knew they weren't safe at home. A stray box would immediately attract Mother's attention. Keeping an eye on things that entered our apartment came naturally to her. So I rented my own small storage box—finding a place she hadn't used in the phonebook. I knew all the ins and outs of storage rental and my unit was hardly bigger than the size of a foot locker. But it was large enough for now. I badly wanted to talk with someone. Daddy? Grandmother? Aunt Linda? None of these possibilities felt right. These people had all jumped headlong into the murky waters Eve stirred years ago. Each had sins to cover, their own guilt or innocence to protect. None would want to admit they'd aided and abetted Mother in her crimes.

Of course, I'd played a bigger role than most of them. It was my childish handwriting on the returns; I claimed to have murdered her lover; I sat home with Ryan while she bilked Charlie Kowalski out of tens of thousands of dollars.

So Jason became my confidante. We sat in his car with the box between us. Where else could we go? I passed him documents, one after the other, watching the expression on his face. Every so often he exhaled his disbelief, but he didn't say much. Just asked a sporadic question.

"Who's this guy?" he asked when he got to the antique cars. I told him what I knew—which was little. We knew his name from the signatures and an address. I could only remember a few words here and there about "poor Charlie." I hadn't paid enough attention to her since I had begun to acquire a life of my own.

"My grandmother will fill me in. Mom kept house for him for a while."

Although I'd never called my mother anything but Mother, my use of the word always raised Jason's eyebrows. So I began to amend it. Mom. Somehow it put a larger distance between us. Me and this "mom" had less history.

Jason shook his head. "She kept more than that. I don't know much about the price of antique cars, but it sure looks like they took him for a bundle."

"Do you see why killing her might be the easiest thing? Do you see why I want to?" I didn't know if or how I would, but the thought was still there. Always there.

"If getting Ryan out of her clutches and into yours is your primary goal, you can't do it from a jail cell." It always came back to Ryan. I'd gone from saving my mother to saving my brother without a beat in between.

When Jason was finished looking through the documents and papers, he looked up. "So what are you going to do about this? Go to your father? The cops?" He swallowed hard. "Or her?"

By now, I think he was as scared of my mother as the rest of us.

"My father knows about a lot of it. Certainly about the Wanamaker's thefts. Probably about all of the return business since he had to pay people off." I thought for a minute, trying to put it together. "I know he bailed her out once or twice for small things. Greased some wheels, filled a few pockets. Probably not about the cars though. And whatever's going on now. Did you see the new TV?"

"So she's done some time?" he asked.

I nodded. "And done some time in hospitals." I sounded breathless—I'd been trained so well that saying this aloud was hard.

But I'd already told him most of it after all. "Your father probably doesn't know about her record as a teenage shoplifter. Can't imagine your grandparents sharing that information with the prospective groom." I shook my head. "So you really think she's up to something now? Something with Bud."

"Yes."

It was going to be harder than I thought to betray my mother. I already had a sick feeling in my stomach. Telling Jason was the first step on my road toward disclosure to someone official. I was practicing for what would be my ultimate act of disloyalty. It was coming and coming quickly. I wasn't sure what would trigger it. What would push me over the line? And what would happen to Ryan? Would I be able to take care of him? Would I be allowed to keep him? Would I have to prove I didn't really murder anyone—that I was her original puppet?

Or a ventriloquists' dummy perhaps, only speaking the words I was primed to say. I wondered if Cy Granholm was still around. Was it possible he'd admit to the truth? Not unless he was willing to hand over his license, be disbarred.

"One thing," Jason said, closing the lid. "You have to be sure you're out of harm's way. You know from experience she'll try to pin it on you. Make like it was your math skills that helped her—that are helping her now." He squinted as the sun broke through the clouds.

I had told him about Jerry Santini too. It was the first time I had said the words aloud to anyone other than that fruitcake doctor. Six years of silence.

I don't think he quite believed it, coming from a normal family as he did. I don't think he believed a mother would pin a murder on her twelve-year old. He reached out and put an arm around me.

"I think you should go to your father. He's dealt with her in the past, right?"

"But only to paper things over usually. He was her husband during most of it and maybe didn't have much choice. But he hasn't been her husband for a long time. I'm in college now and Ryan's not his kid to worry about. Or probably isn't. Why would he get involved with her again?"

"He won't want you to get into trouble whether you're eight or eighteen"

Jason didn't know Daddy at all. Had never met him. Coming from his family, he couldn't begin to understand mine. Didn't know about the years when Daddy was quite content to have me raised by whoever came along. I couldn't see Daddy saving me, and most of all, Ryan. Things between us were better now, but it didn't rewrite the past.

"So you think you should go to the police?"

"If it comes to that," I said.

I'd go immediately if I knew what would happen with Ryan. I couldn't take a chance that ratting her out would make his life worse. I had to figure out how to avoid it.

I could see Jason thought I was being too hard on my father. "I'm going to tell you something," I said, swallowing hard. Thinking about all of it had a way of making bile creep up my throat. "Daddy never once asked me what happened the night Jerry Santini died. Never asked if the story I told the police was true though he knew what Mother was capable of." Jason shook his head. "Now does that sound like a father to take this tale to?"

CHAPTER
Twenty-Eight

The edge I'd be pushed over was still a few days away. I came in unexpectedly and found Ryan dressed in a sailor outfit.

"Why's he dressed like that?" I asked, finding Mother in the bathroom applying makeup. "Did you enlist him while I was out?"

Her hand moved expertly—the line across her lid was perfect. My brother was wearing a particularly elaborate suit with a matching coat and hat. It boasted epaulets on the shoulders and anchors on the socks. Ryan outgrew clothes in a few months at his age, and I thought he looked ridiculous— like one of those miniature poodles old ladies dress. He was sitting on the floor like a nineteenth-century doll, getting more agitated by the minute.

"I'm hot," he told me. He began struggling to undo the buttons. "Mommy!"

"Wait a sec, baby. Doesn't he look darling?" she asked me through the mirror. "Everyone raves about him."

"Who's everyone?" I was close enough to hear her breathe.

There was no *everyone* in our lives. Or no one I knew anyway.

She took a long pause as she capped the eyeliner. "Oh, you know. People at the businesses where I go." She saw it wasn't enough information to satisfy me. "Bud's patients mostly."

Now it was me who caught my breath. "You're pimping him, aren't you?

"Bud?" she said, not getting my meaning. "Bud's no pimp." She turned around when I didn't respond. "What the hell are you're talking about." The menace in her eyes was palpable as she began to get my meaning.

"Ryan," I said. "You're pimping Ryan."

In a flash, she raised a hand and slapped me. It wasn't a hard slap—I was too close to her for her to get much arm into it—but it still stung. I think it may have been the first time she ever hit me, not that she hadn't done far worse. We both stood there silently. I fought back a strong desire to grab a razor blade from the medicine chest and slit her throat. It was mere inches away. The image of the blood running down her neck was mesmerizing.

Finally, she said, "Sorry, Baby. I shouldn't have done that. I don't think you realize what the word means. But when you put it together with Ryan's name like you did, well, it made me see red. Do you know what a pimp is?"

For years she'd treated me like I was years older than I was. Now the pendulum had swung. I was too immature to understand anything.

I groaned. "Certainly, I know what it means. You're using Ryan in whatever it is you're doing to get money. Whatever scheme you and your boyfriend have put into motion. You're taking him along to divert people. Curry favor. Something like that. That's what pimping is. It's not always sexual." I put my hand to my stinging cheek. "Or perhaps you're too immature to understand that. Too uneducated."

Sighing, she closed the medicine chest door and stepped back, taking a last look at her face. She hadn't broken a bead of sweat over my accusation.

"Look, I need to earn a living and I can't leave him with your grandmother all the time. So I take him along. It doesn't hurt things if he looks cute. You're right about that part." She stepped out of the bathroom and I followed her. "It's not like you're Johnny-on-the-spot. Not since Joseph came along."

"I'm here now," I told her. "Professor Meek canceled class. I can watch him today."

"Oh, he's all ready to go now. Look at him." She walked into the living room with me one step behind her. "I hate to disappoint him." She swept him off the floor and carrying him under her arm like a football, headed for the door. "We enjoy our little mother and son outings. Don't we?" She was practically cooing.

I felt faint, but kept up with her. "Wouldn't you rather stay with me," I asked Ryan. This was the clincher: this was the moment of decision.

"No. I wanna go with Mama." He hadn't even hesitated.

It was Ryan's Jerry Santini day; he'd fallen for Mother Love too. Mother was the glamorous one, the one to be courted. I remembered that special feeling well—the heart swell I felt when Mother returned from wherever she was, replacing Mrs. Murphy or Aunt Linda in my life. Now it was Ryan's turn to feel it.

I didn't know where they were going or what they were up to, but Ryan was being used like I was, time and time again. I'd thought our bond—Ryan's and mine—was the more important one, but I'd fooled myself. I could never match Mother's ability to seduce. She had honed it for forty years. Her electricity may have dimmed a bit but mine was no competition. And never would be.

Mother smiled, saying, "Of course you do, Ryan. Christine can stay here and work on her schoolwork. That's the most important thing to her. Getting those A's her Daddy likes. Getting *educated*."

Speechless, I watched her bundle him into a stroller and head out the door. At the window, I saw Bud Pelgrave waiting for them in his flashy new car. I picked up the phone and called Jason. "They're leaving right now."

"What?"

"Ryan was dressed like a Victorian doll. I've got to find out what she's up to."

"If I'm going to follow them, Christine, I'll need some notice," he said. "It's not like I live around the corner."

I thought about this. "You're right," I said. "It'll have to be me." I paused. "Could I borrow your car for a day or two?"

CHAPTER
Twenty-Nine

It was a week later. I watched them enter and exit four department stores out on the Main Line. Packages under an arm or in the stroller coming out, packages hauled back into another store fifteen or twenty minutes later. It didn't take a criminal mind to figure it out. That night when I returned his car, I told Jason, "She must be using Ryan as a diversion. And there's probably more going on—stuff I can't spot. I wonder if we could get into his office."

"Whose office?"

"Guess?"

"Now how are we going to do that?"

"I bet anything she's got copy of his office keys. She's a key junkie—you should see the ring she carries. She can probably let herself into houses and offices up and down the coast."

It was easy to eliminate some of the keys on her chain—our door, the car keys, Grandmother's house, the key to her safes and storage units. I was shocked to see there were almost a dozen. Some looked old, but others were shiny new. While she was taking a nap one afternoon, I made copies of the remaining ones. The storage keys were easy to ID, tagged with the unit's location.

It only took a few tries before I got the knob on Bud's office door to turn. Bud and Mom were out for the evening so Jason and I brought Ryan with us. "What are we looking for," Jason asked. "Any specific ideas?"

"Some proof of—of whatever the deal is," I said, making a play area for Ryan by moving some chairs and cushions around. I handed him a bag of his plastic animals, which he immediately began to set up in this exciting new environment. Smiling encouragingly, I said, "Whatever she's up to now 'cause I know it's the biggest scam yet. So let's hunker down and find something to turn over to the cops. Or to my Dad before she brings the roof down on us."

We began going through drawers. Bud had a lot of them— half of his back room was filled with file cabinets. It was nearly all patient records inside.

"Old Bud certainly has a thriving business," I said. "Hard to believe such a sleazy guy could attract so many patients. I've never been sure what it is he does either. Is he masseuse to the stars?" Suddenly my hand froze. The name on the top of the file in my hand read *Adele Hobart.* "Grandmother," I said uneasily. "Jason, look. This is my grandmother's file. I can't believe she came to this guy 'cause she hates him as much as I do. Is he billing her for treatments she didn't have?"

Jason came over and took the file from my hand. A few seconds later, he whistled. "Not her, Christine. Medicare. He's billing Medicare for treatment. He's billed them for nearly a year's worth of visits from her. Twice a month. For her spine problems." He started shuffling through the file. "I wonder how many of these other so-called patients are on Medicare." He whipped around. "All of them. Look at their dates of birth.

Somehow he's gotten hold of their Medicare numbers and billed treatment." At the back of the drawer, he found a long list of names and Medicare numbers. "I think Bud's managed to get his hands on their social security numbers. He could be stealing from them too."

"How'd he get them?" I asked. "Maybe my mother gave him my grandmother's information, but what about the rest."

There had to be a hundred files like my grandmother's.

He flopped into the chair, thought for a minute or two, and pretended to pick up a phone. "Mrs. Brown," he said. "This is the Medicare office in Harrisburg. We're issuing you a new card next month and want to verify your social security number, address, and other relevant information. Can you read it from your current card to me? Certainly. I'll be happy to wait while you go get it."

I gagged, sinking onto a stool. "Do people fall for it?"

"Sure," he said. "Especially if he targets older seniors, the ones who aren't as clear-headed or ones not as skeptical of telephone calls. A caller with an authoritative voice is very effective with older people. Try sending them a letter with a fake letterhead and they're toast. They have no idea how easily something like letterheads can be faked." He thumbed through the files again. "There are literally hundreds of names in here. Does he have a copier?"

"Yes."

"Well, let's make a few copies. Don't need to do them all. Just enough records to be persuasive."

But who were we going to be persuasive with?

Jason and I pieced together what must have been going on in department stores too and showed up at Daddy's house a few days later.

"She met someone with a greater vision," he said, when I'd finished telling him about the trips to department stores. "That's always been a concern. I didn't worry about Mickey too much—he was satisfied with his lot. But Bud..."

The box of cheap bracelets in the basement persuaded us she was buying expensive jewelry, but returning low-priced things for a refund. Choose a busy clerk and how attentive would they be to the quality of a bracelet or sweater or handbag if a price tag was attached. It'd taken me, the fount of suspicion, a minute or two to realize the gold on the bracelets was paint. Some were brass. Not hard to imagine she'd pulled the same stunt with cashmere sweaters, alligator shoes, and who knew what else.

When we'd gone through the entire battery of bad deeds we'd come across in the basement and at Bud's office, we sat back, giving Daddy a minute or two to take it in.

"I knew about a lot of the early stuff. Saved her ass more than once." There was a tinge of pride in his voice you couldn't mistake.

"But a lot of this stuff's new to you, right? You never heard about it before?" I sensed a certain bristling going on from Jason's corner. He'd told me more than once he couldn't understand why my father had tolerated so much. It was hard for him to understand the different sort of pressures Daddy had—the expectations placed on him by his parents. His primary responsibility as far as they were concerned was to make his wife behave. And if that failed, to keep her misdeeds under wraps. My mother had brought so much disgrace to his family Daddy was reluctant to allow any more to surface.

"It's gonna come out, Daddy," I told him. "She's bound to get caught. I don't know how deep she's into this Medicare fraud, but the department stores are sure to get wise. She and Bud have so many balls in the air, one's bound to crash."

"So what do you want me to do?" Daddy asked. "Go to the

cops? Confront her myself? I'm not sure what you're asking. How many times do I have to bail her out?"

I was a bit taken aback by this coolly delivered reply. I'd expected rage. What I got instead was a tepid and largely unsurprised response coupled with a limp self-defense. He wasn't her husband anymore, but her deeds predated his escape. Did he expect me to overlook all the evidence we placed at his feet because it might be inconvenient to him?

"I think you should ask your attorney how to handle it. Let him advise you—us," I said. Jason was nodding in the background—this had, in fact, been his idea.

Daddy shook his head. "As an officer of the court, he'd be obliged to report it. We have to be sure what we want to happen before I approach him. Be certain we want her to go to jail—for perhaps as much as a decade. Look, you're out of it, aren't you? Move into a dorm—I'll give you the money. Put some distance between you."

Move into a dorm? This was his response? I realized it was how he'd handled it over the years. Send her off to her mother's house. Slap her in a hospital, find her a place to live well out of his orbit. Let his sister take care of things. Let his daughter. He'd written letters to get her jobs he knew she was ill-suited for. Bribed—who knew how many people?

Well, *did* I want to see my mother in jail? If it meant getting Ryan out from under her influence, the answer was yes. I went in with my big guns next.

"She killed Jerry Santini," I said, tears in my eyes. Jason moved quickly, covering my hands with his. "I might as well tell you this too, Daddy. She shot him while I was sleeping in the next room." I stopped to catch my breath. "She was the one who pulled the trigger and then made me take the blame. Shouldn't a murderess be in prison?"

My father's mouth started to form words, but then he

hesitated. "You mean… for not stopping… you, right?" Hadn't he heard what I said? He was looking everywhere but at me as he broke into a sweat.

I realized it then. He knew the whole story and had known since it happened. Had let me go through with my lies, let me make my appearance in that judge's chambers, spend the year in therapy, and never blinked. That was his method for dealing with his wife. Or ex-wife. Hand her off to his daughter.

"You knew, Daddy! You knew! I don't know why I didn't realize it before now." Or had I? Had I been as eager as he was to obscure the truth?

He was staring at his feet.

"Why didn't you do anything?" I asked him. "Daddy?"

"My attorney, one I no longer use by the way, talked it over with the fellow she used for her legal woes. Sid… something."

I didn't bother to fill in the right name. Both of my parents forgot names that proved embarrassing.

"Well anyway, the two of them talked over the various scenarios. Eve would've gone to jail for years if she confessed. Maybe for life. Or gone back into a facility, at the very least. If you took the blame—they figured—and rightly as it turned out, the judge would do exactly what he did. He'd come down easy on a kid. Almost think of your action as heroic—trying to save your mother." He cleared his throat. "We thought it was a better plan all around. You would've lost your mother." His voice was defensive, whiney. "You forget how attached you were to her in those days. Those first years—you two were inseparable. She couldn't keep her hands off of you." He looked up. "More than once, I was jealous. Jealous of my own kid."

"That's not it at all," I said, shaking his pap off. "That's not why you went along with it. Your family would've been affected by Mother's conviction. Been disgraced again. It might've hurt the business. Got you booted from some boards, your clubs."

It was a wonder his eyes hadn't burned a hole in the floor. "With me as the murderer of record, it all got covered up."

I hated him—even more than I hated my mother, who was clearly a sick woman. He was a coward. A coward who'd never once put me first.

He cleared his throat. "Maybe if you tell Eve all the things you know, she'd stop. If you lay it on the…"

I could tell he didn't believe this. Both of us knew she was powerless to give up her junk: anything else, including me, came in second.

"So what are you going to do?" he asked.

I didn't answer. I wondered if I'd have anything to say to him again. Suddenly a new thought popped into my head. "What about Grandmother Hobart?" I asked. "Did she know about me as the sacrificial calf too?" Had she gone along with it all too— never saying a thing about it? Where was her Christianity?

"Absolutely not," he said. "We never considered telling her the truth. She didn't enter into it at all."

He looked me straight in the eye, and I believed him. At least there was that then. One person had believed me to be a murderer but didn't abandon me.

Jason and I drove home, neither of us saying much. I couldn't help but wonder if he was regretting what he'd gotten himself into with me. I would have.

CHAPTER
Thirty

My mother was paging through a magazine when I came into the house carrying the same attaché I'd taken to my father's a few days before. She was probably the only person in the world searching for the ads rather than the articles in a magazine. The little slap each turning page made was sickening in the state I was in. She didn't look at me, didn't notice the attaché, probably mistaking it for my usual book bag.

Earlier that day, and somewhat unconsciously, I'd decided this was the right time. Life had come to a complete standstill. I couldn't study or think of anything else. The newly spawned hatred of my father was eating away at me. I wanted to be done with both of them—done with the two people who were supposed to care for me but hadn't.

Jason gave me little prods as well, telling me putting the confrontation off was not the way to go.

"Get it over with," he said. "You'll feel much better. No matter what the outcome."

The outcome. I could hardly imagine an end to it all—hardly think of a life without the burden of my mother dogging my every step. What would it be like not to expect horrific things to happen whenever the doorbell or the telephone rang. How would it feel not to expect the police car on the street to be heading our way?

"She's a parasite," Jason told me.

But was I too? We'd lived off each other for so long.

"Who died?" Mother asked now as our eyes met across the room. My face must have betrayed my apprehension.

"Ryan in bed?" I asked, hanging my jacket, my back to her. I could sense her nod, imagine her licking her finger to turn the page. "Keep him out all day again? He should apply for working papers."

I couldn't manage to keep my mouth shut about what were now inconsequential things. Nerves were doing that to me, and my voice sounded edgy to my ears.

"He spent the day with your grandmother." Slap, slap. "Bud and I went to see his accountant."

I could tell she regretted admitting as much immediately and her voice tapered off.

She invented an elaboration—one of those quick lies she usually excelled at. But this time it carried no heft. "We had some mutual business matters to discuss." She slammed the magazine down and stood up, stretching.

Mother probably would've liked to slap more than the pages of LOOK magazine. But having done it the week before, it seemed like a stale idea. I could imagine her sorting through the ways I'd failed her in recent months, figuring out what had caused the change, and blaming both my enrollment in that fancy college and my relationship with Jason for it. I'm sure she considered the time I spent with my father and grandmother as sources of friction too. How she would've loved to know that those days with Daddy had ended.

"Have you noticed things aren't as close between us as they were a year or two ago," she said, reading my mind. "Is it because of Bud?" She'd spotted the truth immediately. "Because he took me under his wing in various… deals? Well look, sweetie, he made our lives a lot easier. You might think about that fact before you roll those eyes again, before you accuse me of whatever it is you have in mind."

Her voice had risen in volume, and we both heard Ryan stirring in the next room. She continued in a more subdued voice. "We're living a lot better now than we have any right to—after what happened with Mickey. And it's mostly thanks to him. To Bud," she said, as if it needed clarification. Her voice sounded reverential almost. "It's not like your father—or Mickey—is helping us out. It always falls on me." I could see her weighing whether to include me on the list of unhelpful people too.

Whine, whine, whine. Blame, blame, blame.

Now I did roll my eyes, but Mother sunk in her own pity pit didn't catch me.

"Look, Mother, getting back to what you said about mutual business matters—deals between you and Bud—I saw a lot of paperwork at Grandmother's. You know, in the boxes in the cellar."

Her eyes flashed a warning, but I ignored it. There'd be no turning back. "I was working on a project for school." I decided to use that story again, "and I ran across a lot of documents that looked—well, strange. Letters, police and school reports, deeds, titles, diaries. Perhaps I misunderstood some of them," I added to quiet her.

"How dare you go through my papers. What business is it of yours?" Mother began to pace the room, her heels clicking on the bare floor, quieting when she reached the carpet, and then clicking as she turned.

"Some people might say it became my business when you forced me to say I shot Jerry Santini," I told her, preparing to open the attaché. "The day you had me sit in a judges' chamber and lie. When you made me lie to the police, to my father, to my grandparents, to everyone." I paused a minute to collect myself, struggling to control my voice. Any detection of weakness wouldn't help me.

"I've been expecting this moment for years," my mother said, sounding unsurprised at what I'd said. "The moment when you'd claim such a thing." She dabbed at her dry eyes. "Oh, the doctors warned me you'd want to disown the incident at some point. You were in such a fugue state that night—you must hardly remember what happened." Her voice took on a soothing quality—as if she was dealing with someone mentally disturbed.

"I remember it well," I told her. "But I needn't have. I wrote everything down, in fact. All the details of our ruse. Our little plot to get you off."

Mother drew herself in. "Something written years after the fact is worthless," she said, coming to stand behind me. "Maybe you don't understand. Both legally and personally worthless. You might as well be writing fiction." She started to reach for me, stopping as I stiffened.

"I didn't write it years later." I lied—but a lie I'd worked on for days— running it by Jason for practice. "I wrote it a few months after it happened. Cy Granholm— that wretched attorney who crafted the story— advised you to keep a record, I overheard him— and I thought it'd be a good idea if I did the same. So I wrote it all down and eventually left it at Grandmother's house—in a box of my own." I patted the attaché. "I guess even then I realized I needed something to protect myself. Even if I was only a child."

"I don't believe you."

But I knew she did. I knew she could imagine me writing away at my desk, wishing she'd supervised me more closely. Wrongly thinking that driving me to the shrink was enough supervision. Wondering if he'd been in on it too. That getting into my head earlier would've been a good idea.

She looked at the attaché curiously. "That bag's awfully thick. What else do you have in there?" Her voice had lost some of its coolness. Her hand started to reach for it.

I held it tighter, shrugging. "About a million pieces of paper documenting your life. Records going all the way back to childhood indiscretions. Accounts of things that happened to you as far back as middle school. You kept careful records and what a help it was."

She made an overt grab for the briefcase.

"It doesn't matter, Mother. These are all copies. Copies of report cards, letters from the parents of children you played with, police records, car sales, department store purchases, stays in hospitals, phony Medicare claims. I can't begin to enumerate the entire history of your activities. It took us hours to make the copies."

"Us?" Mother turned on her heel and walked over to the closet, opened it and made to reach for her coat. "Do you mean Jason or your father?"

"Are you running away, Mother? Leaving Ryan and me to ourselves?"

This was one scenario I'd envisioned. The best one too. I held my breath. But I was still a fool, still didn't know the depths of her wickedness.

Her voice was muffled. I stifled a scream as she came out of the closet holding a gun. It wasn't poised for shooting, but it wasn't slack in her hands.

I hadn't thought of this though I should have. A gun had solved things for her once. The penalty for its use had been so slight she was bound to try it again.

"Is that the same gun you used on Santini or did Bud rearm you?" I asked, straining to keep calm.

I didn't think she'd use it, but I knew there wasn't much she wouldn't do to protect herself. I girded myself and began to think about how to get it out of her hands. Did it occur to her that her other child was twelve feet behind her—through wallboard only inches thick? Would she ask him to take the fall after she killed me? Say she caught him playing with her gun after it was too late. Of course, she would. I could almost see the story forming in her head.

She was talking again, telling me her plan. "This is what I'll tell them—these people you plan to go to—whoever you have in mind," Mother said, aiming the gun. "I'll say you were going through something tonight—sort of reliving the night it happened. Bud was here too, and you were ready to kill him— kept calling him Jerry." She paused, needing a minute to catch up with her own story. "He'll back me up. I've heard of such things—people reliving a terrible moment. Unfortunately— there was no choice—and we had to shoot you. Maybe Ryan came out of his room and saw it. Or maybe there was a struggle and the gun discharged. Something like that anyway. Bud can be here in five minutes. He'll help me make a plan."

She said this smugly. As if it solved all of her problems. Had she forgotten I wasn't alone in the world anymore? Chances were both Jason and Daddy would know why I was here. She had no way of knowing Daddy has disowned all my actions.

"You don't think it'll look suspicious. Another body found dead on your living room floor." It was ludicrous. "And anyway, Jason knows. Daddy knows—has always known." I didn't mention my father's lack of support. "It's too late, Mother."

"Your father?" Mother lowered the gun incrementally. "Cy told me he knew what happened, but I didn't believe him. Said he'd keep quiet." She bit her lip. "I guess he did. What did he say about me?"

"He said he'd back me up," I lied. "Whatever I decided to do with this — stuff — was okay with him." I waved the case at her.

"And you decided to come to me first rather than go straight to the cops? Why, I wonder?"

"It seemed fair."

"You expected me to take off after you told me, didn't you?" The gun was waving in the air, shaking with her anger. "Leaving Ryan to your tender care. Some people might call it incestuous — the strange love you have for him. I remember when you insisted on him sleeping in your room the day he came home from the hospital."

I made a move toward my mother, wanting to rip her head off, shut that damned mouth of hers, stub her out like a spent cigarette. I wished I'd decided to kill her — made a plan for murder instead. She stepped away from my lunge, tripped on a toy Ryan had left on the floor — how apropos — and the gun went off.

I'm not sure what happened next, but the bullet skimmed my shoulder on its way into the wall behind me. I felt it down in my soul somewhere too. We both stood there stunned — for what seemed like forever.

"You almost shot me," I said, not at all surprised.

"Well, you tripped me — or backed me into a corner." She set the gun on a table. "You should know better than that. You can't make any sudden moves when I'm agitated. Why did you have to get me so upset?" She paused and asked quietly, "Are you okay? God, I'm sorry. I never would've fired it."

"How could I have forgotten about you and your corners?" I examined my shoulder. "I wasn't there when Jerry Santini made his move, you know. I was sound asleep." She'd managed to phrase it as if Jerry's *move* was made on her—and not part of his futile attempt to call the cops.

She nodded wearily. "I barely remember that night, you know. I wasn't myself, of course." She laughed lightly.

"I know."

"What will you tell people if I take off? That's what you have in mind, right? Your arm is all right, isn't it? You do know I wouldn't have shot you except for the toy I tripped over. I only meant to scare you."

I bet she'd had the same thing in mind six years earlier. I nodded. "I'll say you couldn't stomach the idea of raising another child. Something along those lines anyway." I paused. "There aren't many people to explain it to."

"You'll tell your father that story?"

I nodded. "He won't question it. And listen, Bud has to go too. And all remnants of the stuff you've been up to must disappear."

"I wouldn't go without him."

"So this is the deal. Leave enough money behind to keep us going for a while—a year or two. You do have enough money to do that?" She nodded. "You'll never come back—no matter how tempted you are. No matter what happens. When Grandmother dies, you won't return. I don't want your address after you get there—but give it to Daddy just in case—once you are permanently settled at least. He can keep it somewhere. He's used to keeping family secrets."

"Maybe jail would be better. My term would have an end date."

"It's up to you," I said, waiting.

"You'd actually turn me in."

I could see she still didn't believe it. Didn't believe her faithful dog was lost to her. I wasn't sure either but I had to appear adamant—sure of it.

"In a heartbeat." My voice was strong. "And another thing, you have to go far away. Maybe the west coast. I don't want any accidental meetings."

"I've always wanted to see San Diego," she said. "I'm not used to being without you—we've been through so much... I hope I can do it."

I covered my ears— literally—something I should have done many years earlier. "You have two weeks to get yourself together, but I'm taking Ryan to Daddy's tonight."

For the first time, yes, the very first time, she started to cry.

"He really is Mickey's kid, you know." She dabbed at her eyes with the back of her hand. "I never cheated on Mick."

I wonder if she thought it mattered to me.

"I don't know how he got it into his head. Maybe it was only his excuse to leave because I was never the promiscuous type. He knew that."

She paused. "And you, Baby. You are the love of my life. You know that. Right, Christine?"

I think she believed it. And some part of me did too. We'd been through so much together. Most of it bad but still it was our story. The only one we had.

We tiptoed into Ryan's room together. I packed a few of his clothes while she watched him sleep. I packed a few of mine too. Ryan didn't wake up when I lifted him from his bed. His head settled into my shoulder like it had been made to fit there.

I put on my jacket, and struggling with the weight of my brother, picked up the packed clothes, and the attaché. Of course, there was no asking her to help me. There never had been. I could sense Mother standing at the open door, could feel her hoping I'd relent, turn back, something. Relent and be the love of her life.

I can't say no tears slid down my cheek, or that her stricken face wasn't seared on my brain. But out on the street, Jason was waiting for me, the car running. Ryan and I climbed in and none of us looked back.

The End

Acknowledgements

When writing acknowledgements at my age, the people to thank is very long indeed. But I will limit this list to those who inspired me to keep working on a novel.

To my friends and family: I love you so much.

To my writing groups: heartfelt thanks and gratitude.

To my teachers: M.L. Liebler and Chris Leland-dispensers of courage and advice

To three special writers/friends who read my work in many stages: Anca Vlasopolos, Dennis James, and Dorene O'Brien

To Jason Pinter, Brian Lindenmuth, and Bryon Quertermous, editors extraordinaire

And most of all: to Sandra Scoppettone and Philip Abbott, my midwives. I love you.

About the Author

Patricia Abbott is the author of more than 100 stories in print, online, and in various anthologies. In 2009, she won a Derringer Award for her story MY HERO. She is the author of two ebooks of stories: MONKEY JUSTICE and HOME INVASION (through Snubnose Press). She is the co-editor of DISCOUNT NOIR (Unteed Reads). She makes her home in Detroit.

CONCRETE ANGEL is her debut novel. Visit her online at pattinase.blogspot.com and follow her on Twitter at @ Pattinaseabbott